Mission in India

Determination and Hope for Our Onward Journey

Mission in India
Determination and Hope for Our Onward Journey

Edited By

K. Jose SVD

SANSKRITI
2019

Mission in India: *Determination and Hope for Our Onward Journey* – jointly published by the Rev. Dr. Ashish Amos of the Indian Society for Promoting Christian Knowledge (ISPCK), Post Box 1585, Kashmere Gate, Delhi-110006 and Sanskriti - North Eastern Institute of Cultural Research, Guwahati-781017.

Online order: http://ispck.org.in/book.php

Also available on amazon.in

ISBN: 978-93-88945-22-6

Cover picture credit: Internet sources

Laser typeset by

ISPCK, Post Box 1585, 1654, Madarsa Road, Kashmere Gate, Delhi-110006 • *Tel:* 23866323

e-mail: ashish@ispck.org.in • ella@ispck.org.in
website: www.ispck.org.in

Dedicated to the loving memory of
late Fr. Dr. Thomas Chacko Ezhuparayil SVD (56)
who met with a car accident on 11th January
and passed away on 17th January, 2019

May He Rest in Peace

Contents

Foreword

The King of Canute from the 10th century in Europe set his throne by the seashore and commanded the incoming tide to halt and not to wet his feet and robes. Yet the tide, continuing to rise as usual, dashed over his feet and legs without respect to his royal person. Then the king leapt backward, saying: "Let all men know how empty and worthless is the power of kings, for there is none worthy of the name, but he whom heaven, earth, and sea obey by eternal laws." He then hung his gold crown on a crucifix, and never wore it again "to the honor of God the almighty king." The King realized his human conditions and the fragility of his kingly power. Realities of the world speak for themselves and we all come to face to face with them. To understand the present realties in India needs ability, intelligent readings and requires unbiased analysis. This is also a demand for the missionaries, it is not only to understand the realities of the people and the environment but it is our duty to respond to the realities and we cannot live in closed doors, in the vacuum or untouched by realities.

This volume on **"Mission in India: Determination and Hope for our Onward Journey"** is a collection of research papers which bring forth how the Divine Word Missionaries have lived and ventured into various missionary activities responding to the local situation. This journey has been undertaken with dedication, innovation, enthusiasm and preference. Some had taken the road less travelled and others in a common stream, yet with adequate focus and determination. We are indebted to all the pioneers, thinkers and workers in the vineyard of the Lord. It may be also fitting here to place on record that the previous volumes by Mission, Education and Research (MER) India - **Migration and Mission in India,** and **Ad Gentes Mission and inter Gentes Mission** were also largely appreciated by the mission researchers and others.

India is the world's seventh-largest economy, sitting between France and Italy. By 2050, India's economy is projected to be the world's second-largest, behind only China. Although there are a lot of positive initiatives, the unemployment of youth is a worrisome factor. Corruption is the virus that pervades all sectors, slowing down economic growth as well as the morale of the people. Amidst many social and economic problems, the respect and safety of women has received the hardest hit; the increasing cases of abuse of girls and rape are disturbing factors in the country. A few scandals of the Church personnel have added to the burden. The political scenario is also a worrying factor; there is manipulation, manufactured lies and consent, careerism, personal gains, use of caste and religion in politics and so forth. In this scenario, the welfare of all the people, creating a just society with equality, justice and integrity are not being achieved.

India is a secular country and it values democratic principles. The Constitution of India promotes the secular nature of the country and gives rights to all peoples equally irrespective of their religion, culture, language, caste or creed. But the freedom of religion is uncharacteristically curtailed. The following articles of the Constitution of India describe the rights of religious freedom: Article 25, Freedom of conscience and free profession, practice and propagation of religion; Article 26, Freedom to manage religious affairs; Article 27, Freedom as to payment of taxes for promotion of any particular religion; Article 28, Freedom as to attendance at religious instruction or religious worship in certain education institutions.

But due to political manipulation and craving for power, some political parties and some fringe groups in India have assumed the narrow ideology of fundamentalism, and thus they have systematically negated the freedom of other religions. Hindus are the majority in India, consisting of 80 per cent of the people. To appease the majority and to get the votes from these people for their political gain, the major political parties like Bharatiya Janata Party, Siva Sena, and major organizations like Rashtriya Swayamsevak Sangh, Vishwa Hindu Parishad and other fringe fundamentalist groups design and execute various programs with Hindutva ideology to oppress the other religions, even with physical violence. The fundamentalist groups, in collusion with political parties, methodically exercise this domination over others now.

The Delhi High Court verdict on the freedom of doing missionary work is an important judgement for the Church. Although it will be challenged by some groups in the higher courts, it still paves the way for hope and freedom. On 8 January, 2019, the Delhi High Court ruled that there is no law that prohibits any person residing in India from carrying out missionary work. The petitioner in the case, Dr. Christo Philip, challenged an order dated 01.08.2017 of the Consulate General of India (CGI) Houston by which his Overseas Citizen of India Card (OCI Card) was cancelled on the ground that he was "involved in missionary activities which is against the law of the land." He also challenged the order dated 22.12.2017 of the Appellate Authority (Ministry of Home Affairs, Foreigners Division) which had rejected his revision application holding that he had "suppressed the real purpose of his visit to the country to carry out evangelical, medical missionary and conversion activities against the interest of the general public leading to unrest and law and order problems."

Reminding the central government authorities, Justice Vibhu Bakhru stated that India is a secular country, noting that the Delhi High Court has observed that missionary activities are not prohibited as the fundamental right to religion is not restricted to citizens, but is available for all persons. Justice Vibhu also held that a person has a right to practice his faith and his rendering medical service, even if it is for furtherance of his religion, cannot be denied. The Court also added that the assumption that missionary activities are against the law of the land is fundamentally flawed. The Court also observed that there is no material to hold that the Doctor was indulging in conversion activities or that any of the activities have led to public unrest and law and order problems.[1]

The Christian mission has experienced a lot of wounds in its missionary activities in recent years. Christian personnel and institutions have been attacked by fringe groups, which malign the members of Christian community with fabricated lies and bi-partisan attitudes. In effect, they intimidate the activities of Christian community. In the process of curtailing the freedom of religions in the country, in actual practice, the rich and the dominant caste have gained power and wealth, but the marginalized, the excluded and the oppressed are neglected. The Conference of Catholic Bishops of India (2019) reminded us, "Every baptized person is obliged to joyfully preach, practice and propagate the Gospel in all circumstances." Further they stated, "We see the urgent need to further strengthen our faith, and we hope to continue extending our loving service to all people — in particular, the Dalits, tribals, women, migrants and refugees — so as to remove all traces of injustice, exploitation and oppression in our society and in the Church."[2] To continue God's mission in today's context is a challenge; we need to adopt new methods, new orientations and new vigor to heal these wounds as well as to reach out to all peoples.

Pope Francis often has stated that the Church needs to "go forth," "to be in the margins," "to smell of the sheep," and to experience the sufferings of the people. He also reiterated that everyone is called to holiness and for the consecrated persons, being holy is to live our commitment with joy (GE 14). The indwelling of joy comes when the mission is realized, which can happen when one experiences the love of God, transforming the persons and impelling them to transform others. Pope Francis says each one of us needs to realize,

"I am a mission on this earth; that is the reason why I am here in this world. We have to regard ourselves as sealed, even branded, by this mission of bringing light, blessing, enlivening, raising up, healing and freeing. All around us we begin to see nurses with soul, teachers with soul, politicians with soul, people who have chosen deep down to be with others and for others" (EG 273). Thus, being with others and for others indicate the ways or dimensions of being and doing our mission.

Divine Word Missionaries set foot in India in November 1932, from then on, we have grown constantly and we now have four provinces and one region; out of 950 members from India, nearly 250 members are working in foreign countries and the rest are serving in India. We have ventured into several states, started many missions, engaged in diverse apostolates beginning with schools, hostels and primary evangelization, experimented with special apostolates like anthropological centers, communication centers, missiolgical centers, retreat centers, health promoting centers, counselling centers, etc. We have put our hand in all types of apostolates according to the need of the local Church. As missionaries, we are primarily engaged in developing and assisting the local church. At this juncture, what is the future? Where are we going? What is the direction? What is the newness? These are some of the questions that come up, but these need to be answered collectively by the provinces and region. However, research bodies like MER has great role to play in reenergizing this collective search for reinventing the original mission mandate.

The general chapters and provincial chapters give directions, and the reality of the country impels us to discern and respond. The 18th general chapter states, "As Divine Word Missionaries, we are inspired and compelled to commit ourselves to carry out the work of the *Missio Dei* to become transforming missionary disciples of Christ in each place, among every people and for all cultures" (#13). Growing as transforming missionary disciples seems to be a powerful way today for effective mission in today's context. Such disciples "engage in mission as partners with the Triune God, whose way of dialogue and prophetic witness and utterance call the whole world into the fullness of being that will be experienced both in global consciousness and local concreteness."[3]

Being missionary in an effective way of transforming ourselves and the society is a big challenge. Certainly transforming ourselves concerns personal growth, conviction, our life-style and so forth. Living a reflective life on the Word of God and discernment would help each one us to change our habits, our prejudices, our relationships, our unwanted desires - towards the glory of God and to become more human and holy. Holiness is living out one's own vocation and mission on the earth (GE 19). As religious missionaries we are called to transform others, and this involves that we live our prophetic element. To be prophets in India today is not easy since the situation in the country would stifle the individuals and institutions; thus what is the intricacy of being prophet today? How can the SVDs assume a prophetic role in transforming the society? Prophetic dialogue gives direction to our mission, and the identification of our dialogue partners and doing mission with them is important. The four characteristic dimensions are the way to realize our mission effectively. They are distinct aspects of our being and doing. Some of the success stories as well as the challenges are highlighted in this volume.

In the context of a fast-paced and changing world, our engagement with the environment and digital world may demand that we relook at our mission methods. Lay partners in mission are another important dimension in our life, because they are co-responsible people in mission today. Being with them and partnering with them in mission calls us to open our doors to the lay partners, sharing responsibility and leadership and also being transparent in our mission engagement.

The challenge to curtail the fundamentalist's ideology is an uphill task. The Christian mission needs work out new strategies to reach out persons of goodwill from other religions and work for all the people bringing justice and peace. In this context, understanding

Evangelii gaudium, Laudato si' and Misericordia et misera, Pope Francis' orientation of mission offers us some models to follow: being an attractive church—an attractive community of an inclusive church, a culture of generosity—share with others what you have, a culture of relationship—establish relationship with all peoples, a culture of forgiveness—show mercy to all, a compassionate church, moved by the suffering and injustice in the world, a church whose mission is to accompany humanity with the leaven of the Gospel in order to bring about radial conversion of hearts and the worldly systems and institutions, and a transformative missional praxis that brings about integration and salvation through solidarity with the poor and marginalized, and a prophetic commitment to human and cosmic flourishing. In India, constructive dialogue with other religions through concrete actions would help to build bridges with others. Reconciliation and dialogue with proactive measures are important elements in healing the wounds among people. Among other priorities, common projects for the peoples and a common orientation towards national progress would help for peaceful co-existence in the county.

Lazar T. Stanislaus, SVD
Mission Secretary, Rome

Endnotes

[1] "Missionary Activities not Prohibited In India as Rights Under Art. 25 Available to All," https://www.livelaw.in/news-updates/india-is-a-secular-country-missionary-activities-are-not-prohibited-delhi-hc-read-judgment

[2] CCBI Declaration, "Announcing the Joy of the Gospel to all," XXXI Plenary Assembly, January 7-14, 2019, Chengalpattu, Tamil Nadu,https://cbci.in/detail_Slide1.aspx

[3] Stephen Bevans, "Theological and Missiological Reflections," in *Missionary Discipleship in Glocal Contexts*, Lazar T. Stanislaus, SVD and vanThanh Nguyen, SVD (eds.), Siegburg: Franz Schmitt Verlag, 2018, 150.

Introduction

Today we place at your disposal this book which originally evolved from the third Mission Education and Research (MER India-Subzone) Conference in Atma Darshan, Mumbai from 3rd to 5th September 2018. Before this important event of SVD in India took place two of our passionate mission researchers passed away to their eternal home – Fr. Dr. Augustine Kanjamala SVD & Fr. Dr. Thomas Vadackumkara SVD. We remember them with much affection and love. Therefore, in this third edition of the conference we were very fortunate to have a memorial lecture in honour of the senior researcher Fr. Kanjamala. And after the third conference we are pained once again to have lost another young researcher, Fr. Dr. Thomas Chacko SVD, who met with a tragic road accident and passed away. We dedicate this volume to his loving memory, and pray that God give them all eternal rest in his heavenly abode.

During Arnold Janssen's time he has responded to the various existential situations with reference to numerous mission needs. He said: "The Lord challenges our faith to do something new, precisely when so many things are collapsing in the Church." Till the day of Arnold's death on January 15, 1909 his life was filled with a constant search for God's will, a great confidence in divine providence, and hard work. No one in the Society of the Divine Word doubts that his work has been blessed abundantly by the good God in manifold dimensions.

In this context we gratefully remember that SVD in India, one of the pioneers in breaking new grounds in missions which often proved to be of far reaching consequences. This zeal and dynamism is not merely a thing of the founding generations of missionaries in our country, but it has been a story repeated time and again. This journey has to continue with determination and hope. That was the heartfelt prayer when a select group of mission researchers from all the provinces and region gathered together to grapple with the given theme of the conference – A critical Appraisal of SVD Mission in India: Contemporary Challenges and its Prospects.

Here below we shall take a brief look at the concept note of our conference.

All the Synoptic Gospels have 'mission' and 'conversion' as the focus and culmination of Jesus' life and teachings. Jesus "appointed twelve ... to be with Him and to be sent out to proclaim the message" (Mk 3:14). The Mission Command, as recorded in Mt 28:19, "Go, therefore, make disciples of all nations," defines mission as "making disciples of all nations". In Luke, Jesus commissions the disciples to be witnesses to all nations (Lk 24:47-48). They are to preach repentance for the forgiveness of sins. The preaching is a call to repentance. In the fourth Gospel mission is shepherding the flock. Jn 21:15-19 is a unique dialogue between the Risen Christ and Peter, in which Peter receives the commission to shepherd the community. Jesus the Good Shepherd (10:11) sends the disciples to continue the same mission. The mission mandate is not merely a command, which Jesus gave just before departing from this world, but Jesus the messenger was himself the message. The mission of the Church is to proclaim Jesus, the Good News.

Because of the present multi-religious reality in India, we can neither follow the past *Ecclesiocentric* model of evangelisation nor the *Theocentric* model, proposed by some pluralist theologians. We can follow the model that has a temporal reference to the future, that is, popularly known as the Kingdom-centred Model. Evangelisation-centred on the Kingdom/Reign of God is the building up of a new humanity. The plan of God is leading everything towards a final fulfilment to which all are called. All are called to transcend, by the work of the Spirit, their present structures built by the religious creeds, codes and cults. He integrates in a holistic manner all that is good and true in all faiths and ideologies. Evangelisation in India needs to aim at a mutually complementary double process:

1. Communion with Christ, in which Church and people of different faiths and ideologies share their experience of their ultimate values.

2. An exchange of brotherly and sisterly love in a tangible form, as they strive together and cooperate with each other for a common end, that is, fuller and authentic human life.

Creation and redemption find their final realisation in the new heaven and the new earth. As Divine WORD Missionaries, we need to look at the Bible as a form of a story that begins with creation (Gen 1:1) and ends with creation (Rev 21:1-4). Therefore, we are called to be partakers in enhancing the quality of life from the first creation (Gen 1:1) to the last creation (Rev 21:1-4). This broad understanding of evangelisation, meaningful in the general Asian context, is contained in documents of Vatican II (GS, NA, DH and UR). Putting these insights together we can conclude that evangelisation today is the leavening of the world, considered as a leavening of gospel values and as making it easier to reach the final goal of building up a new humanity. The XIII General Chapter of 1988 spoke about these same matters in terms of 'passing over' at the 'frontiers' of class, culture and religion.

Since the religions are at the service of the world, inter-religious dialogue cannot be confined to the religious sphere but must embrace all dimensions of life: economic, socio-political, cultural and religious. It is in their common commitment to the fuller life of the human community that they discover their complementarities, the urgency and relevance of dialogue at all levels, socio-economic, intellectual, spiritual, among the common people in daily life as among scholars and people with deep religious experience. Pope John Paul II in *Redemptoris Missio* describes the vast horizons of mission for which there are different tasks and activities. Pope Paul VI in *Evangelii Nuntiandi* acknowledges, "Today we face a religious situation which is extremely varied and changing" (32). God has placed us in this world, and he has given us a variety. Moreover, it is part of the mystery of God that there is variety that can be complementary and that it can contribute to the totality.

The prophetic dialogue calls us for a new way of being missionaries in the context of diverse religious traditions, secular ideologies, vibrant cultures, and the teeming millions of poor *dalits* and tribals. The SVD's distinctive call is to commit ourselves to the four-fold prophetic dialogue in frontier situations. The characteristic dimensions of our missionary life and service, namely Bible Apostolate, Mission Animation, Justice, Peace and Integrity of Creation (JPIC) and Communication are quite novel in SVD terminology. These dimensions were already concerns of our father and leader, St. Arnold Janssen, although these developed through the years as characteristic dimensions of our charism and emerged from the responses of our missionaries to the mission challenges in all four zones and at different periods of history.

The present day national scenario demands a relook at the way we SVDs engage in the God's mission with all its challenges and its possible Prospects as well. Present day realities in our mission contexts in our country call for deeper awareness, data based analysis and possible strategies. Therefore, MER India organized this national conference in view of charting out new and innovative paths in consonant with the contemporary national movements – we have done it based on the data from the mission fields of each researcher who took part in this national event. The major sub-themes they were invited to consider are also given below.

Sub-themes

- Christian teachings and its rootedness in India

- Christianity and Post Modernism: Challenges and Pathways in India

- Christianity in India: Emerging Context of SVD Mission Undertakings

- Identity driven Movements and their social repercussions in India

- Impact of Christianity on India: Contemporary Challenges and Responses

- Policy Making in India: Impact of Christianity

This is the third national conference organized by MER India, from its inception. The first one was in the year 2005 and the second one in 2015. We are glad to publish all the innovative and data based full length research papers in this comprehensive volume in English. As members of the SVD, we are heirs to a valuable, multi-disciplinary tradition of mission research. The changing situation of mission challenges our various research institutes and all SVD mission researchers to be in very close collaboration, and to focus their study and teaching on concrete issues that can help improve our missionary service, and make it responsive to present needs...... (Cfr. In Dialogue with the Word, No. 105 & 106, Vol. No. 1 – September 2000:45-46). Certainly, as partakers of Mission in India we are all invited to rekindle that determination and keep the light of hope burning brightly so that our onward journey will definitely be remarkable.

As our country is still grappling with many challenges we need to recapture with determination and hope our mission strategy. For example when India has 1.3 billion people and about 5 per cent of them living in extreme poverty we know there is a need not only of mere good intentions but adequate interventions. Or, when we hear that a lot of women in India still are not able to get adequate health care, we are called to rethink our mission undertakings for the better. Yet again, every one of us are aware that there is enough room for building up good will among various communities as social discrimination and disparity are growing wider. As Pope Francis reminds that "evangelization takes place in obedience to the missionary mandate of Jesus: "Go therefore and make disciples of all nations….." (Mt. 28:19-20). The risen Lord empowers you and me to launch out with manifold initiatives of contemporary relevance. We pray his ever abiding accompaniment empower us with the ability to reflect, critique and once again rededicate ourselves as a disciple of the divine master in today's context.

We place on record our gratefulness to all the collaborators of this conference beginning with the SVD Generalate team for their whole hearted support, SVD provincials and Regional in India who guided us in its various stages, the committed paper presenters, director and his colleagues at Atma Darshan, Mumbai who provided us with a very conducive venue for this three days engagement, the financial assistance from our Society headquarters, the short but fitting foreword by Fr. Lazar T. Stanislaus, SVD Mission Secretary, Rome, the ever available consulting editors – Fr. Surendra Kumar Kanher SVD, Banderdewa, Arunachal Pradesh and Dr. Bhaskar Das, Dibrugarh, a fantastic collaborator and an eminent professor-anthropologist, other editorial consultants and the ISPCK Publishers, New Delhi for bringing out this volume in an elegant manner – all of them deserve our heartfelt thanks. Yes, we appreciate your timely interventions, and may God bless and accompany you in your multifarious undertakings.

K. Jose SVD
Director, Sanskriti

Restoring the Credibility and Legitimacy of Christian Mission

Thomas Malipurathu SVD

1. The Implications of Being a Church-in-Mission

Our awareness of the implications of being a Church-in-mission,[1] like our Christian faith itself, must grow in time and must attain clearer and clearer levels of articulation giving due place to the particularities of the place we inhabit. This is a fact that needs to be considered as a matter of prime importance particularly in the contemporary scenario unfolding before us. In fact, that the articulation of the Church's missionary task has been evolving from the time it was launched is undeniable.[2] Down the centuries a number of models have been proposed and followed such as the "saving the souls" approach, "bringing the light of civilization to the uncivilized peoples" approach, the "planting of the Church" (*plantatio ecclesiae*) approach, the "conquering of lands for Christ" (conquest) approach, the *ad gentes*, *inter gentes* and *cum gentibus* approaches, etc. These were not necessarily models one replacing the other with the passage of time. Many of them were existing side by side and vestiges of most of them still remain alive in the missionary consciousness of a good number of the practioners of Christian mission in our days. But surely a missionary approach that seeks "to bring enlightenment to the unenlightened", for example, cannot anymore be maintained without reducing ourselves to an object of utter ridicule today. No self-respecting people would tolerate attempts by others to consider them as unenlightened, or much less, as uncivilized!

1.1. The Credibility Question

What that points to is the need to formulate and present to the world a missionary approach that is credible on the one hand, and acceptable on the other, to the people we interact with as part of our missionary outreach, sometimes referred to as our partners in mission. Some of the ideas we were perceived as championing in the past had been assessed by the followers of other faith traditions as aggressive and intimidating. That is the reason for the scathing criticism of the missionary efforts of the Church in certain parts of the world today, particularly in our country. On occasion, objections are raised with quite extraordinary ferocity even at the very mention of the word "mission". Many of the staunch adherents of ancient and well-established religions are suspicious of our motives. They often conclude that Christians want to increase their numerical strength by covertly and overtly poaching on their turf. In their assessment proselytizing is the only driving force of all Christian missionary interventions. This feeds the frenzy of the fanatical fringe groups among them and leads to escalating social tension and even sporadic cases of physical violence. It is in this context that the credibility of our missionary approach moves into contention.

1.2. Mission's Legitimacy Issue

When it comes to the legitimacy of our missionary effort, it can be firmly established only by reasserting the fact that it is quintessentially an effort to bring alive the mission of Jesus in every succeeding generation. By emphasizing that it aims at continuing, as it were, the unfinished agenda of Jesus. While subjecting Jesus' mission to a closer examination the focus often falls on such redoubtable mission commands as what we find in Mt 28:16-20; Mk 16:15-16 Lk 24:46-49; Jn 21:21-23 and Acts 1:8. In fact, much of the mission theology of the past had been formulated using these passages as foundational texts. But there is a problem here. Very frequently in the past there was a kind of exaggerated emphasis placed on the first of these: the so-called "Great Commission" text in Mt 28:16-30. Interpreting it simply as a powerful mission mandate by detaching it from its actual location in the narrative continuum of the Gospel and ignoring its post-Easter context, mission-thinkers have indulged in questionable exegesis paving the way for a distorted understanding of the practice of mission.

In recent years, however, another Gospel text has moved into sharper focus in discussions relating to the legacy of mission bequeathed to us by the life and work of Jesus. It is the passage dealing with Jesus' visit to Nazareth recorded in Lk 4:16-30, which in that Gospel represents the inaugural moment of the Lord's public ministry. My effort in the following pages will be to have a closer look at this passage in view of establishing its pivotal role in understanding the basic tenets of Jesus' mission and establishing it as providing the veritable foundation for the mission of his followers of every age.[3]

2.   The Defining Thrust of Jesus' Mission Brought to Evidence in Lk 4:16-30

More than perhaps any other New Testament passage of missionary import, Lk 4:16-30 contains decisive pointers to what Jesus intended his followers to take up as the missionary challenge he was handing on to them. That the evangelist wanted it to be read as a programmatic text is clearly established both by the content and the context of this passage. Programmatic in the sense that Jesus is presented as placing before his audience the programme of his mission and also in the sense that it contains in a nutshell the entire programme of Luke's two-volume work (the Gospel and Acts). Its place as the opening scene of Jesus' public ministry is profoundly significant. The content of the passage, when elaborated by taking into consideration the unique elements of the Jesus Movement obliquely set forth in the Third Gospel, will bear clear testimony to its central role in the narrative.

2.1. The Internal Coherence of the Passage

For all its pivotal significance the interpretation of this episode poses serious problems. To begin with, the internal coherence of the passage is a much discussed issue. The problem is the abrupt and not-so-easily explainable change in the mood of the audience. Verse 22 speaks of a very positive response from the gathering. But in vv. 28-29 we learn of a radical change in the approach of the people. Suddenly they turn enraged and violent. The situation leads to extreme hostility and mob violence. This change is too sudden to explain. There are commentators who say that two separate stories of Jesus' two different visits to Nazareth are fused into one here by the author and it has resulted in the incongruities that it presents. Jesus' comment on the unfriendly stance of the co-citizens vis-à-vis a prophet from their own midst and his words about God's preferential treatment of the "pagans" and the marginalized seem to have triggered the fury of the crowd. This motif may have been deliberately added by the evangelist to make it a programmatic introduction to the ministry of Jesus.

2.2. The Quote from Prophet Isaiah

The words of prophet Isaiah quoted in 4:18-19 constitutes the quintessence of Jesus' mission: "The Spirit of the Lord is upon me, because he has anointed me to bring good news to the poor. He has sent me to proclaim release to the captives and recovery of sight to the blind, to let the oppressed go free, to proclaim the year of the Lord's favour".

The citation from the book of Isaiah is not a direct quote. It is called a "conflated quotation". Luke uses the Septuagint version (the Greek translation of the OT) of Isaiah. First, Is 61:1-2 is used, but one phrase from it is omitted, i.e., Is 61:1d ("to bind up the broken-hearted"). In its place is added a phrase from Is 58:6d ("to set at liberty those who are oppressed"). Another omission is the last part of Is 61:2 ("and the day of the vengeance of the Lord"). This kind of rearranging the text was unusual in the context of a synagogue service.

Synagogue service in the days of Jesus had a fairly fixed format consisting of the following elements:

1. Recitation of the *Shema* (Deut 6:4-9; 11:13-21)

2. Some formulaic prayers (18 benedictions, etc.)

3. A reading from the Torah (*seder*)

4. A reading from the prophets (*haphtarah*)

5. The singing of a Psalm

6. Sermon (usually introduced by short introductory reading from the prophets or writings [*pethita*])

2.3. Modification of the Isaian Quote

Jesus' reading mentioned in the passage in Luke refers to the *haphtarah*. Although there was some flexibility allowed (such as dropping a verse or two), the rearrangement of the text as evidenced here could not have come from Jesus. Such freedom was unusual. Particularly striking is the omission of the phrase in Is 61:1d ("binding up the broken-hearted") and its replacement with the phrase from Is 58:6d ("to set at liberty those who are oppressed").

Several explanations have been offered to account for the reworking of the quote. Some say it is done to safeguard against the spiritualizing interpretation of the manifesto of Jesus implied in the context. The omission of the "broken-hearted" of Is 61:1d and the inclusion of the "oppressed" from Is 58:6d in its place is the case in point. "Binding up the broken-hearted" is clearly amenable to a spiritual interpretation whereas the patently social thrust of "to set free the oppressed" cannot be overlooked. One is reminded of the spiritualized version of the Matthean beatitude in Mt 5:3 ("Blessed are the poor in spirit") in contrast to the originally strongly social beatitude that we find in Lk 6:20 ("Blessed are you poor").[4]

Another more likely explanation has to do with Luke's concept of the work of the Spirit. He had a prophetic understanding of the Spirit. The gift of the Spirit (or the anointing by the Spirit) was for the prophetic tasks of being a medium of divine revelation and being a proclaimer of inspired message. "Binding up the broken-hearted" does not fit in with these Spirit-inspired tasks.

Still others content that the inclusion of Is 58:6d ("to set at liberty those who are oppressed") was most probably made as a result of the verbal linkage with the preceding verse "to proclaim release to the captives and recovery of sight to the blind". It is to be noted that "to proclaim release" is expressed through the use of the accusative case of the noun *aphesis* (*aphesin*) and to denote "to let the oppressed go free" the same noun in the dative (*aphesei*) is used.

There are commentators who hold that the jubilee motif is at play here. There was the practice of general amnesty for slaves and condoning of debts attached to the jubilee celebration. Other scholars say that Luke wanted to emphasize the idea of "forgiveness of sins" (*aphesis*), which Jesus, inspired by the Spirit, proclaimed. In the liberating power of the mission of Jesus, the aspect of forgiveness of sins was of crucial significance.

Another notable modification of the original Isaian text is carried out through the omission of the phrase "and the vengeance of our God". This omission again could have been due to Lucan redaction. Luke probably wanted to avoid any negative element from the mission manifesto of Jesus. In this carefully crafted pericope (with the "conflated quotation" from Isaiah that he builds into it), which Luke wanted to present as the cornerstone of his theological programme, the concept of vengeance did not fit. He is the evangelist of "compassion" rather than of "vengeance".

2.4. Revision of the Chronology

Luke has moved the story of Jesus' visit to Nazareth found much later in the ministry of Jesus in Mark (thus effecting a change in the chronology of Jesus ministry). This could have been in the first place to ensure that the Nazareth event happened close on the heels of Jesus' reception of the Spirit at his baptism in Jordan (Lk 3:21-22), thus to highlight the significance of Jesus' Spirit-anointing for his entire ministry. We notice for instance that in Acts 10:38 Jesus' baptism is interpreted as an "anointing" in view of his mission. Thus Luke establishes the fact Jesus' reception of the Spirit at baptism was the means by which he was equipped to carry out his mission.

The anointing mentioned in Isaiah 61:1-2 thus becomes a very relevant detail. In 4:18-19 Luke reworks the Isaian text to make it the signature statement about Jesus' mission. For this Luke follows the rabbinic method of enhancing the meaning of one text (Is 61:1-2) with another text (Is 58:6). It is important to note that this Isaian quote is the only significant OT citation that Luke makes use to serve a key function in his entire narrative. Hence the build-up is uniquely Lucan.

2.5. The Motif of Liberation

The liberation motif clearly present in Isaiah 61:1-2 refers to the institution of the sabbatical year (cf. Ex 21 and 23: Deut 15) and its subsequent development into the concept of the Jubilee Year (seventh sabbatical year – Lev 25). Restitution of the land taken in mortgage, remission of debts, freeing and ransoming of slaves (general amnesty) presupposes the fact that every Israelite is equally dependent on Yahweh, the sovereign, who is the ultimate owner of the land. The vision underlying the Jubilee Year legislation (cf. Lev 25) was the fundamental equality of people. Debt relationships were temporary in nature (no one could be permanently held as debtor). The cancellation of debts in the Jubilee Year restored relationships.

However, lofty as the ideal was, there is no evidence that this legislation was at any time actually put into practice. Nevertheless, it helped to underscore Yahweh's sovereignty over Israel and its consequence for mutual relationships among the people. The principle that it indisputably established is that God is sovereign over Israel. The structure of social and economic life must embody people's affirmation of God's sovereignty. In other words, God's reign (the Kingdom of God) and humankind's liberation go hand in hand.

2.6.   The Signature Statement of Jesus' Mission

Luke sees this principle (which can be rephrased as "God's parenthood and human brotherhood/sisterhood") as representing the core of Jesus' message and brings it into sharp focus by working the Isaian quotation into Jesus' inaugural sermon, thereby making it the "signature statement" of his ministry. The Jubilee Year motif strongly emphasized the call for social justice. This also belonged to the core of Jesus' message: "I have been anointed to bring good news to the poor..."Against this background it becomes easier to understand why Jesus' message was truly "good news" to the poor.

However, the jubilee concept is to be interpreted not as a legal prescription but as a symbol of the vision of the new age. The jubilee concept with its liberation-perspective provided the conceptual background for Jesus' exorcisms and healings and his radical concern for the poor and the marginalized. This is a typically Lucan insight.

Is 61 belongs to the book known as the "Trito-Isaiah" (Is 56-66). Its backdrop is the situation of the people who had just returned to their homeland from the exile in Babylon (in the late sixth or early fifth century BCE). The people were in deep distress. The high expectations raised by the end of the exile did not materialize. The socio-economic situation in Palestine which they encountered upon return from the Exile was shockingly miserable. People were living in penury. These are the "poor" mentioned in Is 61:1 and 58:7.

In the social plea echoed in Is 61 and 58 Luke found a powerful scriptural metaphor to convey the essential thrust of Jesus' mission, a fact that would make it particularly appealing to his community. Most probably the community he was addressing his Gospel to also was financially in dire straits which made their situation parallel to the Isaian community. That could be the reason why he decided to formulate the "signature statement" of Jesus' mission using the Isaian quotation.

Jesus' words after the reading is completed are subsumed in just one sentence: "Today this scripture has been fulfilled in your hearing". Some say these are the introductory words of Jesus; the rest of the sermon remains unreported. Others say it is the concluding line. The word today (sēmeron) has a special resonance in Luke, who uses it frequently (cf. 2:11; 4:21; 19:5; 19:9; 23:43). It is a word linked to "salvation". Interestingly, the very first word that proceeds from the mouth of Jesus as an adult, apart from the words of the reading, is "today"!

The words quoted by Jesus were of the prophet. There was nothing new there. What was new was the word "today"; the assertion that God seeks to become a reality in the present, to aid all those who are oppressed (Lk 14:21), the Gentiles (Lk 4:25-27), the prostitutes (Lk 7:36-50), the tax collectors and sinners (Lk 15:1) and criminals (Lk 23:40-43). That is where the message of Jesus begins.

Jesus announces that the age of God's reign is here. The end-time, the final decisive period when God's promises are fulfilled and God's purpose comes to fruition (the *eschaton*), has finally dawned. There will be change in the condition of those who had waited in hope. Those changes for the poor and the oppressed will occur today. This is the beginning of the jubilee. The time of God is today! The ministry of Jesus—and of the Church after him—ensures that "today" continues. Throughout Luke-Acts, such "today" is never allowed to become "yesterday"!

2.7.   Lucan Reconstruction of the Thrust of Jesus' Mission

The way Luke has reported the incident surely is more than a historical account of an actual visit of Jesus' to his hometown. On that level it is difficult to explain the extreme hostility he provokes among his townsfolk on the occasion, especially considering that it was his maiden public appearance after his baptism. In reality this episode foreshadows the final outcome of Jesus' ministry which would happen in Jerusalem. Jesus' eventual rejection—Luke indicates here—is because of the profound significance of the mission he was launching. Jesus and his ministry were the harbinger of a new era, a new vision which embodied good news for the poor and the marginalized. But by the same token, it became a threat to the establishment. People who built their careers on the status-quo which ensured a comfortable life for them were obviously alarmed.

The vision contained in the jubilee motif (God's parenthood and human brotherhood/sisterhood) is the foundation of the vision Jesus proposes through the ideal of the "Kingdom of God". It is this vision for a renewed humanity that he announces at the Nazareth synagogue as his "mission-statement". Jesus' agenda proposed through the inaugural sermon at the Nazareth Synagogue envisages an integral mission that is stunningly down-to-earth as a programme of action, liberative in its scope, favouring the poor and the marginalized and inclusive of all.

The liberative thrust of the Isaian text (evidenced through its "jubilee motif") is the linking point with Jesus' proclamation of the Kingdom of God. Both emphasize that God's sovereignty and human liberation go hand in hand. If one accepts God as the supreme power guiding one's life, one cannot remain indifferent to the plight of one's needy neighbour. Thus, the vision of a renewed humanity which Jesus proposed through the metaphor of the Kingdom of God has in it a strong element of social justice, making it truly good news for the poor. The Jesus' movement's preferential option for the poor was captured with its full implications by the evangelist Luke because of the situation of the community (its *Sitz im Leben*) he was addressing his Gospel to.

3.   Translating Jesus' Vision into Life Models

3.1.   Programme of Mission Rendered Alive in Jesus' Ministry

An attentive reading of the Gospel narrative will reveal how the manifesto presented in 4:16-30 was progressively unfolded through the ministry of Jesus. Everything that Jesus said and did after his inaugural sermon at the Nazareth synagogue was a continuous effort to translate the vision he announced into a living reality. His activity of proclamation and teaching, healing and exorcisms, his feeding of the hungry crowds, his curing of the blind and the lame, his reaching out to the dreaded victims of leprosy, his table fellowship with the outcasts and tax collectors, his forgiving of perceived sinners, etc., were distinctive moments of his missionary outreach. It was such activity he would suggest as providing clear evidence of his messianic identity. When on one occasion the disciples of John the Baptist wanted to have a definitive proof that he was indeed the Messiah, he convinces them not by a lengthy discourse with scriptural proofs, but by drawing their attention to the scenes of missionary engagement unfolding before their eyes at that moment in which he insisted there was an unassailable evidence of his identity (cf. Lk 7:18-23). The fact that he always made sure that his apostles and other disciples were present with him when he carried out his mission showed that he meant to instruct them in the ways of mission to ensure that they would be fully prepared to continue his mission once he was taken away from their midst. His missionary efforts he also intended as a paradigm for their future mission.

Equally strikingly, the movement that was taking shape through his ministry—the Jesus Movement—which in fact turned out to be by and large a collective of the poor and the disinherited of the land, he made sure was rendered distinct by the practice of certain outstandingly sublime values. Having originated in the new and radically liberative religious experience of Jesus it became a radical movement leading its adherents to an authentic conversion—the dislocation of the familiar patterns of perception and behaviour and a shift to a totally new way of experiencing reality and responding to it. Such a conversion would inevitably result in the emergence of a new community with its own worldview and values, with its own particular life style through which these values were expressed. Moreover, this new community emerging from and embodying the *abba* experience of Jesus would have an archetypal significance for the succeeding generations of Christian communities. It was a community that was free, all-inclusive, open to sharing, ready for service and practising genuine equality.[5]

3.2.   The Emergence of a New Humanity as the Goal of Mission

The ultimate goal of the Kingdom ministry of Jesus was then the emergence of a new humanity suffused with values such as freedom, inclusiveness, sharing, service-mindedness and equality. His efforts in this direction started with his momentous declaration in the Nazareth synagogue that "Today in your hearing this scripture has been fulfillied" (Lk 4:21). That "today" continued throughout his public ministry and was passed on to the post-Easter apostolic community and the later Christian communities of the early days. They understood the mission entrusted to them by Jesus as progressively actualizing his vision by continuing his mission taking the cue from the example he provided during his ministry.

Only through an earnest attempt to refashion our missionary efforts in the Jesus-mode we will be able to reclaim legitimacy for our work as disciples of the Lord today. That alone will bestow credibility on it as it will not be judged as aggressive or intimidating by anyone. We will then be able to place before the world an understanding of Christian mission that is radically inclusive in vision, integrally liberative in scope and deeply respectful of the sensibilities of the people we reach out to.

Endnotes

¹ Whereas other papers in this volume may be more specific in their treatment of the basic theme "SVD Mission in India: Challenges and Prospects" my attempt is to piece together a few reflections on the general question of the legitimacy of Christian mission. Such revisiting of this fundamental premise is, I believe, an imperative especially in the face of the new challenges the field of mission is facing.

² Pointing out the fact that models of mission and ministry have been considerably reconfigured in various epochs of the Church's onward journey, Robert Schreiter reminds us that this happened partly due to the changing self-understanding of the Church and partly from realizing how context-bound the various received models had been; cf. "Preface" in William Jenkinson and Helene O'Sullivan (eds.), *Trends in Mission: Towards the 3ʳᵈ Millennium* (Maryknoll, New York: Orbis Books, 1991) xiv.

³ Many of the ideas for the following interpretation of Lk 4:16-30 are drawn from Herman Hendrickx's brilliantly argued little book *A Key to the Gospel of Luke* (Quezon City, Philippines: Claretian Publications, 1992).

⁴ Cf. George M. Soares-Prabhu, "Good News to the Poor: The Social Implications of the Message of Jesus" in Scaria Kuthirakkattel (ed), *A Biblical Theology for India, Collected Writings of George M. Soares-Prabhu*, Vol. 2 (Pune: Jnana-Deepa Vidyapeeth Theology Series, 1999) 262.

⁵ Cf. George M. Soares-Prabhu, "Radical Beginnings: The Jesus Community as the Archetype of the Church," in Francis X. D'Sa (ed.), *Theology of Liberation: And Indian Biblical Perspective, Collected Writings of George M. Soares-Prabhu*, Vol. IV (Pune: Jnana-Deepa Vidyapeeth Theology Series, 2001) 143.

A Critical Appraisal of SVD Mission in India:

Contemporary Challenges and its Prospects

Joy Thomas SVD

Introduction

All the Synoptic Gospels have 'mission' and 'conversion' as the focus and culmination of Jesus' life and teachings. Jesus "appointed twelve ... to be with Him and to be sent out to proclaim the message" (Mk 3:14). The Mission Command, as recorded in Mt 28:19, "Go, therefore, make disciples of all nations," defines mission as "making disciples of all nations". In Luke, Jesus commissions the disciples to be witnesses to all nations (Lk 24:47-48). They are to preach repentance for the forgiveness of sins. The preaching is a call to repentance. In the fourth Gospel mission is shepherding the flock. Jn 21:15-19 is a unique dialogue between the Risen Christ and Peter, in which Peter receives the commission to shepherd the community. Jesus the Good Shepherd (10:11) sends the disciples to continue the same mission. The mission mandate is not merely a command, which Jesus gave just before departing from this world, but Jesus the messenger was himself the message. The mission of the Church is to proclaim Jesus, the Good News.

Mission for SVDs in India

Because of the present multi-religious reality in India, we can neither follow the past *Ecclesiocentric* model of evangelisation nor the *Theocentric* model, proposed by some pluralist theologians. We can follow the model that has a temporal reference to the future, that is, the *Basileiacentric* one, popularly known as the Kingdom-centred Model. Evangelisation-centred on the Kingdom/Reign of God is the building up of a new humanity. The plan of God is leading everything towards a final fulfilment to which all are called. All are called to transcend, by the work of the Spirit, their present structures built by the religious creeds, codes and cults. He integrates in a holistic manner all that is good and true in all faiths and ideologies. Evangelisation in India needs to aim at a mutually complementary double process:

1. Communion with Christ, in which Church and people of different faiths and ideologies share their experience of their ultimate values.

2. An exchange of brotherly and sisterly love in a tangible form, as they strive together and cooperate with each other for a common end, that is, fuller and authentic human life.[1]

Creation and redemption find their final realisation in the new heaven and the new earth. As Divine WORD Missionaries, we need to look at the Bible as a form of a story that begins with creation (Gen 1:1) and ends with creation (Rev 21:1-4).

This broad understanding of evangelisation, meaningful in the general Asian context, is contained in documents of Vatican II (GS, NA, DH and UR). Putting these insights together we can conclude that evangelisation today is the leavening of the world, considered as a leavening of gospel values and as making it easier to reach the final goal of building up a new humanity. The proclamation is realised in the mutual self-gift and consequent mutual enrichment of Dialogue,which the SVD XV General Chapter (2000) renamed as a four-fold **Prophetic Dialogue** with faith seekers, with people of other faith traditions, with people of other cultures, and with the poor and marginalised. "The XIII General Chapter of 1988 spoke about these same matters in terms of 'passing over' at the 'frontiers' of class, culture and religion. Even a cursory look at contemporary church documents and missiological works makes clear that the matters addressed in our four-fold dialogue are at the heart of the *ad gentes* mission."[2]

Since the religions are at the service of the world, inter-religious dialogue cannot be confined to the religious sphere but must embrace all dimensions of life: economic, socio-political, cultural and religious. It is in their common commitment to the fuller life of the human community that they discover their complementarity, the urgency and relevance of dialogue at all levels, socio-economic, intellectual, spiritual, among the common people in daily life as among scholars and people with deep religious experience.[3] This reflection of the Federation of Asian Bishops' Conferences gives full backing to the SVD Chapter's redefinition of its mission as prophetic dialogue today. Number 8 of the conclusions of the seminar on 'Prophetic Dialogue' attended by representatives from the SVD and SSpS Provinces reads:

> The Church's mission of imparting the Good News is based on the dialogue of salvation initiated by the Triune God and revealed in Jesus Christ. Dialogue is "the characteristic mode of the Church's life in Asia" (EA 3). We have to discern signs of God's presence and purpose in the world in a spirit of dialogue (GS 11). Dialogue must always be prophetic. "What is expected of us missionaries is to listen, to follow, to give witness to, and proclaim the Word of God, and to denounce without fear all that is opposed to the Gospel and the Kingdom of God" (IDW-2/31). Prophetic dialogue is the deepest and best understanding of one's vocation. Missionaries are called to enter the four-fold prophetic dialogue today.[4]

In his reflections on the 'Spirituality of Mission', Fr. Thomas Ascheman, former SVD Mission Secretary, describes the fruits of this prophetic dialogue in these words: "In dialogue with faith seekers there is the fruit of welcome, witness and discipleship; with the poor and marginalised there are the fruits of solidarity and empowerment; with people of different cultures there are the fruits of Inculturation and the promotion of life-giving values; and with people of different religious traditions there are the fruits religious tolerance, respect and inter-religious collaboration."[12] These four fruits can create, as he calls it, a kind of "unusual friendship", which may release the present situation of 'anxiety' which militant terrorist attacks have created all over the world. The unholy alliance between religion and violence has turned religious fanatics into extremists. Terrorist organisations are threatening the social order even in India today, and this has an impact upon communal politics, ethnic mentality, religious sensibility and cultural identity. There is a widespread suspicion of the claim of religions to be peace loving, unity fostering and brotherhood upholding, for the reality is often very different. In such a situation, prophetic dialogue is the mission of the Church in India.

Pope John Paul II in *Redemptoris Missio* describes the vast horizons of mission for which there are different tasks and activities (Chapter IV). Pope Paul VI in *Evangelii Nuntiandi* acknowledges, "Today we face a religious situation which is extremely varied and changing" (32). God has placed us in this world, and he has given us a variety. Moreover, it is part of the mystery of God that there is variety that can be complementary and that it can contribute to the totality. Therefore, if we want to evangelise a world, where the complex phenomenon of violence has become almost a way of life, we have to work with other religions and their insights.[5]

The prophetic dialogue calls us for a new way of being missionaries in the context of diverse religious traditions, secular ideologies, vibrant cultures, and the teeming millions of poor *dalits* and tribals. The SVD's distinctive call is to commit ourselves to the four-fold prophetic dialogue in frontier situations. The characteristic dimensions of our missionary life and service, namely Bible Apostolate, Mission Animation, Justice, Peace and Integrity of Creation (JPIC) and Communication are quite novel in SVD terminology. These dimensions were already concerns of our father and leader, St. Arnold Janssen, although these developed through the years as characteristic dimensions of our charism and emerged from the responses of our missionaries to the mission challenges in all four zones and at different periods of history. The Statement of XV SVD General Chapter of 2000 captures this important realisation that there is something historical about these dimensions:

> Our characteristic dimensions invite us to deepen our experience of the Divine Word in multiple ways. We get to know the Biblical Word whose story is told in Scriptures. We proclaim the Animating Word who calls everyone to share in mission. We commit ourselves to the Prophetic Word who announces peace, justice and the transformation of all creation. We share the Communicating Word who seeks only to be poured out in self-giving love (CS 74).[6]

Moreover, the Chapter likened these four characteristic dimensions to SVD family traits that make both the community life and the missionary activity unique. They somehow belong to our identity our history and our Charism.[7] They do help to round out the picture of our missionary vision.

Endnotes

[1] *SVD Characteristic Dimensions*, (Rome: SVD Publications, 2002), 29.

[2] Cf. BIRA III/7, *For All the Peoples of Asia* (Manila: 1984).

[3] L. Stanislaus and A. D'Souza, eds., *Prophetic Dialogue – Challenges and Prospects in India*, (Pune: Ishvani Kendra/ISPCK, 2003), 153.

[4] *Ibid.,* 17.

[5] Cf. Jerome D'Souza, "Religion and Violence," in *The Church in India in the Emerging Third Millennium*, ed., Thomas D'Sa (Bangalore: N.B.C.L.C., 2005), 257-271.

[6] Antonio M. Pernia, *Foreword* to "SVD Characteristic Dimensions" (Rome: SVD Publications, 2002) 23.

[7] *Ibid.,* 61.

A Critical Appraisal of SVD Communication Mission in INC:

Contemporary Challenges and its Prospects

Clarence Srambical SVD

Introduction

The SVD Central Indian Province articulated quite aptly a vision-mission statement at the beginning of the 3rd millennium. The statement is as follows:

The Vision: "That they all may be one" (Jn 17, 21).

The Mission: : As members of the Central Indian Province of the Society of the Divine Word, we strive to foster unity and harmony in our multi-cultural, multi-religious and diverse situations fragmented by ethnocentrism, fanaticism, discrimination and inequality, through dialogue of life and action with all people and become bridge builders. We endeavor to involve all in planning, decision-making and implementation of projects, promotion and evaluation of apostolates to make the poor and the marginalized communities to be self-affirming and self-reliant.

The vision sets the goal for us in INC; it is clearly and simply identifying with the vision of Jesus himself in whose footsteps the INC members have been going forward in these parts of the country. And as such, it is a valid and suitable goal for anyone in the mission.

As part of the preparation for the 2018 General Chapter, our members became aware that we need to engage in the process of renewal of oneself, community life, and mission. The 18th General Chapter also made an effort to re-found the Congregation back to its roots – the Word of God. No doubt, the Capitulars in this Chapter felt that "OUR NAME IS OUR MISSION".

This identification of our mission with our name is what Marshall McLuhan said years ago, the medium is the message. The medium – our life and activities with our identity thus becomes our message to the world at large. We ought to be people of the Word and become fully identified with the Word if we have to have any impact with our life and activities among the people we live. Already the 15th General Chapter while talking about the Society, identified communication as a characteristic dimension that every SVD ought to live and communicate. This is a constant challenge for all Divine Word Missionaries, specifically for those who are trying to be media professionals.

In the light of the above, I would like to scan and scrutinize the communitarian initiatives and activities to examine how far they mirror or are close to the target of achieving in practice the evangelization goals that SVD has set in INC. The vision calls for unity as the aim. The INC Mission statement was articulated taking into account the fissures in the 'multi-cultural, multi-religious and diverse situations' existing among the people. And in this context, the confreres here have generally identified their vocation - to be bridge builders.

To be bridge builders, then, they ought to be exposed to and related to people of different religions and become acceptable to them. The bridge builders should become icons of dialogue of life and action. Only then could we become people who usher in unity in the communities and societies, we live and interact. It calls forth creativity and pioneering initiatives in a vast field to meet and accept the challenges as opportunities for Mission.

Dialogue of Life and Action

In the past, INC was credited to have taken several initiatives to reach to people of other faiths. In Madhya Pradesh, other dioceses looked at Indore and learned from its initiatives. Today, initiatives are being taken equally by others but several of us have become maintainers of status quo! But, there is nothing wrong about it, as long as, we are sincerely identifying our life and activities with our characteristic dimensions and get across to others as genuine persons and communities.

From 1969, the state government brought in "the Freedom of Religion Law"; and later with the arrival of BJP governments in the state and the center, direct proclamation almost ceased even in our rural missions. This, despite the fact, the law does not forbid us from sharing the message of the Gospel publicly. It has only put in restrictions on the way of someone wanting to become a Christian.

Even before we experienced oppositions, we wanted to reach out to caste Hindus and upper class people through dialogue. But dialogue ministry got a fillip when opposition from fundamentalist forces became quite open and made life difficult for missionaries to move freely among the villages. Pundits made distinctions and talked about the dialogue of life, and action especially valid in the context of mission herein these contexts, let us look at some of the challenges and opportunities that come on the way of SVD in INC.

Use of Information and Traditional media for Dialogue

At the beginning of 1960(,) Indore Diocese launched Masih Vidya Bhavan, Information Center in Indore, with the precise objective to reach out to urban and literate higher classes. It opened a library cum reading room. Initially this center was managed by diocesan priests but from 1972 onwards it is managed by the SVD personnel. Frs. Clement Moolankuzhy, James Mariakumar, Varghese Nediakalayil, Prasad Kuzhively and now Raju Sastya have contributed much for the growth of various activities here. Since we took over the management,

'Correspondence Course' in collaboration with IHS Centre Poona organized by Jesuits, has been developed further by printing and distributing additional material from here. These materials were dispatched to anyone who expressed a desire to know more about Jesus Christ and the Church. Since several years, this program is being run in collaboration with Holy Spirit Sisters. Masih Vidya Bhavan gradually became the best run center in the country that had almost 30000 persons as correspondents. However, for the last one to two decades those seeking information have come down but still it mails materials approximately to 15000 people annually. The advantage of the above method is to reach out to those who have expressed their interest and desire voluntarily.

The center is also actively pursuing Inter-religious dialogue and ecumenism through two associations. One, Sadbhavana Prathishtan started by Fr. Prasad Kuzhively and other, United Christian Forum whose chairperson is Fr. Clarence Srambical but whose secretariat is based in Masih Vidya Bhavan. Regular meetings are organized for prayer and sharing of views through both from time to time during the year. On an average about 30-40 people are regular participants from different communities for such programs. However, people join in hundreds for protest meetings, prayer for the nation and Christmas programs. The Centre also organizes the Unity Octave week in different Churches. Through these activities, some of us SVDs reach out to people of goodwill from various religious communities as well as from the churches and forge lasting friendships. These certainly help us to take initiatives to build bridges across Religions and Churches in Indore.

In the past, Masih Vidya Bhavan also organized several exhibitions in the city on the themes: 'God in search of Man' and on 'Salvation History'. These exhibitions drew thousands. Now, the Cathedral parish displays exhibits of large flex pictures on Salvation History during the Christmas season on Cathedral grounds that attract annually thousands of people.

Maitri Sadan Udaipur

Initially Maitri Sadan organized 'Correspondence Course' for the people in collaboration with Holy Spirit Sisters. But gradually, starting with Fr. Prasad Kuzhively, they moved to organizing prayer sessions and meetings with people of goodwill of all communities.

Presently Maitri Sadan Udaipur under the leadership of Fr. Norbert Herman has been making waves in Rajasthan and beyond through his music and singing concerts and *Sarva Dharm Sammellan*. Regular inter-religious meetings are organized by Maitri Sadan that bring hundreds of people in contact with the staff and establish lasting relationships.

USE OF MASS MEDIA IN INC

Satprakashan Sanchar Kendra, Indore

Individual members of INC used to occasionally write articles, publish books and give radio programs. They also used mobile units of short films, slide-programs, and feature films to communicate the message of the Divine Word. But more concerted efforts in this direction began with the founding of Satprakashan Sanchar Kendra in 1980 by Fr. Clarence Srambical.

Since then, Satprakashan Sanchar Kendra, Indore, has been playing a pivotal role in Madhya Pradesh in the use of mass media to communicate the message of the Gospel. It functions as Regional Communication Center. Subsequent directors and their team have left their mark on the activities of this center. Presently the team led by Frs. John Paul, Lawrence Fernandes and Antony Swamy Swamikkannu have taken several initiatives to build on the activities of this institution especially on Internet and traditional media like music and dance.

Publication of books, audio-video programs and related activities

Initially Satprakashan started to publish much-needed books on religious, spiritual, devotional and development areas. During this time, Satprakashan published Bible stories for children and thus tried to reach the Word of God to them. Later, it began publishing the Hindi Bible for the entire Hindi belt. During this time, the center also started a bookshop, a lending library of feature films, videos for use in the mission. The staff from the center went to screen "Daya Sagar" feature film on the life of Christ that brought the staff directly to people. All the book releases or audiocassette releases were media events that brought a few hundred people in contact with the staff.

Radio Satyaswar, through Radio VERITAS, Manila

Satprakashan grabbed a timely opportunity for evangelization and dialogue when Satprakashan signed a contract with RVA Manila to produce daily Hindi programs. Socio-cultural and Bible themes were prepared in Satprakashan studio and sent to Manila for each day where another Indian SVD confrere was responsible for the broadcasting accordingly, in1988 Satprakashan launched radio programs in Hindi with Frs Joseph Kayany and Dominic Emmanuel as coordinators of the program in Indore and Manila. Later Frs Deepak Sulya, Norbert Herman, John Wakhla and Herman Bandod served as Coordinators at Manila. The program was aired under its banner "Radio Satyaswar" morning and evening on short wave in collaboration with Radio Veritas Asia, Manila. It has been on since then till today. The feedback from the listeners was primarily through postal letters. On an average more than 5000 letters were received annually. Through them, one could gauge the popularity and acceptance of the programs. Generally, Satprakashan was able to enter into dialogue with listeners through letters and through programs that had certain transformative value for quite a few listeners.

Lately, the Radio Satya Swar is available 24 hour on the Internet and through Aap. Presently the Radio programs have approximately hundred thousand listeners for one or the other programs in a week. People are free to select what they would like to listen. Satprakashan has also launched sharing the Word of God through Internet independent of radio programs. These too have thousands of readers and listeners.

Video Studio and production of videos and films

The 1980s saw the expansion of mass media especially television with its cable networks, posing new opportunities for the Divine Word Missionaries. Satprakashan expanded its activities by adding further facilities for Video studio and rooms for participants to stay for training programs. Fr. Sony Kadekelil began the work of directing and the production of videocassettes for cable networks of Indore. Christmas and Easter programs directed by him were telecast on a routine basis through these networks. After him came Fr. Geo George who produced several short films and later his major undertaking, the release of 'Khristayan' written and produced by Geo George in Hindi. Presently the Video Department is managed by Fr. Lawrence Fernandes who too keeps producing short films from the center as well as produces films for our partners who seek our collaboration.

Thus Satprakashan studios both audio and video are regularly being used to record audios and videos. They bring in several people into contact with the institution. Further, the customers for books, religious articles, audio-video CDs, training programs draw several people regularly to the premises.

Training programs

Besides the above, Satprakashan has started for those interested to get training in traditional media like music and dance that regularly bring several young budding artists to the premises. Along with these specific programs that the center conducts, it also organizes training programs for M.P./Chhattisgarh Church personnel both lay persons and missionaries. The Satprakashan team also conducts media education and media training programs at the Centre and elsewhere, in order to make people critical and intelligent consumers of media.

Through all these media activities, the staff of Satprakashan enters directly and indirectly with thousands of people who avail of its services regularly. They certainly get information and specialized services in above areas.

"The Word Among Us"

"The Word Among Us" an Indian edition of the biblical family magazine started by Fr. Mathew Chennakudy, is presently edited and published by Frs. Clarence Srambical, George Thottian and Alfred Fernandes from Sat Prachar Press, Indore. It has been in circulation for the last seventeen years. It has a regular subscriber-base above nine thousand and as per the calculations of media specialists with every subscription there are several readers. Therefore, a very conservative estimation would indicate that we reach with every issue of the Word Among Us above fifty thousand regular readers. The feedback from the readers and their commitment to continue the subscriptions are indications that we are filling a basic need through this publication.

Prison Ministry in Indore and Udaipur

SVD personnel involved in Media activities have also got interested in the prison ministry in both Indore and Udaipur. In Indore, Fr. Clarence Srambical and in Udaipur, Fr. Norbert Herman is also engaged in coordinating prison ministry for their respective dioceses. Regular programs for the prison inmates bring in great satisfaction not only for the inmates of the prison but also to all volunteers who regularly organize such programs. In Indore, the volunteers not only conduct regular classes for prisoners who are illiterate, or teach English; and support those who want to go for higher education while they are in the prison. The group also organizes cultural events and even medical camps for the inmates of the prison. The volunteers also involved in rehabilitating released prisoners or assist their children for education.

Divya Vani, Bhopal

Divya Vani Bhopal initially situated in Indore was started by Fr. Joseph P Xavier and developed by Fr. Augustine P.A. has been making the Bible in audio-format, first through audio-cassettes, then in CD and now on the Internet. Presently, its director is Fr. Thomas Peringalloor assisted by Fr Thomas Ottrackal is trying organize some training programs.

Critical Evaluation

With a limited number of SVD personnel directly involved in providing above services, our personnel in collaboration with lay staff have shown multi-tasking abilities, definitely shown elasticity to shift their roles from inter-personal communication to group media, and then to mass media. These certainly have certain dividends. Through these activities we reach out, on the one hand to thousands of people, on the other, we are able to foster friendship with a limited number through group and inter-personal meetings and programs. In this way, certainly, the media personnel are engaged in sharing information, attitudes and values with vast number of people.

However, we are far from the ideal that we have set - to be bridge builders. Vast majority of the people still do not accept us, including those who have been exposed to our programs. They are suspicious of our motives and therefore, unless, there is significant shift in their entrenched attitudes, while collaborating with us at a certain level, still will have reservations to go deeper to accept us as bridge builders and inspirers for their lives.

Some Challenges and Opportunities

Having taken panoramic view of some of the scenes of the communication activities in INC, it would be worthwhile to identify some of the challenges and opportunities that are before us.

Today, we are increasingly feeling the biases and prejudices that have come forefront through the media, especially through TV channels. In order to score points or in line with their political bosses, the comperes of programs either exaggerate or generalize particular incidents to malign an entire community. Naturally(,) such media set the agenda what is important and accepted by vast majority of people. Often majority of the viewers and listeners are silent and do not volunteer to defend the Church personnel when we are in such difficult situations.

The basic prejudices that prevail towards the mission of the Church and the missionaries are very much entrenched in wider Indian society. They have field day on such occasions. Our presence in such media is limited and even when one or the other is called to voice our concerns, our voices are silenced by the loud cacophony or shouting matches of other panelists, including sometimes of those who function as comperes. It is not necessary to dominate the media with the use of our vocal chords or to have a shouting match but we need to be present to express our views cogently.

The above also go as far as secular print media is concerned. Neither the clergy nor the lay persons from the Christian Churches are regular contributors to secular print media and so, when negative reports or so called "fake news" are highlighted, our absence is significant.

Another aspect is that generally we do not write in secular papers and air views in secular TV channels about various issues that the larger society grapples with. We give news about our programs or give features during Christmas or Easter. Precisely because of this, our opinions are not sought on major social, economic or political, cultural issues. If our educationists, social development activists collaborate instead of running parallel programs, join forces with other secular agencies, certainly opportunities will knock on our doors.

In this context, it is important to stress net-working not only among media people but net working with all other SVD personnel and people of good-will who are actively present in various apostolates. For net-working not only among ourselves but also with others of good will make a significant difference.

In Indore, annually, a gathering is organized for the media personnel during Christmas season. Major newspapers and channels are represented in such gathering. They do cover Christmas and other religious programs during the year. But, rarely some of them have made any effort to know our point of view when we are on the receiving end.

It is clear that our presence in the mainstream secular media is extremely limited especially in the Hindi belt. We are still running parallel periodicals, small monthlies, weeklies or parallel channels on Internet. It is because of this, most likely, that we are unable to become bridge builders in the society at large where it matters most.

Is this because we find more comfort being in our shells? Is our training and formation makes us to be separate from the mainstream? Is there something wrong with the entire formation program that isolates us from the main society for very long periods of time? Even our lay persons are hardly present in the secular media in significant positions to make a difference. Do we as a whole cultivate a ghetto mentality?

Many of us function as bureaucrats. We are not much different from them. We are transferred like bureaucrats after a few years in a place or in an institution. Naturally, we do not take roots in a place in terms of building up permanent relations and friends. Long innings ina place is needed to build lasting relationships to instill confidence among the people to accept one as a mediator or as bridge builder.

In the north India, vast majority of the missionaries hail from other parts of India and so, we are considered 'foreigners'. Our command over language and local culture is wanting despite lot of goodwill. We have working knowledge of the language and culture but that is not enough to inspire people deeply. Therefore, we need to inspire local lads to join the society for its future in a significant way.

Formation of our Lay Partners

SVD has been encouraging and in some provinces forging relationships with other religious and lay partners to be present in the wider world. In this regard, we have to do much more here in INC. We also need to become proactive with our lay persons and assist in their formation right from cradle to grave!

Our expectations would be that the Catholics who are thus exposed to the worldview and values to the Kingdom would be fully immersed in the life of the nation. They ought to become builders of bridges across communities through life and activities. However, sadly this is not true. Vast majority of our Catholics are inward looking, as most of us, missionaries are equally inwardly looking. And extremely, a few would get involved in the life of the village or town or state. Most keep themselves comfortably within their own ghetto.

Catechesis is primarily concentrating on the faith formation of young people who are already baptized. In fact, formal training in faith formation for Catholics more or less stops with marriage preparation course. But, informal education goes on through Sunday liturgy, basic or small Christian communities and several seminars and programs that take place through various forums in the parishes, dioceses and on the SVD level. We need to begin adult catechesis for Catholic lay professionals at various levels to enable them to come out of their shells and be active in the mainstream of society.

In the Church, there have been some efforts to provide training for lay persons but much more need to be done in this sector especially because vast majority of our faithful are drawn from traditionally oppressed communities. Therefore, they need to be highly inspired and empowered to take leadership positions in the secular field!

Conclusion

We have taken a panoramic view of different media apostolates from traditional to most modern media we engage in INC; and how we have to actively take up those opportunities that come our way for dialogue of life and action. In Hindi belt, vast majority of the missionaries hail from other parts of India. We are considered as outsiders and we get hardly involved in the life of the wider society. Therefore, though we would like to become bridge builders and peace makers, we are not anywhere on the scene when it matters most. We need to be Spirit filled people to become mavericks and not just prudent persons who seek security in the world. Only the Lord can give us the security, until then, such responses will continue to plague us!

A Philosophical Foundation for Interfaith Dialogue: The Lonerganian Perspective

Thomas Chacko SVD

Introduction

Vatican II, affirms the yearning of men and women of our times to draw closer in bonds of friendship *(Nostra Aetate* 1). However, we are also aware of the forces at work in our society to divide people on the basis of nationality, religion, caste, creed, ideology, language etc. In such a complex context church recognises the importance of dialogue for its life and mission. *NA* states "The Church rejects nothing of what is true and holy in these religions …" The church, therefore, urges her sons to enter with prudence and charity into discussion and collaboration with members of other religions (*NA* 2). Many other Council and Post Council documents corroborate this new outlook of the Church.[1]

S V D and Dialogue

For Society of the Divine Word dialogue is an inalienable aspect of our missionary activity today. The key term that emerged from the 15th General Chapter was 'dialogue', four-fold prophetic dialogue. For the 16th General Chapter dialogue was chosen as its theme: "Living Prophetic Dialogue: Spirituality, Community, Formation, Leadership, Finances".[2]

Who is Bernard Lonergan?

Bernard Joseph Francis Lonergan, an Irish Canadian, was born on 17 December 1904, at Buckingham, Quebec, Canada as the eldest of the three children born to Gerald Lonergan and Josephine Helen. In 1918, at the age of thirteen, Bernard went as a boarder to Loyola College, a Jesuit school in Montreal and left it in 1922 to join the Society of Jesus. The consequent formation followed a pattern more or less normal for Jesuits: classical studies (Guelp in Ontario), philosophy (Heythrop College in England, with specialization in languages and mathematics for a degree at the University of London), theology (Gregorian University in Rome), and second novitiate or "tertianship" (Amiens in France). Graduate studies won him a doctorate in theology (at the Gregorian again), and he began his professorial career in 1940 at L'Immacul'ee- Conception, the Jesuit Theologate in Montreal; then Regis College, the sister Theologate in Toronto, midway through the year 1946-1947; and then the Gregorian in Rome in 1953. His most important work *Insight* was published in 1957. He died in 1984.

The contributions he made, in 80 years of his life, both to philosophy and theology, to say the least, is indeed remarkable. Meynell in his *An Introduction to the Philosophy of Bernard Lonergan* says: "Lonergan's philosophy is one of the outstanding achievements of our time, and applicable to a vast range of pressing intellectual, moral, social, political, educational and religious problems."[3] Bertrand Russell's remark that it takes a good part of our lives to enter into the thought of any first-rate thinker is absolutely true of Lonergan. While *Insight* is regarded as a profound and brilliant treatise on philosophical subjects, written in our times, it is also a difficult book. This has led Collin Brown to characterize Lonergan as "a thinker to be wrestled with."[4] However, any serious-minded reader who is willing to study Lonergan with patience will have no difficulty in understanding the general import of his philosophy. He will gain the reward that comes to any person who makes himself at home with one of the master minds of our times.

Lonergan's cognitional structure

Lonergan's cognitional structure provides a philosophical foundation for interfaith dialogue. His cognitional structure is developed as a response to questions for intelligence and questions for reflection. Questions for reflection ask 'is it so?' of what is understood in response to the questions for intelligence and are answered by 'it is' or 'it is so' / 'it is not' or 'it is not so'.[5] However, between the reflective question 'is it so?' and the answer 'it is so' there is much activity involved: a process of marshalling and weighing of evidence. At certain stage of this process one recognises or grasps the sufficiency of evidence to make a prospective judgment. This recognition or grasp of the evidence as sufficient for a prospective judgment is to recognise or grasp the judgment as virtually unconditioned.

It is at the third level of cognitional structure, which is the reflective moment, that one advances from thinking an object to affirming it in judgment and, thus, knowing it as a being, as a reality. It is the activity of critical reflection and the attainment of virtually unconditioned that transforms our knowing into truly human knowing.

Towards the Virtually unconditioned

The cognitional process that begins from experience and finds its final partial increment in judgment is grounded in the virtually unconditioned as far as its truth content is concerned. But prior even to cognitional process is the sense of wonder, the desire to know that is natural to man. We begin our discussions of this section with a consideration of this sense of wonder, which is a dynamic drive, the object of which as we shall see is being.

The Pre-eminence of the Dynamic Drive

As the term 'towards' in the title of this section implies, the attainment of the virtually unconditioned is the result of a process. There is much effort and activity involved before one attains the virtually unconditioned. Differing from all other animals it is human beings alone who ask questions. What these questions manifest is the dynamism, the drive to know, the sense of wonder which are natural to the humans. This dynamic drive to know, this sense of wonder is prior to cognitional process; in fact, it is this drive, this wonder that sets the very process in motion and is operative at every stage of the process.[6] The cognitional operations themselves are prepositional, pre-verbal, pre-judgemental, pre-conceptual[7] but the drive to know is prior to all these.[8]

The Notion of Being

Lonergan's central concern has been to know what 'is', that is to say, to know being.[9] What the dynamic structure of human knowing intends is being. In the cognitional process, which consists of experience, understanding and judging, it is being that is intelligently grasped and reasonably affirmed because apart from being there is nothing. Anything that is non-being is nothing, is non-real. "As answers stand to questions, so cognitional activities stand to the intention of being."[10]

Intentionality Intends Being

Unlike other animals humans do not cease to have interest in his sensations even when his sensitive demands for food and drink and need to mate are met. The inherent drive, the desire to know, the cognitional dynamism, which is commonly called intentionality, naturally tends to understand what is given in experience. Let us consider the example of the experience of a lunar eclipse: at the instance of such an experience one wants to understand what an eclipse is? Once he understands what eclipse is he wants to make sure what he understood is true. So he asks, 'Is it so?' The critical enquiry ends in the grasp of the virtually unconditioned and in an affirmation, 'it is'. The 'is' of 'it is' stands for the real, the being, the true. The intelligent and rational inquiry is an inquiry for the real, for the being.

> All marshalling and weighing of evidence, all judging and doubting, are efforts to say of what is that it is and of what is not that it is not. Accordingly, the dynamic structure of human knowing intends being. That intention is unrestricted, for there

is nothing that we cannot at least question. The same intention is comprehensive, for questioning probes every aspect of everything; its ultimate goal is the universe in its full concreteness. Being in that sense is identical with reality: as apart from being there is nothing, so apart from reality there is nothing: as being embraces the concrete totality of everything, so too does reality.[11]

Proper Object of Human Knowledge

Though, as we saw above, human knowledge tends towards unlimited being the proper object of human knowledge is material being or reality.[12] That is to say, it is the material reality alone that is proportionate to the mode of knowing that is proper to humans because, "man's desire to know is unrestricted while his capacity to know is limited..."[13] Or, "Man's unrestricted desire to know is mated to a limited capacity to attain knowledge."[14] Human understanding is experience-dependent (limited by what one experiences), *intelligere sensibili* (insight into the sensible) and human judging is understanding-dependent (limited by what one understands).[15] Thus, human knowledge, though tends towards unlimited being, the absolutely unconditioned, knowledge of everything that *is*, what, in fact, it knows is, indeed an unconditioned but not formally or absolutely unconditioned but the virtually unconditioned. It has the status of an unconditioned because its conditions are fulfilled. Thus, in every judgment we make, it is being, real, the objective that is known because every judgment is grounded in the virtually unconditioned. It can be said, "being is whatever can be grasped intelligently and affirmed reasonably."[16] What is grasped in the virtually unconditioned is grasped intelligently and rationally; the virtually unconditioned results from intelligent search and rational affirmation. Moreover, what is intelligently grasped and reasonably affirmed is real, is true.

Reflective Moment

This is the third moment of the cognitional structure, the first and second being empirical and intellectual, respectively. As has been clear by now, with the question for reflection the reflective moment of the cognitional process begins leading to the knowledge of proportionate being. The operations of the rational consciousness or of reflective moment could be understood as consisting of Critical Reflection, Reflective Understanding and Judgment.

Critical Reflection

Just as intelligence, coming up against data of experience, spontaneously and naturally enquires into data seeking the intelligible in the sensible so also rationality seeks for evidence or for the rational basis of what is understood before affirmation or denial is made in a judgment. As Lonergan would say, "The formulations of understanding yield concepts, definitions, objects of thought, suppositions, considerations. But man demands more. Every answer to a question for intelligence raises a further question for reflection."[17]

A question for intelligence urges us on to enquiry, understanding and formulation of concept. Similarly, a question for reflection urges us on to a different kind of insight and to judgment. What is understood has to be judged as to be so or not so. The distinction between fact and fiction, logic and sophistry, philosophy and myth, history and legend, astronomy and astrology, chemistry and alchemy emerges only when a judgment is made.[18] It is at this level we judge something to be true or false, certain or probable. Thus, there is the need to gather sufficient evidence before we make a judgment because we judge something to be true, false, certain or probable depending on the sufficiency of evidence. Lonergan summarizes it thus:

> Questions for intelligence presuppose something to be understood, and that something is supplied by the initial level. Understanding grasps in given or imagined presentations an intelligible form emergent in the presentations. Conception formulates the grasped idea along with what is essential to the idea in the presentations. Reflection asks whether such understanding and formulation are correct. Judgment answers that they are or are not.[19]

Reflective Understanding

It is an insight that is gained in response to a question for reflection and is similar to direct and introspective insight which is gained in response to a question for intelligence.[20] The end result of reflective understanding is a judgment and that of the other a definition or a formulation. While reflective understanding grasps the sufficiency of evidence for a prospective judgment the other grasps a unity, system or an ideal frequency.[21]

All of us have at some time deliberated on, for and against, some issues before we passed a judgment, before we made up our mind. At certain stage of this deliberation, in making up our mind, we are confident that we have sufficient evidence to pass a judgment in a certain way or to make up our mind taking a specific stand. When we have the confidence about the sufficiency of evidence for a prospective judgment we have performed an act of reflective understanding. However, in order to distinguish what exactly occurs in a reflective insight much introspective analysis needs to be done.

Judgment presupposes a question for reflection, 'Is it so?' The only meaningful answer to this question is, 'it is so' or 'it is not so' which is a judgment. However, between the question and the judgment there is a process of marshalling and weighing the evidences. "To marshal the evidence is to ascertain whether all the conditions are fulfilled. To weigh the evidence is to ascertain whether the fulfillment of the conditions certainly or probably involves the existence of occurrence of the conditioned."[22] The judgment is made only when there is a grasp of the sufficiency of evidence and, in fact, "to pronounce judgment without that reflective grasp is merely to guess; again, ... once that grasp has occurred, then to refuse to judge is just silly."[23]

The Virtually Unconditioned

With the question 'Is it so?' the reflective moment of the cognitional process starts. The aim of the process is to reach a stage of confidence with regard to the reasonableness of the ground, based on which the answer 'it is' or 'it is not' is given. Here a point needs to be taken note of; the answer 'it is' is not limited by any conditions because before the judgment is made there is a grasp of the fulfilment of conditions. In other words, before the answer 'it is' is given there is a grasp of the reasonableness of the ground based on which the affirmation is made. Because the conditions are fulfilled, because one is convinced of the reasonableness of the ground, the 'it is' is unconditioned. According to Lonergan, the affirmation "involves an element of the *absolute*, the ground of what we mean when we speak of the *eternality of truth*."[24]

Judgments on the Correctness of Insights

We have seen that it is the reflective understanding (reflective insight) that grasps the evidence as sufficient in order to make a concrete judgment of fact. Now, the question to be asked is, how do we know the reflective understanding is correct? The judgment would be correct, only if the reflective understanding is correct. Thus, simply put, here the issue is, how do we know our judgment of fact is true?[25] A summary answer to this may be given: at the level of rational consciousness the critical reflective task should be performed in such a way that all the data that would be relevant to the object thought has to be presented in the sense experience.[26] Critical reflection should also make sure that none of the data that is presented in experience, which has relevance with regard to the insight, is overlooked.

In his discussion on the correctness of insights, Lonergan makes a distinction between vulnerable and invulnerable insights. "Insights are vulnerable when there are further questions to be asked on the same issue."[27] It is an insight but there are further questions that arise which are relevant to the insight. These questions may give rise to further insights that compliment, qualify or even may modify the present one. The present one may give rise to a cluster of insights. But in the course of time it can reach a stage when there are no further relevant questions that may give rise to insights that compliment, qualify or modify the present insight. Such an insight is an invulnerable insight.

Based on our analysis the immanent law of cognitional process can be formulated as follows: "such an insight is correct if there are no further pertinent questions."[28] From this it follows that if there are no further pertinent questions for the prospective judgment, then we can be confident, the conditions are fulfilled. However, it is not enough that further questions don't occur to me. I might have lost interest in the matter or I may be more obsessed with satisfying other drives rather than the drive to know. To pass judgment in such cases would be rash. I need to wait for and welcome the questions from others too; questions which are pertinent to the insight.

This offers a philosophical foundation for dialogue. Other faiths, other religions may have questions which are pertinent to the insight that I have of my faith and religion. I am open to, interact and dialogue with people of other faiths and religions so that I may not overlook and be ignorant of any questions which would jeopardies my insight from gaining the status of an invulnerable insight

Lonergan and Inter-Faith Dialogue

In this section an attempt will be made to demonstrate the praxis potential of Lonergan's cognitional theory for inter-faith dialogue. This will be done by developing the intersubjective side of Lonergan's cognitional theory, as intersubjectivity is a constitutive element of dialogue.

Lonergan's Pragmatics of Insight

It may be noted that Lonergan's approach has much in common with formal pragmatics. Here, by "pragmatics" what we mean is an analysis at the level of practice or performance, in contrast to semantic and syntactic levels of analysis.[29] Since Lonergan's cognitional account in *Insight* is more concerned about what knowers do, rather than on the specific concepts they must have in order to know, it represents a kind of pragmatics. His analysis is "formal" as far as it surveys different contexts of knowing in order to arrive at the formal structures governing a broad spectrum of cognitive acts, the general process or operations any knower in any field of inquiry must undertake in order to arrive at a judgment.

A contrast with Kantian epistemology can further clarify the pragmatic nature of Lonergan's approach. When Kant, in the *Critique of Pure Reason*,addresses the question of how objective knowledge is possible, he is primarily interested to show how a claim covering all empirical reality can count as knowledge, given that one can never investigate more than a part of such reality. His effort to find a solution ends when he locates universality and necessity, and, thus, the objectivity of scientific knowledge, at the level of "categories of understanding," fundamental semantic structures comprising the necessary conditions for the possibility of meaningful experience on the part of a rational subject. Precisely because the "categories of understanding" or the *a prioris* are universal and necessary structures of experience, they provide criteria of objectivity and, thus, make objective knowledge possible.[30] Thus, Kant's analysis highlights the role of concepts or semantic structures in the constitution of knowledge. The important work is done not so much by the process of judgment as by the fundamental categories that organize experience.

Lonergan, by contrast, defines knowing and objectivity not by semantic structures but by the dynamic *process* driven by the desire to know and capped by judgments.[31] Once again, the pragmatic or performative focus is evident: to understand how knowledge is possible, one must look not so much to fundamental categories or concepts for organizing experience as to the active process in which potential knowers engage in order to satisfy their desire to know, the process that first generates fundamental concepts to begin with. According to Lonergan, this desire to know, if suitably unleashed from other interests, does not rest content with a given set of concepts, but drives beyond these to ask whether they are actually correct, i.e., to ask whether they are the most appropriate categories for understanding reality or not.[32] It is the point at which Lonergan introduces his "is it so?" question, a question that sets one on a path of gathering sufficient evidence, in order to reach the virtually unconditioned, before one judges "yes" or "no." Lonergan would say, one puts an end to his gathering of evidence when he grasps that there are no further pertinent questions, with regard to the direct insight, of which, the "is it so?" was asked.[33] Lonergan, at this point, makes a distinction between invulnerable and vulnerable insights: such direct insights, of which there *are no* further pertinent questions, are called invulnerable; and such direct insights, of which there *are* further pertinent questions, are vulnerable.[34] Lonergan's insistence on attending to all pertinent questions, now shall be shown, point to the intersubjective dimension of insight.

Insight as Intersubjective

Direct and reflective insights[35] have an intersubjective dimension. This may be most evident with direct insights. Any individual's direct insights owe their existence to a background of meanings the individual shares with others. One possesses most of these meanings as a member of a specific language community, others are specific to a particular subgroup such as a religious community, and still others are inherited from those who have previously worked on a specific problem. Although, direct insights certainly depend on the individual's creative synthetic efforts in arriving at new ideas for solving a problem, such insights presuppose a much wider and deeper dependence on others. As a result, direct insights only occur within traditions of meaning and prior insights.

At first glance, the intersubjective character of reflective insight is less obvious. For, when I judge that a direct insight is correct, is it not I and I alone who render judgment, who take personal responsibility for what I affirm? Lonergan provides the first clue that matters are more complicated than the obvious: "It is not enough to say that the conditions [for correct judgment] are fulfilled when no further questions *occur to me*."[36] There should be enough space for others to pose such questions.[37] Thus, according to Lonergan, correct judgments depend on a grasp that all the further, pertinent questions have been answered and as we have seen, such questions come from others too. Lonergan's concept of insight in this intersubjective context may be reformulated thus: "One can grasp a given answer or prospective judgment as probably correct to the extent that one has the reflective insight that there are no further, pertinent questions to be raised in an unhampered discussion of the currently available information, arguments, and counterarguments by all those who are competent on the matter at hand."[38]

Now what remains to be done is to bring into focus, the impact, the intersubjective elements of Lonergan's cognitional structure have in the evolving understanding of Church, with regard to its relation to other faiths.　Church's growing openness to other faiths has been officially inaugurated with the Vatican Council II.　However, as we have seen, much before Church officially declared its openness to other faiths, Lonergan through his intersubjectivity had suggested such a shift in perspective. Lonergan had completed *Insight* in 1953, though it was published only in 1957, just a few years prior to the commencement of the Council in 1962. One cannot fail to notice the similarity of intersubjective dimension of the *Insight* of Lonergan and the evolving opinion in the Church with regard to its stand on dialogue with other faiths.[39]

Intersubjectivity as the Ground of the Possibility of Dialogue: Towards a Lonerganian Paradigm

There exists unity among human persons that antedates and precedes the distinction between 'I' and 'thou.' This unity is primordial and foundational; this "is as if 'we' were members of one another prior to our distinctions of each from the others."[40] This prior 'we' is the ground of intersubjectivity and it is functional. One is familiar with the spontaneity with which one would raise one's hands to ward off a blow against one's head. It is with same spontaneity that one would reach out to another to save him/her from falling.[41] In one's reaching out, perception, feeling, and bodily movement are involved, but the help given to another is not deliberate but spontaneous. One is moved to such spontaneous action not before it occurs but while it is occurring.[42]

Intersubjectvity is not only at the level of actions but also at the level of feelings. Borrowing Max Scheler's[43] ideas Lonergan distinguished community of feeling, fellow-feeling, psychic contagion, and emotional identification.[44]

Besides the intersubjectivity of action and feeling, there are also intersubjective communications of meaning. This may be illustrated by attending to the phenomenology of a smile. We smile naturally and spontaneously; it does not appear as the end product of reflection and thought. Further, there is no laborious effort involved in learning to smile as well as to learn the meaning of smile as is the case with words and gestures.[45] The spontaneity with which we smile is similar to the spontaneity with which we reach out to support someone who is stumbling. The meaning that one grasps of a smile is trans-cultural. Thus, a smile does have a meaning and one is able to grasp the meaning of a smile on the face of someone else. A smile is not just a combination of certain muscular movements of lips, eyes, and face. It is a combination with a meaning. It is named a smile because its meaning is different from that of a frown, a scowl, a stare, a glare, a snicker, and a laugh. It is the underlying fundamental intersubjectivity that makes it possible for one to understand the meaning of someone else's smile immediately and spontaneously.

What is evident here is that there exists a primordial, foundational intersubjectivity at the level of action, feeling and meaning that opens up the possibility of dialogue among people of different cultures, traditions and religions. Different, though, we are, there are levels at which we are akin to one another in reaching out to help another, in feeling with another and in understanding the meaning of what another is communicating. Dialogue is possible because of similarity and the same is called for because of difference.

Dialogue of Faiths: Lonerganian Perspectives

Lonergan calls our attention to the changed understanding of theology and, thus, the need to enter into dialogue with other faiths and even other disciplines. Theology cannot be considered, merely, as the product of the religion it investigates and expounds but also of the cultural ideals and norms that set its problems and direct its solutions. Christian/Catholic theology in the thirteenth century adapted to its age by assimilating Aristotle and in the seventeenth century resisted its age by enclosing itself in the dogmatic corner. Theology of our time too is engaged in an encounter with its age. Whether it will triumph or will wither to insignificance would depend, in great measure, on the clarity and the accuracy of its grasp of the external cultural factors that undermine its past achievements and challenge it to new endeavours.[46]

Christian/Catholic theology was deductive in the sense that its theses were conclusions to be proven from the premises provided by Scripture and Tradition. Today it is considered an empirical science in the sense that Scripture and Tradition now supply not premises, but data. The data is viewed in its historical perspective. It is interpreted in the light of contemporary techniques and procedures. Lonergan maintains: "An empirical science does not demonstrate. It accumulates information, develops understanding, masters ever more of its materials, but it does not preclude the uncovering of further relevant data, the emergence of new insights, the attainment of a more comprehensive view."[47] Lonergan's intention with regard to theology is evident here. As an empirical science, he wants it to be ever open ended, accepting relevant data whenever it emerges and be ready to enter into dialogue with other disciplines and religions thereby gaining more and more comprehensive perspectives. This is further emphasised by Lonergan: "… a contemporary catholic theology has to be not only catholic but also ecumenist. Its concerns must reach not only Christians but also non-Christians and atheists. It has to learn to draw not only on the modern philosophies but also on the relatively new sciences of religion, psychology, sociology, and the new techniques of the communication arts."[48]

Lonergan goes a step ahead and lists seven principal areas of unity that can be discerned in the major world religions of our time.[49] The first in the list is the reality of the transcendent, the holy, the divine, the 'Other'. Second, the divine, while transcendent is also immanent in human hearts. Third, this reality, transcendent and immanent, is for human person the highest good, the highest truth, righteousness, goodness and beauty. Fourth, the reality of the divine is ultimate love. Fifth, the way of human person to God is the way of sacrifice. Sixth, they teach not only the way to God but, always, also the way to the neighbour as well. Finally, while religious experience is as manifold and varied as the human condition itself, the superior way to God is love. This list of unity, as is evident, provides a meaningful platform for religions to enter into dialogue.

Lonergan is not content with merely giving an account of what is common in the major world religions. He says: "… it is not Christian doctrine that the gift of God's love is restricted to Christians."[50] He takes support from the Epistle to Timothy as it says that it is God's will that all men should find salvation and come to knowledge of the truth (1 Tim. 2:4). Lonergan draws a bold conclusion and says: "… since grace is necessary to salvation, grace sufficient for salvation is given to all men."[51] What Lonergan says in clear and simple terms is that salvation is offered not only to men and women who are within the Church but to all; it is not necessary to be a member of the Church in order to be saved. The boldness of such a stand would become apparent only when we consider the times in which he took such a stand, that was, within a couple of years immediately after Vatican Council II, a time by which such views had not become vogue in the Church.[52] Lonergan was really ushering in a paradigm shift in the Church in its understanding of itself and of other religions and faiths. If truth and salvation are not the exclusive privilege of those in the Church, it is mandatory for Church to work towards dialogue with other faiths and religions.

We may conclude this section by indicating how Lonergan's intersubjecctive dimension of insight became a force in bringing about paradigm shifts in the Church. Insights, both direct and reflective, are intersubjective for any direct insight is dependent on persons' background of meanings and prior insights and every reflective insight has to take into consideration the questions that come from others. This philosophy of insight is seen to be effective in the case of theological insights as well. Every insight in theology is dependent on prior insights, the universe of meanings within which it occurs. No insight is absolutely context independent or occurs in an absolute vacuum. What the paradigm shift demonstrates is the forward moving drive of the detached, disinterested desire to know. This paradigm shift also bears testimony to the praxiological effectiveness of the intersubjective dimension of Lonergan's cognitional theory.

Endnotes

[1] See: Paul VI, Encyclical, *Ecclesiam Suam*, 1964; Asian Bishops, *Evangelization in Modern Day Asia,* 1974; Paul VI, Apostolic Exhortation, *Evangeli Nuntiandi*, 1975; John Paul, Encyclical, *Redemptoris Missio*, 1990; A joint statement by the Pontifical Council for Inter-religious dialogue and the Congregation for the Evangelization of peoples, *Dialogue and Prolclamation*, 1991.

[2] See: Antonio M. Pernia, "Prophetic Dialogue: From the XV to the XVI General Chapter. Advances, Difficulties and Challenges".

[3] Meynell, *An Introduction*, 185.

[4] Brown, *A Man to be Wrestled With*, 47.

[5] The question for intelligence, man asks, is an expression of man's intellectual dynamism and the question for reflection an expression of his rational dynamism. Over and above these, man has also a moral dynamism which is revealed in the question he asks in reference to decision, the question of 'what should I do?' This is his orientation to good. We will not be discussing this third aspect of human dynamism, here, as we have limited our study to that of man's intellectual and rational dynamisms.

[6] Lonergan, *Insight*, 34, 372-373.

[7] Lonergan, "Change in Roman Catholic Theology," 36. The Larkin-Stuart Lectures at Trinity College, Toronto, were given by Lonergan on four successive days, November 12 to 15, 1973. The titles of these lectures were, in the order in which they were given, "A New Pastoral Theology," "Variations in Fundamental Theology," "Sacralization and Secularization," and "The Scope of Renewal." His general title for these lectures was "Revolution in Roman Catholic Theology?" Three months later, on February 11, 12, and 13, 1974, Lonergan delivered the first three of these lectures in the Thomas More lecture series on the campus of Yale University, New Haven. To this series he gave the title, "Change in Roman Catholic Theology."

[8] Though, Lonergan does not acknowledge his indebtedness to Kant, Could it be that Lonergan's 'pure desire' or 'dynamic drive' is inspired by Kant's *a priori*? The similarities are obvious: for Kant, it is the *a priori* element that makes true knowledge possible (trans. F. Max Muller, *Critique of Pure Reason*, 98-109); for Lonergan, dynamic drive or pure desire is the very basis of any true knowledge. Again, for Kant, true knowledge becomes an actuality only when *a priori* is combined with *a posteriori* (trans. F. Max Muller, *Critique of Pure Reason*,109-117); for Lonergan, knowledge becomes an actuality only when pure desire encounters an object of experience. Further, for Kant, *a priori* as *a priori* is not dependent on any experience (trans. F. Max Muller, *Critique of Pure Reason*,2); for Lonergan too, pure desire as pure desire is not dependent on any experience.

[9] In reference to Lonergan's concern for being, Crowe says: "I have to state that all the intellectual activity and production I have laboriously and perhaps tediously described was only a provisional and transitional concern. If there has been a preoccupation with method and the knowing subject in almost all his works, it was subordinate to a long-range purpose of knowing better what is, of returning methodically to being. His present concern with the world that is constituted by meaning is perhaps a sign that the long transitional phase is almost over and that now he will turn to greater concentration on the object of ultimate concern which is being. His ruling passion, you might say, is being. He calls the built-in dynamism that is our fundamental drive a 'notion of being.'" Crowe, "Exigent Mind," 29.

[10] Lonergan, "Cognitional Structure," 235.

[11] Lonergan, "Cognitional Structure," 235. Lonergan says: "Objects are what are intended in questioning. What is this intending? It is neither ignorance nor knowledge but the dynamic intermediary between ignorance

and knowledge. It is the conscious movement away from ignorance and towards knowledge. When we question, we do not know the answer yet, but already we want the answer. Not only do we want the answer but also we are aiming at what is to be known through the answer. Such, then, is intending and, essentially, it is dynamic. It promotes us from mere experiencing to understanding by asking what and why and how. It promotes us from understanding to truth by asking whether this or that is really so. It promotes us from truth to value by asking whether this or that is truly good or only apparently good. As answers accumulate, as they correct, complete, qualify one another, knowledge advances. But answers only give rise to still further questions. Objects are never completely, exhaustively known, for our intending always goes beyond present achievement. The greatest achievement, so far from drying up the source of questioning, of intending, only provides a broader base whence ever more questions arise.

Intending then is comprehensive. Though human achievement is limited, still the root dynamism is unrestricted. We would know everything about everything, the whole universe in all its multiplicity and concreteness, *omnia, to pan*,and, in that concrete and comprehensive sense, being. To that object our cognitional operations are related immediately, not by sensitive intuition, but by questioning. Lonergan, "Natural Knowledge of God," 123-124.

[12] According to Harvanek, "Classical intellectualism ... maintains that the first and proportionate object of human knowledge is the sensible world. This sensible world however, is potentially intelligible, since it is the product of the first intellect, or the mind of the creator. This potential intelligibility of the world is brought to actuality for and by man through the activity of his intellect on the data received from the senses. The intellect intelligizes the sensible data and then expresses a truth about the world by forming a judgment. This interior judgment is then expressed in external speech in one of the various languages developed by man." Harvanek, "The Community of Truth," 68.

[13] Lonergan, *Insight*, 666.

[14] Lonergan, *Insight*, 662.

[15] By this it is not meant that humans have no way of knowing the transcendent realities, realities that lie beyond the sensible sphere of this world. Human intentionality is capable of and does inquire about, understand and affirm of what is beyond our sensible sphere. However, this foray into what is beyond is based on what it knows of the proportionate being. Transcendent being is affirmed on the basis of the material being. In virtually

unconditioned we have the knowledge of the existence of proportionate being. But it does not say anything about why it exists. As a contingent reality another contingent reality could be pointed out as the reason for the existence of the first one. But the question of why something contingent exists at all is not answered; the question is only shifted. As an ultimate reason for the contingent, we need to posit a transcendent being, the reason for the existence of which is not anything other than itself. Lonergan has made an attempt to address this problem in chapters 19 and 20 of *Insight*.

[16] Lonergan, *Insight*, 662.

[17] Lonergan, *Insight*, 298.

[18] Lonergan, "Cognitional Structure," 231. See also Lonergan, "The Dehellenization of Dogma," 31.

[19] Lonergan, *Insight*, 300.

[20] Carruthers says that the terms 'question' and 'insight' are used analogously. In the case of questions for intelligence, by the term 'questions' what is meant is, 'what', 'why' and 'how often' questions; whereas, in the case of question for reflection, what is meant by 'question' is, 'is it' or 'is it so' questions. The analogous use of "insight" is seen in this, that the direct or introspective insight is a grasp of unity, system or ideal frequency whereas the reflective insight grasps the sufficiency of evidence for a prospective judgment. Carruthers, *Dialectic in Lonergan's Insight and Method in Theology*, 76.

[21] Lonergan, *Insight*, 304.

[22] Lonergan, *Method*, 102.

[23] Lonergan, *Insight*, 304.

[24] Lonergan, *Understanding and Being*, 118; emphasis added. Michael Vertin has shown that Marechal too affirms the real objectivity of human knowledge. He says: "Marechal's approach to the question of the real objectivity of human knowledge, then, is simply to argue that even at a very primitive level of awareness the human subject makes judgments that are indeed discursive or affirmational. On the basis of what purportedly is a transcendental analysis, Marechal avers that a transcendental condition of one's having some concrete intelligible as phenomenally objective is that one affirm, at least implicitly, that concrete intelligible as fundamentally really objective, really existing, related to the ultimate objective term of intellectual finality. But it is undeniable that one frequently has concrete intelligibles as phenomenally objective. Consequently, says Marechal, the real

objectivity of human knowledge stands essentially vindicated, and the critical problem is dissolved." Vertin, "Dialectically Opposed Phenomenologies of Knowing," 3. Newman too, voices the same opinion. He says: "it has been my object therefore in good part of my volume to prove that there is such a thing as *unconditional assent*." Newman, *Letters and Diaries of John Henry Newman*, 375.

[25] What the question asks for is a criterion, a yardstick to determine the truth of judgments I make. The context demands a word about the notion of truth. Our own position is that the content of what is known through experience, intelligent grasp and reasonable affirmation is true. Besides this there are other ways of conceiving truth. (i) Logical truth: Every judgment has, besides the explicit content of what is affirmed or denied, an implicit content. That content is truth. In my affirmation of 'it is so' I, at the same time, imply that 'it is true that it is so'. Thus, truth, properly speaking, is a quality of the judgment, of the internal expression. It is a relation of knowing to being. Logical truth is the conformity of my affirmations and negations to what is and is not. (ii) Ontological truth: It is the intrinsic intelligibility of being. We saw that reality or being is what is known by intelligence. What is known by intelligence is the intelligible. For something to be it must be intelligible. Earlier, while discussing inverse insight, we gave the example of a 'square circle' which is absolutely unintelligible and, thus, such a 'thing' simply cannot be. Such a 'thing' lacks ontological truth. (iii) Moral truth: If what I say is a faithful representation of what I internally judge then I have what is known as moral truth. The opposite of moral truth is lie, in which, what I say is at odds with my judgment. (iv) Error: The opposite of logical truth is not a lie, but an error. When my judgment is not conformed to reality, it is false. I am mistaken. Lonergan, *Insight*, 575-577.

[26] In the context of his discussion on the question of interpreting a text or an author, Lonergan says: "What the interpreter was doing, was building up the evidence for an element in the history of the theology of grace and, while he can arrive at a grasp of the main movement and an understanding of many details, he rarely achieves and never needs an understanding of every detail. Judgement rests on the absence of further *relevant* questions." Lonergan, *Method*, 166.

[27] Lonergan, *Insight*, 309.

[28] Lonergan, *Insight*, 309.

[29] Rehg, "From Logic to Rhetoric," 153-172.

[30] Kant, *Critique of Pure Reason*, 104-105.

[31] Lonergan, *Insight*, 383-388.

[32] Lonergan, *Insight*, 388-398.

[33] Lonergan, *Insight*, 309.

[34] Lonergan, *Insight*, 309.

[35] See chapter 3, section 3.3.5.2.

[36] Lonergan, *Insight*, 309; emphasis added.

[37] William Rehg says: "Habermas's concept of 'rational motivation' presupposes something like Lonergan's notion of insight and the 'reasonableness' in which it is grounded... For Lonergan, as a prospective knower I can take a judgment as correct once I grasp that the direct insight formulated in the judgment is invulnerable, i.e., that there are no further pertinent questions. For Habermas, as a hearer I can be rationally motivated to accept a truth claim inasmuch as the speaker guarantees that the claim can be vindicated on the basis of good reasons. Such vindication implies that potential challenges to the claim can be answered, hence that there are no further pertinent questions or at least no questions that will prove unanswerable and thus overturn the claim. Thus, Habermas's notion of rational acceptability – at least at its ideal limit – would seem to presuppose Lonergan's account of reflective insight – the grasp that there are no further pertinent (or valid but unanswerable) questions on an issue." Rehg, "From Logic to Rhetoric," 164-165.

[38] Rehg, "From Logic to Rhetoric," 166.

[39] "All men form but one community... [God's] providence, evident goodness, and saving designs extend to all men." Vatican II, "*Declaration on the Relation of the Church to Non- Christian* Religions" (*Nostra aetate*), 1965, §1.

"The catholic Church rejects nothing of what is true and holy in these religions... the precepts and doctrine which, although differing in many ways from her own teaching, nevertheless, often reflect a ray of that truth which enlightens all men." Vatican II, "*Declaration on the Relation of the Church to Non- Christian* religions" (*Nostra aetate*), 1965, §2.

[40] Lonergan, *Method*, 57. See also Lonergan, *Philosophical and Theological Papers*, 96.

[41] Lonergan narrates a personal experience of his own: "Leading up to the Borghese Gardens in Rome, where I usually go for my favorite walk, there is a ramp. Coming down the ramp was a small child running ahead of its mother. He started to trip and tumbled; I was a good twenty feet away

but spontaneously I moved forward before taking any thought at all, as if to pick up the child. There is an intersubjectivity, there is a sense in which we are all members of one another before we think about it." Lonergan, *Philosophical and Theological Papers*, 96.

[42] Lonergan, *Method*, 57.

[43] Scheler, *The Nature of Sympathy*, 256.

[44] Lonergan says: "Both community of feeling and fellow-feeling are intentional responses that presuppose the apprehension of objects that arouse feeling. In community of feeling two or more persons respond in parallel fashion to the same object. In fellow-feeling a first person responds to an object, and a second responds to the manifested feeling of the first. So community of feeling would be illustrated by the sorrow felt by both parents for their dead child, but fellow-feeling would be felt by a third party moved by their sorrow...

In contrast, psychic contagion and emotional identification have a vital rather than an intentional basis. Psychic contagion is a matter of sharing another's emotion without adverting to the object of the emotion. One grins when others are laughing although one does not know what they find funny...

In emotional identification either personal differentiation is as yet undeveloped or else there is a retreat from personal differentiation to vital unity. Undeveloped differentiation has its basic illustration in the emotional identification of mother and infant... Retreat from differentiation ... occurs in sexual intercourse when both partners undergo a suspension of individuality and fall back into a single stream of life." Lonergan, *Method*, 57-59.

[45] Lonergan says: "Both the meaning of the smile and the act of smiling are natural and spontaneous. We do not learn to smile as we learn to walk, to talk, to swim, to skate. Commonly we do not think of smiling and then do it. We just do it. Again, we do not learn the meaning of smiling as we learn the meaning of words. The meaning of the smile is a discovery we make on our own, and that meaning does not seem to vary from culture to culture, as does the meaning of gestures." Lonergan, *Method*, 59-60.

[46] Lonergan, "Theology in Its New Context," 58.

[47] Lonergan, "Theology in Its New Context," 59.

[48] Lonergan, "Theology in Its New Context," 62-63.

[49] Lonergan acknowledges that the list is not an original contribution of his own but adapted from an essay published by Heiler. Lonergan, "The

Future of Christianity," 149-151. See also Heiler, "The History of Religions as a Preparation for the Cooperation of Religions," 142-153.

[50] Lonergan, "The Future of Christianity," 155.

[51] Lonergan, "The Future of Christianity," 155.

[52] Church, for long, thought of itself as the sole possessor of the saving truth is clear from the old and familiar adage 'Outside the Church no salvation'. In this ecclesiocentric model of the Church, salvation was deemed available to people only through faith in Jesus Christ explicitly professed in the Church community. This model excludes any possibility of dialogue as Church has nothing to learn or receive from others but only to teach or give.

Interfacing Mission and Cultural Research:

A Road Less Travelled by Divine Word Missionaries

G. Lazar SVD

Introduction

Consistency is the key to a great brand of a product in market economy today. Brands that manage to remain steadfast to their core principles, but also consistently innovate and stay relevant in a mercurial market are the ones that make for success stories. Trusted brands sustain a loyal consumer base and add new consumers to the fold by maintaining stringent quality control, excellent after sales service and by keeping abreast with the market's evolving needs. Over the years, consumer needs and expectations in the field of 'Mission-evangelization' have evolved – traditional missionary methods have given away to newer platforms. Advances in post-modernism and religious fundamentalism have led to challenges, but have also created greater opportunities. New brand of missionary methods need to tap into the potential of this rapidly changing market while keeping their ethos intact. Against this backdrop this paper is a humble attempt to analyze the tension between the traditional missionary methods against the post-modern brands of *missiodei* with the lens of the Society of the Divine Word in India. I limit myself in offering some insights for the readers to reflect from post-modern socio-cultural point of view. Lastly, this paper also will propose a few areas as means of culture-identity integration through hermeneutic intercultural processes for effective mission methods.

The world has turned to be a place of pandemonium, plagued by terrorism, riots, lynching, rapes, threats of a nuclear war and other events that endanger our life on earth. The reason behind all these one could say is an irrational dislike, vengeance and hateful feelings – towards an individual, group, nation or community. Prejudice is one of the great enemies of active communion with the 'other' in the modern world.[1]

To start with, one of the main reasons for traditional irrational dislike or hateful feelings against the 'other' in India is socio-cultural perspective that could be explained with the reference to the economic, historical and social conditions. Some scholars address this problem from a sociological and anthropological perspective focusing on the sociocultural factors. They emphasize that the existing differences within the cultural conditions can bring about further conflicts, whereas, other scholars focus on the existing situations, which influence the attitude of prejudice or dislike. For example, rapid social changes, competition, difficulty in compliance, family attachment, migration and so on.[2]

Culture –A Principle to understand the other

Culture, as a concept, is 'wriggly', amorphous, often unseen and diverse, open to interpretations and is observed only in the demonstrated behavior of people that live in a society and often subject to exogenous or endogenous shocks that mutate or transform it.[3] In contrast to this(,) we see in India today that the rise of social and religious groups gripped with a particular understanding of culture in violent mode against human and democratic freedom of Indian citizens as is observed in the assault and harassment of women in Sabarimala temple case. Such things happen because the Right-wing parties have gained electoral prominence in India either by pseudo promises or by misinterpretation of Indian Philosophy pampered prejudices that appeal to many middle-class, upper-caste, socially conservative people. This is demonstrated violently and publicly with the pretense of 'nation-saving or 'nation-building' slogans. This serves as a concrete attempt to keep society unequal and hierarchical with discrimination. Electoral politics in India are structured to evoke prejudice and manufacture distrust between people that do not resemble each other in terms of gender, caste, religion and sexual preferences. It also forcefully restructures and stereotypes peoples' behavior and reimages a cultural identity. For example, the inter-caste or inter-faith marriage is a threat because they prove that religion is at best a residual category in affairs of the human heart.

In the modern world, pluralism is used as an ethnical, cultural and religious term, seeing it as a clash of diverse cultures and religions among themselves. Instead, pluralism is at the basis of any cultural process that is living. The meeting and mixing of cultures, processes that have been going on forever in asymmetric and unequal ways, has become more accelerated today due to the extension and speed of human mobility, merchandise and information. In this 'global city' in which all are both interconnected and interdependent, new citizens' rights are necessary, rights which are guaranteed and protected by a government that is international, responsible and in solidarity with all.

Cultural Differences

One of the chief concerns of missionaries is the set of problems arising out of human variation. Among other things, missionaries had to face the question of religious differences. How do you relate to non-Christian religions? Are they totally evil, and, therefore, to be wiped out? Do such religions contain partial truths on which the missionary can build? Such questions have led to extensive discussions.

Missionaries, like anthropologists, are confronted with other cultural differences. People in other societies built different types of houses, spoke different languages, organized different kinds of families, had different concepts of right and wrong, and believed in different values.

Cultural variance also raises some knotty philosophical and theological questions. It appears that all cultures "do the job" that is, they provide a basis for orderly, meaningful human life. How then can we judge one culture to be better than another? What criteria can we use to compare and evaluate customs? What right do we have to try to change other people?

For a time, many anthropologists staked out positions of total cultural relativism, holding that all customs of all cultures are equally good. However, such relativism raises equally difficult questions. Are, in fact, all customs equally good? For example, in curing diseases, is magic as effective as modern medicine? Should we refrain from helping people if they desire it or if it is to their benefit? Are there no absolutes, no biological, psychological, social or moral principles underlying all human life? Is there no Truth? Today, few anthropologists take a completely relativistic position with regard to cultural variance, but there is little consensus on what the criteria for evaluation shall be.

Missionaries have had to face questions of cultural variance. Many of them wanted to make people Christians, but does this also mean wearing clothes, using western medicine, having one wife, giving up segregation based on caste or race, and giving up headhunting? If not, where does one draw the line between Christianity and western culture?

The relationship of the Christian message to cultures is complex. On the one hand, the message must always be expressed in cultural terms in a language, cultural symbols and behavioral practices that will, in part, mold the message. On the other, Christianity claims that its message is universal and transcends any one culture.

The theological question raised by cultural variance goes further. The events of the Bible took place in specific cultural contexts. How do we determine what is the universal message to be proclaimed to all people everywhere, and what part was addressed specifically to the people and culture of that day? To say all parts of the Bible apply equally to everyone is to evade the question. Few, if any, modern Christians put adulterers to death (Leviticus 20:10), or stone blasphemers (Leviticus 24:14). Not many practice the holy kiss (1 Thessalonians 5:26), require women to pray with their heads covered (1 Corinthians 11:13), or lend money freely without expecting its return (Luke 6:35).

Finally, cultural differences pose basic epistemological questions to missionaries and anthropologists alike. How do we relate to those who believe differently than we, but who also claim to have found the truth? As anthropologists point out, we must avoid uncritical ethnocentrism - the tendency to automatically assume our own beliefs and customs are right and then to use them to judge other people and cultures to be wrong. Being ethnocentric blocks understanding and communication, and in the end each only stands up and declares himself right.

So, how do we relate to people if fundamental differences between us persist? Can we still accept others as persons and maintain relationships with them?

Cultural Overhang

Dr. Donald McGavran has introduced a term into the discussion of missionary work. He calls a certain manifestation, cultural overhang.[4] He points out that missionaries tend to bring their own cultural habits and understandings into the work that is being done. The carrying over of the culture from the missionary's own background tends to confuse the issues involved and to hinder the reception of the Gospel.

There is a further consideration that concerns cultural overhang. This is the effort to perpetuate methods and mores used in missionary work in one section when engaged in another area. It may be, moreover, that work used in one generation will determine the procedures of the next generation. More specifically, methods pursued in rural work are not usually the ways for mission work in the city. Or the mode for mission activities in the normal city of the past may not at all fit into the present burgeoning city life. Neither should we expect that the methods used by the missionaries in the colonial days of India will be necessarily effective today. These are general examples of cultural overhang. The missionary must exercise perpetual care that the things he does and the ways he recommends are not overhangs of another time, another place, and another culture. He must ever be alert to be relevant in terms of the environment where he is working and in terms of the timeless Gospel.

In the post-modern world, there is a need to reconsider the issue of relationship between an individual identity and culture, especially with a view toward educational and rational integration and for 'understanding the other person'. It allows individual journey for on-going formation to enable each individual to constructively internalize otherness with its diversity, especially from the cultural perspective. There is a need to reconsider the issue of relationship between an individual's identity and culture, especially with a view towards educational and formational integration. In order to carry out correct educative intercultural processes, which begin with understanding the other, it is necessary to outline ways for a critical and continual re-elaboration of one's own those cultural signs that are part of one's roots.

Following this above philosophy, the de-culturation process through two internal strategies, namely, recognizing (acceptance and contact with the other) and relativizing (cross-cultural openness), and one external strategy – optimizing (promote differences and the other), and reduce the attitude of prejudice of the culturally formatted humans. This is done by de-programming the collective 'mental software' (cultural identity through in-culturation)[5] or cultural encapsulation.[6] This calls for de-automatizing the culturally formatted human, or better, a deconstruction of the one-sided cultural identity – that should lead towards acculturation through cross-cultural experiences.

Mission Musings

Keeping these above philosophies in mind Pope Francis has given a very timely and relevant message on World Mission Day (2018). At the very outset, Pope Francis quotes Pope St. John Paul, "Mission Revitalizes the Faith". Just three words from *RedemptorisMissio* (No.2) addresses to all Christians and indeed to all men and women who want to live as children of God. Mission indeed revitalizes our Faith, and St. James would say faith is dead without work (Jas 2:17). Pope Francis tells the people of God that the Lord Jesus has a special message for them, and through them, all the world communities.

Every Christian is aware of God's mission. However, the Pope goes much deeper: he says, "every man and women is a mission". This is the reason why we are on the earth. This powerful statement is reminiscent of *Evangelii Nuntiandi*, which is considered as a parting gift to the Church bequeathed by Pope Bl. Paul VI, The Church exists in order to evangelize the world, he said and Pope Francis reminds us of that, to joyfully accept this great challenge. "I am a mission on the Earth, that is the reason why I am here in this world" (EG 273).

The Kingdom of God

According to the gospel of Mark, when Jesus began his public preaching he starts with a declaration: "The kingdom of God has come near; repent and believe in the good news (Mk 1:15).The disciples, of course, did not understand this. It was only after his resurrection that they slowly understood that the goal of Jesus was not an earthly kingdom, but a community of people. The first community at Jerusalem provided a model by pooling its resources, loving and serving each other and praying together (Acts 2:44-47).

Interestingly, a few theologians and church-men still think that the Church in the world is the kingdom of God. They imagine that if the church spreads across the world and the whole world becomes Church, then God's kingdom will be fully established with Christ as the King. The Second Vatican Council, however, specified that the

Church "receives the mission of proclaiming and establishing among all peoples the kingdom of Christ and of God, and she is, on earth, the seed and the beginning of that kingdom" (The Document on the Church, no, 5). Today we are also becoming aware that God, the Word and the Spirit are present everywhere, also in the believers of other religions. St. John Paul II, in his encyclical, *The Mission of the Redeemer,* says: "It is true that the inchoate reality of the Kingdom can also be found beyond the confines of the Church among peoples everywhere, to the extent that they live "Gospel values" and are open to the working of the Spirit who breathes when and where he wills (cf. Jn 3:8). Asian theologians have started saying that the believers of all the religions are co-pilgrims towards the kingdom of God.

In this context, the kingdom of God, the sphere of God's activity in the world, is seen as wider than the Church. The Vatican II document on Church says: "The Church, in Christ, is in the nature of sacrament – a sign and instrument, that is, of communion with God and of unity among all men" (No. 1). In less material and more human terms, the words 'sign and instrument' can be translated as 'symbol and servant'. Therefore, we can say that the Church is the symbol and servant of the kingdom of God, which reaches beyond the Church, to include all people of good will.

Isaiah's vision in the Old Testament is beautiful: that of the "mountain of the Lord's house." This is not a house whose entrance is meant to be guarded by sentinels, bull-headed bouncers who check "the guest list" at the door to determine one's entrance. Instead, we hear "all nations shall stream toward it." All are welcome! Our Church continues to emphasize this vision. As *Nostra Aetate* (the Declaration on the Relation of the Church with Non-Christian Religions) reads from the Second Vatican Council, "In her [the Catholic Church's] task of fostering unity and love among humanity, and even among nations, she gives primary consideration in this document to what human beings have in common and to what promotes fellowship among them." (n.1) Pope Francis goes on to say, "the Church will be ever more committed to travel along the path of dialogue and to intensify the already fruitful cooperation with all those who, belonging to different religious traditions, share her intention to build relations of friendship and share in the many initiatives to do with dialogue."

God revealed within differences

At first, differences in our dialogue ministries of Research Centres were viewed as obstacles to our Church's goal. Later, we have been discovering the variety and beauty of languages, faiths, cultures and living conditions. The dialogue-cum-research centres have begun to feel and know God's work. These centres have transformed the understanding of 'difference' and 'oneness'. While this mission work has a profound influence on others, the missionaries involved with dialogue and research have come to recognize that they are equally influenced through the interactions and contacts. As one of the professors from a popular University stated: 'When the heart is touch by direct contact, the mind may be challenged to change' The Society of the Divine Word continues to carry this mantle passed on from St. Arnold Janssen to this day.

This is much more than just tolerance of religious difference (or any difference, for that matter). This is about celebrating the gift that the other is to our world, and can be to our life, if we are open to it. Our Dialogue-cum-Research Centres in India conduct research seminars, workshops, animation programmes and dialogue with those who identify as Hindu, Buddhist, Catholic, Muslim, Lutheran, and Sikh. They report that the experience has been one of "warmth" where they felt "seen" and "fed" by authentic interactions with several people who attend. This is what heaven on earth is like. We don't bemoan the fact that we must *tolerate* each other, but, as the Psalmist says, we "rejoice" in the gift of being able to actually *celebrate* each other.

If we can do this well, perhaps the beautiful vision of Isaiah of beating "our swords into plowshares" and our "spears into pruning hooks" actually has a shot and we can use these new tools to reap the bountiful harvest of gifts that come from a human family that savors the beauty of "the other" and feast "at the banquet of the Kingdom of heaven." (Mt 8:11).

Indian SVDs have understood that planned change is central to the missionary task. Early anthropologists were concerned primarily with the broad evolution of culture and with the diffusion of ideas around the world approaches that raised theological questions but had little to say to missionaries in their work. Structural-functional approaches tended to view cultures as static. Change was seen as essentially harmful. Today, anthropologists and mission scholars are studying the nature of both planned and unplanned change avoiding stereotyping an age.

The following analysis will depict how the Divine Word Missionaries have launched into new challenges of evangelization by cultural studies with the involvement of the people of other faiths following the missiological dimension of *inter gentes.*

SANSKRITI – NORTH EASTERN INSTITUTE OF CULTURAL RESEARCH–GUWAHATI

Director: K. Jose SVD

SANSKRITI started off with the aim to work with a vision of providing reliable and researched data on Indian Culture, Religion and Society with special reference to North East India, towards the goal of building a just, inclusive development driven and humane society. Accordingly, *SANSKRITI* placed its thrust on: Cultures and Religions, Cultural Symbols, Cultural Change, Languages, Peace Studies, Tribal Studies, Social Unrest, Endangered Cultures, Development Studies, Indigenous Resource Management, Folklore of Ethnic Communities, Etc.

SANSKRITI–North Eastern Institute of Cultural Research, Guwahati is a Research Centre in Anthropology, Sociology, Folklore and North East India Studies. It was founded in 2006 by Divine Word

Society (SVD). This society is well known around the globe for its contributions to the field of Anthropology through ethnographic and cultural studies. Over the years the faculty members of *Sanskrit* have done primary research on people of North East India with special reference to Assam, Tripura, Meghalaya, Manipur and Arunachal Pradesh. A number of research papers are published by its faculty members in the leading journals and books. This Institute has been hosting regional and national seminars and workshops on different subjects related to the cultures and religions of the people of North East India.

Following the great traditions of late Dr. Wilhelm Schmidt SVD, the founder of Internationally acknowledged *Anthropos* Institute, Germany and his long time collaborators in SVD and other academic fraternity, and late Dr. Prof. Stephen Fuchs SVD, the founder of Institute of Indian Culture, Mumbai and a number of renowned faculty members and great stalwarts like Archbishop Emeritus Thomas Menamparampil SDB and others we are in the process of establishing this Institute for scientific study of the people with special reference to North Eastern Region of India. From its inception *Sanskrit* has been working with a vision towards providing reliable and researched data on Cultures, Religions and Society as a whole with special reference to North East India with an aim to promote a just, peace loving and humane society. In this effort the institute networks with other research institutions, universities, NGOs and Government departments to preserve, promote and disseminate various cultures through research, documentation and publications on languages, fine arts, cultural symbols, indigenous knowledge systems of people to promote development in view of socio-cultural, economic, political and religious advancement of people. The main objective of this Institute is to disseminate and advance knowledge by providing quality, data based research/facilities in such branches of social sciences which may play a positive role in the socio-economic, cultural and religious development of the people of North East India.

ANNUAL NATIONAL SEMINARS 2007 – 2018 /VOLUMES PUBLISHED

2007: National Seminar on Tribes & Castes of North East India (1 Volume).

2008: Regional Seminar cum Workshop on Tribal Development in Tripura: People's Participation, NGOs and Government (1 Volume).

2009: National Seminar on Social Unrest and Peace Initiatives in North East India (2 Volumes).

2010: National Seminar on Concept of God and Religion: Traditional Thought and Contemporary Society (1 Volume).

2011: National Seminar on Anthropology in India: Retrospect and Prospect (2 Volumes).

2012: National Seminar on Indigenous Resource Management in Tribal India (2 Volumes).

2013: National Seminar on Endangered Cultures and Languages with special reference to North East India (2 Volumes).

2014: National seminar on Verrier Elwin: Contributions to Contemporary Anthropology and Ethnology (1 Volume).

2015: National seminar on Syncretism in India: Cultural and Religious Dimensions (1 Volume).

2016: First Decennial Conference on Re-Imagining Social Science Researches: Contexts, Perspectives and Priorities (1 Volume).

2017: Customary Laws as Discourse: The Northeastern Perspective (1 Volume in Press).

2018 North East India: Changes, Meanings and Transformations (1 Volume in Press)

North East India - Land and People Series

So far four titles (Riang, Lepcha, Karbi, and Lisu) have been published. Work is in progress for the volumes on Nyishi, Manipur tribes and others.

JOURNAL: *Anthropos India* (ISSN NO.: 2394-8396) E-mail: anthroposin@gmail.com

Other research publications which are in various stages of completion include about 15 volumes in English on various contemporary themes on the North East India. Most of these will go to press by the end of the year 2020-21.

This research institute net-works with Anthropological Survey of India, Indian Council for Social Science Research, Indian Council for Historical Research, Indian Council for Philosophical Research and other social science research institutions, state governments and Universities with special reference to NE India.

During the past ten years, *Sanskriti*-North Eastern Institute of Cultural Research, Guwahati, Assam has been trying to become an agent of rejuvenating this herculean enthusiasm in doing pertinent researches involving both senior and time tested professors and emerging younger scholarly fraternity side by side - to focus better, and achieve the goal with more precision and tenacity.

SANSKRUTI KENDRA - Tribal Cultural Center (TCC), Sundargarh.

Director: Ignatius Soreng SVD

Sanskruti Kendra – The Tribal Cultural and Research Center[8] was started by - The Society of the Divine Word in 2011 with a Vision to do integrated service to the tribal people through cultural initiatives. The vision of the institute has been to: Protect, Preserve and Promote Tribal Culture and the objectives are to:

1. Document and preserve tribal heritage, i.e. culture, tribal folk lore, dance, songs, music, arts, crafts etc. in various forms.

2. Set up a library and archives of tribal literature and tribal related books and other printed or non-printed materials.

3. Set up a museum of tribal articles, art and artifacts.

4. Bring out tribal print, audio and video productions and publications.

5. Conduct research on tribal social and cultural topics.

6. Educate and train the people specially the youth and children on tribal socio-cultural heritage through Training Programs.

7. Develop tribal language and literature.

8. Conduct and facilitate Education and Higher Education on tribal disciplines.

9. Conduct and organize tribal demonstrations, competitions, seminars, workshops, feasts, festivals and memorial days.

10. Facilitate display and sale of tribal goods and articles.

11. Organize and Conduct Tribal Awareness and Motivation Programs.

12. Conduct tribal cultural connectivity activity among various tribal groups.

13. Promote Tribal games and sports through coaching, training, competitions and tournaments.

14. Take tribal troupe for national or international presentation, demonstration or competition

15. Facilitate tribal socio-economic development programs.

Activities presently going on in the Cultural Center:

1.   Tribal Cultural Activities

a. Co-organizing tribal programs with various tribal groups, mainly annual tribal assemblies of four tribal groups every year – Oraon, Munda, Kisan and Khadia.

b.   Tribal dance festival with tribal song and dance competition. This is one of the crowd pulling activity, where over a thousand people attend.

c.   Celebration of memorial days of tribal heroes (four of them – Birsa Munda Jayanti, TelengaKhadia Jayanti, Budhu Bhagat Jayanti)

d.   Celebration of tribal feasts and festivals – like, Cattles' feast, New grain feast

e.   Documenting in audio and video form tribal dances and songs especially those that are getting extinct.

f.   Documenting Tribal medical practices by conducting consultation with traditional medicine-men, documenting in audio, video and print form medicines and medical practices.

2.   Tribal Cultural Research

a.   Research on backward tribal groups and some Particularly Vulnerable Tribal Groups (PVTG) from sociological and historical perspective

b.   Research on dance and songs, customs and practices of the tribal groups

c.   Research on various aspects of the Indigenous People

d.   Publishing books and booklets on tribal themes

Tribal life, society, culture and tradition are in disarray in our area today. Industrialization, urbanization, globalization, education and present civilization have virtually destroyed and destabilized the tribal world. Tribal culture, language, art, artifacts, song, dance and music along with socio-cultural values are virtually lost. The present day youth and children have turned their back on these things, as the result of which tribal riches and heritage are forgotten and abandoned.

But, humanity needs them because they possess principles of integrated human life that hold humanity together. Egalitarian values, unity, peace, harmony, human respect, charity etc. are still strong in the tribal communities. Humanity cannot afford to lose them. The tribal riches and heritage need to be protected, preserved and promoted, so that the tribal communities will survive, and their values benefit the world.

Conscious efforts are needed in order to protect, preserve and promote the tribal culture, so that coming generation will know them and take pride in them. Today, means and methods are available to assist protection, preservation and promotion, and concrete programs are possible, but they require initiative and adventurous steps to actualize them.

SANSKRUTI – Institute of Dravidian Culture and Research (IDCR), Hyderabad.

Director – G. Lazar SVD

SANSKRUTI – Institute of Dravidian Culture and Research, is an academic association of the Society of the Divine Word, in the province of India Hyderabad Province. The vision of the centre has been to foster and promote indigenous cultures and civilization and thus stand to protect the rights and cultural heritage of minority communities of India. The aims of the institute are to disseminate advance knowledge by providing data based research facilities in such branches of social sciences which may play a positive role in the social, economic, cultural and religious development of the people of India in general and south India in particular.

Since its inception in 2012 the centre is being patronised by the eminent professors, scholars, NGOs and marginalisedpeople from grassroots. The Institute organises national, international seminars and colloquiums periodically, publishes research papers.

On-going programmes of the Institute

1. International Seminar, "Methods of New-Evangelization for India Today" August 4-6, 2014.

2. All India Seminar: "Dimensions of Indian Civilization" January 23-25, 2015.

3. All India Seminar: "Tribes of Contemporary India: Issues and Challenges" January 24 and 25, 2016.

4. All India Seminar: "Caste-System in Contemporary India: Issues and Implications" January 27 and 28, 2017.

5. International Seminar, "Indigenous Knowledge System Interfacing Modern Digital Knowledge System in India: Practices and Policies", January 18, 19, 2018.

6. National Seminar, "Women among Marginalised Communities of India: Issues and Challenges", February 2019.

7. Regular Inter-Religious *Satsang* with Muslims and Hindus held in Nizam College Grounds, Hyderabad.

8. Periodical Dialogue meeting with different Cultural groups in Hyderabad during the festivals of Dassera and Diwali.

9. Inter-faith dialogue/*dawat*with Muslims of Hyderabad on every June 25.

10. Annual *Namaz* and *Iftar* gathering with Muslim brothers and sisters, in Ambarpet Mosque during the month of Holy Ramadan.

11. Research on backward tribal groups and some particularly de-notified Tribal Groups (DNTG) from sociological and historical perspective in the tribal settlements of Adilabad, Telangana.

Publications

1. *Missionary Mandate of Christ in the light of New Evangelization,* SANSKRUTI Publications (2013).

2. *Beyond Religion: Towards a new Theology of Dialogue,* Satprakashan, Indore (2013).

3. *Dimensions of Indian Civilization,* B.R Publications, Delhi, India (2016).

4. *Tribes of Contemporary India,* Omsons Publications, Delhi, India (2017).

5. *Caste System in Contemporary India,* Mittal Publications, Delhi, (2018).

6. *Indigenous Knowledge System Interfacing Modern Digital Knowledge System in India: Practices and Policies,* Mittal Publications, Delhi, (2019).

7. *Syncretism and Religious Dialogue* (edited), (2016).

8. "Touch-Points" *SANSKRUTI* publications (2015).

In partial collaboration with Anthropological Survey of India, Mysore *SANSKRUTI* – periodically organises lectures and Symposiums by eminent professors, scholars and NGOs from the Universities of Delhi, Kolkata, Mumbai, Chennai, Hyderabad, Osmania, Ranchi, Bangalore, Pondicherry, Mysore, Gawahati and Arunachal Pradesh.

In order to encourage young sociologists and Anthropologists to achieve excellence in their chosen field of specialization the centre has instituted an award for excellence in honour of Dr. Ambedkar. The award is bestowed to the presenter of the best field-based research paper on the seminar theme during the seminars organised by SANSKRUTI. Students and scholars from Osmania University, Hyderabad Central University, St. Francis Girls College, Kasturba Ladies College, St. Pius College, and Little Flower College, have been actively participating in the academic exercise of the Institute.

Conclusion

The mission work is often culture-bound. Most religious researchers' have observed that the church often seems to be on the lagging boundary of culture, rather than on the leading edge. One of the reasons why the church fails to minister creatively, and the para-church groups do so, is because the church is plagued with cultural paralysis. Tillapaugh in his book, The Church Unleashed,[9] tells how the Baptist and Methodist denominations grew rapidly in the 19th century by responding to the changes in society. As the population moved west, there were not enough trained ministers to plant and pastor the Churches, which were required. The Baptists responded creatively by supplying 'farmer-preachers' while the Methodists had their 'circuit riders'. The result was the rapid growth of these churches, due to their responsiveness to the changes in their culture. The church of today is so culture-bound that it finds change difficult and distressing if possible at all. The typical symptom of this cultural severity is the protection, since we have always done it that way before, the church needs to be able to become aware of changes in the culture around it and to respond creatively, yet biblical to them. Creativity in ministry is, in part, due to appropriate understanding of culture and its relationship to the gospel.

Society of the Divine Word (SVD), in India has taken this mandate seriously and the newly established cultural centres of the Divine Word Missionaries meet these challenges and guide the missionaries on the road that is less travelled.

Endnotes

[1] The term 'other' is used to identify the other human being/group, as 'different' from the self/group being dissimilar to and the opposite of self/us.

[2] Cf. Allport G. and Kramer M., *Some Roots of Prejudice,* in *Journal of Psychology,* (1946, n.22), pp.9-39.

[3] Cf. Vasundhara Sirnate Drennan, *A Culture to be built on Prejudices.* The Telegraph, Kolkata, March 15, 2018.

[4] Donald McGavran, *How Churches Grow* (London: World Dominion Press, 1959), p. 85 ff.

[5] To understand this concept better, cf. Greet Hofstede, *Culture's Consequences.* (Delhi: Sage Publishing, 2nd Edition, 2016).

[6] Cultural Encapsulation is the lack of understanding of another's culture and its influence in the current world view.

[7] The author thanks Fr. Jose K, SVD, Director, for providing information about *SANSKRITI*, Guwahati, ING Region.

[8] The author wholeheartedly thanks Fr. Ignatius Soreng SVD the Director of *SANSKRUTI*, Sundargargh for the information given above.

[9] Frank R. Tillapaugh, *The Church Unleashed*, Regal Books, New York, 1982, p. 67.

SVD Mission in an Inter-Religious Context

Libnus Kullu SVD

The mission of Divine Word Missionaries is to, "to be with Him and to be sent out to proclaim the message" (Mk 3:14). To be a relevant missionary today is to proclaim the relevant message in the given context. What is the message that we are called to proclaim? Through our message, we build up a new humanity with gospel values. We are called to be on the move, as mission is never static, always dynamic. We are familiar with the terms of 'passing over' at the 'frontiers' of class, culture and religion (XIII General Chapter of 1988). In fact since Vatican II there is a new paradigm shift in the understanding of our mission: from 'frontier situation' to 'partners in dialogue' – from place to people. This necessitates the cultivation of genuine friendship as one important way to facilitate dialogue.

Over the years the Chapter Documents of the Society remind its members to enter into a life of universalism and inclusivism, much more than before. "Listening to the Spirit: Our Response Today" was the theme of XV General Chapter (2000). The theme of XVI General Chapter (2006) was, "Living Prophetic Dialogue: Spirituality-Community-Leadership-Finances-Formation". XVII General Chapter (20012) had the theme, "From Every Nation, People and Language: Sharing Intercultural Life and Mission".

Recently concluded General Chapter (2018) has invited us to reflect on the theme, "The Love of Christ impels us (2 Cor 5:14): Rooted in the Word, Committed to His Mission." We are to foster a process of a spiritual rekindling, bringing us back to the Word of God as the source of our life, vocation and mission and our religious missionary commitment. Following the General Chapter documents, as members of MER, we could give direction to our members, so as to be effective missionaries in India. As SVDs where can we be found today? What can we be doing? What do we emphasize in our apostolic work? What kind of spirituality that inspires us today? In the context of India, what is it that God wants us to do?

We try to reflect on our position and response in the wake of recent developments in the Indian scenario. Fr. Heinz Kuluke, former superior general, in his report to XVIII General Chapter (2018) invited us to reflect: We continue to ask and to determine "What characterizes us as SVDs, as individuals and as communities?" "What makes us SVDs different from others?" "What distinguishes our SVD ministries/apostolates?" "What do we want to be known for?" Four characteristic dimensions in fact specifically characterize our life and ministries as SVD individuals and communities. These characteristic dimensions are the attitudes that every SVD should cultivate in his life and ministry.

Through the first characteristic dimension – Communication, we want to reach out to others, to be close to people of all walks of life – living *inter gentes* – sharing in people's suffering and joys, making ourselves and our institutions available for the people. By our involvements in JPIC concerns, we contribute to transform the world, making it a better place to live for the present and future generations. With the Mission Animation, we closely collaborate with all our mission partners, especially the lay partners. We value their contributions and expertise. In the words of Pope Benedict, the lay mission partners are not mere 'collaborators' but are truly 'co-responsible' for making God's presence felt in our world. The fourth characteristic dimension – Biblical Animation gives identity to the name of our Congregation. It places Bible as the center of all that we believe and do; our spirituality and actions; our prayers and ministries. We apply these four characteristic dimensions in our mission.

Today we are living in an ever increasing world of plurality – cultural, religious, linguistic and ethnic. Pluralism is a sign of perfection, which should be appreciated and given a positive value. Diversity is not something to be regretted and abolished, but to be rejoiced over and promoted, since it represents richness and strength. On the one hand while we celebrate diversity, at the same time, we find the world dwindling with regard to its ideologies in finding commonalities in all its diversities. The world presents a fragmented reality in terms of economics, social, cultural, political and religious aspects of life. Due to unjust distribution of wealth and corruption, we find millions of poor people in rural and urban areas of our universe. Socio-cultural oppression, gender inequality, migration, ruthless economic exploitation of the environment, have immensely affected the people.

Though the scope of pluralism has enlarged to its great extend, humanity has not been able to take advantage of such situation and to celebrate its uniqueness. Definitely there is a situation of contrast and contradictions in the world we live. As we involve in the lives of the people, we take into considerations the challenges of today: various conflicts and violence, mobocracy, massive poverty and inequality, increasing number of migrants and refugees, pollution and environmental crisis, corruption and moral degradation, breakdown of social cohesion, terrorism and all forms of fundamentalism. These challenges are our opportunities to be effective in our ministries.

The Context

From time immemorial, religions have always been an integral part of mankind's life. There were certain questions with regard to life and death, natural calamities and disasters, which fascinated people to form an idea of religion, developed their own system of religious beliefs and practices. People began to claim that there are certain objects that posses invisible and holy powers like huaca of the Incas of Peru, fetishes of the Africans, shamans of Africa, North and South America, Eskimos and Chinese, totems and animism which is considered as the most primitive form of religion. Man's belief in gods has usually reflected his view of the world and how it was created.[1] Early civilization like the ancient Egyptian, appear to have adopted a multiplicity of gods and goddesses. Monotheistic faith is traced from the religion of Hebrews. Greeks were enthusiastic about variety of gods who were considered to be closely involved in the daily lives of the people. We cannot think of human existence without belief in the presence of god.

India is deeply a religious country, though having secular constitution. Plurality of religions is a blessing. But at the same time, a lot of violence is perpetuated by these various religious adherents. Some of the faces of violence that we find in every day walk of life could be: physical, political, structural, ecological or psychological violence. But the need of the hour is to experience peace, harmony and acceptance. Religions are capable of giving birth to these, if all these religions congregate and work together. Inter-religious dialogue and inter-religious communities play a vital role in this process.

Asia is a unique continent that the people are heirs to ancient cultures, languages, beliefs, religions and traditions. Our continent is the cradle of world's major religions – Judaism, Christianity, Islam and Hinduism. It is also the birth place of many spiritual traditions such as Buddhism, Taoism, Confucianism, Zoroastrianism, Jainism, Sikhism, Shintoism and many other tribal religions. Sri Lankan theologian Aloysius Pieris would speak of double baptism that the Church in Asia must undergo to fulfill its mission. It is baptism in the Jordan of Asian religiosity and baptism on the Calvary of Asian poverty. This double baptism in fact forms the core of an Asian Theology of Liberation.[2] The people of Asia have concern for religious and cultural values, respect for life, compassion for all beings, closeness to nature, filial piety towards elders and a highly developed sense of community. These values make inter-religious dialogue a reality in the Asian scenario.

The demographics of India are remarkably diverse and interesting, as India is the second largest populous country in the world. It is the home of more than two thousand ethnic groups and major religions of the world – Hinduism, Islam, Christianity, Jainism, Buddhism, Sikhism, Zoroastrianism, Baha'ism, and Judaism. Constitutionally, India is a secular republic that upholds the right of citizens to freely profess, practice and propagate any religion or faith. Generally Indians are tolerant and retain the secular outlook, though at times there are sporadic incidences of religious violence and fundamentalism, which are due to politics. In the spirit of dialogue, a number of inter-faith groups have been formed and are actively involved in the overall progress of the country. In many places multi-faith gatherings, multi-faith consultations, inter-faith services, and *sarva dharma snehasammelan* are organized to create greater awareness of living together in harmony and collaboration.

Muslims too have taken serious initiatives to enter into dialogue with people of other religious faiths. A decade ago, in October 2007, about 138 Muslims leaders and scholars wrote an open letter to the world Christian leaders, called *A Common Word Between Us and You*, inviting both religious leaders to promote peace and harmony in the world, as Muslims and Christians together make up over half the population of the world. It is in fact, a beautiful gift to engage in dialogue, as both these religions, acknowledge in a creator, ever living and loving God. As believers in one God, we are impelled by our faiths to move out to others to experience such God in one's individual life.

When one is rooted in his own religious beliefs and practices, the person finds spiritual nourishment in other religious traditions too. One such person whom I have come across in my life very closely is Fr. Paul Jackson SJ. He is one of the rare committed Catholic Priests who is a pioneer in the area of Christian-Muslim dialogue in India. His spiritual journey with Sharafuddin Maneri, a fourteenth century Sufi, is an example for everyone to be open to learn from other religious traditions. He recounts the fascinating story of his spiritual encounter with the Sufi, in his book, *The Sharafuddin Maneri: The Hundred Letters*. Later we find his thesis published as, *The Way of a Sufi: Sharafuddin Maneri*. In the words of Fr. Paul Jackson, "Many changes took place within me during those long months. I was often astonished at the depth of Maneri's spiritual insight and the beauty of its expression. I realized that there was a whole process of interiorization going on within me as I met God dwelling in the heart of Sharafuddin Maneri."[3] His in-depth study on the life and teachings of the sufi, made him to acknowledge the Sufi as a God's great saint. Fr. Paul Jackson is able to go 'beyond dialogue' to experience transformation at a deeper level and as a catalyst help others to experience the same in life. It is in the concept of interreligious dialogue that we undertake a spiritual journey.

Understanding of Dialogue

In the context of multi-religious milieu in the world today, the scope of inter-religious dialogue is intensified. Engaging in dialogue mission is an essential part of the Church's mission. It is not just one of the ministries in the Church, but it is the priority of the Church. Pope Paul VI declared in 1964, 'Dialogue is the new way of being the Church.' Genuine dialogue leads to mutual understanding, mutual transformation, mutual enrichment and mutual communion. Today we perceive dialogue as an historical imperative in view of today's world which is fragmented by postmodern secularism and conflictive religiosity. We engage in dialogue with other religious traditions as it is an evangelical and missionary imperative, breaking down all types of divisions and barriers. Inter-religious dialogue is an integral dimension of its mission and service. Encounter between religions can be mutually prophetic and transformative and such encounter can lead to mutual enrichment. It is possible when the followers of religions are rooted in God-experience.

Existence of different religions is a motivation to engage in dialogue. Over the years, theologians, philosophers and social scientists have made an attempt to define dialogue. According to Habermas, for dialogue to be effective and credible, we must realize and understand the points of convergences and divergences in different traditions. In fact the consensus rests on the inter-subjective recognition of criticiseable validity. Through dialogue we aim to achieve, sustain and review certain consensus. For Panikkar, dialogue is our way of being. It is opening oneself to the other so that he might speak and reveal my viewpoints. Gadamar explains that genuine dialogue is to recognize oneself in the other and find a home abroad. It means to find otherness in oneself. Martin Buber's proposition is that we address existence in two ways: first, that of the 'I' towards an 'It', second that of the 'I' towards 'Thou'. In the former, there is a movement towards an object that is separate in itself as an experience and the later the movement is towards an existence of relationship without bounds. It acknowledges a living relationship. Human life finds its fulfillment in relationships. All our relationships Buber contends, brings us ultimately into relationship with God, 'Eternal Thou'. Thus when we enter into relationship with the other, we enter into a new relationship sustained by a mutual love and appreciation.

In dialogue there is mutual sharing and listening to each other's beliefs, each other's religious experiences with openness, eliminating all kinds of prejudices, intolerance and misunderstanding. "This does not mean that we give up our convictions about one's religion. It only means that, firmly holding to what we believe we listen respectfully to others, seeking to discern all that is good and holy, all that favors peace and cooperation."[4] For me personally, dialogue stands for, "Activity and Attitude of Committed and Convinced People." BIRA (Bishops' Institute for Interreligious Affairs) of FABC defines dialogue as, "a process of talking and listening, of giving and receiving, of searching and studying, for the deepening and enriching of one another's faith and understanding".

The Church and Dialgoue

The paradigm shift in the Catholic Church took place after Vatican Council II. With regard to the approach to other religions, she has moved from exclusivism to inclusivistic attitude. "The Catholic Church rejects accepts all that is true and holy in other religions" (NA 2) and "But the plan of salvation also includes those who acknowledge the Creator, in the first place among whom are Muslims; these profess to hold the faith of Abraham and together with us they adore the one, merciful God, mankind's judge on the last day" (Lumen Gentium, no. 16). It is only an example to show that the Church is sincere in its approach and teachings. The Catholics are clearly urged to engage with people of all faiths, to foster and facilitate a better understanding between people of all religions.

The Second Vatican Council, through its document, *Nostra Aetate* gives new impetus for its followers to engage sincerely in dialogue with other religious traditions to foster positive approach. The document affirms that God is present in all religions that all things are true and beautiful and that should be preserved and promoted, that all humans form one community with one origin and a single destiny guided by God. Dialogue is the best way acknowledge this truth and maintain a Godly relationship with all. The official teaching of the Church on dialogue is also found in other postconciliar documents such as: EvangeliNuntiandi (1975 by Pope Paul VI), Redemptoris Missio (1990 by St John Paul II), Dialogue and Proclamation (1991 by Pontifical Council for Interreligious Dialogue) and Papal Letters: Tertio Millenio Adveniente (St John Paul II) and Novo Millenio Ineunte (St John Paul II). Each religion plays a vital role in the development of humankind, for universal peace and promotion of human and spiritual values. Through dialogue, we bear witness to the values of God's reign and are called towards mutual respect and acceptance, build bridges, heal memories of historical wounds, break down the walls of religious fundamentalism and fanaticism. To be human is to be in dialogue with 'the other'. The option to dialogue is an option to be human.

Today we are living in the world of dialogue. Even after 50 years of the Vatican Council II, many Christians do not have the real understanding of the term 'dialogue'. Some consider it as merely talking to people of other faiths. Some recognize dialogue as an intellectual affair where experts / scholars of various religions come together, present their views of religions followed by discussions and finally by end up by bringing out statements. Most of the times, such statements do not percolate to the ordinary masses. The Church's approach to dialogue is much broader, where she encourages the followers of other religious traditions to engage in an existential approach.

We realize the importance of openness towards the people of other religions and the indispensable role of witness to the kingdom of God ever growing in the heart of people. Through our sincere commitment to dialogue, "Jesus Christ will be better known, recognized and loved." In his encyclicals *Redemptoris Missio* Pope John Paul II writes: "A vast field lies open to dialogue, ... for integral development and the safeguarding of religious values; from a sharing of their respective spiritual experiences ... believers of different religions bear witness before each other in daily life to their own human and spiritual values, and help each other to live according to those values in order to build a more just and fraternal society" (No 57).

Forms of Dialogue

There is a misconception that dialogue is confined to only the elite and intellectuals in a conference hall. The broad perspective of dialogue, leads to four different forms of dialogue, and there isn't one superior to the other: the dialogue of life, action, experts and spirituality. In a way as Christians, they interact with others at the levels of being, doing, thinking and reflecting. These forms of dialogue express various dimensions of our life as Christians which we share with the followers of other religions. It involves interaction at the levels of being (dialogue of life), doing (cooperation of social issues), thinking (study, discussion of theological issues) and reflecting (sharing of religious experiences).

When we truly involve in inter-religious dialogue, it becomes a clear sign that God's spirit is active in the Church. While meeting the Bishops of Chad on October 3, 2006, Pope Benedict XVI encouraged them and said, "Continue to collaborate in a spirit of sincere dialogue and mutual respect, to help everyone lead a life in keeping with the dignity received from God, with concern for authentic solidarity and the harmonious development of society." Genuine dialogue leads to recognition of the dignity of everyone, of the identity of every human and religious group and of their freedom to practice their religion, forms part of the common values of peace and justice that must be promoted for all and in which everyone must have an important role to play.

Dialogue of life is central to Christian life. We truly carry on the mission of Christ, when we participate fully in the social and cultural life of others among whom we live, and in turn appreciate the values found in others' faith. Such dialogue of life brings about openness and respect for people of other religious traditions and cultures. Dialogue of action finds its concrete expression in our creative response to the existential situations of life – in the midst of poverty, ignorance, sickness, injustice, exploitation, social evils... Promotion of justice becomes integral dimension of interreligious dialogue. In dialogue of life people work together to promote whatever leads to unity, love, truth, justice and peace. In fact it is a life-giving and life-nourishing movement that enables us to see God's face in the suffering humanity.

Pope Francis in his post-synodal exhortation *Amoris Laetitia*, writes, "Keep an open mind. Do not get bogged down in your own limited ideas and opinions, but be prepared to change or expand them. The combination of two different ways of thinking can lead to a synthesis that enriches both. Or, "Fearing the other person as a kind of 'rival' is a sign of weakness and needs to be overcome." The words of Pope Francis, though is in the context of family, can well be understood in the context of dialogue. On November 3, 2016 while addressing the representatives of different religions, Pope Francis invited them to work tirelessly to bring about peace in the world. He said, "Here, our responsibility before God, humanity and the future is great; it calls for unremitting effort, without dissimulation. It is a call that challenges us, a path to be taken together for the good of all and with hope. May the religions be wombs of life, bearing merciful love of God to a wounded and needy humanity; may they be doors of hope helping to penetrate the walls erected by pride and fear."

The reality of today invites us to engage in dialogue as witness to Jesus, who shared his life with the poor and marginalized in a kenotic way. Michael Amaldoss in his paper on 'The Challenges and Opportunities of Dialogue with Other Religions' mentions some of the obstacles against dialogue as: communalism, religious fundamentalism, sense of identity and historical memory. One needs to overcome these obstacles and work for peace and justice in the society through dialogue. It is our vocation to build bridges and establishing communities of love and peace. So dialogue is not just a mission, but a lifestyle and spirituality. It is not only what we do, but also about who we should become and how we relate with God.

Attitudes in Dialogue

According to FABC document, following attitudes foster interreligious dialogue: openness and sensitivity, receptivity, honesty and humility of spirit, sincere disinterestedness, cordial love, openness to overcome suspicion, fear and other negativities and willingness to learn from other religious traditions. In dialogue there is mutual acceptance, respect for each other, build bridges, break down walls of jealousy, hatred superiority, pride and prejudices. Commitment to one's faith will lead to a deeper and fruitful dialogue. When we listen passionately to the personal commitment of faith and witness of the other partners, we are enriched and grow in our faith and spirituality. Matured and deeper level of dialogue will enable us to avoid all sorts of obstacles such as: prejudiced attitudes towards the other, lack of knowledge, fear of conversion, triumphalistic attitude and stubbornness, religious fundamentalism.

According to Panikkar, there could be four attitudes in Dialogue: Exclusivism, Inclusivism, Parallelism and Interpenetration. The first three indicate certain negative attitudes. It expresses sense of superiority, making compromises, considering others not equals, and insensitive to other religious traditions. Panikkar is in favor of the fourth attitude: Interpenetration. It helps a follower to go beyond one's tradition. Though it is the right attitude, according to him, it is only a wishful thinking.

In inter-faith dialogue the partners commit themselves to search and to stand for truth. Definitely, in this context, truth cannot be reduced to a mere quality of some proposition. It is participatory and not speculative. Paul Lehmann puts it as, "It expresses a movement and a relation in which men are caught up and involved."[5] Truth is something to be 'in' and to be 'of'. It is a relationship to be entered into. While the partners seek truth, they participate in the Mission of God, by speaking truth in love, by being open to each other in all honesty and sincerity, affirming and criticizing when needed. The ultimate goal of dialogue is the coming into being of a common human community willed by God. It is witnessing to, discerning and working together with persons of other faiths that we are truly involved in both mission and dialogue. Only then we can find the true meaning and purpose of our inter-relatedness, 'that all may be one' (Jn 17:2).

Co-Relatedness in Dialogue

We understand our responsibility to immensely involve transforming the world. We concentrate on the Bible, as a form of a story that begin with creation (Gen 1:1) and ends with creation ((Rev 21:1-4). At the beginning of the world, there was creation and as the world progresses we contribute our share in the process of re-creation, enhancing the quality of life. However efficient we may be, we must value the transforming presence of God in the world. God is the author in building the Reign of God on the earth. We are the companions with God. The Trinity is communication in its nature and dialogue is one of the essential aspects of the Trinity in communication. God reveals to us in dialogue. We consider it as our mission in dialogue with our partners, which is a necessity and not just an option. It is necessarily dictated by three realities: our membership in the Church, our relationship with God and our being human being. We do not exclude anyone, rather in the wake of negative characteristics of marginalization and globalization, we witness to the universal and inclusive love of God, by accepting universality and diversity.

Two saints from medieval India are examples of this level of dialogue – Sant Kabir of Banaras (15th century Indian mystic poet and saint) and Lal Ded (Lalleshwari) a mystic of Kashmir. Both of them were deeply spiritual persons who had profound experience of God and build bridges between Hinduism and Islam. Attitudes of solidarity, respect and love would break barriers and open up communications. Some of the qualities of dialogue persons are: being rooted in one's wholeness and uniqueness, having free and frank acceptance of the other and their views, listening to the other well, treating them with utmost respect and seeing the other with the eyes of God, seeking the truth and common values to promote justice, peace and harmony.

Spirituality in Dialogue

Spirituality is embedded in dialogue. St John Paul II, in his address in Chennai to a group of religious leaders in February 1986 said, "By dialogue we let God be present in our midst; for as we open ourselves in dialogue to one another, we also open ourselves to God ... as followers of different religions we should join together in promoting and defending common ideals in the spheres of religious liberty, human brotherhood, education, culture, social welfare and civic order." When people collaborate in promotion of the common human and spiritual values, God becomes the common origin and goal of all peoples. In fact, Pope John Paul II envisages that when believers of various religions encounter each other, their encounter take place in the presence of God.

The inter-religious context makes one to realize one's understanding of God, giving due respect to every religious tradition. Every religion is concerned about God and teaches the followers to find their belief in God strong. There is a difference between religion and spirituality. Religions denote differences, historical diversifications, while spirituality denotes the underlying harmony among religions. It is the spirituality of religious essence on which religions are built and it gives meaning to our life and understanding of God. In dialogue we find that the religions are related and interconnected. There is a constant flow of movement from inside to outside and outside to inside. Spirituality is at the core of every religion.

In October 1986, when leaders of different religions were invited to Assisi to pray for peace, the very fact that they came together to pray is a positive sign that they can be in contact with God and that God would hear their prayers. In 1974, the Federation of Asian Bishops' Conference, during the plenary assembly in Taipei, Taiwan accepted the other religions as significant and positive elements in God's economy of salvation. "Every authentic prayer is prompted by the Holy Spirit, who is mysteriously present in every human heart" writes St. John Paul II in *Redemptoris Missio (No. 29)*. When we realize this fact, our human solidarity is strengthened and deepened. We truly become the voice of the voiceless, poor and the marginalized, victims of injustice and oppressive structures.

Salvation means participation of the whole universe in the life of God. God is gathering up all peoples into unity (Eph 1:3-10) till God will be 'all in all' (1 Cor 15:28). In this cosmic project all people belonging to various religions discover themselves as fellow wayfarers towards the kingdom. 'God wishes that everyone be saved' (1 Tim 2:4). Here salvation means that everyone be made whole, without any exception. God manifests himself in various ways and means, in various forms and at various times. Each one is a collaborator in this project and none is enemy to the other. Religions are the outcome of human response to God's self manifestation. We have the common pursuit to unravel the mysteries regarding God, world and man leading to mutual learning and enrichment between religions.

According to St. John Paul II, 'The kingdom of God is a concern of everyone; working for the kingdom means acknowledging and promoting God's activity. Building the kingdom means working for liberation from evil in all its forms' (RM 14). The Church's appreciation of other religions has led to a realization of the presence and action of God in them. In his general audience on September 9, 1998 St John Paul II said, "The 'seeds of truth' present and active in the various religious traditions are a reflection of the unique Word of God, who 'enlightens every man coming into the world' (Jn 1:9) and who became flesh in Christ Jesus" (Jn 1:14).

Each religion by its very nature is unique. When religions encounter each other there is mutual enrichment. Enrichment is possible only if the focus is on God-experience in these religions. One should also be enriched by the God-experience in other religions too. As a Christian I am enriched by the way Muslims express their love for religions by meticulously following the traditions of the religions, not only externally but with real commitment and faithfulness to God. Gandhi was a staunch Hindu. He was influenced by the experience of Jainism, when he spoke and practiced non-violence. His experience of Christianity and the Bible made him to be reflective and generous. The French Benedictine, Swami Abhishiktananda remained a Christian while he experienced the non-duality of the Advaitic philosophy[6] and built bridges with Hinduism at an authentic level and inspired many Indian Christians to discover another relationship with Hinduism. It is possible that the entire humanity can be brought together under one umbrella to recognize one God, if not in their individual symbols and rituals, in common prayer and silence.

Dialogue is essentially a process through which one partner- through mutual encounter with another – helps awaken in the other the very human depth which was hitherto latent.[7] In the process of dialogue, there is mutual sharing and all that separates are made to known, and genuine disclosure is made possible. The two horizons of dialogical partners fuse in such a way that they are enveloped by the Supreme Being, God. The spirit of truth and love is manifested in the dialogue partners and they recognize it in each other. The very presence of the Spirit in the dialogue partners makes dialogue a spirituality and part of God's mission. Witness is an essential dimension of dialogue, for it seeks invites the partners to be transparent before each other.

Our Unique Mission

For about two decades, SVDs have been reflecting on our mission as 'Prophetic Dialogue'. It is a call to radical way of life. Prophecy is essential to religious missionary life. Pope Francis says: "Prophecy announces the spirit of the Gospel" and then further "Prophets know God and they know the men and women who are their brothers and sisters. They are able to discern and denounce the evil of sin and injustice. Because they are free, they are beholden to no one but God, and they have no interest other than God. Prophets tend to be on the side of the poor and the powerless, for they know that God himself is on their side". We understand Prophetic Dialogue as being rooted in the Divine Word and inspired by the Holy Spirit, we commit ourselves to encounter and relate with our dialogue partners in friendship by witnessing to the values of universality and diversity.

Multiplicity, fragmentation, migration, religious and economic exploitation have become normal situations of the day. As *ad gentes* missionaries, we are to enter into prophetic dialogue with such wounded partners, bearing witness to the universality and promote diversity of God's people. Such prophetic dialogue would be marked by the characteristic dimensions, as mentioned earlier. The story of God's mission in the Bible invites us to conversion and urges us to witness to the universality and openness of the Reign of God. Our call to mission through Communication is a call to build up among ourselves a missionary, religious community that gives an ever more credible witness to the Reign of God. Through Mission Animation, we invite our communities to remove barriers to faith seekers, and we promote attitudes of religious tolerance and openness with people of other faith traditions. We incorporate JPIC by sharing the reason for our hope and inviting faith seekers to share in witnessing to the Reign of God. Within the mission of the Church, we are to bear witness to the universality and diversity of God's Reign. Through our ministries we invite everyone to share their gifts and treasures in realizing God's plan.

There are two global processes that are reshaping our life today, that affect our mission partners in India too – the marginalization of the poor who are kept away from the 'free' market economy because they do not have the technological know-how and the purchasing power and globalization that eliminates diversity and promotes uniformity. In such a society we are called to witness to the universal and inclusive love of God though our community life. Through our life of witness we transcend all bias and prejudices to make dialogue an ongoing transforming experience.

As qualities of a prophetic dialogue persons - we are to be rooted in our wholeness and uniqueness; to initiate and create a friendly atmosphere to welcome the other; to make efforts to know the other, listen to the other, treat others with utmost respect and see the other with eyes of God; and to seek the truth and common values to promote justice, peace and harmony, giving witness to the Reign of God. Frustrations arising out of painful experiences are inevitable in life and mission. Regular prayer, friendship, attitude of forgiveness, daily reading of scripture would be effective antidote to frustrations and pains.

We are to commit ourselves to interreligious dialogue because it is God's plan that unfolds itself through Word and Spirit, embracing the whole world and all peoples. The contribution of all religions is indispensable today for universal peace and promotion of human and spiritual values. It is to become integral part of our mission. Through dialogue we, Divine Word Missionaries give prophetic witness to the values of God's Reign and are called towards mutual respect and acceptance, build bridges, heal memories of historical wounds and break down the walls of religious fundamentalism and fanaticism.

We continue to involve in apostolic activities with a contemplative presence among God's people. To contemplate is to look within, to listen, to discern, to respond and to collaborate. We meditate on the presence of the Word and dialogue within ourselves before we choose to speak or not to speak to the other. It enables us to treat the other with extra ordinary respect and with the eyes of God. We cultivate a genuine fraternal community life within our communities. This will teach us prophetic dialogue with the poor and marginalized, by passing over from egoism to solidarity. We are to foster a welcoming community life that embraces diverse styles of prayer and religious expression.

Our Founder had a dream: 'May the Heart of Jesus life in the hearts of all'. Today we share that dream - that all peoples may live in a network of affirming and challenging relationships. This dream inspires us to walk together and motivate us to look to the future with hope. Our spirituality nurtures our dream through contemplation, conversion and communion. Contemplation helps us to see the world through the eyes of God and our understanding of 'WE' keeps on growing and expanding. In conversion we participate in the Paschal Mystery that casts our fears and helps us cope with frustrations. We understand communion as abiding in the spirit that guides us in our efforts to dialogue. We sustain our missionary spirituality by engaging with our dialogue partners, having intimacy with the Word of God in our communities, and by remembering and including our dialogue partners in the liturgies and celebrations.

Conclusion

We wish that we better be called as 'prophetic dialogists'. It includes our very essence of our being as Divine Word religious missionaries. It is not mere theoretical involvement, but in every practical sense, we engage ourselves in dialogue with our mission partners. Pope

Francis while addressing the Bishops of Asia on August 17, 2014 said, "Authentic dialogue also demands a capacity for empathy. We are challenged to listen not only to the words which others speak, but to the unspoken communication of their experiences, their hopes and aspirations, their struggles and their deepest concerns. Such empathy must be the fruit of our spiritual insight and personal experience, which lead us to see others as brothers and sisters, and to "hear", in and beyond their words and actions, what their hearts wish to communicate".

Today evangelization is understood in a holistic and integral way. It includes being with the people, responding to their needs, being sensitive to the presence of God in cultures and in other religious traditions and witnessing to the values of God's kingdom through our presence, solidarity and sharing. The only way to be effective missionaries in India is by being an ardent Prophetic dialogist.

Prophetic Dialogue is necessary for peace in the world. It affirms that all of us are 'inter-beings' and that we relate and co-relate with each other, for we are created in the image and likeness of God. We journey together, work together and build together a just society. We continue to involve in interactive pluralism – which implies the attitudes of listening, discerning and enriching, and by being sensitive to God's presence and action in other religious traditions. Presence of many religious traditions is in no way to be deplored bur rather acknowledged as a divine gift. Through prophetic dialogue, we are privileged to have the divine presence and experience. Today our mission is prophetic presence, service, collaboration and cooperation. In the present scenario in India, we need to revitalize our Interreligious Dialogue Centers and train more confreres to engage in this noble ministry. May we continue to be rooted in the Word and committed to the Mission.

Endnotes

[1] David Stent, *Religious Studies Made Simple*, Heinemann, London 1983, p. 10.

[2] Quoted by Peter C Phan, "Take and Read: An Asian Theology of Liberation", in National Catholic Reporter, March 7, 2016.

[3] Paul Jackson, *A Jesuit Among Sufis*, Gujarat Sahitya Prakash: Anand, 2017, p. 24.

[4] Pope John Paul II, *Address to the Representatives of Other Religions and Christian Confessions*, during his Apostolic visit to India, November 7, 1999. No 3.

[5] Paul Lehmann, *The Transfiguration of Politics*. London: SCM Press, 1976, p.63.

[6] Swami Abhishiktananda, *Ascent to the depth of Heart*, Delhi: ISPCK,1998

[7] R. Panikkar, *Myth, Faith and Hermeneutics*. Bangalore: Asian Trading Corporation. 1983. pp 242-3.

Bibliography

A.   Books

Abhishiktananda, Swami. *Ascent to the depth of Heart.* Delhi: ISPCK, 1998.

Amaldass, Michael. *Making Harmony.* Delhi: ISPCK, 2003.

Bongiovanni, Ambrogio (ed). *Windows On Dialogue.* Delhi: ISPCK, 2012.

Edwin, Victor (ed). *Journeying Together in Faith.* Anand: Gujarat Sahitya Prakash, 2008.

Fernandes, Angelo. *Experience of Dialogue.* Anand: Gujarat Sahitya Prakash, 1994.

Jackson Paul. *A Jesuit Among Sufis.* Anand: Gujarat Sahitya Prakash, 2017.

Lehmann, Paul. *The Transfiguration of Politics.* London: SCM Press, 1976.

Panikkar, R. *Myth, Faith and Hermeneutics.* Bangalore: Asian Trading Corporation, 1983.

Stent, David. *Religious Studies Made Simple.* London: Heinemann, 1983.

Suresh, A (ed). *Sarva-Dharma-Sammelan.* New Delhi: Commission For Interreligious Dialogue, 1998.

Tirimanna, Vimal (ed). *Harvesting from the Asian Soil.* Bangalore: ATC, 2011.

Wilfred, Felix. *From the Dusty Soil: Contextual Reinterpretation of Christianity.* Madras: Jyothi Printers, 1995.

B.   Articles

Amaladoss, Michael. "Indian Christian Theological Issues in the Context of Interreligious Dialogue."

_____: "The Challenges and Opportunities of Dialogue with Other Religions."

Arulsamy. "Mission of the Church and Dialogue with Religions", *Vidyajyoti Journal of Theological Reflection 66* (2002): 674-688.

Doss, Mohan. Dialogue: "A New Way of Being Church in India Today."

John Paul II, *Address to the Representatives of Other Religions and Christian Confessions*, during his Apostolic visit to India, November 7, 1999. No 3

Kroger, James H., "Milestones in Interreligious Dialogue", *Review for Religious*, Vol. 56. No 3 (May-June 1997): 268-276

Machado, Felix. "The Development of Theology from Vatican II to Our Days: A South Asian Perspective", *Vidyajyoti Journal of Theological Reflection 63* (1999): 559-574.

Michel, Thomas. "Dialogue in the Context of Consecrated Life: Working with Others for Justice and Peace."

Painadath, Sebastian. "Theological Perspectives of FABC on Interreligious Dialogue", *Jeevadhara* (1997): 275-276.

Peter C Phan (Quoted), "Take and Read: An Asian Theology of Liberation", in National Catholic Reporter, March 7, 2016.

The SVD Mission among Tribals:

Challenges with a Special Reference to INM's Raigad –Mangaon Mission

Richard Quadros SVD

Introduction

In the major tribal belt of Indian sub-continent, the SVDs have various interventions for tribal emancipation. Education , pastoral, Socio-economic empowerment, Research etc. being some of the major work areas through which the SVD mission is spread over states like Madhya Pradesh, Gujarat, Orissa, Jharkhand, West Bengal, Maharashtra and North Eastern States. The focused interventions in the tribal communities have such overwhelming results and indicators of growth, development, empowerment etc. that the tribal literacy rate, leadership, socio economic, cultural growth etc. have shown an upward movement. Through pastoral interventions, the community has spiritually benefitted.

Exploitation and marginalization of the poor, underprivileged, illiterate etc. groups and communities are the open secrets, which doesn't need a layman to do deep research but life experiences of the tribal communities come in good stead as reliable proofs. Most of the tribal communities are poor and vulnerable and marginalized from the colonial era till today; so the Church's interventions in tribal communities has brought a ray of hope towards a vertical movement;

in terms of upward socio-economic growth, assertion of rights, participation in good governance and active politics. The right and fight of tribals over (*3Js*) *Jal* (water) *Jungle* (forest) *Jameen* (land) is legitimate as they are indigenous communities whose rights were not given but acquired by the very fact of their ancestral lineage in a particular habitat. This paper focuses on the SVD Mission among Tribals: Challenges and Prospects with a specific reference to the Katkari tribe in Maharashtra with and for whom the SVDs are working for about 10 years in Mangaon, Mahasala and Tala taukas of Raigad district, Maharashtra state about 160 k.m south of Mumbai and 140 k.m west of Pune; the two commercially sizzling cities that sandwiches the tribal community with limited resources, landlessness, illiteracy, distress migration etc.

1.   SVD Mission

1.1.   The word 'Mission' Hijacked

'Mission' has become a significant word. During the colonial era, 'mission' was predominantly seen as the intervention of the Christian missionaries in the mission territories. When the second half of the twentieth century ushered in a new world order, the missionaries' monopoly of the word 'mission' was splintered. The duty assigned to an eavesdrop or a criminal investigation officer is referred to as his or her 'mission' to their organization, institution or society. In this sense, people like Nelson Mandela, Mahatma Gandhi, and Mother Theresa had their definite mission of liberation, independence and service. Different religious groups and political establishments have come up with their specific mission agendas viz. Islamic Mission, Chinmaya Mission, Ramakrishna Mission, Bahai centres propagating faith, Buddhist Missionary Society, Sarva Shiksha Mission (Literacy Promotion Mission), Swachata (Cleanliness) Mission etc. What were once the methodology and motivation of the Christian missions are now efficiently imitated by the mission attempts of most non-Christian religions. Many commercial and business establishments viz. Amway, Amazon, Coco Cola, Microsoft and Pepsi etc. are outdo get the global market with a missionary zeal! The word mission derives from a Latin word*missionem* (nominative mission) that means "to send." Jesuit missionaries (1590s) who sent members of their order overseas to establish schools and Churches first used it. Before sending, the dedicated and committed members, they were well formed oriented, motivated and inspired by the teachings of Christ who also sent his disciples to proclaim the Word of God...i.e. Good News to the poor and exploited, liberation to the captives, peace and justice to those suffer due to injustice and disharmony, Knowledge and information to the ignorant, message of love and forgiveness even to the extent of forgiving one's own enemies. With this mission, orientation a missionary is sent. All those who were sent to proclaim the above values were convinced that they were working to bring God's kingdom on earth. But, today one must ask a specific question as to how these values are promoted in the mission strategy of other religious and political establishments. What is the defining moment for mission strategy of these establishments? What is the missionary zeal? If the missionary strategy and zeal are synergized then what is the ultimate goal? Is it for promotion of God's Kingdom? Or is it for yielding maximum business profits? Or is it to promote radicalism, fundamentalism or for aggressive agendas?

For the Church's interventions mission relates to God's salvific involvement in creation. The created order- both nature and humanity -has been adversely affected due to misappropriation of mission strategy and conveniently appropriating for one's own ulterior motives. Christian mission essentially implies the educating of the membership of the church to responsibly involve in the world order along with God as His agents in the process of new creation in Christ. In the whole process of adding value to the fractured world is very difficult but not impossible as the Lord invites us to be salt of the earth and light of the world. Therefore, the mission of the Church is not just only the act of faith formation in the individuals, but the act of actualizing the formed faith. How does one do that? Simple, having built a dam around the water we never congest the water to be stored without any outlets. The stored water is given enough outlets, ventilation to be flown and get actualized in its natural flow. Having said that the dam remains safe and the flow of water for various purposes is being actualized. In that sense the Church over the years has formed and is forming faith among its members so that the formed faith is not expected to be stored without actualizing it and purposefully actualized in their daily life. So the actual mission of the Church is not just storing the Faith but living, actualizing. This purposeful action of the Church essentially invites members who are committed, dedicated and inspired. Only then, the actual meaning of the mission strategy will get realized in its result lest the word mission will be hijacked for someone's vested interest.

1.2. Our Name is Our Mission

In the last three General Chapters of the Society of the Divine Word, we perceive an attempt to identify our mission in the present world and our specific role within the church. With the expression "prophetic dialogue" the 15th General Chapter (2000) provided a concept to identify our vocation and mission today. The 16th General Chapter (2006) focused on prophetic dialogue "as a lens to focus some aspects of our life as Divine Word Missionaries". The 17th General Chapter (2012) spelt out an action plan known as 'Congregational Direction' to address several challenges faced in our mission ad extra and our life ad intra. In the 18th General Chapter (2018), our Society is engaged in a process of renewal of oneself, community life and mission. In this Chapter, we have had the Chapter theme "The love of Christ impels us (2 Cor 5:14): rooted in the Word, committed to his mission". This Chapter has given an impetus to all the members of the Society to deepen our Trinitarian and Incarnational (Word becoming Flesh) spirituality that will bring us close to God and closer to our brothers and sisters especially the poor, the last, least and lost, the vulnerable viz. tribals, refugees, poor etc.

Every member of the Society of the Divine Word who is rooted in the Word needs to spell out the mission in the company of Christ for he is a Divine Word Missionary and there is our identity: our name is our mission. Having borne that name every Divine Word Missionary is sent out from one continent to the other, one country to another and one culture to the other. The openness to be sent out is the pre-requisite to be in the mission field. Therefore, we celebrate the internationality, interculturality in the interpersonal growth. Therefore, the spirituality of 'mission' as against the meaning of 'mission' in the secular world is quite distinct, specific, and apparent. So, a missionary and that too a Divine Word Missionary is sent out in the mission field to live up to the theological values of the Word Incarnate. Unless and until the one who is sent out is not rooted in the Word Incarnate, he will just define 'mission' like that of a commercial company or a political establishment. So as a matter of fact, a missionary without a definite mission-definition is just a driver who drives as a functionary; a manager who manages or an administrator who administrates. Therefore, for the Divine Word Missionaries, the name itself encompasses the spirituality of mission. Further to say, Divine Word Missionaries being rooted in the incarnate Word is the greatest inspiration for mission.

1.2.3. 'Mission SVD' Journey Embarked

From the very inception of SVD mission in India way back 1932 till today the mission orientation for the members of the Society Of the Divine Word is 'difficult frontiers'. We need to salute the early generations of the SVDs in India for their visionary approach, commitment and dedication to the mission. Listening to the life sharing and testimonies of the members in the yesteryears and in the present years one has no choice than to conclude that the inner inspiration and rootedness in the 'WORD' made them faithful and successful to bring a logical conclusion to their ministries. While addressing the august assembly of the Capitulars of the SVD 18th General Chapter in Rome on 24th June 2018, the Pope Francis said that "to know the mission of the Congregation go to your roots and cemeteries where the SVDs are buried in faraway Africa or Amazon". Truly, the Pope stirred the shallow commitment and dedication of many missionaries from whom he expects a total commitment. It also invites us to examine our own secured life, comfort zones and makes that hymn resound: "So I leave my boats behind, leave them on familiar shores." In our mission, we are challenged to feel the gory realities from the virtual flashed on digital screens, to the actual on fatal fields.

The vacuum of Indian expatriate is being filled by the native Indian SVDs in all the four SVD provinces and one region. In the growing difficulties of foreign missionaries entering the Indian shores, though internationality is absent in our provinces/regions; we overwhelmingly celebrate interculturality while being in the mission fields as India is a unique country of cultural mosaic. Due to varieties of political conflicts, we are standing on the threshold of a less peaceful and less safe globe. These global realities are experienced in India as well. In the guise of the territorial security of the nation states, there is brazen violence of human rights, rights of minorities, war torn areas that result in refugees fleeing from their home town and getting settled in alien land, culture and language. In this process the tribals, women and children are the most vulnerable. In the history of the church and the Society of the Divine Word, there are missionaries who explored and trekked unknown lands for the sake of the Gospel never to see their own home land, parents and relatives. In another context while giving an interview to a periodical –La Civilta Catolica Pope Francis says the missionaries' faith is not 'lab faith', but a journey faith', a historical faith. God has revealed himself as history, not as a compendium of abstract truths. He further says, "I am afraid of laboratories because in laboratory we take the problems and then we bring them home to tame them, to paint them artificially, out of their context. You cannot bring the home the frontier, but you have to live on the border and be audacious".

Over the years, the SVD mission among the tribals had been very down to earth. The entire central province and Chotanagpur belt of the area had been trekked by the missionaries for more than 75 years and now of course with an underscored mention of the SVDs continuing the legacy of the founding generation in spreading the Word of God in the North Eastern states especially among tribals. In the areas where there was no government presence, the missionaries had taken the lighted candle of education, health services, empowerment process etc. And to enable spiritually, the members of the Society embarked a journey of pastoral care to tribals. Hence, in these tribal belts the literacy rate has shown an upward trend. And a vibrant witnessing community, faith formed Church has grown.

1.2.4. 'Mission-SVD' among Katkaris in Mangaon, Raigad Maharashtra

It was after the bifurcation of the erstwhile India South (INS) Province in two separate provinces India Hyderabad (INH) and India Mumbai (INM) Province, the later contemplated as to extend its geographic mission territory to Raigad district of Maharashtra state in 2004. Having accepted the invitation from the local zonal bishop of Archdiocese of Bombay, the SVD embarked a journey in to the frontiers in 2006. The base was Mangaon taluka. The civil district Raigad is known for the habitat of one of two most backward tribes (formerly known as primitive tribe) Katkaris and Madia Kolam. The tribe Kathkari is derived from their profession of peeling of skin (*kath*) of *kaire* tree, which was used to produce *gutka* type of substance. The tribe- Kathkari is also known as hunter gatherers. Today the government has banned felling and skinning of *kaire*trees and hunting wild animals under the prevention and conservation of wild animal's law. As a result, the hunter gathering community- Katkari has taken up specialized jobs on brick kilns and charcoal kilns as brick bakers. They are also landless agricultural laborers. The district of Maharashtra according to the 2011 census has 25,15,250 population out of which 250,000 belonging to the tribe of Warli, Thakur, Mahadev Koli and Kathkari. Though the former 4 tribes are scantly spread over the district, Katkaris are thickly populated in southern district of Raigad where the SVDs work in 3 out of 15 blocks or taluks of Raigad. There are also other 18 church based NGOs working in the district in other blocks. There is also a good presence of the non-church based NGOs with whom the SVD is working in tandem under its networking strategy.

In 2016(,) while celebrating the decennial anniversary of SVD presence in Raigad district a short study was done by the SVD run organization Sarva Vikas Deep (SVD)- a Human Resource Development and Training Centre- as to mainly make a comparative assessment with that of the base line study done in the year 2009. The study showed a remarkable inroads by the SVD venture in the tribal belt of the district in terms of conceptualizing the interventions, setting the goals, vision-mission and objectives 2020.

The baseline study of the 2009 showed a aghast results of 80% distress migration to distant places for livelihood, literacy rate as low as 10.3% as against 25% government literacy rate, and among the tribal women only 8% literacy rate and among men 20%. Though tribals identify themselves with land, water and forest; all these three aspects of their lives were flicked away by the colonial rule before independence under the guise of protecting and preserving forest and that is being carried out by the independent India government till 2006: Right to Forest Land Act 2006 was enforced. Due to landlessness, the tribals migrated to neighboring states or within the state on brick kilns or charcoal kilns risking their own lives and leaving their spouses and children in the high vulnerable situation at the destination point of the migration. In the migration process the children, were forced to discontinue schooling which had resulted in high illiteracy rate among them. Malnutrition cases were on the rise due to lack of nutrition, clean and potable water, rampant child marriage. In a predominantly patriarchal Katkari tribal society, the woman had very little opportunity to take decisions due to lack of access to resources, economic availability, illiteracy leading to low self-esteem and self-confidence.

In 2016, when the organization Sarva Vikas Deep (SVD) in retrospection embarked the study of the same community after having intervened for about ten years, the results are inspiring and heartwarming. The 7 objectives set in the year 2007 were evaluated and found that the 12 different programmes the SVD worked towards the empowerment of tribals and brought literacy rate among the children to 25% by formal Hostel education and informal supplementary education and doorstep schools on brick kilns as against 10% in the base line. Having Vision Mission statement in place and 7 specific Objectives, the organization the SVD dotted a remarkable growth in women's empowerment through sustainable livelihood activities both group agricultural and nonagricultural activities. To implement the Right to Forest Act to acquire forest land, the SVD closely networked with the government machinery by which the 'Mission SVD Acquiring Land' got a whopping success of 2500 acres of forest land in the name of the tribals. Along with forest land rights, the tribals also are accompanied to acquire land under Tenancy Act. Under the same Act a total of 15 acres of land is in registration process. Along the right based approaches, the implementation of Right to Food Security Act 2013 was closely monitored along with government departments. Every village food security vigilant committees were trained as to how they should be watchdogs when ration in public distribution system (PDS) under the right to food security act gets pilferaged. A total of thirty tribal women were trained to be vigilant to regularize the PDS in the villages.

As part of good governance and enabling village parliament (*gram sabha*) training had been held in the villages to generate awareness on decentralized power and a special reference on women's role and gender equality in gram panchayat elections and preparing women *sarpanchs*' and elected members' trainings were held under 73rd amendment of the constitution of India. A total of 3 tribal women *sarpanchs* and about 10 tribal men and women were elected to the post of gram panchayat as committee members in the past ten years as against hardly any before 2006.

The indicators of mission tribal empowerment is seen in reduced distress migration as low as 10% to 20% in twenty villages out of eighty villages through the intervention of sustainable local livelihood, marketing of minor forest products (cashew nuts, *karvandasetc.*) have created opportunities for the tribals in the village itself. Similar initiatives are on to curb migration in other villages through sustainable livelihood generation initiatives.

2. Challenges to the SVD Mission

To learn more about ourselves, we must test our limits and capabilities. That helps us to take new ventures, challenges. So, challenges become opportunities on our way. To lead an authentic life, we need challenges that help us to stretch our life. There is a lot of risk in taking challenges, but an authentic person doesn't mind that because through these risks one has learning, unlearning and relearning process built up. Risk in taking up challenges is like crossing a river on stepping stones-there is always a possibility of getting wet. The question is not how we lead a life in which we don't feel the fear of failure but rather how do we move forward in spite of fear. In this sense, both in the past and present the Church and SVDs did fear the challenges, but the second question how do we move forward despite fear had been a reflective question to get into innovative mission methodologies to limit the fear of risk and challenges. The challenges to the SVD Mission have been both *ad extra* and *ad intra*. As part of the *ad extra*, the following challenges can be listed as follows:

Ad extra Challenges

2.1. Building the gap between the rich and poor

One area that challenges us is increasing divide between the rich and the poor. More number of industrial corridors, SEZ etc. is not actually benefitting the tribal population. They are actually marginalized and rich are becoming richer. The purchasing parity has a huge gap. Land alienation was once upon a time a big problem, now displacement becomes biggest problem. The quest for justice roots itself in the basic provision of equal rights for all. Human Rights movements have sprung up in different settings. Explorations to discover means of alleviating poverty have become top priority in the mission focus of the many relief and development agencies. As an undercurrent, there is the cry for 'justice' and 'human rights' emerging as mission themes for us in the tribal belt of Raigad district.

In simple terms, there are 200 millions of people struggling for their basic needs who are identified as people who live below poverty line in India. I agree with Amartya Sen, Nobel Prize winner in 1998 for economic philosophy, when he says the "poverty cannot solely be determined by the economic income of a particular person rather by the freedom that person has to earn his basic needs within a particular environment". According to Sen, "being a poor does not mean living below an imaginary poverty line, such as an income of two dollars a day or less. It means having an income level that does not allow an individual to cover certain basic necessities, taking into account the circumstances and social requirements of the environment". He then focuses on the other factors that enable an individual to find income to cover or not to cover the basic necessities. He goes on to say, "There are geographical, biological and social factors that amplify or reduce the impact of income on each individual.

2.2. Corruption

Corruption is another challenge that poses umpteen obstacles to the mission. For Mission-SVD corruption is a challenge - but one hears the question: 'how can the church help clean up a nation when there is enough corruption within its rank and file?' For the Church corruption becomes a challenge both at *ad intra* and *ad extra* level. The two powerful forces keep stoking the fires of corruption: selfishness and greed. A selfish person will try to amass more and more wealth through corruption. This becomes a way of life for such selfish people. He also becomes greedy for amassing wealth and money. In the process of corruption the most affected are the poor and marginalized. As corruption snowballs, it becomes more acceptable until it is finally a way of life. Today it has become a way of life for many politicians, industrialists, businessmen, the so called spiritual leaders etc. Many anti-corruption laws have been enacted enforced and amended in the history in several countries. But, the evil of corruption is haunting every society leading to difficult situations.

2.3. Doctrines and Dogmas and Church's Ecumenism

Today in India, we are faced with religious fundamentalism, linguistic chauvinism, caste exploitation, political vengeance and ideological conflicts in different parts. The Church across denominations is not united due to dogmatic and doctrinal issues. Catholic Church being the largest institutional church, is always been targeted by fundamentalist for any contentious issues emerging from any small church denominations. The lower rung of the fundamentalist groups have either not done or not interested to do a baseline study as to what are the dogmatic teachings of different denominations and how they streamline the mission strategies and methodologies in a particular Church. A few Christian denominations do have an aggressive agenda for which the Catholic Church has to pay a heavy price. Ecumenical meetings may remain only coming together and do not yield a concrete step to address the growing communalism in the country. Hence, ecumenical unity in the given dogmatic teachings is a major challenge. Church ecumenism leading to Cultural Ecumenism would be one of the ways that the different Churches can work together in addressing present day situation. But, the way forward is still unclear.

2.4. Biased media

Present day media is one sided and virtually bought by the political parties. Such media has any freedom to be courageous in its journalistic profession though profess so. They have been bound by the political parties for their ulterior motives and sharp polarization of electoral in the country. When someone is biased against, then in whatsoever one does good will not be reported and published as balanced news.

The biased media will always looks at the Church and its contribution through the lens of communalism/conversion etc. and try to establish a narrative that defames the Church and its institutions. This is another challenge that church has to fight against the giant media house in India.

2.5. Government apathy towards development and non-willingness to work with Church based organizations

Due to lack of political will, the governments are apathetic towards people's development. That results in lack of growth in vulnerable communities, lack of access to government schemes. Those Church organizations that work with the government machinery find it difficult to dispense government schemes through its platform as there is lack of proactive support and willingness to share valuable information, which can be disseminated to the village tribal community.

2.6. Tribals Losing their Cultural Identity to the Dominant Cultures

The dominant culture influencing the tribal society is another challenge to conserve the age-old cultural heritage of tribals. The tribal feast and festivals, dance, music and folklore have been replaced with non-tribal feast and festivals; tribal dance has been replaced with DJ and Bollywood music and dance even during the tribal feast and festivals. The younger generation is feeling shy when the traditional cultural dance and music is discussed in the schools and hostels. Conservation of tribal cultural is a challenge in the wake of modern, western dance and music.

2.7. Insufficient Research integration into Interventions

Very often, the interventions to address the issues among the tribals are with a charity top down approach. The end result is treating the symptoms and not the cause. Research must be integrated into the SVD interventions while working with the tribal community. This would also help the members of the Society of the Divine Word to chalk out proper strategies and methodology and work towards accomplishing the objectives rather than activities.

2.8. Oppressed emerging as Oppressor

Paulo Freiere in his book "Pedagogy of the Oppressed" speaks about how once oppressed individuals, groups emerge as Oppressors. The social upward mobility of some of the leaders within the community is leading into oppression of their own community members.

Ad intra Challenges

2.9. Priestly formation: Increasing culture of comfort zones

For an innovative mission strategy to work among the tribals one also needs proper orientation, formation, aptitude and specialization. Institutionalization of our mission has gone to an extent that the members work as managers and administrators and not as animators or facilitators in the mission field. Comfort zone created by some mission strategies become attractive or easier for the members to be in the comfort zone than enter into 'difficult frontiers'. The priestly formation needs these issues to be addressed in the formation.

2.10. Sustainability in the Mission Task

One of the questions unanswered by many church organizations/congregations is how to handle the issue of frequent transfers of the members from some specialized mission work areas. Mission needs continuity and sustainability. Many times, the mission tasks especially in JPIC context are started by either one or two individuals' initiative. When they are transferred before the goal posts are set properly, the mission doesn't get a proper direction. Often transfers without preparing the second rung of leadership would mean setting the new goal posts. One cannot change the goal post every now and then. Often the goal posts are changed without any reference to previous programs, activities, plans etc. Every person sets his or her own goal post. As a result, there is no baton carried forward in the relay race of the Mission Task. This needs a special attention as well.

Conclusion

In summery then, the mission ventures must be practical praxis: learning from the past, reflecting on the present, and reaching out to the future. Thus needs a holistic analysis of our Mission Interventions at all levels. The 'SVD Mission' ventures, strategies, objectives are not fool proof that they are written in a compendium once and for all. They need to be visited and re-visited. Therefore, it is a process. In theorizing, the Mission without praxis is next to planning an event but not implementing it. We are Divine Word Missionaries who carry out the mission not to construct literature but to put it in practice. Therefore, our Name is our Mission.

Bibliography

Raja, Joshva 2002, *Communication, Reconciliation and the Culture of Dialogue*, a paper presented at Kualalumpur for Asia Region WACC Congress, Kualalumpur.

Raja, Joshva. 'Relevant and Effective Theological Education in the Twenty First Century India', 2002a, January, *Ministerial Formation* WCC's Publications Geneva.

Raja, Joshva. 2002, *Internet, Mission and Ecumenism*, Published as Document of EMS, presented for Mission societies in Stuttgart, November

Michale Kinnamon and Brian E Cope ed, The Ecumenical Movement. An Anthology of Key Texts and Voices. WCC Publications, Geneva, 1997.

Andreas Gross, A Brief Survey of Mission Discussions and Its Importance for the Theme, in New Horizons in Christian Mission: A Theological Exploration edited by Victor Premsagar, Chennai: Gurukul Lutheren Theological College, 2000 - 106.

Scherer James A and Bevans Stephen B ed, New Directions in Mission and Evangelisation 1 Basic Documents. New York: Orbis, 1992.

Chomski, Noam.2002, Clash of Civilizations? Seminar, Vol.509, January.

Mission to Transform Societies:

North East in Context

Babu Karakombil SVD

Introduction

I consider it a privilege to be involved with the MER group that routinely assemble together and think aloud on contemporary issues that confront our mission in India. And this seminar gains greater significance in the light of its context in which we all think together for better effectiveness of our mission intervention. And the context is to pay homage to the late Rev Dr Augustine Kanjamala SVD who in more senses than one, was one of the leading architects of the contemporary missiological landscape in India.

For Dr Kanajamala an accomplished Sociologist and Missiologist has been a path finder in the complex socio-political scenario of India, and he did it in the most appreciative manner is more than evident from his many years of splendid service rendered at Ishvani, a pioneering missiological institute in India, as well as his many publications. He was not one who always towed the familiar line of thinking not only of the Church but even of liberal secular thinkers on a wide range of social and religious issues. As for instance his article on the alleged 'failure' of Christianity in Asia was severely critiqued by a cross section of Christians in India (*Rf. Christian Mission in Asia complete Failure: Catholic Priest in Matters India Dec 30, 2014*).

His book, 'The Future of Christian Mission in India' created a flutter not only among the Indian theologians and but even in the US it was taken note of. Dr Kanjamala argues that even after 400 years of Christian presence and work in Asia only about 3% of its large population has accepted Christianity and this certainly shows that it has been a failure here. He goes on to argue that although the Church has invested huge amount of resources and personnel in this part of the world, the results have not been encouraging. By saying this he has not discounted the good that the Church has done and continues to do for the socio-religious development of people especially those belonging to the margins of the society.

His lectures and writings always called for transition and transformation of the manner in which Church has to get rooted in the Asian context. For far too long the Church has been presented in the European garb and hence it faced perpetual suspicion among the Asians who already have their traditional religions and spiritual traditions. Hence it has always been a challenge for Christianity to make its presence and relevance felt in Asian context. This is the same challenge we are facing today and therefore our efforts to find new ways to move on with our mission.

Struggle between Tradition and Transformation

At any given time of history one can always witness a struggle between the forces that support tradition and that push for transformation. On one hand there is always a tendency in a given society at a given time of history the urge to maintain status quo, and fierce resistance to change. Be it in the area of morality, social norms, political institutions, financial practices, economic activities, art and art forms, there is always a section of the society that wants to retain the familiar ground and resist any attempt to bring in change and transformation.

On the other hand there is also the irresistible urge to bring in change and transformation in all spheres of life. This is particularly so in societies that have hitherto been fortified from other cultures and societies. When such cultures are exposed to more contemporary liberal cultural mores, they tend to realign themselves to the latter: at times they completely identify themselves with the new cultures or they absorb some elements from them while retaining the some of the old.[1] An example of this cultural transformation in the Indian society is the dressing patterns of people especially the youth who are easily drawn to the western patterns of clothing. For some years ago, it was a common sight to see young women in the North India wearing salwar kameez, but that has now given place to jeans and top and a variety of fashionable clothes. This trend is more pronounced in the north eastern states where the cultures are predominantly Tribal and with the arrival of Christianity they have easily adopted the European cultural elements such as the English language as their link language, European dress patterns and even food habits.

Meeting of ideologies and meeting of cultures

The substratum of any society is its social, religious and cultural ideologies. These ideologies are formed over a period of time with the general social approval and practice of them which in turn are articulated in their myths, fables, art and art forms, life styles, food habits and above all in social institutions.

When we look at these ideologies from a phenomenological stand point, we realize that these ideologies reflected in the social mores have been 'sedimented,' for with each passing generations, these ideologies get reinforced with new elements added or some elements modified. So if we want to view the original ideologies of any society we need to follow the phenomenological deductive process which in other words is the process of unraveling the many layers of features added to the original elements. It is certainly not an easy task for with the passage of time it becomes extremely strenuous to separate each layer of features added to the original but it is a worthwhile exercise to do so that we can decipher the actual or rather as close as possible elements of a culture.

This exercise is important from the point of view of gauging a culture vis-à-vis another culture that has made its inroads into it. As for example, what were the actual cultures of the Tribes of north east which have been metamorphosed into composite cultures in the contemporary time? This has happened because of the influence of Christian beliefs and teachings that many Tribes of the north eastern states have adopted along with their cultural elements. The cultural elements that came along with Christianity in the case of the north east is largely European and American initially and later missionaries from south of India.

With the arrival and meeting of cultures several Tribals cultural elements were either modified or even renounced. As for instance, the Naga Tribes in Nagaland and also in other states of North East have had the custom of head hunting, and that was considered a heroic act in the original Naga culture. But with Christianity making inroads to the Naga society, this practice also got eradicated as it amounts to cruelty to human beings and goes contrary to Christian teachings of holding human life and valuable and precious.[2]

Emerging Composite cultures
The meeting of cultures has inevitable fallout. It gives rise to new forms of cultural expressions, and they exhibit both continuity as well as discontinuity with the existing cultures. It is hardly a total break from the past but more often than not one finds some of the aspects of the old cultures are merged with the aspects of the new culture that bring about a refreshingly new cultural expressions. As for example, in music there are noteworthy examples of blending of eastern and western music thus creating wonderful melodies.[3] Among many contemporary music maestros AR Rahman stands out in his brilliant creations of musical pieces that blend the best of eastern and western classical music. So also in the fashion industry, experimentation is the key word as they keep trying to find global attires that bring together the best in different cultures. Mabel known in her article, *Difference between Eastern and Western Fashion, And*

why we dress the way we do, talks about different mindsets of Asians and Europeans when it comes to the choice of clothes and their colors. As for instance, bright colored clothes are preferred by Asians in comparison to the westerners who prefer single deep colors. For most Asian the black color is inauspicious as it is often associated with death and grief, while it is a formal dress color for Europeans. There is also a difference in the design patterns in clothes that are preferred by the Asians and Europeans.

Dietary habits give us a glimpse of the changing food patterns in a globalised world. Today food is globalised through vast networks of restaurants that serve a variety of foods. While it provides a never before opportunity for people to familiarize themselves with the cuisines from all over the world, it has also a flip side to it. That is the traditional foods of the indigenous people are slowly giving way to the fast food promoted by the transnational corporations. These business giants invest huge amounts of money in creating demands for their products through their targeted advertisements and sales promotions. And following these fads is unfortunately considered as signs of modernity and progress.

Emerging composite culture and the Christian mission

The church and its mission has been the most powerful globalization force in the world. The early missionary expansion was possible because of the large network of religious congregations that spread out into the whole world with a singular mission of reaching out to all with the message of Christ's salvation. 'The Roman Catholic Church actually could be called the oldest global institution, and certainly is continuing that today, although it is very much changing its character,'[4] opines Peter Berger. He further suggests that the globalizing trend initiated by the Catholic Church is now changing for some reasons beyond its control. For one thing, there is a demographic as well as geographic shift of Catholic Church's presence and influence. Demographically the number of members of the Catholic Church is increasing in the southern hemisphere of the world while it is dwindling in the traditionally stronger northern hemisphere. And one of the reasons for this decline in the traditionally stronger areas of Europe and America is the invasion of modern secular ideologies that view religion with suspicion or worse as non essential to human life and society.

Another contemporary phenomenon in the world is the globalization of pluralism. The west which was predominantly Christian is now faced with the reality of the presence of other religious traditions creating social realignments. It is no more a mono religious culture but pluralistic in their very social structures. In this changed pluralistic social context the church has to find its way to negotiate with the demands of such a society. Peter Berger suggests that the 'globalization of religion is a globalization of pluralism. Pluralism, which was a much more geographically limited phenomenon 150 or 200 years ago, has become a global phenomenon, and that has enormous implications'.[5]

For the Christian mission in India, pluralism has never been alien to it; rather it was always the template on which it found its distinctive identity and anchor. For right from the start of Christian presence in India in the first century of CE the church was deeply entrenched in the pluralistic environment of India and that is reflected in the manner in which the Church adapted itself to the cultural mores of the relevant times. Take the traditions of ancient Syrian Christians of Kerala or St Thomas Christians as they are popularly known, for example; they have adapted themselves to the prevalent Hindu cultural modes in their social customs and even in religious worship patterns.[6] This cultural amalgamation is quite explicit in the art forms and architecture followed by the Christian community in Kerala. It is a common sight that a flag post is an integral part of temple as well as Syrian church premises; so also seven-tiered brass lamps within temples and churches. Processions with the presiding deity's statue of a temple and the statue of patron saint of a church are quite common. In short, there are quite a few similarities when it comes to the festivities of both temples and churches in Kerala.

While the Kerala St Thomas Christians have followed a line of cultural amalgamation, it is not the same with the Christianity in the rest of India. The Latin rite Catholic Church and almost all the protestant denominations across India have largely been following the western life style and worship patterns. A case in point is the Christianity in Goa and in the north east where Christians have adopted western ways of dressing, food habits and of course Latin as the liturgical language. This uniformity had certainly its advantages but perhaps more disadvantage in a country like India that often viewed the west and its Christian religion with some measure of suspicion and therefore ignored or worse resisted it.

Besides, the very philosophy of Hinduism opens its doors to a variety of ways (*margas*) to salvation, and under this understanding it is easy to consider Christianity as another way to seek one's liberation. Therefore there is no urgent need to switch one's religious identity; it is more than enough to open one's mind to another philosophy of life. This mode of co-opting and rejecting is well described by Tony Joseph in his article, *Why Christianity failed in India*, "Christianity, probably for the first time, came up against a philosophy and culture that did not feel the need to persecute other faiths, did not find the Christian messiah and his teachings either objectionable or exceptional, and therefore, didn't see why anyone should convert either. This embrace-cum-rejection was such a novel experience for it that Christianity probably didn't know quite how to respond."[7] Tony Joseph's observation regarding the failure or what I would call lack of numerical growth of Christianity in India coalesces with Dr Kanjamala's conclusion that after two millennia Christians remain a miniscule percentage of Indian population.

Catalyst role of Christianity in India

While there are hardly any credible reasons to doubt the claim of Dr Kanjamala or Mr Tony Joseph who opined that Christianity has numerically failed in India, we must also consider other dimensions of the issue of Christian presence in India. What I refer here to is the transformational influence Christianity has exerted in the Indian society at large. Several social reforms in Indian society, particularly in the Hindu society have been initiated by those who followed either Christian religion or were influenced by its teachings and values. As for instance Mahatma Gandhi in more occasions than one acknowledged and endorsed the contributions Christianity has made to Indian society through their education and health institutions and especially those meant to serve the marginalized and disadvantaged. He acknowledged Christian influence on him and attributed his fierce hatred of child marriage and untouchability to Christian influence. He also acknowledged many splendid specimens of Christian missionaries.[8]

Prior to Gandhi was Raja Ram Mohan Roy who was fondly called 'maker of modern India,' pioneered social reforms in Bengal. He called for an end to the cruel practice of 'sati', child marriage, idol worship, caste system, propagated widow remarriage and also emphasized the need to promote western scientific education. He also refers to the influence of Christianity on him and his reform movements.[9] Similar sentiments were also voiced by many other Indian thinkers who appreciated the Christian contribution in bringing about changes in Hindu society, and in particular it is Christianity that has very strongly promoted and practiced the idea of compassionate care of those socially ostracized and neglected. It was the Christian missionaries who opened leprosaria to treat and rehabilitate those suffering from leprosy which was a dreaded sickness and those who were affected were often socially ostracized.[10] It was indeed a big departure from the prevailing Hindu social customs and practices of treating people suffering from leprosy as social liability.

Similarly the Christian missionaries have begun institutions for the physically and mentally challenged, for the destitute, orphans and other deprived sections of the society giving them the light of hope and consolation in an atmosphere where they were treated as nuisance to others. In the contemporary times, it was St Teresa of Kolkata who epitomized this spirit of Christianity to cater to the needs of the poorest of the poor through a number of institutions she and her congregation, MC opened across the country and abroad. Many prominent Indians have lauded her selfless work and have inspired by her indomitable spirit of compassion and care.[11]

Way forward for the mission in India

It is within this complex socio-religious and highly polarized political context that we, the missionaries find ourselves in, and we need to find our way forward to carry on with the mission mandate. This isn't easy, as we have witnessed the recent developments within the country that are not exactly conducive to the growth of Christian community. And in these demanding circumstances we need to make wise choices. For one thing, we know that this is not the first time the Christian community is facing challenges; it has faced them before as well and came out stronger, of course by the grace of God. There has been fierce opposition to the growth of Christianity in India, even from leaders like Mahatma Gandhi who spoke against religious conversion. Such opposition got more institutionalized when after the independence some states of India passed anti-conversion legislations targeting religious conversion to Christianity.

Even in the midst of such legal and other coercive measures adopted by some right wing Hindu organizations in India, Christianity has always found a way forward. Given the geographic spread of India and the sparse population of Christians in it, there is an urgent need to consolidate their efforts to, first of all, secure themselves from the onslaught of the right wingers. The Christians in India need to build a better and broader social support base among liberal and open minded persons of other communities, particularly of Hindus so that they will be a bulwark against the machinations of aggressive religious bigots.

How do we achieve this objective? To my mind it needs a departure from the all too familiar interreligious dialogue exercises. Such exercises may have paid their limited dividends; what we need is the deeper and stronger commitment of people of different religions to create lasting structures that will serve as templates to foster social harmony and fellowship. As for instance, can we take the lead to establish cultural centers with prominent social leaders having their stake in them which can be a meeting place for people of all faiths to consider issues of larger society? More often than not the problem is that we look for exclusivity in ownership and control of institutions and that promotes not collective interest but sectarian consideration.

Secondly, we have been lead players in some social development segments like education and health for a considerable period of time in India. But India has changed; in some ways beyond recognition. Here I am not talking about the physical transformation of Indian cities and towns have witnessed but more so the infrastructure for social development that has marked our contemporary times. Other communities have come forward with more capital and qualified personnel to establish health and education institutions giving us tough competition. Healthy competition is always welcome, because only then can we promote excellence. It is a common sight now that many private education and health institutions established by the majority community have also seized the opportunity to collaborate with overseas institutions thus bringing in competitive edge over others. [12]

Thirdly, and perhaps most importantly, there is a need to work on the perception deficit that we as a community suffer from. Whether or not we like it, there is a popular perception about the Christian community that it has an ulterior motive behind its altruistic works: conversion of people of other faith to Christianity. This perception deficit has created a crisis for our life and activities. This needs to change, and it has to begin with us. How do we do it? One of the ways to do that is to use the media including the social media to begin new narratives about our faith and faith related activities. I often wonder why we shy away from making our work known to people particularly those who are vested with decision making roles. To some extent I think it is the religious structures that we have created and maintain that hinder us from engaging the larger society and its concerns. The point here that I want to drive home is that we as Christian religious personnel need to be socially present and relevant.

Conclusion

Christianity, in India may not have succeeded or failed as Dr Kanajmala would say, in terms of numerical strength, but it has certainly touched the soul of India. In ways that are diverse Christianity has persuaded the majority community to critique itself and bring about changes, some of which have been radical in content and form. India would not be what it has become today if not for the presence of Christianity and its social intervention. Although the hard liners among the majority community want to erase any trace of Christian presence and influence on India, - and this is quite evident from the fact that they have published school text books denigrating Christianity thereby transmitting misinformation – history is an eloquent witness to the fact that Christianity has decisively changed India in ways that no force today can eradicate. Dr Babu K Varghese in his path breaking book, 'Let there be India' boldly speaks of the manifold contributions Christianity has made in this country. And, if not for the presence and contributions of Christianity, India would have been poorer in terms of development of its various dialects and languages, culture, education, health care systems, social service initiatives, care for the differently abled and socially ostracized.[13] It is Christianity that has undoubtedly brought the values of social equity and respect for human beings *per se* to the centre stage of Indian social discourse and ethos. Social equity has not been a high point in Indian society which is quite hierarchical and therefore respect for a human person is to a large extent determined by his caste identity. It is in this context Christianity has played a crucial role to reinforce the value of human beings solely on the fact that they are created by God and are therefore worthy of respect.

The unique role of Christianity in India cannot be substituted. It has still has a long way to go; it is still work in progress. And the journey should continue however bumpy the ride might be. For we have a mission on hand – to unite all things in Christ.[14]

Endnotes

[1] A clear case of this tendency is very much visible in the north eastern cultures which have accepted Christianity and their life style has been significantly westernized. At the same time it is also the fact that they have kept up their Tribal customs of village administration, family customs and other social institutions.

[2] The Konyak Tribes if Nagaland is known for their head hunting practice. William Dalrymple, in Financial Times, 30, September, 2016, The Last of Nagaland's Headhunters.

[3] A.R. Rahman is an excellent example of splendid blend of eastern and western classical music.

[4] Peter Berger in a discussion on the topic 'Religion in a globalizing world' Kay West Florida, Dec 06, 2006.

[5] Ibid.

[6] Rajendra Prasad: A Historical-developmental study of classical Indian philosophy of morals, pp. 484-487.

[7] Tony Joseph, " Why Christianity Failed in India," Outlook, 13, April, 2015.

[8] CWMG Vol. 48:121.

[9] Mohan Roy and William Carey were contemporaries and they worked together and that the latter's influence in him was much visible in his social and religious reform movements.

[10] Wellesley Bailey, an Irish national took the initiative to begin the Leprosy Mission in India in the late nineteen century when leprosy patients were totally neglected and ostracized by the society.

[11] Mother Teresa received several awards including Nobel Prize and Bharat Ratna in recognition of her work for the deprived sections of people in society.

[12] As for instance, the Amity university has several tie ups with overseas universities and thereby it has established a brand name for itself.

[13] Babu K Varghese, Let there be India. This book gives a detailed account on the impact Christianity has made on India in various fields of study and services. He claims that the Bible has played a significant role in promoting local languages as it was the Bible that the missionaries translated into local languages.

[14] Eph 1:10.

SVD Mission in Northeast India:

A New Way of Communicating Church

Ivan D'Silva SVD

Introduction

"Colonialism in the Northeast India was seen to assume both the role of a 'politician' and a 'priest' and Christian missions appeared to be a part and expression of western colonial expansion **(Christian Missions and Colonialism, by Lal Dena, 1988, Shillong, p. 1)**. In the most cases, the missionary was far ahead of the government and even of the trader. In a backward region where a state of barbarism or savagery existed, the missionary usually ventured to work. The selfless services, which he rendered in terms of his expert knowledge and moral influence tended to have a soothing effect on the peoples among whom he worked and lived.

Process of Conversion in Northeast India

From the Christian (missionary) point of view, conversion is of three kinds: religious, psychological and spiritual. Religious conversion is a process by which one migrates from one religion to another religion, involving merely outward identification with the new religious community. Psychological conversion is deeper than religious conversion. It often comes upon a person's or persons' deep appreciation of the doctrines or teachings of a particular religion by rejecting the other. What is most striking and what the missionary emphatically stress is the Spiritual conversion in which one undergoes a mental anguish resulting from conviction of sin and then comes to accept Jesus Christ as his saviour and master.

What influenced the speed and ease of conversion? Why was it that Christianity, despite its newness, came to secure a firmer hold in the minds of the people?

'The new religion also offered to the people a thousand expectation and a new hope for future. A future which would culminate in the creation of 'new heaven on new earth', 'new Jerusalem' where all would live in harmony, happiness, peace and plenty, and in short, with 'no more tears'. On the contrary, the traditional religion offered no hope of this kind and the picture was just the opposite. For instance, only a few people who were declared were eligible for entry into paradise. Thus, there was no hope whatsoever for the rest of the people (p.89).

Among a number of missionary techniques, the two levels of techniques, which were effectively used by the missionaries during the mission period were: Spoken word, which was used in personal conversation and public preaching. This was a two-way process, involving the missionary to study the native language and urging the native people to study the language of the missionary. Personal conversation and public preaching were done with a view to evangelize the people. Secondly, level was the written word. This immediately served the needs of the new education which the missionary introduced and also enriched the literature of the people (p. 9).

"One thing that disturbs many Indians when they hear about NE is, the so-called "change in religious demography" that has apparently occurred in Northeast India. Some speak of region "lost to Christianity". What are actually lost are simple facts. In the most populated state of Northeast India, Assam, which has 66% of the population of the region, Christians constitute 3.7%, In Tripura, the next most populated state of Northeast India, Christian constitute 3.2%. In the so-called Christian majority states of India, Nagaland,

Mizoram, Meghalaya and Manipur, Christians constitute 89%, 87%, 70% and 34% respectively but these states have a total population of about 7 million and about 79% of this is Christian. In the Northeast as a whole, Christians constitute less than one eighth of the population (7 million out of 45 million).

Another popular misunderstanding is that the insurgencies in the region are largely due to their Christian allegiance. It is true that some of the militants are Christians predominant among them the Nagas. But their cause can hardly be called militant movements, especially in Assam and Manipur, which are not led by Christians. If anything, Christianity in the Northeast has contributed to integrate the people into the national mainstream rather than separate them". **(Padinjarekuttu, Isac, *the Catholic Church in Northeast India a Socio- Historical Profile, research paper*).**

Today the Catholic Church in the seven states of Northeast India consists of three Archdioceses and twelve dioceses, having members from practically all tribal and other communities, rendering a variety of services. This is a geographical area in India where people are open to the Christian faith. Ethically they belong to different tribal group of the mongoloid gene, which is different from the 'mainstream' Indian population. Therefore, there exists a sense of alienation due to geographical social cultural, religious and many other aspect of identity as communities. By and large, they have very strong sense of ethnic identities for their survival and growth. There are many tribal groups with different languages, customs, and traditions. How to cross these ethnic boundaries with a punitive faith in Roman Catholic?

Challenges & Pathways

I.   Vocation to the Priesthood/Brotherhood
How to engross Gospel Values to the fast changing times of the cyber world:

Comfort culture with modern gadgets, the excessive pressure of materialism, and the utopian desire for freedom without sufficient discipline. What was upheld values by the early wise men are now out-dated and they don't exist anymore in the families and societies. Things are replaced, such as:

- Rosary to Mobile
- Sacraments to Computer
- Community to Facebook

Degradation of human values is taking place. "We are following the REMM way of life – *Resourceful, Evaluative, Maximizing Model.* Jensen and Meckling said "Like it or not, individuals are willing to sacrifice a little of almost anything we care to name, even reputation or morality, for a sufficiently large quantity of other desired things." He or she is always wanting more and more and therefore each individual is a maximizer. Each individual is an evaluator. *Immorality* is creeping into **analysis** when number of dead bodies or the acres of defoliated jungle are measurable while the worth of a human life is not. We can measure material resources and capital assets but not the characteristics of trust or integrity, why? There is an *Economic Immorality* that is when the economy and the Society are not connected to each other. If this separation is taken seriously then corporations end up creating the costs while society pays the bills. We have consciously or unconsciously accepted *Legal corruption* as a way of life. Rich business people loot the bank and settle in abroad and poor are busy depositing their savings in the banks. There is an **economy exclusion and inequality**. How can it be that it is not a news item when an elderly homeless person dies of hunger and disease, but it is news when the stock market loses two points? This is a case of exclusion. Can we continue to stand by when food is thrown away while people are starving? This is a case of inequality. When the Narendra Modi the P.M of India gives to flood affected Kerala Rupees 600 crores and whereas B.J.P party built a Party house in Delhi which costs 1100 Crores, 2000 crores were spent on P.Ms foreign tour, 5000 crores were spent for P.Ms self promotion and publicity advertisements. The Kerala State which needs more than 20000 crores why the centre government mistreating the flood affected people. This is the case of economy exclusion and inequality.

There is a Challenge to be a real player. For example: Mary Kom must have worked hard to earn that gold medal. After so much sweat, practice, and struggle she has become the real life celebrity. Whereas, Priyanka Chopra becomes 'Mary Kom' in Hindi film to earn much more than what the Mary Kom must have earned in her life time. As aSVD, there can be temptation to be a reel player than the real player. It is more challenging to go to the interior missions, to learn the local languages but it is more comfortable to sit in the office and order. "Amen, Amen, I say to you, unless a grain of wheat falls to the ground and dies, it remains just a grain of wheat… (Cf, Jn 12:24)." When the cell in the body forgets to die, it leads to cancerous. Only when the body dies, the cancerous cell dies.

Eucharist: We priests can make Jesus to come down at the Eucharistic table. He is so obedient, "….even to death on the Cross". He said, "Do this in my memory". What happens to us in our daily life, Holy Mass can become a boring exercise. When the school program comes one would postpone the Mass to evening in order to prepare for the program to make it more perfect. And when the evening comes, some would complain of tiredness after over working and the day's Mass is cancelled. Jesus said, "Mary has chosen the better part" **(Cf, Lk: 10:42)**.

There is a challenge from the **'fixed centre to scattered centre'.** That is why Jesus challenges Martha **(Cf, Lk: 10:41)**, "Martha Martha, you are anxious and worried about many things." That is when a Priest's mind scatters, his focus changes and his commitment diverge then there are questions about his faithfulness. The scandal of sexual abuse by priests and consecrated persons has no doubt unearthed a serious lacuna in the pedagogy of formation of candidates for priesthood and consecrated life. In the wake of scandal of paedophilia, the sexual abuse of children and youth by clergy the image of the Church, particularly of the priests is terribly tarnished. This is because of lack of moral and spiritual integrity. People expect us priests and consecrated persons to be persons of character. Character is formed through cultivation of virtues: truthfulness, honesty, transparency, love, compassion, simplicity, gentleness, mercy. "....Whoever remains in me and I in him will bear much fruit, because without me you can do nothing" **(Cf, Jn 15:5)**. Therefore, Eucharist is the hospitality of God and relationship is the heart of hospitality. Hospitality comes in when the ego is put aside.

Our Identity as Consecrated Persons: There is a strong temptation to relate one's identity to one's functions: educator, social worker, professor of philosophy, theology, scripture, counsellor, doctor, builder, treasurer, Principal etc. these functions require of course specialised training, skills, etc., based on human sciences or even ecclesiastical studies. One can be qualified in all these areas without being a man of moral and spiritual integrity. For example, one can be a professor of Moral theology while wanting in transparency, honesty in matters of money, unhealthy relationships, etc. according to Mother Theresa "Many people mistake our work for our vocation, our vocation is the love of Jesus." Why do people come to us asking for admissions, work, financial assistance, and not for Prayer. Because people mistake our work for our vocation, as a very good teacher, administrator, builder, etc. "Hence it is the need of the hour that we as priests and religious must are clear of our identity: **Disciples of Christ**." Disciple is one who is disciplined. Jesus said to Thomas, "...Bring your hand and put it into my side..." **(Cf, Jn 20:27)**. When a priest touches the Lord in the daily Eucharist and stretches out his hands to others, those are his meeting point with others.

"Pope Francis is reminding us time and again on the importance of being men and women who are deeply rooted in God, having an intimate personal relationship with Christ. Only this God experience will eventually help us to evolve a nourishing spirituality that will motivate our attitude and actions that will resonate with Gospel values radiating the mind and heart of Christ. And this in turn will influence our functions as teachers, social workers, professors with greater apostolic efficacy. Otherwise we will be mere functionaries, bureaucrats and all our works however good and beneficial they will be mere social works for which we need not be priests and religious." **('Consecrated life and psycho-sexual integration' by Fr. Joseph Benedict Mathias, S.J., 18ᵗʰ Sept 2015 Paper presented for IPC SVD Formators, Jharsuguda)**

## II.	Making Christianity an indigenous faith

Another challenge for the SVDs in the Northeast would be how to give the faith that is truly tribal expression by bold inculturation, embodying the values of the tribal cultures. Prior to it, one should ask this question; **what influenced the speed and ease of conversion in the NE?** "It should be noted that Christianity and for that matter any religion could not be applied or propagated in a vacuum. It had to be related to the reality of the objective situations-existential situations of the people in their cultural milieu-might be in terms of individuals, communities or tribes. There was thus an indigenous concept of the Supreme Being which was continuous in its essentials with the Christian concept."

The Church in Northeast India has been accused of transporting the western form of Christianity to the people. Therefore, it should now attempt to recover the basic myths of each tribe giving them the reinterpretation in the light of faith in Christ. There is need to stress the importance and the centrality of symbols in the primeval world, offering a perception of the faith different, and in some senses, richer than that which comes from concepts. In this way, they can rescue ancient celebrations of local festivals and art forms. Liturgical and theological inculturation, fifty years after the Second Vatican Council, has just begun to enter the consciousness of the people.

The SVD has been a body that draws together, persons of diverse cultures who are united by a single charism. Society's primary mission is to inculturate the Gospel in the very diverse settings. SVD communities are being made up of persons of diverse cultures having rich experience of interculturality must be rooted in the cultures wherever he is appointed by learning the local language and doing research. "OUR NAME IS OUR MISSION. This name is challenging us today to do our task. We are invited to be in touch with our experiences of life and to be rooted in the Word today; the Word manifests itself in various forms, places, persons and realities. Discovering the Word is an exercise that animates our life." **(Cf, Arnoldus Nota: August 2018)**.

III. Education for evangelization

One of the reasons why Christianity, despite its newness, came to secure a firmer hold in the minds of the people is "education, technology, material well-being and eventually material consciousness." After hundred years of existence in the region(,) the Church must ask some hard questions. The first concerns education. Speaking before the UNESCO, the secretary of State of the Vatican, Cardinal Pietro Parolin said that, "culture and education have never been considered by the Catholic Church merely as tools for evangelisation, but rather as dimensions of humanity with high intrinsic value." The Catholic Church as an expert in humanity "has placed education at the centre of her mission and continues to consider it a priority". Unfortunately, the Catholic Church has fallen into this trap of allowing education to become primarily an economic activity, a tool to secure finances for the Dioceses and congregations. The simple question is, do we expect the Church to serve our needs or do we serve the Church to help her fulfil her Christ-given mission?

One of the greatest predicaments we face in our modern society is the education that we give our young. Should we cram our children's heads with facts, or educate them for success as human beings? One of the common questions that we put in minds of the young students is, "what do you want to be when you grow up". The better would be, "how do you want to contribute to the world when you grow up? That question changes everything. When you ask a kid, "How do you want to contribute to the world?" you are not putting them down a narrow path; you are having them open up their mind to a whole field of possibilities and to a life that is about meaning and contribution. They are likely to be seduced into a job selling that we don't need. When you ask these questions to your teenager, not the question of, what do you want to be when you grow up, but, how do you want to contribute to humanity, you help them get in the right path, you help them emerge into a life, into a career, that is actually giving back to the human species. And those are the careers that give us the greatest amount of fulfilment. These are the people we need in the world today. We teach children how to solve problems in mathematics, but give them nothing to help them solve the problems they face in their personal lives. We flood them with a tide of facts, and then tell them, as we send them out the door with their diplomas, "It's up to you to figure out what it all means."

The modern age is addicted to factual information. By "addiction" I mean that the fascination has reached abnormal proportions. It is necessary for us, now, to emphasise that facts by themselves cannot bestow wisdom. We forget that the discovery of some new fact concerning a galaxy millions of light years away has very little actual bearing on our lives here on earth. Knowledge, on the other hand, of how to get along with others, and how to be happy, has a great deal of relevance.

Teachers and parents may complain that if we spend too much time teaching children these personal skills, they will be left behind in the race to acquire the information that will fit them to compete in the job market after they leave school. However, this is false reasoning.

Children who learn to concentrate, to increase their awareness, and to channel negative emotions into constructive outlets are able to handle all the factual information they'rethey are taught in school far more effectively. Primarily, what is needed is a system of education that will prepare children for meeting life's challenges, and not only fit them for employment or for intellectual pursuits. Moreover, we need to see the whole of life, beyond the years spent in school, as education.

IV.   SVD mission towards integration of creation:

"The Church has a responsibility towards creation and she must assert this responsibility in the public sphere, said Pope Benedict XVI in the year 2008. Newsweek, one of the world's most popular weeklies, called Pope Benedict XVI, the Green Pope, when he addressed 400,000 youth at the youth rally in 2007 in Loreto, Italy and said, "Learn to sustain the planet before it is too late." **(Mission in Civil Society Challenges and responses, ed. Vellarackal, Paul and Jeyaraj, Dasan, 2015, Gujarat Sahitya Prakash Anand, P. 180)**

The respect for nature, central to the modern ecological consciousness, and so poignantly brought home to us by Pope Francis in his encyclical letter *Laudato Si*, finds a strong ally in the tribal consciousness and it is not surprising that the tribals have been in the forefront of the battle to protect forests and rivers and to stop massive interference with nature characteristic of capitalist culture. However, whether this is the case in the Northeast is to be doubted, where massive destruction of nature is going on unchallenged. Lowering down the hills to fill the mud in marshy land in Assam, felling the pine trees in some parts of Meghalaya, unscientific way of excavating coal mine and lime stones in Jayantia District of Meghalaya, deforestation in Tripura and so on. "Today we need to consider not only social justice i.e. just relations between people, but also ecological justice i.e. just relations between human beings, other creatures and with Mother Earth herself. Creation is now understood as a community of beings interconnected with each other and with the triune God. In the 21st century, ecological integrity is an essential part of all faith traditions and is an important issue around which dialogue, collaboration and mutual understanding revolve.

Tribal Christianity should become the leading force in developing an ecological consciousness so badly needed in our time and the tribals of Northeast India can give a lead in this. (**'The Catholic Church in Northeast India A Socio-Historical Profile', a paper by Dr. Isaac Padinjarekuttu).**

a.   What role can the SVD missionaries play?

"What we need to widen is networking between all people of good will who are working on this issue. We need to be more involved and concerned about ecological issues today because we are capable of reading the signs of the times. We have been taught the right disposition for discernment." (**'The Catholic Church in Northeast India A Socio-Historical Profile', a paper by Dr. Isaac Padinjarekuttu).** "Real ecological integrity can only be achieved with concerted effort on the part of every single human being. The environmental or ecological crisis is essentially a crisis of values, leading to a cultural crisis and in turn to a spiritual crisis."

- Model ways of conserving resources. We need to commit ourselves to a lifestyle that leads the way in conservation reducing, re-using, recycling, etc.

- We are better equipped with more knowledge because of our education, seminars and exposure programmes to understand ecological degradation. We need to be activists and not just Social workers after our MSW degree to write the projects or complete the projects.

- We must invite environmentalists and activists to speak to our school children and our confreres.

- Make efforts to conduct seminars, workshops, and study on eco-spirituality and make eco-spirituality retreat.

- Be activists to work for the displaced refugees, indigenous people, land less people and work for their rights.

The Kokborok Film, Yarwng takes on the worldwide phenomenon of 'displacement of peoples' caused by what is called 'development' projects.

Yarwng *(Roots) 35mm, Kokborok (with English subtitles), 95 mins, India, 2008,* memorializes the trauma suffered by thousands of people that once inhabited the Raima Valley of Tripura but had to move out when the valley was submerged due to the construction of an electricity-generating dam on the Gumti river, about three decades ago, transforming thereby what was once called the 'granary of Tripura' into vast 'catchments of resentment'.

With its byline 'A romance on the idyllic banks of the Raima and Saima, swept away by the floodgates of Change', *Yarwng* is both a protest on behalf of 'the excluded' and a celebration of their unconquerable spirit of survival in the face of extraordinary upheavals.

In the minds of those who once inhabited the lush Raima valley, names like Bolongbasa` raises strong emotional connotations not just of places now non-existent in the records, but of a way of life, now vanished and gone forever. The experience of being uprooted from the earth that one always considered one's own leaves on the psyche of the victim scars that are indelible. He must live forever with a sense of `loss` and nostalgia about a bygone idyllic past.

In one of his pieces about the making of the dam and its consequences well-known journalist, Subir Bhaumik, writes, "The heartburn over steady land loss on a one-to-one basis was further exacerbated by the submergence of huge swathes of arable lands owned by the tribals in the Raima Valley as a result of the commissioning of the Gumti hydel project in south Tripura. This project not only disturbed the fragile ecology of the Raima Valley, but also introduced a permanent sense of loss into the tribal psyche." Mr. Bhaumik points out that "the 46 sq km of the valley area that the dam submerged was one of the most fertile valleys in an otherwise hilly state, where arable flatlands suitable for wet rice agriculture are extremely limited. He quotes official records, which suggest that 2558 families were ousted from the Gumti project area and points out that these were families who could produce land deeds and were officially owners of the land they were ousted from. Unofficial estimates varied between 8000 to 10,000 families or about 60 to 70 thousand tribes-people displaced."

Barnalee Choudhury in an article, 'Development Induced Internal Displacement in South Asia' speaks of a number of Dams in the Northeast that has caused displacement. "The Dumbur dam of Tripura displaced a total of 35,000-40,000 people. The Loktak hydel project in Manipur displaced around 20,000 people as their villages went under water. The Pagladiya Dam Project of lower Assam is going to displace 1, 50,000 people, but according to official estimate it would affect only 18,000 persons. Likewise, Tipaimukh project is displacing 40,000 people. In Arunachal Pradesh more than 20,000 would be displaced by the Siang project."

Yarwng film was shot on actual locations - Bolongbasa and adjoining areas and many of the people who act in the film are real-life victims of displacement. A group of 60 people consisting of the technical crew and artistes spent about a month in capturing through the lens the emotional turmoil of Karmati and Wakhirai and the story of their love torn asunder by the thwarted flow of the legendary waters of Raima and Saima.

The incidents and characters

The incidents and the characters of the film are based on the narratives of the villagers who had themselves undergone the trauma of the displacement. "Sitting in the bamboo huts in the evening, with only a kerosene lamp in the middle, the group of villagers used to narrate the incidents they could recall about those days. As the narration progressed, we could find their eyes moistening and more than once the exercise ended up in tears" remembers Meena Debbarma who was the principal interviewer of the team. "We merely wove together the various characters and incidents that found a mention in their narrative."

Impact of the film on Tripura

1. The film made known to the world not only the Displacement caused by the Dumbur hydel project, but the plight of the indigenous people of Tripura.

2. The then minister for information and Culture, Government of India during the Inaugural function of the Indian Panorama of IFFI at Goa, (where Yarwng was the opening film) publicly admitted that he had never heard of a language called 'Kokborok'. He assured that he would look in to the issue the film highlighted.

3. Perhaps, most importantly, thanks to the film, today there is a more critical approach to developmental projects among the people of Tripura.

Year after year when we look at the famine and suicide of the farmers, when the streets become the rivers and roads are washed out, when heat increases and pools dry, when concrete jungle collapses and human beings buried under the debris, we keep our mouth shut, eyes wide open and lost at the cross roads, not knowing whom to blame. "The earth has enough for our needs but not enough for our greed. It is time to awaken to the naked reality and strive hard to bring forth an environmentally sustainable, spiritually fulfilling and socially just human presence on our beloved Planet Earth."

v.   Learn to combine passion and compassion

Images and Novenas of sacred heart and Divine Mercy are popular among people of NE because it conveys how to be compassionate. Compassion is not an attribute of any one religion. It is a universal principle for happiness and peace. In a world torn by conflict and strife, where violence and not love dictates people's actions, what every person, at every level, of every age needs to learn is the art of nurturing compassion within. Be it a home-maker fulfilling the many needs of her family, an entrepreneur meeting people and clinching deals for her company, a politician passing Bills in the legislature that can change the destiny of millions or an auto rickshaw driver bargaining for higher rates with his passenger –whoever you may be, you need compassion. Compassion should no more lie in the ideologies of philosophers or in the lucrative rewards of theologians (in the afterlife). The voice of compassion needs to be heard in every household, educational institution, office, business unit, shop, mall, and theatre, besides other places and circumstances.

For centuries now, we have reserved compassion to be a prerogative of a chosen few, like a Christ or a Buddha. We have also conceptually dismissed the possibility of someone living and embodying such a quality in the hurly-burly of everyday life. Is it so difficult to live compassionately? Or are we so incapable that we cannot raise ourselves to those standards?

Compassion begins with empathy. Empathy is the ability to feel for another. Those who are sensitive to the motions of life, to the experiences of pain and pleasure, are capable of empathy. Those who have watched the movements of their thoughts, the burden of unnecessary thinking, and the pain of conflicting thoughts know it well. Those who have paid attention to their emotional upsurges, the unintelligent ways of anger, hurt or hate, the irrationality of ear, feel empathy for another who is going through a similar emotion. Hence, compassion begins with attention to one's own life experiences, be it physical or emotional.

Empathy and compassion thus born would naturally blossom into acts of kindness to reach out to others. Jesus would perform miracles because of His compassionate heart. Whether it was the feeding of multitude, giving sight to the blind, cleansing the lepers, raising the dead, not to judge at the sinners, everything surfaced out of compassion. Well-being of the other is the highest priority for a compassionate person; hence, her actions would reflect tremendous intelligence, fortitude, and discretion. It could be a dynamic plunge into action to change the adverse situation of the one who is suffering. It could also be gentle words of love and strength or a heartfelt prayer for Divine help.

Compassion is not the armour of the weak; it is the weapon of the strong. It is irresponsible to think, believe, and preach that anger and violence can solve our problems. Problems at micro as well as macro level arise because of lack of understanding and love between people. Problems that are situation-based are very less compared to those that are emotion-based. Situation-based problems need better strategy and skill to solve them but emotion-based problems need people who are involved in moving out of those negative emotions that are causing them. That is why any constructive change can never be effected through anger and violence. Compassion is the answer.

Fearlessness is a necessary condition for realization of truth. Fearlessness that is accompanied by compassion is the true prerequisite for spiritual attainment. Determination comes from fearlessness but without compassion(,) it can be destructive and selfish. Jesus says, "I desire mercy, not sacrifice" (Cf. Mt. 9:13). That is why Buddha sacrificed all qualities but compassion. Compassion comes from selfless action. Selflessness grows from fearlessness. Jesus fearlessly faced the crowd whom they wanted to stone at woman to death, said "Let the one among you who is without sin be the first to throw a stone at her" (Cf. Jn. 8:7) and to the woman, out came the compassionate words from Jesus, "Neither do I condemn you. Go from now on do not sin anymore" (Cf. Jn. 8:10). As religious missionaries, we run the schools, institutions and ministries with full passion and vigour but if there is no compassion it will be like a salt without a curry. We become good administrators, efficient constructors, well-disciplined principals, orators, preachers and teachers. Work well done, professionally done, work done with great effectiveness but if we don't have compassion then our mission is emptied of any religious spirit. 'All fingers are not same in length but when they bend all stands equal'. Life becomes very easy when we bend and adjust to situations. What is that blocks us not to be compassionate. It is our EGO. It is just like a dust in the eyes without clearing the dust one can't see anything clearly.

Let us nurture the noble virtue of compassion consciously with dedication. Let us see the faces of people who walk into our world with smiles, tears, affection, and wrath. Let us meditate on their feeling to let compassion blossom.

VI. Documentation

Ever heard the saying, "time is money"? We take so much time to locate a specific document because it is not placed in proper place or it is not there at all. With new and more stringent laws with regards to the Schools, Churches, FCRA, land, vehicles, insurance, accounts, etc. will taunt us, if the proper papers are not documented. One of the challenges for the SVD missionaries is to cultivate the habit of proper documentation in our missions and institutions. The SVD Generalate has a written letter to all the PRMs (Province, Regional and Mission superiors) concerning this matter.

"07 November 2017; P08/2017

Dear Fr. Provincial/Regional/Mission Superior,

Last July, from 10 to 11, 2017, the Generalate organized a meeting with the directors of main Communications centers and the directors of Mission offices of our Congregation; then, from 12 to 14, another meeting took place with' only the directors of Communications centers. Those present at the meeting were the directors of Mission offices of Chicago, Saint Augustine, Austria, Switzerland and Australia and the directors of Communications centers of Kairos (Ireland), MCS (DR. Congo), Steyl Medien (Germany), Verbo Filmes (Brazil), Wordnet Production (USW), and the National Communications Coordinator of India. The meeting was headed by Fr. Modeste Munimi, our Generalate Coordinator for Communications.

We are aware that our confreres are doing excellent works in different fields, but many of these works are not known to others because they have not been sufficiently documented. Good documentation is needed for sharing good practices with the rest of the Congregation and with our lay partners, and for raising funds for our mission. In fact, we are challenged to follow the recommendation of Saint Arnold in a letter he sent to Becher on 3 June 1892: *"In order to encourage our missionaries and stoke the zeal of our benefactors it is important that you prepare statistics showing the work of our missionaries. Each year you should send a copy of those statistics to Steyl."*

The main objective of the meeting was to foster the collaboration between the Communications centers and the Mission offices for mission animation and fundraising, as well as to have properly documented our ' projects and activities and to share our good practices and stories with others.

Thus, we ask you, your Mission Secretary and Communications Coordinator to have an active and interactive role in the construction of this initiative already done in various Provinces/Regions/Missions (PRMs). We wish that this initiative becomes a common and normal practice in our PRMs under the coordination of the Generalate Mission Secretary and the Generalate Communications Coordinator. We ask you to encourage each and all confreres to regularly make use of and contribute to these data banks. Using the existing platforms we already have in our Congregation, we put at your disposal and ask for your contribution to these data banks:

1. An SVD data bank for pictures/photos: "www.svdphotos.org" is administered by Fr. Andrzej Danilewicz (POL). At this website, you can download any picture you want. All you have to do is to contact the administrator and you will be given a password to download the pictures. To upload pictures, you can also contact and send to the administrator high-resolution photos(,) which will then be made available to all. To contact the administrator, enter the website and click on CONTACT (at the upper left comer). All the pictures that are already available at various Mission offices and Communications centers would be made available to Fr. Andrzej. At this website, every picture uploaded/downloaded will be copyright free but should be properly acknowledged.

2. An SVD data bank for Videos clips: "https://vimeo.com/svdmission" is administered by Mr. Anton Deutchman, the director of Steyl Medien. To download a video clip: Open the video clip

and click on the "download" button which is directly under the video screen (at the text explanation). For downloading video clips, there is no need to log in or register. However, to upload a video clip, one must request the user name and password from the administrator at: <deutschmann@steyl-medien.de>. All the video clips that are already available at various Mission offices and Communications centers would be made available to Mr. Anton. Again, at this website, every video clip uploaded/downloaded will be copyright free but should be properly acknowledged.

3. An SVD data bank for Stories: "www.witword.org" is administered by Fr. Modeste Munimi, the Generalate Communications Coordinator. It contains short stories and best practices of our mission activities worldwide. We ask your Communications Coordinator, in collaboration with the Coordinators of the other Characteristic Dimensions, to send in the best practices and stories of your PRM to Fr. Modeste. We need short stories of our mission activities with photos.

We would like to thank you, as well as all the confreres and lay partners in your PRM, for your participation and collaboration in this common project.

Fraternally in the Divine Word,
Heinz Kuliike, SVD
Superior General"

We write our projects well and we convince the agencies about the proper implementation of it. What is undone is completion report of the project because it needs the proper documentation with photos and report. The daily chronicles, vehicle log book, inventories, cash book, etc., is the need of the hour.

VII. Increasing intolerance

Media violence has been the cause of numerous crimes among teenagers and adults across India. With the development of the television and the recent popularity in media violence seen on television, it has become a major concern. Today it seems that every home in India has a television and some have it in their personal room too. Both children and adults even have computers and entertainment systems in their own bedrooms. Studies have also found an increase in media violence shown on television shows, movies, and video games. **For example**: one of the video games says that: 'if you kill your pet dog you will get 30 points, if you kill your neighbour you will get 100 points and if you kill your parents you will get 200 points.' Media violence is successfully targeted towards teens and adolescents. More than 60% of TV shows are violent, some violence is lethal, some violence shows no pain and some violent scenes on TV include humour. Media violence is especially damaging to young children because they cannot differentiate between real life and fantasy. They become more fearful and use violence as a solution. Children imitate what they see and relate to the oppressors. Cartoons include major amounts of fantasy. The level of violence during the weekend cartoons is higher than the level of violence during the week days. The main reasons why viewers are attracted to these shows are for the fighters and the quarrels. Children watch, fantasise and imitate. When I question in my media literacy class to the High School students about the 'WWE (world wrestling entertainment)' channel, most of them reply that majority of boys and some girls too watch it along with their parents. And they think that the wrestling telecasted as true and competition. Children who are exposed to these violent scenes beginning from cartoon channels, Shanktiman serial, WWE channel, Action Channels, reality shows with abusive language, daring games such blue whale, films like spider man, bat man, horror movies likely to be more violent. "It increases aggressiveness and anti-social behaviour, making them less sensitive to violence and to victims of violence and increasing their appetite for more violence in entertainment and in real life".

(Stanislaus, L SVD and Joseph, Jose SVD, ed., 2007, Communication as mission: mission in the social communications: challenges for

the Church in Asia, Ishvani Kendra, 2007 (catholic communications in India Strengths and challenges, Henry D' Souza)

Since 2015, many people across the country have fallen victim to incidents of mob lynching related to religious intolerance that commonly results over petty issues. Mob lynches gather for action when the messages are conveyed through the social media. Mob violence has occurred in other cases too, including attacks on Dalits suspected of illegally transporting cows, the killing of alleged child traffickers in Jharkhand, Assam, Tripura and lynching of a police officer at a mosque in Kashmir. Hate crimes, mob violence, communal violence, religion-related terror, the use of force to prevent religious practice, the harassment of women for not conforming to religious dress codes, and violence over conversion of proselytizing is few examples where people are intolerant.

Amidst growing intolerance in India, there is a great challenge for the missionaries to hold our heads high and be firm in our faith and commitment. Mahatma Gandhi who fought for Independence for our nation, propagated non-violence and '*Satyagraha*' movements, that tolerance we don't find anymore. Aggressive way of anchoring the TV news by shouting and yelling at panellists conveying to the nation as to who is right and not what is right. Violent scene on the screen is viewed and clapped, hacking to death at the broad day light is filmed and forwarded by the onlookers, stone pelting has become a new way of protest, ministers in the parliament are often scene shouting and passing cheap comment in the well of the house and gruesome killing in the name of the cow is supported by the mob. And when we see this retaliation and intolerant behaviour what would be our reaction? Will we remain faithful to our master or will we run away just like disciples did in the Gethsemane garden. "….But when the Son of Man comes, will he find faith on earth?" Cf, Lk 18:8)

VIII. Mass Media

Pope John Paul II asserts that, "involvement of the mass media, however, is not meant merely to strengthen the preaching of the gospel. There is a deeper reality involved here: Since the very evangelization of modern culture depends to a great extent on the spread of the Christian message and the Church's authentic teaching. It is also necessary to integrate that message into the 'new culture' created by modern communications. This is a complex issue, since the 'new culture' originates not just from whatever content is eventually expressed, but from the very fact that there exist new ways of communicating, with new languages, new techniques and a new psychology" **(P.4, 'mission in the social communications: challenges for the Church in Asia by Franz-Josef Eilers, SVD, ed. L. Stanislaus SVD & Jose Joseph SVD, "Communication as mission".)**

"Thus also mission is communication, it is the communication and sharing of the faith with others especially those who are not yet reached by this message. It means that our communication training is not just media training of specialists but an essential element of our faith. Does not the Acts of the Apostles remind us how the early Christians were communicating his/her faith? Those who had been scattered preached the word wherever they went. Circumstances of life are seen as challenges for missionary 'activity' in sharing faith experience with everybody around. Reflecting on this, Pope John Paul II wrote in his World Communication Day Message 2000 on "Proclaiming Christ in the Media at the Dawn of the new Millennium": "Having spent time in prayer with Mary and other followers of the Lord, and acting at the spirit's prompting, the apostles begin the work of proclamation at Pentecost (Cf. Act 2). As we read about these marvellous events, we are reminded that the history of communication is a kind of journey, from the pride driven project of Babel and the collapse into confusion and mutual incomprehension to which it give rise (cf. Gen 11:1-9) to Pentecost and the gift of tongues: a restoration of communication, centred on Jesus, through the action of the Holy

Spirit. Proclaiming Christ, therefore leads to a meeting between people in faith and charity at the deepest level of their humanity…"(P.6, **'mission in the social communications: challenges for the Church in Asia by Franz-Josef Eilers, SVD, ed. L. Stanislaus SVD & Jose Joseph SVD, "Communication as mission").**

"The FABC Communication bishops added already 1999 in their final statement of their annual 'Bishops Meet' on 'Megatrends Asia', a new trend which they called "From Traditions to Options." While in the past, young people grew up in traditions of society they now have many options and "in the modern communication situation, where the news is available to everybody in an instant, journalists and Church leaders are not just 'gatekeepers' any more who determine what reaches the audience. They must be 'guides' through the jungle of options, inspired by the principle and visions of Christian faith" …"(P.9, **'mission in the social communications: challenges for the Church in Asia by Franz-Josef Eilers, SVD, ed. L. Stanislaus SVD & Jose Joseph SVD, "Communication as mission").**

'New way of being the Church' was the significant hot debate for the Christians in the Jubilee year 2000 through seminars and workshops. After a decade now the debate would be **'new way of communicating church'.** "The rapid proliferation of cell-phones not only gives places with no phone lines access to the world but also changes the way people relate to each other. Instant text messaging helps to make and develop appointments on short notice and to inform about important events. They help to spread new ideas easily and can invite to common actions on short notice, which might end up in bigger demonstrations. In a further development, images will be added to the text and thus we slowly develop into a total communication environment where everybody will be available at anytime, anywhere. Test messaging also has potentials for pastoral and evangelizing ministry beyond tradition ways of communicating". **(P.10, 'mission in the social communications: challenges for the**

Church in Asia by Franz-Josef Eilers, SVD, ed. L. Stanislaus SVD & Jose Joseph SVD, "Communication as mission".)

a. New technologies

New technologies are developing day by day, and they slowly but surely change our ways of communicating. From desktop to laptops, from landline phone to mobile Internet phone services with voice and images, I-Pad, I-Pod etc. "all these new ways of communicating and new technologies have great potentials for sharing Christian faith and convictions from the monolithic mass media we are moving to an interactive and participatory mode, where everybody becomes her/his own editor and determines him/ herself what and with whom he/she is formation in communication Education and Moral Theology. There are new possibilities and dimensions for sharing Christian faith and convictions with other individuals and communities. Christian faith is communication. Every Christian should become this way a **'cyber-missionary'** fulfilling Christ's command to go up to the ends of the earth. **(Stanislaus, L SVD and Joseph, Jose SVD, ed., 2007, Communication as mission: mission in the social communications: challenges for the Church in Asia, Ishvani Kendra, 2007)**

The challenge is when you are surrounded with lot of technologies and gadgets it might make you more individualistic than a communitarian. confreres who get addicted to these gadgets will have less time to interact with others and less interest to read books. Their machine-dependent habit will make them less participative in the community and more isolated. It will make them late night awake and certainly they will not be fresh in the morning for the rest of the activities.

b. New language

With the new technologies also the language of people and the use of words also change. "We have moved from the language of the alphabet into the language of electricity. The language of the alphabet works on strict rules and logic. If one doesn't understand the rules of grammar and strictly abide by them one is not able to communicate." When we speak the language properly, people love to listen to us. A missionary who speaks the language of the people is welcomed in their village and family. People feel confident to accept him as their own. Where as in the language of electricity, we see connectivity taking prime place in the lives of people. "Because the language of electricity shows us how everything in life is interdependent and interconnected. Whole world becomes the global village. The Internet has broken many walls. It has empowered the individual to the extent that today there are centres everywhere and boundaries nowhere. The language of electricity gives more importance to image and emotion than to logic." 'Visuals speak for itself', that is why youngsters when they buy a mobile they check the camera pixel to take the pictures and selfie. People look out for electricity mobile charging points in the airports, bus stations, railway stations, trains and buses, offices and homes. When Fraters or Brothers sent for mission experience to the far-flung areas two things they look out, one is internet facility and then electricity charging point. They are disappointed and discouraged when these facilities are not available.

Pope Francis in his Apostolic Exhortation *The Joy of the Gospel* he emphasizes the importance of using a language that people understand (EG 21), and not in the "dull categories" which weaken the "freshness of the Gospel" (EG 11). Pope Francis said: "Sad Christians can't transmit the Gospel." During his daily Mass at the Vatican's Casa Santa Marta on June 2, 2013, the Pope invited Christians to embrace happiness and to not live life with a 'funeral face.' The Pope explained that the Holy Spirit brings Christians a special joy that should lead them to praise God.

c.   New way of relationship

Through new ways of communication and new technologies, our relationships also changed. The 21st century will be remembered especially for among other things, the opportunities for making 'contact' beyond the boundaries of country and continent. Social networking sites ensure that we keep in 'contact' with others with the option to "choose a friend" or limit the access of others to our privacy. Friendships and relationships through the Facebook, cell phone and WhatsApp have no geographical limits, no mother tongues required, no cultural background asked, no ethnic and religion is needed. Only to know which SEX you belong. These relationships are sustained by the slender thread of an optical fibre.

Being in contact may often be an addiction that spells disaster for personal relationships. Social networking sites can often become the immunization we take to eschew genuine personal relationships. It may hide the fact that beneath the surface lays the fear of genuine intimacy. Worse, we think we are in relationship just because we are in contact. The hollowness of it all is exposed by some people, for whom virtual reality has become frighteningly REAL.

Contact creeps into our spiritual lives as well. We are happy to be in contact with God multiplying and creatively finding ways of marketing our spiritual wares. Keeping in contact with God through rituals and spiritual practices may just be the balm that soothes our troubled spirit. Online contacts have created the relationships for once own benefits. Online communities, online likeminded groups, online prayers, online Bible reflections, online shopping, online matrimony, online interview, online admission, online food, online studies, online treatment, online counselling and online undertakers are done. Other than birth and death, everything has become online. Today the internet has created different culture and relationship: Use and Throw, have more, sex sells, single parenting, promiscuous relationship, etc. According to Bollywood actor Hrithik Roshan, "relationships today are the mercy of how the typed sentence is interpreted" (**Tripura observer, P.6, 10ᵗʰ August, 2018**). Sunday was meant to be for family. Together go to the Church, have recreation, eat together, watch television, go for outing, etc. But now, the Sunday has become the day of individual activities. Tuition or coaching classes, dance classes, music classes, party meetings, club meetings, and so on, are held on Sunday.

Earlier days Marriage celebration was a celebration of the whole society because of the close relationship with one another. People would come together few days earlier in the marriage house to decorate, to collect the vegetables, to cook, to serve, to dance and rejoice. Now it is reduced to merely contacts and contracts. Contract between bride and bridegroom, between two families, with the decorators, with the band party, with the caterers and with priests to see the marriage is blessed. Marriage and friendship lose much of their meaning when they are reduced to merely being in contact with our spouse or with one another. In a relationship, contact with another through a handshake or warm embrace and gift-giving are meant to be signs of intimacy and the gift of self to each other. During the time of Christmas, birthdays, celebrations we revive the contact with others. We fulfil our religious duties too, making sure that we are as much in contact with God as we are with friends and family.

Prime Minister Narendra Modi's fondness for hugging international leaders seems to have rubbed off on Congress chief Rahul Gandhi as well in the Parliament during the no confidence motion. Modern hug contacts among the politicians are for political purpose and not much to do with lasting relation. Most of the parties like iftar parties, business parties, MacDonald parties, birthday parties, wedding parties, etc. the relationship ends with the parties and nothing beyond than this. Among the rich, bureaucrats and army commanders were caught in '**Honey trap**' because they were the victims to the sensual contacts. Through contacts, emotions are created and reflected with people that we might never see in the reality of life. Youth in the village call it as '**wrong number**' contacts and these wrong number calls are attended without knowing who and how the person is on the other side. Sometimes this relation leads to marriages too. "We establish relationships with people who might finally only be constructions of the mind or creatures of the curiosity of somebody somewhere in Cyberspace".

The cold, distant relationships that the media fosters weaken family relations, making them passive, contactless, hurried and superficial.

There is an urgent need to introduce media literacy especially in school, and other educational institutions. Media literacy teaches people to analyze the message conveyed by the media. In fact, media education aims to make people media-literate and critical. Media education demands a critical evaluation of the mass media.

IX.   Pornography and its challenges

Most of the mobiles today has inbuilt internet access. With internet facilities, these devices allow children to connect to others in ways we cannot even imagine. Many harmful elements like sexting, cyber-bullying, sextortion, pornography and bluewale game are part of the internet use. Pornography is not viewed only by the youth but people of all ages and marital status. The use of pornography has reached to even the rural areas of Northeast India. The influence of pornography has led to the discrepancy in sexual preference. The increasing number of AIDS/HIV case is of grave concern, one that can be blamed of the increase usage of pornography. It is a market-driven industry aimed at making money as much as possible by whatever means. It is not about the ethical value of altruism, generosity, gentleness and liberty. Pornography is one of the reasons and the products of increasing human trafficking in the global society today.

Therefore, SVD missionaries must come out with the plan to educate the children, students, youth and parents about the media education, sex education and health education. The prefer choice for sex educators by the youth are their parents, teachers, lecturers, and doctors. Does this mean that the Church leaders are inadequate and unequipped to deal with this responsibility? Although most parents feel that talking to their children about sex and media is a good practice but most of them are afraid to do so. Therefore, here comes our responsibility to update our knowledge and be the good Samaritans. Sunday schools can be used to teach children and youth the morals and life skills in accordance with our Christian beliefs. We must organize seminars, workshops for parents to educate them about how to handle their offspring and increase their efforts to familiarize themselves with the internet and take steps to protect their children from the dark side of the internet. SVD missionaries do MORE to utilize the resources and platforms it possesses in order to deal with these increasing problems.

X.   Ecumenical Dialogue

The SVD missionaries should develop an entirely new perspective on ecumenism and interreligious dialogue in the spirit of Vatican II's directives and post-conciliar initiatives. Authentic interreligious and ecumenical thinking, attitudes and practices have entered the bloodstream of only a minority of Catholics, whether laity, clergy or bishops in the Northeast India. The SVD mission must become an agent of peace and unity in this region; foster a sense of brotherhood and sisterhood beyond tribal, denominational and inter-church line, to diffuse the bloody rivalry between different denominations.

Conclusion

When we live in this hassle puzzle world, there is a whisper we hear to 'follow me'. It is more challenging and testing. Around me, where luck determines rights and one person's fortune depends on anther's inequality this is the era of capitalism competition and industrial revolution. The era where profit comes before corruption everything is counterfeit production. In these times, we reward ignorance and sacrifice the integrity for acceptance. We wilfully destroy the environment and glorify idiocy over real intelligence. This is the century of Instagram, WhatsApp and Facebook. In this century, you can be ignored for your morals, yet worshiped for your looks because selfishness is portrayed as strength and kindness is mistaken for weakness and the media teaches us to ignore what is important and instead follow what is popular. We have been taught to believe to be successful; we need to be wealthy but real virtues like honour has become irrelevant. Today honour is understood in different way; i.e. 'honour killing' for when someone raises voice against the majority for the right cause, 'beaten to death or out casted' for professing one's religion, 'stripped naked and paraded' for protesting one's rights, 'mob lynching' for eating one's choice of food, 'hanged to death' for loving somebody out of his caste or religion.

And are we truly free? When we can't spend a full day without the Apps on our smart phones? Do schools really teach us how to think? Are degrees desired for education or validation? Why do ideas make people forget their humanity? All we are is humanity and so a person's quality of life should not be determined by their skin colour or ethnicity. Why is kicking a ball around a field worshipped by millions when starving children get little recognition? Why are phones, cars and possessions more of concern than climate change and animal extinction? Why is pop culture and entertainment prioritised over world injustice and hunger? Why are celebrities seen as role models for selling corrupt messages? Why do we make stupid people famous being for vulgar? What is it that we care about now? Status? Image? Titles? Perceived values?

People are now defined by their financial prosperity and famous people are just people who manipulate and trick you. Why do we exploit and kill animals weaker than us because we are on top of the food chain? We do treat some animals well but only on the condition that they offer us the personal gain. It will lead us to the collapse of civilization. If we have not noticed the problem then we have not been paying attention. We need to wake up, because as missionaries we need to be firm in our faith, strong in our vocation and committed to our mission. We are proud to say that we are in the modern world and with modern gadgets to communicate well, yet still there is a famine, poverty, illiteracy and war that exist around us. Is it true that humans are intelligent? Or are we ignorant? Is honest is really a virtue if nobody wants to hear the truth? Don't we encourage a system, which makes the selfish rich and the selfless poor? One percent of the world's population own thirty five percent of all wealth. How can we say this fair and working? Success depends on who you know not what you know. The majority are being exploited this is the reality of everyday. The takers of society bathe in greed, while the common folk slave away. Prosperity isn't earned anymore; it is a privilege dependent on exploiting the poor.

To be a Priest or a Brother in a missionary congregation is very challenging. Soon after you are ordained or professed, Jesus takes you to the Gethsemane garden, there he tells, be awake and pray that you don't fall into temptation. Be awake and celebrate Mass, be awake and sit for confession, be awake and be available to the People, be awake and be accountable. We are aware but most of the time we are not awake. We can be awake and pray, we can sleep off or we can be running away from Jesus, just like the Disciples did.

'Can you be awake with me'? 'I know flesh is weak, though the Spirit is willing", will you leave me and go?

When we begin to doze, begin to fall sleep, that is the time Satan comes and takes us away. Satan is nothing but our flesh, our sensual, we fall prey to it. That's where we bring shame on to ourselves and our Church, that's where we have to go through the humiliation. That's where the disgrace comes to us. We leave the Lord from Gethsemane and run away.

To be a missionary is to share in the "missio Dei" (the mission of God). Thus, our apostolic activity is holy. Jesus did not use the magic wand to heal the people nor did he raise his hand stretched out on the public but have gone personally to heal them. Even though magical media can have many answers for many of our questions but it cannot replace missionaries' personal touch to the people, personal conversation with the people and personal blessing for the people.

Are we disturbed? Disturbance leads to discernment and from discernment flows the decision making from which it leads to direction and all these different aspects leads to Dedication.

The Half Way:

A Story of Hesitant Progress in SVD INE

Ignatius Soreng SVD

A 'Mission' is generally established afresh or acquired from some others with great vision, hope and enthusiasm. In course of time, however, with commitments waning or priorities changing, how much of those factors are fulfilled, is for one to see and judge. The *Gangpur Mission* of the Belgian Jesuits, acquired by the SVDs with such vision, hope and enthusiasm, too is such a case for study.

In this dissertation, I am going to narrate some aspects that will bring forth points that will help us to reflect on the past and present of the mission, in order that some obscurities in understanding may be cleared, and proper steps be taken for benefit of the mission.

SVD takes over a great Mission from the Jesuits

Two prominent reasons made the Jesuits give away parts of the huge mission they had carved out in Chotanagpur: first, it was too large to take proper care; second, due to the Second World War men (missionaries) and money dried substantially, so they struggled in both fronts.

In 1948 SVD took over *Gangpur Mission* from the Belgian Jesuits of Chotanagpur a great Mission, which, at that time Jesuits considered as the best part of their Mission. Catholic population was big – 64,865[1] including baptized and catechumens in five Mission stations – Kesramal, Hamirpur, Gaibira, Jhunmur and Kusumdegi; average number per Mission Station being 12,973.

At the time of handing over to the SVD in 1948 *Chotanagpur Mission* of Jesuits comprised of nine Deaneries – Gangpur, Ranchi, Barway, Biru, Jashpur, Khunti, Noatoli, Palamu, and Udaipur/Raigarh. A glance at the numerical status of all deaneries may give a clearer picture why the Gangpur Deanery (Gangpur Mission of the SVD) was so dear to the Jesuits:

Deaneries	No. of Baptized/ Catechumen		No. of Centers	Average per Center
1. Gangpur	64,865	in	5 centers	12,973
2. Ranchi	28,728	in	6 centers	4,788
3. Barway	39,504	in	6 centers	6,584
4. Biru	69,659	in	7 centers	9,951
5. Jashpur	57,537	in	5 centers	11,507
6. Khunti	26,287	in	7 centers	3,755
7. Noatoli	38,749	in	6 centers	6,458
8. Palamu	22,244	in	5 centers	4,448
9. Udaipur/Raigarh	15,396	in	2 centers	7,698

Numbers spoke for themselves. Gangppur deanery was large and still growing. Besides this, the other factors that made a Mission remarkable were things like vivacity, overall response, faith, and cooperation of the people. Gangpur excelled all these.

Gloom and Sunshine of Jesuits at the handing over

Thus, Gangpur Deanery was so dear to the heart of Jesuits of Chotanagpur, that when it was being handed over to some another Congregation, the Jesuits had a lot of apprehension about the future of the Mission. What would happen to Gangpur? Would the successors be willing to make necessary sacrifices? Would they go ahead and work for expansion? In fact, Bishop himself made it known to the authorities that if the mission field of Gangpur was to be given to a Congregation that would be unable or unwilling to make sacrifices in personnel and resources, it might be advisable to keep the *status quo*.

What a relief it was when they learned that it was S.V.D., the *Society of the Divine Word* that the mission is being given. The reaction of the Jesuits was aptly expressed by Bishop Oscar Severin himself, the then Bishop of Ranchi, "But suddenly, a flash lit up the sky: the gloomy cloud had vanished. News came that Gangpur would have been entrusted to the S.V.D. Fathers. Then our joy knew no bounds. For we knew that nothing would be spared to carry on the work to a successful issue, that *'Verbum Dei non eritalligatum'*, that the mission would thrive and develop and expand as it could not possibly have done had it remained attached as an outlying district, to the vast Diocese of Ranchi."[2]

Such was the hope and expectation of the Jesuits at the handing over of their most promising mission to the SVDs. Their well-founded optimism that the SVDs would do well for the mission was based on a few practical points:[3]

The SVD, with its world resource of missionaries was not hit hard by the Second World War as much as the Belgian Jesuits were hit. Belgium was directly involved in the World War, and consequently suffered severe shortage of both - money and missionaries. As far as SVD was concerned, when Europe was hithard, it would pull resources, men and money, from other parts of the world quite easily and carry on the work. The International nature of the SVD Society was a big strength in such a crisis.

What did SVD receive from the Jesuits?

A huge Mission area, spanning across three feudatory States – Gangpur, Bonai, and Bamra. It was a challenging geographical area, but the Jesuits could not exclude any because these states were inhabited by many Christian migrants from Chotanagpur, whom they primarily targeted for outreach. Their familiarity also eased their initiative and approach in the mission. People under care of the mission belonged to primarily four tribes – Oraon, Munda, Kisan and Khadia. Though there were numerous other tribes, the mission had never approached them significantly.

A clear mission method for smooth running of the mission, where the Parish center functioned as fulcrum of Christian life and activities. Most of the parish centers were well equipped with basic facilities of service, like – church, presbytery, convent, school, and dispensary. Parish center was surrounded by village centers under spiritual care of a catechist. Besides sacramental service, the parish priest would visit the village twice a year – before Christmas and before Easter. Harvest was plenty but laborers were few; but the missionaries organized their sacramental service, house and village visits, conducting mission organizations, and monitoring schools and education with conciderable regularity.

Five well established parishes with beautiful Churches, presbyteries, 125 Primary and 6 Middle Schools, 1 High school, and 2 Industrial schools.[4] Though in the Returns of Gangpur Vicariate 1947-1948 mentioned only two Industrial schools were entered – one in Kesramal and the other in Hamirpur, Gaibira and Jhunmur too had small industrial schools albeit in their nascent state. There were only three Convents of the Daughters of the Cross – in Kesramal, Hamirpur and Gaibira. Jhunmur and Kusumdegi did not have convents.

Well-functioning mission organizations, like – Catholic Sabha, sodalities for men, women, youth and children where hundreds of men, women, youth and children attended twice every month – once in the village center and once in the Parish center. These were great organizations for nourishing and improving the Christian living of all level of faithful. They were great motivating factors, and with proper management they produced great result in the Church.

Well established Social organizations. In line with those social organizations in Chotanagpur, Gangpur mission had well organized social organizations, like – *dhangola (grain bank)*where spare paddy grains were collected after harvest and distributed when in need, *Mission Co-operative Society* where mission managed bank receive deposits from people on banking basis; *Nishasangat*, where drinking prohibition was practiced in an organized manner.

Special social service drives: Apart from these, there was promotion and recruitment of educated Christians for official and industrial jobs in Gangpur. Jesuit missionaries established new villages and colonies in various parts of all the three States that they had ventured in with proper permission from the office of the State.

During the World War, there was substantial recruitment organized by the Mission from among the Christians for World War military service. Hundreds of Christian tribal young men were recruited for this and obtained good profit. There was also promotion and recruitment of labor for Assam tea gardens and Andamans forest clearing sites. Thousands of tribal profited by this drive.

A clear educational policy that controlled the educational activities of the mission. Education was the chosen instrument for progress and empowerment of the tribal. Therefore, it had to be well organized and executed. Today if the tribal of the Ganapur Mission have risen to a level, it is because of this far-sighted and visionary educational policy that was made for the entire Chotanagpur mission. Let's have a glimpse of this policy in order to understand it:

In 1908, with the sanction of the Bishop of Ranchi diocese and the Jesuit superior of Ranchi Province, a mission educational policy was made and promulgated for the entire Chotanagpur mission where the Gangpur Mission too was a part. The gist of it was as follows:[5]

1. Each mission station must have its own Lower Primary School

2. Village schools in the district must be multiplied as many as possible, and they ought to be preparatory to the Lower Primary School of the station.

3. Each Central Station, in addition to the Lower Primary School, must have an Upper Primary School for the whole district. There will be no objection to any other Station opening an Upper Primary School, provided they do not find difficult to find qualified teachers.

4. Boys of other stations who are sent to the Upper Primary school of the central station have to pay for their boarding.

5. Boys who pass the Upper Primary and are deemed fit to continue their studies should be sent to the Central School, Ranchi that has English Middle and High School.

6. In order to make education more suitable to all classes of boys, Middle Vernacular (MV) school and Industrial School too be added.

7. One of the ends of St. John's School was to produce masters and catechists from among the students and even vocation for priesthood.

8. Middle vernacular was to prepare students so that they could do something in life. The Industrial School was principally for those to whom literary education offered no prospect.

Guru Training School: Since Mission ran so many schools, there was need for a Teachers' Training school so that the mission schools would not lack trained teachers. So in 1928 the Jesuit missionaries started Guru Training School in Gaibira, but this ran only for four years – 1928-1032. When Gaibira started Middle Vernacular school in 1932, running the Guru Training School became difficult. And, though initially Hamirpur was decided as the center for Guru Training School, eventually it was shifted to Kesramal in 1933.[6]

High School: In 1944, despite war time financial and personnel crunch, the Jesuits of Chotanagpur Mission had taken a bold step by starting St.Xavier's College, Ranchi, because, for them education was important for the mission. They made their educational program complete networking well with Lower Primary, Upper Primary, English Middle, Vernacular Middle, Industrial School, High School and College.

With St. Xavier's College, Ranchi sitting on the top of the pyramid, High Schools, the next highest were well distributed in the Mission. Though Jesuits were leaving the Gangpur Mission, they pushed for a High School here, and on 24th June, 1947 Rajeshwar High School was started at Hamirpur. At this point, Hamirpur High School was only the second High School in the whole State of Gangpur, the other one being Bhawani Shankar High School, Sundargarh, that had become full-fledged High School in 1921. High School was the highest education offered in the State at that time, and the Mission was proud to have one along with the one run by the ruling chief.

Industrial School: In order to make education more suitable to all classes of boys, Industrial School too was added. This was meant for those students whose academic capability was limited. Initially, this was basically trade oriented, where students were given training in skills like carpentry, weaving, masonry etc. so that they can do something in life. Later on, due to demand of technical knowledge, some basic technical training was added in it.

There were two recorded Industrial schools in Gangpur Mission – Kesramal and Hamirpur. Though there were no recorded Industrial schools in Gaibira, Jhunmur and Kusumdegi, they did have small weaving units that attracted good number of students.

Two Women's Religious Congregations: Along with what directly belonged to the Jesuits, there were two women's Religious Congregations working in the mission as mission partners – The Daughters of the Cross Sisters (F.C.), and the Handmaids of Mary (H.M.). The Daughters of the Cross had come to Kesramal of the Gangpur Mission in 1909, but by the time of handover, they had given it up having started two other convents – Gaibira 1926 and Hamirpur 1941. In both the places, the Sisters were doing excellent work in schools, pastoral field, and in the field of medical care of the poor.

The second Religious Congregation was the Handmaids of Mary, started in Kesramal by Fr. Edmund Harrison S.J. in 1944. After the modest beginning due to the unexpected transfer of Fr. Harrison to Mahuadanr in Chotanagpur, the nascent Congregation was struggling to find a firm ground, but, there was a firm assurance from the SVD that the new Congregation would be looked after.

Thus, at the handing over, SVD received a great mission legacy where a great vision of mission had been displaced by the Jesuit predecessors. No doubt that there was euphoria among the SVDs over this great acquisition, and there was a great sense of commitment to further the mission to its heights.

After acquiring this great mission, did SVD fulfill the expectation? As we are trying to look back to the past, we have to see how this great mission progressed under care of SVD or how much remained wanting.

The Ground reality at the time of takeover

1. At the time of takeover of the Mission from the Jesuits, the turbulent time that had preceded was settling down. The World War II was over in 1945, and its aftermath was visible in various ways world over. Though Gangpur was not directly involved in it, after the end of the war there was some buzz about it due to the fact that some who participated in the *Labor Corpse* in France during the war time had returned and were their memories were making rounds.

2. The Independence of India won in 1947 was gradually having its effects in socio-political life of the people. There was a change in the administration as the authorities people served and feared, i.e. the kings of Gangpur and Bonai, and zamindars of Nagra, Sargipali, Sarapgarh and Hemgir were no longer powerful.

3. With feudal system obliterated, feudal officials in the villages, i.e. gountia, lalu, khamari, kotwar etc. were no longer terrors. There

was a new type of administration and the SVD missionaries had no longer to battle against whims and fancy of the feudal rulers or other personalities as the Jesuit missionaries had to. There were now new administrative names like district, tehsils, blocks and panchayats. There was also an end of prolonged rivalry and power struggle between the Bhuiya zamindars and the ruling family of Gangpur, resulting in permanent peace.

4.   Sundargarh, known as Suadih earlier, maintained its importance after the new political organization. Since the 19th century it was the capital of the State, now it remained as the district headquarters with the office of District Magistrate and all other district administrative offices.

5.   Though out of power, the royal family continued to wield significant influence on the psyche of people, as they had indeed created some lasting memory for themselves with renamed places, i.e. Birmitrapur, Uditnagar, Rajgangpur, Rayboga, Raghunathpali, Deokaranpur etc., and some monumental infrastructure like the Sundargarh Palace, the royal court that was turned into Collectorate, Bhawanisankar High School, Rani Janaki Girls' High School, Regent Market, District Hospital Sundargarh etc.

6.   Ecclesially, in order to serve the mission well, in 1951 a new diocese – the *Diocese of Sambalpur* had been created out of Archdioces of Ranchi, Calcutta and Nagpur.The new diocese comprised of four districts of Odisha – Bolangir, Dhenkanal, Sambalpur and Sundargarh, with Rt. Reverend Herman Westerman S.V.D. as its first Bishop. Though named the diocese of Sambalpur, initially Bishop resided in Kalunga, until he shifted to the new Bishop's House in Hamirpurin 1966.

7.   In the new political delimitation, Gangpur and Bonai Feudatory States had been joined together to construct Sundargarh district, Bonai feudatory state had become Bonai subdivision, most of Nagrazamindary had become Panposh subdivision, and the

Khalsa, and three western zamindaries, i.e. Hemgir, Sarapgarh and Sargipali had become Sundargarh subdivision. This administrative formation had brought in sea change in the attitude of the people and administrative persons.

8. *Beth begari* forced labor that had been a key part of kingship order had ended, and the people were fully on their own. Missionarie of Gaibira, Kusudegi and Hamirpur, who were much involved in brawl with the kings of Gangpur and the zamindars of Nagra over *bethbegari*and cart festival issue were over once and for all. People were no longer harassed on these issues any more.

9. **First wave of Industrialization:**Industrial activities were beginning to show up with Orissa Cement Limited Rajgangpur(OCL) being set up by 1948, and formally start producing by 1951. Steel Plant at Rourkela was being set up for it to become fully operative by 1955. Within a period of a decade, a number of large, medium and small scale and ancillary industries popped up and created huge industrial estates in Kalunga, Kansbahal and Jalda.

10. In addition to some mining units that already existed around Jharbera, Birmitrapur, Bisra etc., now there were many new ones to supply raw materials to the industries, thus generating heavy industrial movement and transport. Industrial towns and colonies began to spring up and finally manifested in the form of Rourkela, Birmitrapur, Purnapani, Hathibari, Lanjiberna, Kalunga, Kansbahal, Jalda, Kuarmunda etc. There was inflow of outsiders in the form of industrial officials, engineers, technicians and other employees into these industrial locations.

11. Mandira Dam was built to supply water to two major industries –RSP Rourkela and OCL Rajgangpur. Built in 1957 a few kilometers up stream on river Sunkh, this damthirty-one villages, and a total of 2400 people, out of which barely 843 were resettled. A great tragedy had occurred.

12. Jesuit preparation and motivation of people bore positive results for quite a few years, as a number of tribal availed small or moderate jobs in the industries, mines and offices. They also settled in the industrial towns and colonies in not so insignificant number. Even in remote jungles of Gangpur, Bonai and Bamra, tribal settlements were established by efforts of the missionaries; this was to prove important in later times.

13. In the towns of Rourkela, colonies like Koel Nagar in Jhirpani, LIC colony in Raghunathpali, Basanti Colony and 7/8 area in Durgapur, Kaling Vihar in Chhend etc. sprang up where mostly non-tribal outsiders came to settle. This created imbalance tribal population and started a total new industrial life and culture.

14. There was a cultural mix in the industrial towns, colonies and settlements. Tribal dominated Gangpur now became a witness to new style of living, cultural trends, and behavioral pattern. Greater amount of money started circulating in the area creating totally new economic proposition. Shops and markets displayed greater variety of goods causing attraction and infatuation.

15. Roads were constructed for industrial movement and transport. All industrial units and locations were connected with proper roads. The *Bengal Nagpur Railway* (BNR), constructed during the time of Maharaja Raghunath Shekhardeo between 1890-1910 period,passed through Gangpur. This railway introduced a significant movement of goods and of people now. By 1950s this movement increased significantly as raw materials from mines and industrial products from the industries were transported to and fro.

16. There was ruthless displacement of local tribal people from the industrial areas, mines and dams; Rourkela Steel Plant and Mandaria Dam were the biggest among them. These two projects alone led to the displacement of 4094 families –2901 families from 33 villages for Rourkela Steel Plant, and 1193 families from 31

villages for the Mandira dam. A total of 25,035.24acres of land was acquired for the purpose of Steel Plant at Rourkela alone. Total number of displaced persons in the said two projects was over 23,400.

17. The rehabilitation and resettlement of the displaced was another tragic, disastrous and heartbreaking story. Despite sweet promises Good alternative sites for settlement, agricultural land, gainful employment, and adequate compensation to be paid for all land, trees, building etc.[7] all that the displaced people received was the bare minimum. On the other hand, there was a cruel betrayal that led hundreds of them to misery and death.

18. The Rourkela Steel Plant (RSP) had four resettlement colonies and 15 reclamation camps farther away, and Mandaria had six resettlement colonies apart from reclamation camps. Some of them were at the periphery of the Plant or the Dam, but some others were far out, away from the place that they left, for example – of the RSP resettlement Sankarla-128 kms, Silikuta-87 kms, and of Mandaria resettlement Lachda-100 kms.[8] Their condition in the new place was heart rending.

19. Mandaria displacement had hit hard the Kisan tribe that had been in that area for generations. Now they were dispersed all over Gangpur, Bonai, Bamdaand even Sambalpur. Known as Gangpuria Oraons by Jesuit missionaries, as Kisansby the rulers of Gangpur, and as Pradhan by the rulers of Bonai, these people had scattered here and there and tried to find new identity for themselves. Those who moved farther away from Gangpur also moved away from the influence of mission!

20. *Adult Training Center* that was a precondition for training local tribal youth to prepare them for the industrial employment had been slyly shifted to Cuttack facilitating training and recruiting candidates from the coastal areas for employment in RSP and other industrial employment. This had deprived the local tribal of the

same, and this was bound to be so for generations thereafter. Late did the tribal of the Sundargarh district realize the game, but by the time they realized it, lasting damage had already been done. Within years the coastal trained persons were being employed in hordes in RSP and other ancillary industries. Rourkela and other industrial towns were being detribalized.

21. Rumour about anti-conversion bill being introduced in the Odisha Assembly was gaining momentum during early days of takeover; so there was anxiety among SVDs regarding its consequence. Indeed, it came to pass within twenty years of the takeover. Odisha was the first state in the country to bring such law named as *Odisha Freedom of Religion Act, 1967*, to provide for prohibition of conversion from one religion to another by the use of force, inducement or by fraudulent means. It was a big challenge to the missionary enterprise.

22. Gangpur had witnessed a massive no-rent campaign in 1939. Discontented with implementation of new rent policy on agricultural land as per proposal of *Indrabilas Mukherjee Settlement Report*, people had come out in protest under leadership Nirmal Munda, and Rani Janaki, the administrative head of the State at the time, had suppressed it with iron hands. It had resulted in inhuman massacre of no less than forty-two tribal at *Amko-Simko*in 1939. Its ghostly memory was still lingering in the minds of the people.There was also as care in the mind of Government that such an uprising may come up any if discontent grows in the minds of the people over the industrial mismanagement.

23. Tribal discontent was indeed brewing in mind of the people because of massive deception and betrayal of faith overthe issue of compensation, rehabilitation and resettlement over Rourkela Steel Plant and Mandaria Dam project. Anytime, there was a possibility of protest campaign in the level of no-rent campaign of 1939. Media was not silent on the issue. Taking two of the

Resettlement Colonies as example: *Lachhada*, about 100 kilometers away within the district,   and *Amgaon* around 120 kilometers away in Deogarh district, or other related matter, they
made case in their coverage indicating the travesty of justice in
the resettlement enterprise of the RSP/Government.[9]

24. Discontent also was arising over the fact that immigration of
    non-tribals into urban areas of Sundargarh District in the name
    of industrial employment was growing. This was threatening tribal
    equation in the district. Also the fact that excess land acquired by
    the Government for industrial purpose was not being returned
    to their original owners as per terms and condition, rather, civil
    settlements for immigrant employees and their families were
    being set up slowly.

25. Mineral-rich Sundargarh district had come to the attention
    of Government as well as under roving eyes of industrial
    companies. From Tensa, Barsuan, Koira in the east to Belpahar
    and Brajrajnagar in the west huge deposits of iron ore, limestone,
    dolomite and coal were identified, and sooner or later they were
    to be exploited. There was a possibility of massive industrial
    concentration south of Sundargarh in the western part of the
    district at par or even bigger than Rourkela.

Thus, we see there was a multi-faceted and volatile reality in the
mission field that the SVD had obtained. To those who were not
concerned, the mission looked just a normal plain, but it was not so; it
was explosive. For a missionary Congregation like SVD, it could have
stirred the mind so that adequate mission policy would be made and
executed. Were the new comer SVDs aware of these situations? Did
they feel the difference in the mission with so many possibilities? A
mission should always be according to existing reality and the signs
of time. We shall see and judge them in the way the SVD responded
to the situation.

What were the directions of SVD as they took over?

True to the international nature of the Congregation, the first batch of SVDs that started work in the mission was multi-national: Fr. Stanislaus Wald, Fr. Alois Kanski, Fr. Charles Smidt and Fr. Clement Beck were from Germany, Fr. Andrew Topol and Fr. Edward Borkowski were from U.S.A., and Fr. Antholy Fleming was from England. Many that followed too were from different parts of Europe, North and South America, and Australia. This was one of the points for jubilation of the outgoing Jesuits – that unlike themselves who depended heavily on Belgium alone for missionaries and money, SVD would pull missionaries from anywhere in the world to meet the need.

SVD set about the work in the mission in some concrete direction; Apart from Evangelization, two of them being prominent – Consolidation and Expansion. In this dissertation, I shall highlight these two; for the sake of brevity and relevance I shall avoid the third – Evangelization.

Consolidation: First and foremost, the mission had to be consolidated. Firm as the mission was, it was too extensive for a limited number of personnel to properly take care. Thus many areas as well as many details were unattended. In order to attend to these needs, many new mission stations needed to be started so that areas of operation will be minimized, and more personnel could be appointed. Urgency was felt so much, that, in a matter of twenty years of the takeover, i.e. 1948-1968, twenty-one new parishes in all – fourteen in Sundargarh district, and seven in Sambalpur and Bolangir districts were opened: Birmitrapur 1950, Jharsuguda 1950, Kalunga 1951, Sundargarh 1952, Kantapali 1953, Majhapara 1953, Telendih 1957, Madhupur 1957,Barilapta 1959, Jhorabahal 1961, Bargarh 1961, Rajgangpur 1961, Gudrapara 1963,Sikajor 1966, Bondamunda 1968, Gomardih 1968, Jalda 1968, Phalsa 1968, Singarmunda 1968,Amlikhaman 1968, and Sambalpur 1968.

Apart from the urgency in consolidation drive, another factor that drove the SVDs to hasten in opening new mission stations was the anxiety over Anti-conversion bill that was being rumored to be imminently table in the State Assembly; and this created panic. There was a fear, that, once it is passed and promulgated, opening new mission stations may not be possible. So, there was hurry. In 1967, the *Odisha Freedom of Religion Act, 1967* was indeed brought up, and before it came to effect by 1968, all these new mission stations were erected. It is noticeable that in 1968 alone not less than seven mission stations were opened up - Bondamunda, Gomardih, Jalda, Phalsa, Singarmunda, Amlikhaman, and Sambalpur.

In Sundargarh district, all the five centers opened by Jusuits were consolidated by way of opening new parishes, but by far, Hamirpur and Gaibira,being extensive, drew more attention as they received five and four new parishes respectively: *Hamirpur* received Kalunga, Barilapta, Kantapali, Bondamunda, and Jalda,and *Gaibira* received Sundargarh, Phalsa, Sikajor, and Telendia. On the other hand *Kesramal*got two – Rajgangpur and Gomardih, *Jhunmur*got two – Birmitrapur, Kantapali, while *Kusumdegi* got just one – Singarmunda.

Opening new mission stations was not the only way of consolidation of the mission; but the other aspects, especially Pastoral Service were consolidated as per the Pastoral method established by Jesuits, such as sacramental service, catechumenate, sodalities, and social work initiatives etc.

Along with Pastoral service, educational service too was widened by opening Primary schools, Middle English schools, and High schools in all the new parishes. In order to raise the school education up to High school level, four High schools were opened in four important centers so that the entire mission would be served adequately: *Hamirpur* for Bonai and Nagra, *Kesramal* for its adjacent areas south of river Sunkh, *Jhunmur* for parishes north of the Sunkh and Koel rivers, *Gaibira* for the entire territory in the west of the Mundagaon-Kiralega hill range, and *Kusumdegi* for its adjacent areas east of the hills.

There is great role of women religious in service of a mission field. They complement the enterprise in unique way, participating with the missionaries in all that is necessary, and at the same time add their own specialty according to their charism. *Daughters of St. Anne(DSA)* Sisters had come, served in Gaibira and Hamirpur and gone back by 1941. The *Daughters of the Cross (F.C.)* were already in the mission since 1909 doing great service, but there was also a newly founded Congregation in the diocese – *Handmaids of Mary (H.M.)*, founded by Fr. Edmund Harrison SJ in 1944. After his transfer to far away Mahuadanr in Chhechhari, Chotanagpur, this Congregation was languishing. Therefore, Bishop Herman Westermann revived it and nourished it with paternal care, gave them new life and vitality, and engaged them in the service of the mission.

English Education started in the diocese as Bishop Herman had brought in the Apostolic Carmel (A.C.) for this purpose. They established the Carmel English School, Hamirpur, Rourkela, 1957, and thus became pioneer of English Education for girls in the diocese. Later, SVD started St.Paul School, Hamirpur, Rourkela, 1964, and engaged in English education for boys.

In the following years, the H.M.s played big role in supporting the mission with their dedicated service, especially in pastoral, educational and medical ministry. Being indigenous of the place, they had their appealing ways that suited the mission needs. They were great proponents of women's education in the district with two big Girls' Highschool – St. Mary's Girls' Highschool, Sundargarh, and St. Mary's Girls' Highschool, Rajgangpur. With these two landmark ventures, women's education in the district flourished greatly.

As far as women's education is concerned, there was a Girls' Highschool run by the F.C. Sisters in Hamirpur. Bishop Westermann SVD then took initiative in bringing the Apostolic Carmel Sisters in 1957to Hamirpur for English medium education of girls. With these four girls' school – St. Mary's Girls' High school Sundargarh, St. Mary's Girls' High school Rajgangpur, St. Joseph's Girls' High school

Hamirpur, and Mount Carmel English school, Hamirpur, Rourkela, women's education in the mission progressed in leaps and bounds.

Expansion: Expansion of the mission was the other major task that the SVD undertook during those days. Jesuits had concentrated mainly on Gangpur while crossing over a bit into the Princely States of Bonai and Bamra. SVD, however, straight away went on an overdrive and ventured into ex-Princely States of*Sambalpur,Bonai,*and*Bamra*: into *Sambalpur* with a parish at Jharsuguda 1950, Madhupur 1957, Bargarh 1961, and Sambalpur 1968; into *Bonai* with a parish at Kantapali 1953;and into *Bamra* with three parishes – Majhapara 1953, Gudrapara 1963, and Amlikhaman 1968.

One noticeable fact in this expansion was that SVD had gone beyond the tribal alone concentration of mission by opening a mission station at Madhupur, which was basically a mission among the *dalit* people belonging to Ganda caste. This was a significant departure from the normal way treaded by the predecessors so far. This was also a great enrichment to the mission as it added a significant dimension.

Between 1968 and 1972 there was quiet regarding opening of new mission stations, but after this it picked up again. Once the anxiety over *Odisha Freedom of Religion Act, 1967* was overcome, mission stations started to spring up, and beginning from 1972 up to 1979, in a period of eight years not less thannine mission stations were started – Barsuan 1972, Kahupani 1972, Salangabahal 1972, Bagdehi 1973, Ghoghea 1974, Bodmal-Rairakhol 1975, Talcher 1975, Balangir 1976, and Kiralega 1977.

In 1979 the diocese was bifurcated into Rourkela and Sambalpur diocese. Sundargarh district as a whole became the Rourkela diocese with Bishop Alphonse Bilung SVD as its first Bishop, while the rest became Sambalpur diocese with Rev. Raphael Cheenath SVD as its first Bishop who resided in Sambalpur.

1980 onwards, SVD expansion widened further more as with opening of mission stations in Deogarh 1980, Thakurpali 1980, Pal

Lahara 1981, Gopinathpur 1985, Duburi 1993, and Jajpur Road 1989, mission among the *Ho* tribe was ushered in. This mission, again, could be subdivided into two identifiable groups – ones belonging to industrial areas, i.e. Jajpur Road and Duburi, and the others belonging to the natural rural surroundings, i.e. Pal Lahara and Gopinathpur. This was a refreshing development, because, it is here a new tribe had been taken into the mission enterprise by the initiative of SVD; the other tribes in Gangpur, Bonai and Bamra were Oraon, Munda, Khadia and Kisan, people who were contacted by the Jesuits.

Much later, in 2008, with a new beginning in Bezda, in the west Midnapur district of West Bengal, another tribal group came under care of the SVD – the Santhal, that belongs to the Munda group of tribes. This was all together another State too – West Bengal, and thus provided cultural and linguistic variety to the mission.

SVD enterprise in Puri was the lone mission remarkable for its service among the caste Hindus. Though this mission was not one that was pioneered by the SVD, rather was taken up in response to an invitation from most Rev. Raphael Cheenath SVD, Archbishop of Cuttack-Bhubaneswar Archdiocese, this was a great departure from the otherwise tribal only mission in the Province. Fr. MarianusZelazek SVD, the parish priest and pioneer of a few other land mark mission activity like SatyaSandhan Kendra Dialogue Center, leprosy clinic etc. created a significant mission thrust in the place.

The biggest venture, however, that he undertook in Puriwas the leper colony where he deployed his dream and committed himself to the care of lepers. Along with medical care, mercy kitchen, rope making cottage industry for lepers, school for their children, a small spirituality center etc. it developed into a multi-dimensional mission service. Now, at the vicinity of the leper colony, Ishopanthi Ashram has become a full-fledged spirituality center, and Beatrix school has grown to be a sought after school educating children from all walks of life along with the children of the lepers.

Second wave of industrialization

RSP and OCL dominated and still now dominate the industrial activity in the district because of their massive capability. However, late 1980s and particularly 1990s saw a spate of industrial activity in Sundargarh district, and during this time, not less than seven more Cement factories and fifty Sponge Iron factories (including those working, under construction, and Project under implementation) sprang up.[10] Of course, many of them were declared sick, or were closed later, and the latest confirmation by the Government of Odisha shows 39 large scale industries and medium enterprises that are operative in the district now.[11] That's not alone, these industries are supported with mineral goods by not less than 41 mines (albeit 4 of them closed) that are spread all over the district now.[12]

This was a time of mad rush of industrialization of the district, but this was to be so because the Industrial Policy of Odisha prompted such activity in the name of development and economic growth of the State. Industrial Policy 1980 clearly states the thrust as follows:

"The State of Orissa is rich in mineral, marine and forest resources. Its vast mineral deposits, extensive coastline, lush green forests and varieties of agricultural products provide an ideal base for rapid industrialization of the State. During the last 30 years investment in industries and infrastructure has created an industrial base but a dynamic industrial culture is yet to emerge. The vast resources of the State have to be efficiently harnessed for creation of a sound industrial base.

i.   The State is committed to an integrated economic development within a fixed time frame through efficient development of resources for optimum growth. A coordinated push will be given to promotion of major, medium and small industries so that each sector promotes and nourishes the other. Greater emphasis would be given to mineral based, engineering and agro-based industries. Effective steps would be taken to provide infrastructure in all areas for industrialization as per the availability of raw material and other locational ensured through dispersal of investment."[13]

Thus, there was an industrial urgency in the State. Sundargarh district was ideal for industrialization because of its vast mineral resource. North-western part of the then Sambalpur district, what is now the district of Jharsuguda, was equally resourceful. Therefore, along with Sundargarh district, Jharsuguda district too picked up heavy mineral and industrial activity. Consequently, today there are in Jharsugudano less than ten mines and eleven large scale industries including Bedanta Aluminium Ltd., Bhusan Steel and Power (P) Ltd.[14]

Subsequent industrial policy of 1986, 1992, 1996, 2001, 2015 of the State enhanced the determination to further industrial progress. Thus, districts of Sundargarh and Jharsuguda, that have maximum possibility of industrial and mineral activity thrived in this direction.

Both the districts created such dizzy industrial activity, that, they became massive employment opportunity for the current generation of local youth and job seekers, provided that they had at least the minimum of required qualification. Quite a few of these posts were availed by them, but the rest were seized by the people of other parts of Odisha or other States of India.

A great miss? Why?

Such opportunities come rarely, but when they come, they have to be used, for if they are missed and others take advantage, one has only to rue and regret. That is what has happened for many of the local youth, particularly those under care of the mission. The boon period of industrialization of two districts – Sundargarh and Jharsuguda went abegging and the people we promote did not profit by them in a way they should have.

They were just not ready. Industrialization of the districts caught the mission unawares. The Mission looked even indifferent to the wave of industrialization with 'who cares' attitude, as if it just didn't matter. Our youth did not have adequate qualification to enter into the privileged employments. Mission had neither program nor infrastructure for providing qualification that would help them to claim the job opportunities.

There was lack of foresight so as to identify the movements of the Government that went on such a massive drive. We had no knowledge of the movements of the Government and industrialists. When the action started, there was no time to wait for training; because all those who were ready, were absorbed.

There was no pre-emptive preparation for forthcoming opportunity. At this level, perhaps an Engineering College and authentic ITI Training Institutes would have been of propelled the youth to industrial level. If not run by own capacity, proper motivation given to go for such trainings in the available Government or non-government facilities would have met the need. That too was lacking.

In contrast, we had seen well planned preparation for availing opportunity during the RSP, OCL and related industrial and mineral period. Those days, the mission knew in advance the movement of the Government, anticipated the event and prepared the youth the best way possible for maximum benefit. This was lacking this time.

After seventy years of running, even today education has not risen beyond High School level. Matriculation was an employable degree in 1960s or 1970s, it was not so after that. When requirement rose for post-matric degree, technical expertise and digital excellence, the Mission was found lacking in promoting that. The Mission had no less than fourteen High Schools under the *Catholic Board of Education*, apart from a few English Schools by the year 2000, but for post-matric education, there was nothing other than one independent +2 college apart from the upgraded +2s in English Schools. There wasn't or till now there isn't any Degree College from the Mission to meet the need of Higher Education for the marginalized that we serve. The Mission has left the pursuit half way.

The Pyramid of education system created by the Jesuits where St.Xavier's College, Ranchi, sat at the top, was chopped off on the top when new Gangpur Mission was formed. In the education pyramid of Gangpur Mission, the +2 remained at the top. Literates grew but proportionately educated who would lead the populace toward height were missing. The Mission could not accompany them to the top. For this reason, though tribal population may be high here, people on the top are proportionately less.

Education in the Mission remained just in the academic level. Old industrial schools of Jesuit period had disappeared; and nothing new had been started. Technical training school in Hamirpur and the workshop at Kalunga died down quietly. Dinabandhu 1982, Upaya 1998 were too little too late. By that time the storm of industrialization had passed by. A great miss due to indifferent response!

There was and still is a visible lack of vision and clear road-map to progress. It has been a maintenance mode, where something started way back in the past is routinely maintained and consolidated; it wasn't and still isn't taken to a higher level. Where Graduation and Post-Graduation, technical and digital excellence is the required qualification today, the mission has stuck to academic matriculation and intermediate, and refrained to rise any further. It is stuck on the half way, serving moderate purpose.

Concurrent concerns emerging from industrialization

Ghost of past haunts the present frighteningly. Ghost of some glaring miss and non-involvement of the mission haunts the minds of the people greatly even today. The people of the Mission, who have been accustomed with missionary accompaniment so much, that, when odds are on, they always looks to the missionaries for direction and help. There was a huge issue of Rourkela and Mandaria displacement and resettlement in early 1950s, and simple tribal people did not know how to go about it. These issues were so tragic that they cannot be forgotten so easily.

Simple unsuspecting tribal villagers were just uprooted from their land, loaded and carried on trucks, taken to most inhospitable jungle of Lachda and just dumped there. As the trucks went back, and their touts departed, the people wailed en-mass in that jungle, for, what they were shown as their new house were nothing more than a few lines of thin bamboo sheds. The report of the President, District Displace Persons' Action Committee says the following:

"The tribals were simple and illiterate. They did not know whom to approach for resettlement. Bulldozers came along with big trucks, brought down house roofs with tiles, wood and bamboos together, and loaded them in big trucks. Then the police forcefully loaded the goods, utensils etc., pushed the family members in the truck together with their cows, goats, dogs, cats, chicken etc. The truck reached them to a dense forest (supposed to be rehabilitation colony) about 100 kms away from the RSP. There after unloading them they left. There was absolutely no arrangement for human living. There was no house, no water, no land, no road, no school, no health facility and no electricity. It was absolutely a strange land."[15]

Were the missionaries aware of it? Didn't they have any role to play there? It was about ten years after the SVD had taken over that this tragic thing took place. Displacements were done from three parishes – Kesramal, Jhunmur and Hamirpur where SVD was in-charge. And, Lachda, the horror rehabilitation center was under Kantapali parish, where the SVD was in charge. Did the missionaries know these movements?

Addressing the concurrent concerns emerging out of industrialization was a half-way attitude of the Mission. Industrialization brought in a horde of issues that proved to be great concerns for the people of the districts – land alienation, displacement and resettlement, migration and human trafficking, domestic workers in big cities, demographic deterioration, and cultural degradation etc. All of these were acute in their own right and created devastating effect on the tribal society of the district of Sundargarh.

In response to these concerns, sporadic and lukewarm efforts were seen in the Mission, and till today, there is neither a concrete program nor established structure to deal with them. Even with well defined Characteristic Dimensions, the result is not extraordinary. JPIC, one of the Characteristic Dimensions, is active and is making remarkable contribution, but it is not able to address big issues adequately. There are diocesan effort and there have been some positive results and remarkable success on the way. There are some Religious Congregations that have taken up some burning issues, and have been able to contribute to the wellbeing of the underprivileged.

The post-modern youth, men and women overwhelmed by virtual world, artificial knowledge, IT explosion, social media etc. need a different education, training and motivation. Their perk and prerogative is different, if not higher. At this stage sticking just to the primary academic matriculation doesn't manifest a commitment to a progressive Mission.

Most of the tribal elite, educated in general colleges, have distanced themselves from the common tribal folk in the villages. Their interest has been their own career, job security and affluent living achieved by alleging faithfulness to their Government, Private orCorporate authorities. Gratitude toward the mission and responsibility toward the common folk is basically missing. The elite, educated and employed have not come to the aid of the struggling majority.

Contentment with a little has been another hindrance on the way of progress. Typical unambitious mentality of the tribal is very much in display here. The people themselves too have not longed for anything higher. Excellence and efficiency requires commitment, hard work and perseverance. With a little rise, 'that's enough' mindset has kept the tribal on the half way.

Conclusion
The SVD obtained a great mission field from the Jesuit pioneers. We have done tremendous job maintaining, consolidating and expanding

the mission. Pastoral focus has been praiseworthy. But, we have not raised the mission higher with daring initiative. Opportunities have come our way in great measure, but there have been huge miss all the way. Looking for the same avenues elsewhere, when we were offered on the very threshold, we have been allowed to pass by. There has been hesitation to dare and to spearhead. The world has gained speed, and it is ever changing. Some tested ways, though good, have outgrown their time. When frequent updating of vision, mission, goal and objectives are the order of the day, refraining from them is tragic. Sadly, that is what we are seeing and experiencing in the mission today.

Endnotes

[1] Sacred Return of July 1947-1948.

[2] Severin, Oscar, Gloom and sunshine, Golden Harvest, p.4 (Golden Harvest is the Golden Jubilee souvenir of the undivided diocese of Sambalpur in 1998?).

[3] Fr. Liam Horsefall SVD, late Regional Superior of the then Sambalpur Region, now INE, was emphatic on these reasons.

[4] Returns of Gangpur Vicariate, July 1947 – June 1948.

[5] Waelkens H, Our Schools in Chotanagpur 1910-1925, (Report), Calcutta, April 25, 1910.

[6] Soreng Ignatius, History of the Gangpur Mission, Society of the Divine Word INE, 2008, p.281.

[7] Press Note, Government of Orissa, Industry Department, dt.27.6.1955

[8] Rath S.N. &Behera D.K., Displacement and Rehabilitation: Data from the resettled colonies around the Steel Plant at Rourkela. p.124.

[9] LakshmiranjanMuduli, "What did the people get", Newspaper feature in 'Sambad' daily, 25,........., p.4.

[10] Govt.Doc., Detail DIC-wise information on Large & Medium Industries in the State, June 2005.

[11] Brief Industrial Profile of Sundargarh District, Government of Odisha, 1916-1917.

[12] Center for Environmental Studies, forest and Environment Department, Govt. of Odisha, 2016-2017.

[13] Industrial Policy 1980, Government of Odisha.

[14] Center for Environmental Studies, forest and Environment Department, Govt. of Odisha, 2016-2017.

[15] Letter to the President of India, from the President, Sundargarh District Displaced Personas Action Committee, 18/7/2002 pp.4-5.

The Hegemony of SVD Missionaries through Education:

Revisiting Gangpur Mission and Contemporary Challenges

Nirmal Lawrence SVD

Introduction

Society of the Divine Word or *Societas Verbi Divini* missionaries (SVD's) entered the Gangpur- Sambalpur mission with five parishes handed over to them by the Jesuits in the year 1948 viz., Kesramal, Hamirpur, Gaibira, Junmur and Kusumdegi. After seventy years of its mission work the SVD mission has expanded its wings to about forty-one parishes in Rourkela diocese¹alone and twenty one in Sambalpur dioceses. This mission catered to the spiritual, social, cultural and psychological needs of the Oraon, Kisan, Kharia, and Munda tribes of Rourkela and Sambalpur diocese, and especially to the Dalit community of the Sambalpur diocese. Many people from these groups adopted Christianity as their religion.

In a broader sense, the Mission was meant to bring about the kingdom values of Christ to its people. The values of Christ's teaching were to be shared and propagated by the missionaries. It was mandatory for the missionary to express Christ's philosophy through their life style and preaching. Since mission was always 'Kingdom centred' and the means and methods used by the missionaries were invariably used to attain this end.

By the dawn of 1951 and 1955, industrial activities started in the towns of Rajgangpur and Rourkela respectively, which opened new avenues for development. With the coming of the Rourkela steel plant, mining gained strength along with the building-up of dams within Sundergarh district. Establishment of educational institutions, and innovative future prospects with new-found enthusiasm also began. The SVDs being the only religious congregation for men had ample chance to set up new schools and institutions to educate the tribals. Though there were schools for girls in the diocese run by the women congregations, the SVDs did not have a single one. So, a boys' school was started in 1955, in the western part of Sundergarh district at Gaibira. The new school, named 'New Orissa High School', at Gaibira, added possibilities of education to tribal students from the western part of the diocese. With the beginning of this school, the SVD along with their pastoral ministry also entered into the educational ministry.

As per the record of the school (2016-2017) from Gaibira; in these sixty years of its existence the school has educated around 20,298[2] boys. With the help of the religious missionary congregations, schools for boys in Hamirpur and Gaibira (1955) and St Mary's school for girls in Sundergarh (1950, 1953) and Rajgangpur (1964) many young men and women of Sundergarh district received education. Today, because of these schools there are many who have received employment in various public and private sectors. Thus, education has so far proved to be a fulfilling accomplishment of the mission. Nevertheless, we need to briefly examine if the purpose of education extended by the mission has really benefitted the people.

We propose to examine the purpose of education, pedagogy usage, the results and current situation of schools, concluding with challenges ahead.

I.   Purpose of Education

A.   Education a tool to make *Ek Accha Nagarik*

In the traditional society the process of education was very simple. An individual was usually required to learn from the elders. In today's modern industrial society, the situation has become more complex and difficult. Hence, when one is involved in the activities of the society the individual is expected to learn diverse roles by oneself. Thus, education becomes an activity which goes beyond the boundaries of a school or college.

So, the purpose of education according to the sociological view point is 'to look towards the future, to maintain the process of social control, cultural change and to maintain one's status quo. It is also to have relationship with social class and other groups and to have an impact on the behaviour and personality of an individual who is in the educational system (both teachers and the students) and finally to teach oneself how to socialize in a given society within the peer group' (Ruhela and Vyas, 1970:29 -31). Thus, education must become an instrument in preparing a person to live a peaceful life and letting others live peacefully.

This kind of learning is called moral learning. For Thapan, 'moral education is something that is given by both the family and the school. These are the main agents of the socialization of the young into the norms, values, and beliefs of the society. Society both nourish and sustain the wellness of its people' (Thapan 2000:3715). Thus, moral education given in the schools is called not to be "grounded on petty politics or trivial pursuits", but work for the common good of all. It is an earnest call to be free from 'prejudices, inequality and being insane, but being just and inclusive, firmly based on rational truth (Thapan, 2000:3716).

Such Education acts as an agent of changing a social process and never is a static reality, so that it becomes a culture in itself and plays a major role in teaching culture to children, shaping them, helping them learn new patterns of behaviour and relationship (Jayaram, 2015). This period in life (of an individual) is very important, where one learns about 'counter culture and subversive culture'. Therefore, an essential aspect of education is to make an individual 'a good citizen.' In schools, the notion of citizenship i.e. what constitutes a good citizen or a normative definition of citizenship", 'Ek Accha Nagarik' is given.

B.   Education imparts morality

Therefore, education as a whole is called upon to impart moral values. The collective nature and the essential task of education are to transform an 'individual human being' into a 'moral human being'. According to Bourdieu, "School is both the repository of culture, an institution that gives culture a sacred value and also reproduces it through its practices" (cited in Thapan, 2006:4195). This sacred value is morality. Schools become the primary institutions through which sacred values and norms are simultaneously constituted and reproduced in a student who lives in the society. Therefore, in essence it means, "Creating a system that enables individuals to learn to know, learn to do, learn to live with others and appreciate independence and diversity and above all learn to act with an ever-greater autonomy, judgmental and personal responsibility" (Ramachandran, 2007:3918).

Thus, Schools should not only teach worldly knowledge but try to instil significant social and moral values, such as honesty and civic responsibilities because almost "every activity like, discipline, drill, assembly, rules, uniforms, classroom seating arrangements, obedience, punctuality, cleanliness, tidiness, asking questions for doubts, clearance in the schools are meant for teaching them values both social and moral" (Chopra and Jeffery, 2005:29). This personal morality indeed leads to social stability and national integrity.

C.   Education as a tool to build National integrity

Education has to be a tool in building personal and national integrity so as to win the heart of every citizen. Schools have been seen as centres in building of identities of nationalism and citizenship. It is done through text book syllabus meant to inculcate the idea of patriotism in the students. "Education however, behaves as the primary institution through which values and norms are simultaneously constituted and reproduced in the society. The methodology used in the school is therefore a process of communion through which knowledge and culture are communicated, contrasted, revised and appreciated or challenged" (Thapan, 2003:1450).

Therefore, the whole purpose of education is to impart the 'core values of self-respect, hard work, competition, achievement-orientation, self-discipline, and inclusivism. It prepares students for important roles in the society, helps students to be innovative, and teaches national integrity, social integrity, nationalism, equality, and patriotism, equal reverence for all religions and to think independently and creatively. It stimulates intellectual curiosity and the ability to debate and critically evaluate all systems of knowledge and finally to channelize their resources into a productive enterprise (Abraham, 2006: 183-184).This enhances life.

D.   Education as a tool for preparation for life

Human beings are conscious beings and are in a permanent state of moving towards productive enterprise. So, the purpose of education should primarily be a "preparation for life" where constant relationship with the world and the things in it brings knowledge to us(Neill, 1986:36 reprint). This, interaction with the reality transforms us. Education should indeed behave as an element of transformation which could, 'integrate People with the consciousness of God and that of the community in which one lives, thereby prompting and propagating the perception' of "unity of spirit and spirit of unity" (Mallik, 1961:37).

Therefore, it is very crucial for an individual to fulfil his/her potential to learn things out of everything that one encounters. However, education is more than mere means for learning or earning a livelihood; it involves living a life for oneself and for others. As the human society desires to change or modernize itself, it has to employ or use institutions, agents or agencies and instruments to achieve this desired goal. Thus, education must help us to get rid of or cut down, rationalism, superstition, ignorance, backwardness, and help bring democratization, secularism, national integrity, as well as economic prosperity.

Thus, education should become a tool in preparing an individual to makeup one's life worthy. This worthiness improves the quality of life. The quality of life gives an individual, "not only literacy but enlightenment in all aspects of life. It paves the way for an individual's social mobility" (Sachchitananda, 1979:328), and sustains economic development of the nation' and helps "to make pupil think" (Venkataraman, 2007:3449). Therefore, 'sustainable development becomes the concern of education and not just the one which provides only employment skills' (Visaria, 2014:38).

Thus having discussed the purpose of education, we now move on to critically analyse the methods and means used by the SVD to bring about life in the Gangpur mission through education ministry. A critical analysis is what follows.

II.   Education as a mission by SVD's in Gangpur

As per the present-day statistics stand, the SVDs have ten schools and a junior college of its own and have handed over 50 schools that were started by them, with those 136 schools, to the diocese of Rourkela since its beginning (1948). As a result of this endeavour, jobs and employment opportunities for the educated became possible and through them the growth to the country in its economic, social, political, cultural and spiritual spear of life. The living standard of many tribal members of the four groups (Oraon, Kisan, Munda and Kharia) has also improved. The SVD mission has been the backbone for this transformation in the lives of the tribal members for the past sixty years in the diocese of Rourkela.[3] The SVDs worked in the mission with four-fold dimension of evangelisation. They are, Pastoral cum Biblical apostolate, Education apostolate, JPIC ministry (justice, peace and integration of creation) and Communication apostolate.

However, in using various means and methods to work through the apostolate assigned to them, individual personality and cultural background of the individual missionaries, the cultural aspect of the Christian faith, the atmosphere of the world around, the accepting nature of the people, the passivity and innocence of the people from the mission, the ignorance of the Adivasi about the new faith, the arrogance of having 'the truth' by the Christian missionaries and the cunningness of the other faith followers who lived alongside the Adivasis were some of the reasons that brought about a vast number of change in the lives of the Adivasis. The emergence of a new culture was the fruit that was reaped.

The interaction between the tribals and the missionaries paved the way to bring about changes in the lives of the Adivasis, both positive and negative. The Gangpur mission of the SVDs has contributed economically, spiritually and socially to the growth of the tribals. Yet in the recent times, a kind of identity crisis and moral decline in the lives of the tribals is also observed. We propose to discuss as to why, in spite of education given to them, such things have happened among the Adivasis.

A.   Medium of education through dominant language

The most important aspect of one's identity is one's own mother tongue. It carries, "unique philosophies, folklores, histories, rituals, ceremonies and irreplaceable environmental knowledge of bio-diversity accumulated over a long period of time and it is essential to human heritage. Each and every language embodies the unique cultural wisdom of a people. It unite people, helps generate and evolves a sense of unity among the community. It helps an individual to think, articulate and express one's ideas and feelings fearlessly. It is the only way by which one can express ones being" (Bera, 2015:26-27).But loss of a language is the loss of a knowledge system and life system says the linguistics.

In the above background, we may analyse the teaching methods used in our schools. For example, the medium of instruction for the first-generation learners (or) the first-time school going child led to an uncomfortable zone, where the child found it difficult to relate to its own mother tongue as he/she had to wade through an ocean of a foreign languages.

The knowledge imparted by the teachers in the schools reflects that if the child studies in one particular language alone, that he/she can become a great person in one's future. Therefore, the use of dominant language for education has become the norm. In this condition, the already confused child-finds it difficult to comprehend when the language of teaching is different from its mother tongue and so, denial of one's own language in schools' results in the denial of their culture. So, their "language (of the tribal) dies, something irreplaceable (of theirs) dies. A complete perspective of the (their) world goes away" says Ganesh N. Devy a linguist (Cited in Griffin: 2018:2).This is what happens to the tribal child when he/she is in the school. A tribal child confused with multiple languages somehow copes up with the new situation and learns something new.

In the schools run by the Church and the Government, the medium of instruction is the state language. The students who speak their own mother tongue in the school campus were reprimanded.[4]Such methods were initiated by the Jesuits and were continued by the SVD's. With this a complete perspective of the world of the community died off once the language was lost. This is the truth of Gangpur mission today. Our field study too reveals that many youths of the community hardly know their mother tongue. During our field visit to Kurukh speaking villages, we came across only the elderly people who were using Kurukh in their conversation, while the younger generation was competent in using Oriya or Hindi. The Church run schools have also been an agent to such a situation in Sundergarh district.

Meanwhile, "Knowledge being socially constructed and decisions of inclusion or exclusion of a particular content in the school curriculum has taken place, the organisation and presentation reflect the distribution of power and principle of control of a society in the schools" says Nawani (2018:14). The Church insisted that the medium of instruction shall be either in English or in the state language, perhaps thinking of the future gains at the expense of the loss of the tribal language. When the language of instruction becomes foreign to the students, the knowledge handed over to them is not comprehensible. Analysing a subject becoming difficult, the students just memorise the subjects just to get through. Thus, neither knowledge nor the capacity to critically analyse has been taught in the schools. Thus, the child remains unproductive. He or she just repeats like a parrot. This is the reality in our SVD run schools too. Rote learning has become the only pattern of education now in rural schools.

B.   The Pedagogy at schools

Today, education through text books has become the central pivot around which school education revolves. It constitutes the 'be-all and end-all' of the school learning, the most dependable resource for both the teacher and the student" (Nawani, 2018:12). When this become the fundamental basis for education, rote learning becomes mandatory for getting through and moving ahead. The teachers just try to explain the text books and the student just memorizes the portions for the exam, where intellectual growth takes the back seat in this process of learning.[5] Hence the common pattern of teaching in the school is that the students have to listen and learn whatever the teachers say/teach. The teacher is supposed to be 'all- knowing' and the knowledge he dumps on the students is absorbed by them without even questioning and reproduce it in the exams. Under this system, the capacity and ability of questioning and analysing the facts are not brought out in a child.

Therefore, knowledge or education given to the child is bookish. The books contain knowledge about the world outside and not about the tribal world and its nuances. The contents of the books are designed by a group of elites who hardly know the ground reality of the tribal people. The contents glorify the heroic deeds of some elite group and its heroes and not about the local leaders who fought for the rights of the tribal people.[6] Thus, the cognitive development of the indigenous children and its society has undergone a severe cultural loss. This leaves their lives at cross-roads where they cannot appreciate, but dislike their own culture as a part of their knowledge system (Singh, 2008:512-513 and Tirkey, 1998:16).

Our SVD schools in the Gangpur mission are no exception to this situation. The teachers follow the syllabus prescribed by the government. The children learn what is taught and reproduce it in the exams to go ahead to the next class. The pedagogy and the examination method heavily depend on the government text books which decide what a student should study so as to secure their future. Neither the teacher has the freedom to teach nor does the child have the freedom to learn using its own creativity. Such freedoms are curtailed. Thus, a single way thought process is imposed upon the students and they are branded intelligent, good, average or poor according to the performance in the exam that is conducted keeping the syllabus as the end-all of knowledge production.

The problems involved in this method adoption in educating the tribals are external, internal, socio-economic, cultural and psychological constrains. The external problems originate at the planning level, policy level, and administrative levels. Internally, the problems are associated with the school system, content, curriculum, pedagogy, medium of instruction, teacher-related problems, academic supervision and monitoring. The socio-economic problem involves poverty. Culturally the problems cover the ethos, social customs, lack of understanding and awareness spread, conflict and gap between the home and the school, economic corruption, and mismanagement of money by the facilitators of the schemes. Psychologically, the problem relates to the gap of understanding and intelligence between the tribal and the non-tribal students (Sujatha, 2008:62-68).

With such complications in the implementation of the pedagogy in schools for the tribal groups, one can technically say that development is given far more importance than issues concerning the welfare and interest of the tribes. In fact, more often than not, the goals of national development are at loggerheads with the interest and welfare of the tribes and the interest of the latter are invariably sacrificed in the name of the former" (Xaxa, 2003:387).

III. Result obtained by the Adivasis through Education

With the usage of a single pedagogy and single language in the school teachings, changes become inevitable. Whether this change is for good or for the worse, none of us are able to comprehend. However, every culture having an 'integrated dynamic world view of life, common values which was embodied and transmitted through language, status and role system, mode of behaviour, music and dance through a long tradition either through oral or written literature has the capacity to influence the society today' (Tirkey, 2008:166).But, economic liberalisation, modernisation, globalisation and educational improvements in the 21st century have been affecting the world at large. The Adivasi culture in Gangpur is no exception. In so far as the tribals are concerned, a constant change began to occur in their society, in a rudimentary way from the beginning of the entrance of the Christian missionaries and in a full-fledged way in the wake of Indian independence, mainly due to education, modernisation and industrialisation process and community development programmes.

Having analysed the works done by the SVD's will help us to see the changes that have taken place in their lives. The changes are as follows.

A.   Entry of Alien culture

While the positive results have been stated above, certain negative results have also emerged; for example, a negative attitude of some of the missionaries towards tribal and other faith worshipers. Evangelisation being the main mission of the Christian missionaries, education ministry became an important means and a tool through which they could do evangelisation work. Missionaries taught their religious beliefs and practices to the students in the schools through moral education classes and in the hostels through religious prayers and Eucharistic celebrations. In this process they made the individuals be involved in the prayers, recite them and follow the ritual of the catholic Christian faith, thus leading many tribal members to lose contact with their own religious rituals and faith.

Since education in the mission was given by the missionaries who belonged to an alien culture, they always insisted that the knowledge that they possessed about the world and God was 'the truth' and maintained that the knowledge of the tribal world was only primitive and even false. Thus, the process of ethnocentrism by them led the missionaries to look down upon the cultural aspect of the tribals and insisted that they leave away/abandon even their cultural traits like rituals, nature worship, dancing, singing, playing drums, and the languages they spoke and follow the language and culture of the missionaries 'for better growth and better living.

Secondly, the missionaries considered the tribal worship as pagan and instructed the converted Christian tribals not to practise their older religion and its rituals. This brought about inequalities and divisions within the once united tribal communities. Their actions and words showed little respect to the Hindu and Tribal customs. Padel (2015:206) writes: "evangelical Christianity often has the appearance of a religion of intolerance and hypocritical self-righteousness that could not be further removed from Christ's teaching. The idea that people are either to be saved or damned and that only the true followers of

Christ can be saved, has led many Christians to divide people into 'good' and 'bad' categories, and become completely closed to other spiritual traditions. This is particularly true for missionaries".

To propagate such ideas, the missionaries used schools and hostels. The consequences of the usage of such methods in the field were revealed in our study. The converts considered their own non-Christian tribal brethren as devil worshipers[7]. This has led to exclusion, hatred and division within their own tribal communities. The consequences of such divisions created by the missionaries are very much visible in the Chota-Nagpur area even today.

B.   Singing, Dancing and Music

Singing and dancing gives the whole idea of communitarian attitude, egalitarian concept, unity and joy of a tribal.[8] It was not only the expression of joy but also an expression of conquest over sorrow which they experience in their daily lives (Bose, 1971:74). Xaxa (1999a:1520) says, "Tribes are said to take direct, unalloyed satisfaction in the pleasure of the senses, in such as food, drink, sex, dance and song, whereas caste people maintain certain ambivalence about such pleasure". "It is an intense feeling of pleasure" said Roy (1984:159).It is in this singing and dancing that we get to know them. "Songs are the outlet of their emotions and imaginations; it helps them to easily remember their memories and dance brings out the highest expression of sense of order, rhythm and delight" (Kundu, 1994:68-69). In spite of such beauty, the missionaries insisted that the tribals give up their song, dance and music.

The strict ban over singing, dancing and playing music by the missionaries on the tribal community, in the hostels, schools and villages led the children to forget their songs which carried a lot of oral history and tradition. The present generation hardly knows any single song of their oldest history. While programs are conducted they switch over to recorded songs and dance hearing it. These days there are more onlookers than participants in the dance; something very strange in a tribal community. Such a change is seen mostly among the educated youths because of the influence of the outside world.

According to Didakus' and Mary teacher's[9] version one comes to know, 'that today's boys and girls are not as innocent as we were'. This was a revelation of what Ghurye wrote way back in 1959. He writes, "Aboriginal dancing has sensual associations; it provides the sexes with an opportunity for illicit intercourse" Ghurye (1959:68). The Christian missionaries too considered it to be such and banned them among the Christian converts in the hostels and in the villages. This has led to the vanishing of their expressions of their own history and tradition. The influence of the modern multi-cultural society, the closer presence of technology among the people of the younger age has led from homogeneity to heterogeneity, simple to complex, informal to formal life style among the tribes. This influence has affected the socio-cultural life of the tribes too.[10]Thus, their identity as a different group of people has seen crisis.

C.   Identity crisis

Developmental opportunities have paved the way for a major crisis among the tribes looking for greener pastures and moving out of their country. Then again, the very existence of the Adivasis identity is being threatened by the influence of the non-tribal entrance into the tribal areas through different ways and means. Hence, the Adivasis needs to assert his/her identity for survival as a distinct ethnic and cultural unit within the larger pluralistic Indian society. The essence of their identity expressed through their language, culture and traditions are under threat. In the present times, they are really uprooted from their village community, culture, customs and village structure. Change has occurred for some of them so suddenly that they are not able to keep themselves with their community and its cultural practices.

On the other hand, they are compelled to mix with non-tribals with whom social interaction becomes a matter of necessity (Lakra, 1999:10). In the second half of the twentieth century they have been migrating to cities, towns and other industrial centres, which are a hub of modern economic activities and have posed a threat to their culture. According to Xaxa, "the process of migration and the mixture of people for many decades make us question 'who an indigenous person is'?" (Xaxa, 1999b:3587). Beteille defines migration and its impact on the Adivasi as follows: "we can't simply define a tribe as an isolated, self-contained, primitive or socially homogenous anymore, because today we can find few tribes no more isolated, self-contained, primitive and homogenous. "They have largely been 'incorporated' within the main stream because of their co-habitation with the other members of the country" says Beteille (1998:187). Therefore, the idea of indigenous people needs to be redefined now.

D.   Loss of Mother tongue usage

Due to migration one has lost one's touch with one's Mother tongue. This mother tongue helps us to identify a person's place of residence and his cultural identity. This language embodies the unique cultural wisdom of a people. Therefore, loss of a language is a loss of all humanity" (Jose, 2015:82). Considering the above references of their co-habitation and co-relation with the other cultures, we see that the Adivasis have lost touch with their mother tongue. Not all tribal members speak their mother tongue. For instance, the Oraons of Gangpur mission, who are Christianized, hardly speak Kurukh because of the influence of Oriya, Hindi, English and Sadri.

The Davidian language traditionally associated with the community as their first language is less used in the Gangpur area. Today, more and more of them speak Sadri which is the local variant of Hindi with a large admixture of Mundari, Kurukh, and others. This is a sign that they are losing the purity of their language. Further, Hindi and Sadri in Jharkhand and Chhattisgarh, Oriya, Hindi, and Sadri in Odisha and English in almost all other parts of the country have acquired importance and has taken over as the languages for communication and education. This is not only valued for their utility but also for the status that they confer. So, by and large, today most of the Adivasis write Oriya as their mother tongue in Odisha, which is in itself a pick-up point for the outsider to deny the identity of tribal-hood to them, and which in turn denies them of their basic rights offered to the tribal.

E.   Religion divided the community

Next to one's identity crisis, the acceptance of different religious faiths have brought division within the tribal community. The influence of Christianity and other religions in the area of Chotanagpur has made deep inroads in the tribal society in general. Christianity, Hinduism, Islam, Bhagatism and a few other small religious sects that had contacts with the culture of the tribes divided them from their main trunk. Social differentiation due to religion is seen at various levels in the tribal community. Today, particularly conversion from traditional religion to Christianity has been one of the most marked processes of change. This process is alleged to be primarily responsible for the rupture in the cohesion and solidarity within the tribe (Kujur, 2012:160). Conversion to Christianity widened the gap between the Christianized and the non-Christianized tribal members of the same community (Minz, 2004:149). The Christianized tribals look down upon the 'Hinduized' or the 'Sarna' (nature worshipping Adivasi) and consider themselves as better Adivasis. They also consider the rituals and customs of their kinsmen as devilish. Concept of purity and pollution entered into the tribal system also in the Hinduized Adivasi mind because of the conversions that had taken place. Along with these religious influences emerged divisions in the tribal society.

F.   Inequalities and Exclusion within the community

Schools are supposed to be places where individuals are taught about issues like identity, citizenship and national building. Values of secularism, citizenship and modernization within the class rooms and school premises should have been the end result of education. But research indicates that there is a gender-based ideology and bias still prevailing in school education and it is a danger in itself for the good growth in a country like ours. In an article "Opening the Black Box" Nambissan (2013:93) explains: 'The schools indeed have created and strengthened new inequalities. Such things became a possibility only because of the presence of outsiders (teachers) in the marginalized areas where the teacher looks down upon the environment from where the child comes and even have discussed that the child comes from a Valmiki (monkey) home environment and blamed their uneducated and innocent parents for the child's backwardness'.

Nambissan (2014) reveals that the schools teach inequalities and deprivation to the students in various ways based on class, caste, gender and age in the lives of an individual in our country. These factors promote 'symbolic domination' over culture by the privileged classes. Exclusion in schools was traced to the out pouring dominance of the dominant group/cultural members/policies presence in the tribal areas, especially through the educational field. Their movements, attitudes towards tribal culture and life, their imposing of their cultural value system, their interest in teaching the Adivasis, the methods that they adopted to teach them degrading the tribal value system and using dominant language for teaching has become a stumbling block for the growth of the Adivasis. They mentally overpowered the students with inequality and inserted an inferiority complex in the child's mind (Madan, 2013:136-153).

Thus, the feeling of being an alien in the midst of the crowd in the school and an attitude of cultivating an inferiority complex in the life of an Adivasis child has been till now an outcome of the educational system. This attitude of looking down upon the Adivasis in the schools in terms of social, religious, and cultural entities has led to exclusion. In Gangpur, education has confused, disoriented, and divided people in terms of educated and non-educated, as also in terms of converts and non-converts. Greed, selfishness in terms of economically high and low classes has led to fight for better economic life.

Education which was once considered as a science is now transformed into a business activity. Consumerism and market economy has influenced education. The teachers have lost their autonomy and their professional dignity to consumerism'. Hence, the schools and educational institutions put the secular ethos under strain and create an uneasy feeling among the students and teachers belonging to the minority community. 'Neo liberalization has degraded the way of educating people.

G.   Educational institutes as havens for alcoholism

In this new liberal state of affair of the world, economic status of the tribal is getting better, but consumption of alcohol has influenced the younger generations in the tribal areas. The young students from schools are becoming attracted to drinking. Its effects are also very much visible in the schools that are run by the SVD's. In the recent times, the students (especially many tribal boys) of the schools and colleges have become addicts. How do we see this kind of behaviour among the tribal boys in this area? In general, why has consumption of alcohol risen in the life of the tribal people? Joshi gives us an answer, "When life is so systematically destroyed, when religion, language and culture are suppressed, problems like alcoholism are sure to arise" (Joshi, 1993:16). Such destruction is very much evident among the educated of the Adivasi community in the Gangpur mission. This is what we saw in the foregoing pages.

The above account shows that our educational policies, with a dominant nature, have in a way systematically destroyed the life style, religion, language and culture of the Adivasis. Every culture has a hold on its members. Though drinking is part of the tribal food habit, there was a controlling system within it. For generations, youth of the Adivasis community respected their elders and stuck to the customary laws. However, students in the schools and in the hostels hardly respect or obey their teachers and care takers. They misuse the opportunities given to them for studies to loiter around, wasting time doing unwanted things. Getting used to alcoholic drinks is one among them. Thus, alcoholism has seen its rise in the tribal community, and at a tender age itself they become addicts. The teachers and the missionaries are not in a position to have a control over the youth nowadays. Thus we could see the youth going astray to a large extend.

Conclusion

As a concluding remark we could say that, many authors of tribal studies agree that Christianity was the initial force to motivate tribal people to join formal education activities. Though it was a good move on the part of Christianity, the consequences of this move are very scaring today. The educated tribals are the ones who bring in lot of changes in their lives as Adivasis. Their characters, customs, cultural traits are changing rapidly. "Education has destroyed many traditional practices that were part of the community living, as the missionaries brought in the western individual way of thinking that was detrimental to the community living. Conversion to Christianity widened the gap between the Christian and the non-Christian tribals" says Minz (2004:149).

In an advanced industrial society, education provided by the state as a matter of right for all its citizens has a set of prepared curricula which the students have to follow. This system of education is highly brain oriented, meaning to say 'to memorize and omit, as it is depicted in the text books. Here the students use only their rational mind. Formal education, in the tribal society was different. The young people learned their lessons for life largely from elders and by doing the daily chores with them. Knowledge and skills were usually learnt informally by imitating the elders. Though adults sometimes instructed the young, they did so as part of their everyday routine. Here an individual learns things which are especially pertaining to life. They used their rational mind as well as the intuitive mind to work on with one's life.

When we analyse the above two types of educational systems and compare it with the present situation and its outcome, we may refer to what Albert Einstein said: "The intuitive mind is a sacred gift and the rational mind is a faithful servant. We have created a society that honours the servant and has forgotten the gift". This is very much true because, industrial revolution and economic liberalisation of the world and education which is economy oriented has concentrated mainly on profit and has failed to look into the aspect of feeling and intuition of a human person. Thus, the formal sector of education seems to have been given more emphasis and the informal sector of education which goes beyond schooling is left out.

While the whole world is changing, tribal communities also experience a change in their beliefs, rituals, and socio-cultural, political and economic matters. Though everything may not change at the same speed, one can notice ripples of change that touches every aspect of the lives of not only the learned and sophisticated but also the remotest tribal communities. Nevertheless, without change a society or community will remain fossilized. But over the years many tribal communities have faced tremendous confusion and conflict due to the transition from tradition to modernity. We SVD's also have contributed to this change both positively and negatively.

But, we also agree with Bishop Thomas who laments: "Change is inevitable, uncontrollable. Change is a must and a need. Yet in this process, must all that is precious be thrown over-board as old and out-fashioned? Who will come to the rescue of the tribal soul? Who can salvage at least all that is left of these once glorious traditions? If the protecting of natural resources beneath the soil is so important, and if preservation of song, story, dance, and festivals is equally important, the survival of genuine tribal value is the most important of all." (Menamparampil, 2015:107).

The Challenges for us today
- While we have committed mistakes in the educational process, it is our duty to correct it. How can we restore the corroded cultural identity of the tribals? It is a big challenge.

- We have divided the tribal groups in terms of religion; now uniting them all 'under one fold' for the cause of tribal betterment is a major challenge.

- Curbing alcoholism especially among the youth of the community is the biggest challenge that is in front of us today.

- It is a challenge to work with tribals on an equal footing and not with authority. Can we become servant leaders in a world atmosphere of master-slave, rich-poor, educated-illiterate and work 'with them' rather than 'work 'for them'?

- Can we help the tribal Church in its fight for people's rights by involving ourselves in politics?

- It is a challenge to start a Degree college to uplift the poorest of the poor from the tribal community;

- It is also a challenge to provide computer education and provide job opportunities within their territory, so that they do not migrate from their places;

- "It is difficult to change the teaching strategies and methods besides introducing tribal languages in the school curriculum;

- It is quite challenging to give importance to and with a renewed focus on tribal culture, and finally,

- It is a challenge to develop vocational training and skills among the tribal children" (Jojo, 2013).

Endnotes

[1] Today the SVD's are in charge of only seven parishes. Remaining 34 parishes are handed over to the diocesan clergy of the Rourkela diocese.

[2] From the New Orissa High School register, Gaibira.

[3] Soreng. Ignatius, "Indian East Province", in Kanjamala. Augustine,(ed.,), (2007:175).

[4] Didakus Beck, a tribal from the village of Lulkidhi from Sundergarh district of Orissa, narrated: "In our schools/ hostels we were not allowed to

speak our mother tongue. The one who was caught speaking their mother tongue was compelled to carry a placard around his neck reading *"Kurukh (or one's mother tongue) bathe karne wale Gadha hai" (the one who spoke Kurukh (their mother tongue) is a donkey)*. This made us to be very cautious not to speak in our mother tongue because carrying the placard on our necks was so disgusting and embarrassing. This kind of treatment even in the schools run by our missionaries actually made us to think twice about using our mother language for conversation. This finally led us not to express ourselves in our language. We were afraid of expressing our oral traditions and our culture, as we were afraid of their punishment."

[5] As a teacher I myself have observed such a pedagogy usage in our college in Gaibira.

[6] In Orissa teaching the history of Oriya freedom fighters to Adivasi and failing to give an history about their own tribal leaders who fought for freedom is what we enumerate here, for example; teaching a tribal about Gopubandu Das than Birsa Munda (who is a tribal leader) is like teaching somebody else's history and asking one to memorise and obtain knowledge.

[7] Villagers from Busurdumi, Gadatoli of Lulkidhi ward from the Balisankara block of Sundargarh district, Orissa, expressed this point when there was a meeting with the Abba's and Aayo's (Fathers and mothers) group discussion during the field study of my PhD studies.

[8] But now-a-days in the villages and in the tribal communities we do see many boys and girls, men and women becoming more an onlooker than a participant in the dance. The researcher has ever heard a few of them saying, it is boring and not interesting to sing and dance.

[9] Interviewed Didakus on 20/08/2016 and Mary teacher on 20/07/2016 respectively.

[10] Today many young members of the community don't like to express their cultural traits through dance and singing. We also find hardly any young boy or a girl play their tribal instruments during festivals and cultural programs. We always see tribal youth dance according to the recorded songs with a worldly meaning in it. Such songs are played in the school and college cultural programs, to which the young boys and girls dance with a modified silo dance.

Bibliography

Abraham, Francis. (2006), "Contemporary Sociology: An Introduction to Concepts and Theories", New Delhi: Oxford University Press.

Bera, Gautam Kumar, (2015), "Endangered Paradigms in Indian Society", in, Bera, Gautam Kumar and Jose. K. (ed.,), "Endangered Cultures and Languages in India", Guwahati: Spectrum Publications, pp. 24-30.

Beteille. Andre, (1998), "The Idea of Indigenous People", Current Anthropology, Vol, 39. No. 2, Pg. 187-191.

Bose, Nirmal Kumar. (1971), "Tribal Life in India", New Delhi, National Book Trust.

Chopra, Radhika and Patricia, Jeffery. (ed.,), (2005), "Educational Regimes in Contemporary India", New Delhi, Sage Publications.

Ghurye, G.S. (1959), "The Scheduled Tribes", Bombay, Popular Press Private Ltd.

Griffin, Peter. "All Others: Two words that changed my life", in 'The Hindu", March 11, 2018, Pg. 1-8, Mumbai Edition.

Jayaram, N, (2015), (2nd (ed.,), "Sociology of Education in India", Jaipur: Rawat Publications.

Jojo, Bipin. (2013), "Decline of Ashram Schools in Central and Eastern India: Impact on Education of ST Children" In Social Change, Vol. 43, No. 3, Pg 377-395.

Jose, K. (2015), "Cultures with Special Reference to Language Vibrancy and Endangerment: A Scenario from North East India", in Bera, Gautam Kumar and Jose. K. (ed.,), "Endangered Cultures and Languages in India", Guwahati: Spectrum Publications, Pg. 82-90.

Joshi, Sharmila. (1993), "Life on the Rez", in "The Illustrated Weekly of India", Feb. 20-26, Bombay, Bennett Coleman.

Kanjamala, Augustine (ed.,), (2007:175), "History of the Divine Word Mission in India: 1932-2007", Indore, Sat Prachar Press.

Kujur, Joseph Marianus. (2012), "Christian and Tribals: The Dynamics of Schedule Tribe Status in the Field", In "Minority Studies", (ed.), Rowena, Robinson. New Delhi, Oxford University Press.

Kundu, Manmatha. (1994), "Tribal Education: New Perspectives", New Delhi. Gyan Publications.

Lakra, Christopher. (1999), "The New Home of Tribals", Faridabad, Haryana, Om Publications.

Madan, Amman, "Does Education Really Change Society? Theoretical Reflection on a Case Study", in Nambissan and Rao. (2013), "Opening Up the Black Box: Sociologist and the Study of Schooling in India", New Delhi: Oxford University Press.

Mallik, Gurdial. (1961), "Gandhi and Tagore", Ahmedabad, Navajivan Publications House.

Menamparampil, Thomas, "Weakening of tribal cultures: Threats to ethical values", in Bera, Gautam Kumar and Jose, K. (2015), (ed.,), "Endangered Cultures and Languages in India", Guwahati, Spectrum Publications.

Minz, C. Vijay. (2004), "Oraon Culture and Christianity" in "Tribes in Transition: Indian Christian Reflection on the Original Inhabitants of the Land", F. Hrangkhuma, Kothanur, (ed.,), Bangalore, SAIACS Press.

Neill, A.S. (1986 reprint) "Summerhill: A Radical approach to child Rearing", England: Penguin books.

Nambissan, Geeta. (2013), "Opening the Black Box: Sociologist and the Study of Schoolings in India", In. Nambissan. G and Srinivasan Rao, (ed.,), "Sociology of Education in India", New Delhi: Oxford University Press, Pg. 83-102.

Nambissan, Geeta. (2014), "Sociology of School Education in India: A review of research 2000-2010", in "Development and Change", by Yogendra. Singh, (ed.,), "Indian Sociology", Vol. 2, New Delhi, Oxford University Press.

Nawani. Disha, (2018), "Modifying School Text Books: Disregarding Children's Experience", in Economic and Political Weekly, July 21, Vol. LIII, No. 29, Pg 12-15.

Padel, Felix. (2015), "Sacrificing People: Invasions of a Tribal Landscape", New Delhi, Orient Black Swan.

Ramachandran, Vimala. (2007), "The Great Number Race and Challenge of Education", Economic and Political Weekly, September, 29, Vol. 42, No. 39, Pg. 3917-3919.

Roy, Sarat Chandra. (1984), "The Oraon's of Chotanagpur: Their History, Economic life and Social Organization", Calcutta: The Brahmo Mission Press. (Reprint).

Ruhela, S.P and Vyas. K.C., (1970), "Education and Social change: A Sociological Analysis", In "Sociology foundation of Education in Contemporary India," Delhi: Dhanpat Rai and Sons.

Sachchidananda. (1979), "The Changing Munda", New Delhi: Concept Publishing Company.

Singh, Deoranjan Kumar and Mahendra, Kumar Mishra. (2008), "Addressing the Marginalized Tribal Children: Multilingual Education in Odisha", in Najunda, D.C. (et al.), (ed.,), "Ignored Claims: A Focus on Tribal education In India", Delhi, Kalapaz Publication, Pg. 509-538.

Soreng, Ignatius, "Industrial Violence in the Sundargarh District of Orissa, India and the Struggle of the Tribal people for Survival", In, Gesch, F. Patrick (ed.,), (2009), "Mission and Violence: Healing the Lasting Damage", Madang, DWU Press.

Sujatha, K. (2008), "Education among the scheduled tribes in India: some observations", in Najunda, D.C. (et. al.), (ed.,), "Ignored Claims: A Focus on Tribal education In India", Kalapaz Publication, Delhi. pp. 53-77.

Thapan, Meenakshi. (2000), "Moral education in the contemporary World", Economic and Political Weekly, Oct. 14. Vol. 35. No. 42. pp. 3715-3716.

Thapan, Meenakshi. (2003), "Pedagogy and the Future Citizen", Economic and Political Weekly, April. 12, Vol. 38, No. 15, pp. 1450.

Thapan, Meenakshi. (2006), "Docile bodies, Good citizens or agential subjects? Pedagogy and citizenship in contemporary society", Economic and Political Weekly, Sep.30, Vol. 4, No. 39, pp. 4195- 4203.

Tirkey, Agapit. (2008), "Cultural Change among Tribals and Christian Response in Chotanagpur", in S.M. Michael and Chittatukalam, (ed.,), "Cultural Challenges in Christian Mission: In the 21st Century", New Delhi, Pub: CBCI Commission of Education and Culture, Media House.

Tirkey, Livinus. (1998), "Tribals: Their Languages and Literature", Ranchi, Don Bosco Publishers.

Venkataraman, Geeta. (2007), "Teaching Students to Think", Economic and Political Weekly, August, Vol. XLII, No. 34, pp. 3449-3451.

Visaria, Leela. (2014), "Population, Education and Development", Economic and Political Weekly, November-8, Vol. 49, No. 45, pp. 38-43.

Xaxa, Virginius, (1999a), "Transformation of Tribes in India: Terms and Discourses", Economic and Political Weekly, June, Vol. 34, No. 24, pp. 1519-1524.

Xaxa, Virginius, (1999b), "Tribes as Indigenous People of India", Economic and Political Weekly, Dec, 18, Vol. 34, No. 51, pp. 3589-3595.

Xaxa, Virginius, (2003), "Tribes in India", in Das, Veena, (ed.,), "The Oxford India Companion to Sociology and Social Anthropology", New Delhi, Oxford University Press, pp. 333-408.

Revisiting The Mission Called 'Me':

Towards A Paradigm of Greater Authenticity

Dixson Lawrence D'Souza SVD

Introduction

Mission had its relevance at every moment of Church history when the authenticity of the Gospel was murdered at the onslaught of various philosophies, heresies, socio-political-religious developments, and contradictions between the Gospel preached and the Gospel lived. After the vocation and consecration of Israel and the prophets and the example of the early Christian community, 'Mission' makes God's reign visible and tangible at every epoch. Today, authenticity in mission is at its lower ebb. Increasing complexity of ecclesiastical structures, cut-throat criticisms, escalating scams, decline in the number of vocations, and a tendency for comfort culture leads to 'mission buffering' causing authenticity in mission enter into the category called "endangered species". The evolution of the understanding of Mission over the years has shifted from 'doing' without to 'being' within: from *missio ad gentes*, to the popular phrase by Pope Francis "I am Mission", leading to the prophetical announcement of the 18th SVD General Chapter, "Our Name is our Mission". When the anti-Christian structures of our country try to damage every fibre of our mission we all get deeply engrossed only in tackling these challenges *ad extra* while forgetting the challenges *ad intra*. Thus emerges amidst all challenges a dire need to revisiting the mission called 'me'.

Today when authenticity in mission is at stake, this paper, having clarified the concepts of mission and the spectra of authenticity down the Church's history presents *imago dei, missio-dei,* and *imitatio Christi* as the fount and foundation of mission for all times, ages, and seasons. Revisiting the mission called 'me' provides a critique over the 'pseudo-authenticity' of mission in our times. The counter-cultural movements, the poverty movements and the Beguine movement of the past emerge as symbols of prophetic authenticity of their times. "We live in a time when much is collapsing and new things must be established in their place."[1]This prophetic conviction of St. Arnold Janssen[2] inspires to spell out how one can embark on a paradigm for greater authenticity. With the Apostolic Letters and Exhortations of Pope Francis to all Consecrated People at its background, revisiting the mission called 'Me' primarily demands an authentic spirituality, an authentic consecration, the establishing of an authentic fraternity and prophetic witness as its hallmark. This paper doesn't provide a 'quick-fix' solution rather serves as an invitation for progressive metamorphosis towards greater authenticity.

1.   Evolution of the Concept of Mission

1.1.   *Imago Dei-Missio Dei-Imitatio Christi:* The Fount and Foundation of Mission

Mission lies in the triple progressive metamorphosis from *Imago Dei* to the realisation of *Missio Dei,* which comes to its completion through *Imitatio Christi,* all of which form part of a continuum. We are created in the image and likeness of God (Gen 1:27) and this is our stated authenticity that we all come from God bearing Himself and His Mission in us, the mission of liberation and sanctification. "The mission of the disciples, the mission of the Church, is to continue this mission of God by prolonging the logic of Jesus' mission in a creative, courageous, and credible way"[3], especially by making "the characteristic features of Jesus-the chaste, poor and obedient one... constantly visible in the midst of the world"[4] The self-emptying of Christ is meant to be a model for imitation rather than a proposition for theological debate...The phrase 'to empty himself' is...a metaphor that holds up a compelling example... From the manger to the cross, the life of Jesus was consistently a life of service.[5]Amidst difficulties and distortions in diverse historical circumstances, there has been a deep-rooted conviction throughout the history of Christianity that "following the way of Jesus is an integral aspect of mission, proof of its authenticity, and the test of missionary faithfulness."[6]

1.2.   Mission down the Church's History

1.2.1 *The Early Christian Community of the First Three Centuries*
The first century took Christianity to the Roman Empire while in the second century Christianity encouraged intellectual exchange between Christianity and Greek culture. The third century Christianity was perceived as a threat to the Greco-Roman society and to the unity and integrity of the empire. Hence, organised empire-wide persecutions against Christians began.The best way to *imitatio Christi* amidst persecutions was 'martyrdom'.

Theologically speaking the Church is Jesus Community, where people responded to the coming of the Kingdom of God in their lives and allowed themselves to be totally transformed beyond cultural barriers. The most important characteristic of Jesus Community was its understanding that they were to continue the mission of Jesus by proclaiming the Kingdom to all cultures, by its *kerygma, koinonia* and *diakonia.*

1.2.2. *Centuries following the Edict of Milan*
With the conversion of Constantine in 312-313A.D., Christianity became the state religion of the Roman Empire.[7] Martyrdom was no longer the perfect way to imitate Christ as there were no longer persecutions. The fifty century Christianity encountered the Germanic tribes while the Church of Persia declared its independence from the rest of Christendom. The sixth century witnessed the Germanization of Christianity. The monks proved to be great missionaries. Under

the control of the Persian Church, Christianity got firmly rooted in various parts of South-Asia like the multicultural India and SriLanka. However, internal contradictions, power struggles, ideological differences, economic and political interests and other factors did not help the full realisation of the Christian vision of life.[8]

The civilisation of the West was closely knotted with the escalation of Christianity. Christian vision of life began to consistently percolate the social, legal, political and other aspects of life leading to an inculturated Christian life in the Western world.

1.2.3. *The Era of Colonialism: The West to the Rest*

The fourteenth century marks the time when the Western Church came in contact with the Christians in India for the first time when European missionaries, travellers and merchants flooded India. Prominent among them are Marco Polo, John of Monte Corvino, the first Franciscan archbishop of Peking, the Dominican Jordan Catalani who was instrumental in the founding of the first Latin diocese in India, the diocese of Kollam (1329), Blessed Odoric of Pordenone (1324), and John of Marignolli (1346).

The fifteenth century is marked by two significant events: the fall of Constantinople (1453) and with it the end of East-Rome and the geographical explorations of the Iberian powers Spain and Portugal and the beginning of the modern mission through colonisation. When the fall of Constantinople blocked the arrival of spices in Europe, the exploration of America by Columbus (1492) and India by Vasco da Gama (1498) marked the opportunity for colonisation and Christianization. The Treaty of Tordesillas of 1494 by Alexander VI provided ample opportunities for intercultural mutuality, reciprocity and dialogue. Missionary movement in Latin America and Asia continue even in the sixteenth century amidst reformation and Catholic reforms. The theology that propelled Christian missionary spirit as proposed by John Sepulved contained three premises: Right to Conquer, Right to Subjugate, Right and the duty to humanise. Except

European culture all the rest were primitive and barbaric. Therefore, the missionary method followed was implantation of European culture "European Implantation" uprooting the culture existing in the area (Hyspenisation).

In the East, the sixteenth century laid the foundation for the modern western mission in India, Japan and China under the leadership of Portugal. St. Francis Xavier's (1506-1552) name will ever remain unwashed in the coasts of India, Japan and China. The mission pattern of Discovery-Conquest-Annexation-Mission led to the capture of Goa followed by the Christianisation of Goa through inter-racial marriages and the rigour of mercy caused the destruction of temples and prohibition of Hindu practices. The Portuguese also came into contact with: the *paravas* of Tamil Nadu (1536-37), the Thomistic Christians of Kerala (that instigated the Latinization of the Thomas Christian community), and the Mughal emperor Akbar (1580, 1591, 1595) which marked the encounter of Christianity and mission in North India.

With British colonialism in India, missionary activities again gained impetus. This century is remembered for the missionary contributions towards the development and enrichment of Indian languages and culture. Notable among them are Joseph Constantius Beschi (1680-1747) for his contribution to Tamil literature, John Ernst Hanxleden (1681-1732) for his contribution to Malayalam literature, and Gaston Coeurdaux (1711-1799) who is credited for the discovery that Greek, Latin and Sanskrit have a common source. Thus Christian message began to get localised. The nineteenth century was the century of missionary extension chiefly by the Protestants. Mission and colonialism were synonymous. The East India Company gave freedom to the missionaries. Many mass movements to Christianity from the dalit and tribal communities in South India, in Chotanagpur, in the North-eastern states were noteworthy. A Church of inculturation and cross-cultural movements were characteristics following these mass movements.

The present day Christianity and the universalization caused by it along its establishment as like a corporate sector with structures, systems, philosophies and theologies is the product of many a century of intercultural interpretation of the gospel within the European and the mid-Eastern background. Western Christianity, in fact, by its political and economic power invaded many of the so-called mission countries and to a great extent denigrated the indigenous people, their language, culture and religion,[9] with some exceptions as noted above who contributed, though in small pockets, to inculturation and accommodation. Expressing his discontentment with the colonial Church, Kuncheria Pathil says:

> Conquest mentality of the colonial powers, superiority complex of the Western European culture and its technological civilization, total ignorance of the value of the cultures and religions of other peoples, lack of insufficient number of local clergy, and ecclesiastical rule exclusively by foreign bishops, all these factors effectively prevented the dialogue and inculturation during this period.[10]

1.2.4. *The Adaptation Mission Model*

The adaptation method of mission was recommended by the Jesuit visitator to the East, Alessandro Valignano that led Matteo Ricci (1552-1610) and Michele Rugieri (1543-1607) to begin a mission based on originality, adapting Christianity to Chinese culture, attracting the attention of the intelligentsia of China. From 1639 the 'Chinese rites controversy' began as Matteo Ricci adapted practices especially the Confucian practice of ancestor worship and the use of Chinese in the liturgy. But Pope Benedict XIV in 1742 prohibited the Chinese rites.

The adaptation method was also followed by the Italian Jesuit Robert de Nobili (1577-1656) who having reached India in 1606 began adapting Christianity to the culture of the high caste Hindus of Madurai. Fr. De Nobili is remembered and widely admired even today for his willingness to adopt Indian customs of dress, food and manner of living, his learning Hindu philosophy and theology, and his determination to show that the Christian faith could be taught and lived in a truly Indian way no longer defined by European cultural values.[11] De Nobili allowed the Brahmin converts to practise some of their social customs like wearing the sacred thread, keeping the *kudumi* (tuft of hair), taking ritual baths, use of the *tali* by women at marriage etc. De Nobili called himself a seer who had come to teach them the "lost" *Veda*. The high caste Brahmins believed that there were five *Vedas* of which one was lost. He equated Bible to the "lost" *Veda* and invited the Brahmins for discussions. De Nobili's critics said: "He incorporates Hindu purifications and rites into Christian liturgical practices; he changes the words of liturgical worship; he gives the impression that his religion is different from that of the other Fathers."[12]

His method proved exceedingly productive. This adaptation termed as 'Malabar rites controversy' was banned by Pope Benedict XIV in 1744. Thus Matteo Ricci and Robert de Nobili emerge as the fine examples for interculturality in the seventeenth century.

1.2.5. *Church before the Second Vatican Council*

The Mission theology operative before the Second Vatican Council basically had two motives: Firstly, the Catholic Church focused on the salvation of souls. Church was considered to be a ship (or ark) in the troubled waters of this sinful and chaotic world. It saw itself as bringing God in a unidirectional movement to people in a lost world and bringing the baptised Catholics safely on board the "ark of salvation". This can be known as the "Ship (Ark) Mission Model". Secondly, the institution of the visible presence of the Church which well thought-out its Western outline as normative and non-Western cultures as inferior. Understanding of mission or 'missions' was in terms of a geographical territory i.e., 'the mission somewhere-out-there'- a situation of primitive status that needed to go through a process of civilisation and humanization.

1.2.6. *Church after the Second Vatican Council: From Western to Universal*

The Second Vatican Council demonstrates a change of the Church's attitude i.e., "a Universal Church, a Church from every nation and a Church for this world."[13] The Church shifted its focus to dialogue and participation. Today's Church professes the universal salvific Will of God (1 Tim 2:4) without which, "the proclamation and mission of the Church make no sense anymore; because the Church stands for the prevenient, unreserved and liberating love of God for all humankind."[14] Church thus bases all its missionary enterprise on *Missio Dei* and recognised the presence of the Word beyond all barriers.

1.2.7 *Intercultural Theology: The Missiology for the Global Age*

Today, the mission of the Church in a pluralistic world is understood as to build bridges between different peoples, nations, religions, ideologies and cultures so that people can cross over to the other side and create mutual understanding, appreciation and acceptance and thus to create a community of communities. The CBCI comments, "Given the pluralistic fabric of the Indian society we need to recognise a pluralistic approach to mission, the paths of interreligious dialogue, liberation of the poor, transformation of the society according to the values of the Gospel."[15]

It is important to remember that the missionary movement was one of the earliest forces that created global networks and new media of communication that were no less powerful than those established by the markets and information technology of the twentieth century.[16] Interculturation recommends a theological and anthropological interface that requests greater inclusivity and interdependence among diverse religious perspectives and secular cultural viewpoints for human well-being ubiquitously in the world. Thus, "there is a dialogical dialectic between faith and culture within a paradigm of authentic Interculturation,"[17] which calls to redefine missiology as intercultural theology with emphasis on mutuality, reciprocity, humility, dialogue, transformation, and liberation of people of all cultures.

1.3. Mission down the SVD History

Mission of the SVDs, until the 18th General Chapter, was understood as a triple combination of *missio ad gentes* (to the nations), *missio inter gentes* (among the nations) and *missio cum gentibus* (among the peoples). Thus our mission is "dialogue WITH people ...encounter BETWEEN people...finding a home AMONG the people."[18] *Missio ad gentes* marked the first phase of evangelisation. Geographical expansion was the primary focus of this missionary stage accompanied by an attitude of going out that moved with great impetus, present in Peter and Paul, the early apostles and the men and women disciples.[19] *Missio ad gentes* basically meant going out to the 'gentes' of a particular geographical situation that was termed as 'mission' or 'missions'. Thus 'gentes' didn't include anyone else; just the people of that set up in which a mission centre was established. The decree *Ad Gentes* reminded "to get out of the castles, towers and Cathedrals and go to the people most in need."[20] From 1982 until 2000, the SVDs in the spirit of *ad gentes* reached out to many countries in Latin America, Africa and Asia. Thus countries were termed as 'mission-sending' and 'mission-receiving'.

The SVD General Chapter 2000 states, "Our discussions in the Chapter have confirmed that our understanding of *ad gentes* mission has shifted from an exclusively geographical orientation to one that includes missionary situations."[21] Fr. Antonio Pernia, the former SVD Superior General has noted how *missio ad gentes* can no longer be identified exclusively with *missio ad extra*. For the 'gentes' are no longer only those who are out there...Often the 'gentes' are also here among us and around us.[22] The 'gentes' may be the family next door, the one beside me in the bus, the person who comes to fix my television, the woman in the market who I buy vegetables from.[23] Mission thus is found in the '*inter*', i.e., the space between what is familiar and different, between unity and diversity, and between the global and the local. Through the incarnation the Word came to dwell among us. But the Word came with the message that "God is with us, to deliver us from the darkness of sin and death, and to raise us up to eternal life."[24] In that space between sameness and difference we are called "to witness to deliverance from the darkness of sin and death, and there lies an important aspect of the prophetic dimension of *missio inter gentes* where at times we are called to take a stand that is not only different from but decidedly contrary to the status quo."[25]

The mode into which mission was switched on to is *missio cum gentibus*, mission *with* the people. Strengthening the dimension 'cum gentibus' (with the people) would help us to be closer to their everyday problems and find the exit door to overcome their existential, economic and social burdens.[26] Fr. Heinz Kuluke, the SVD Superior General, evaluating the present scenario writes:

> Today, one can say an *inter gentes* (among), and *cum gentibus* (with) approach show the way to be effective. Thus, we are called to learn from and collaborate with and among people to bring justice and peace. Here, there is mutual conversion of heart and mind and transformation. People and the missionaries are transformed, and the people of God realise that God is present and loves all.[27]

As missionaries, we experienced many times that our feet lead us to geographical places that we had never imagined to be, but this is not enough, it is necessary to use the head, heart and hands for evangelisation to be truly effective.[28] This is the mission conviction with which Fr. Kuluke defines *missio cum gentibus*. Here the 'gentes' are "not just the object of mission, but also are potential partners in mission."[29] Mission is never a one-way traffic as of old but a dialogue whereby both the gentes and the missionaries collaboratively respond to the challenges of the times, work towards solving the problems enlightened by the Word, enrich one another through a life of prayer and works of commitment thereby journey together towards the new heaven and new earth .

The 18th SVD General Chapter came out with quite a prophetic announcement- "Our Name is our Mission". This slogan that captured the imagination of all the Capitulars in its original form was "Our Name is our Agenda" which along the General Chapter progressed to be as "Our Name is our Identity". The General Chapter theme, "The Love of Christ impels us' (2 Cor 5:14): Rooted in the Word, Committed to His Mission" and the objective to cultivate a process of a spiritual rekindling, bringing us back to the Word of God as the font of our life, vocation, mission and our religious missionary commitment, invites every SVD to move from *missio ad extra* to *missio ad intra*, from *'missio ad gentes'* to *'missio est nomen nostrum'*. That's a prophetic move from 'without' to 'within'.

1.4. The Mission called 'ME'

Pope Francis as a Spirit-impelled visionary missiologist with a combination of simplicity and humility envisioned the Church as a "missionary disciple,"[30] a person than a complex structure who must go in search of the least, the last, and the lost, to the peripheries and to the ostracised, nourished by the light and strength of the Holy Spirit rather than "a Church which is unhealthy from being confined and from clinging to its own security"[31]. Mission thus is to have shoes with the dust of people's joys and sufferings. Without the usage of any generic terms and phrases or repeating the wisdom of the past, Pope Francis exemplifies mission:

> My mission of being in the heart of the people is not just a part of my life or a badge I can take off; it is not an "extra" or just another moment in life. Instead, it is something I cannot uproot from my being without destroying my very self. *I am a mission* on this earth; that is the reason why I am here in this world. We have to regard ourselves as sealed, even branded, by this mission of bringing light, blessing, enlivening, raising up, healing and freeing.[32]

Mission symbolised in and through 'the washing of the feet' as per Pope Francis conveys that authentic power is service after the example of Jesus who "bathed filthy, dust-covered feet that might have been flecked with trace of human or animal waste."[33] Mission is neither a product of one intellect nor a commodity to be traded upon for one's profit instead an ingrained identity as "evangelizers fearlessly open to the working of the Holy Spirit... proclaim the good news not only with words, but above all *by a life transfigured by God's presence*."[34] Mission is not a time-bound compartmentalised activity rather we are called to be "permanently in a state of mission."[35]

2.   Revisiting the Mission called 'ME': An Authentic Prowl

Derived from the late Latin *authenticus* (principal) and the corresponding Greek *authentikos* (genuine), authenticity means entitled to obedience and respect and as "original, really proceeding from its stated source."[36] Authenticity lies in living the crystal clear knowledge of what one is, from where one is and for what one is without any camouflage. A life devoid of any dichotomy, of interior freedom expressed through a transparent life lived in the light is the essence of authenticity.

2.1.   The Challenges to the Mission called 'ME': A Critique over the Pseudo-Authenticity of Mission in the Present

Pope Francis invites all consecrated men and women "to live the present with passion,"[37] and posses few questions: "... are we open to being challenged by the Gospel; whether the Gospel is truly the manual for our daily living and the decision we are called to make."[38] Is Jesus really our first and only love, as we promised he would be when we professed our vows?[39] Are our ministries, our works and our presence consonant with what the Spirit asked of our founders and foundresses?[40] Do we have the same passion for our people.... understanding their needs and helping to respond to them?[41]

Collectively speaking (with a very few exceptions), crisis that has gripped mission today with struggles in discerning whether the call is really religious or blatantly secular is on the increase. The salt seems to have begun to lose its saltiness and mission its authenticity. Joan Chittister talks about a spirituality crisis among religious-"a crisis of meaningfulness and relevance".[42] Donald Senior says, "Diminishing of numbers, uncertainly about the future, a low-grade depression that suppresses hope on the part of many religious, put people in a survival mode."[43] Jacob Parappally confused over the way mission is presently lived exclaims:

3.   Over institutionalisation of the foundational charism, transformation of apostolates into well-structured, rigid, complex, secure, comfortable and often profit-making services like that of secular agencies and even competing with them, worldly values of struggle for power, domination, unhealthy competition, misuse of the means of communication for spreading information and even calumnies about the members of the same religious institutes and others, the dwindling number of vocations to religious life etc,. are some of the symptoms of a crisis in consecrated life. Unfortunately, the religious women and men are called to transform the world into God's Kingdom are being transformed by the world. Those who are called to renounce everything to follow Jesus radically are accused of following "moneytheism" than monotheism.[44]

2.1.1. *Syndromes causing Mission Buffering*

The medical term syndrome *means a combination of symptoms* and signs that together represent a disease process. It would not be an exaggeration to conclude that the mission called 'Me' is in such a disease process today because it vehemently exhibits a host of syndromes and relating symptoms.

2.1.1.1. *The 'Busy Bee' Syndrome:*

This syndrome has the following symptoms: (a) The *'busy-life symptom'* that has filled our days with activities but our hearts unfulfilled which leads "to boredom, resentment and depression"[45] (b) The misleading *'work is worship symptom'* has stolen away spiritual exercises and *lectio divina.* (c) The *'workaholic symptom'* with no time for spiritual silence has given birth to more 'Marthas' over 'Marys'. These symptoms have rendered 'Word-Centered Spirituality', our foundational character, dysfunctional.

2.1.1.2. The 'Touch-Me-Not' Syndrome

This syndrome is exhibited in and through the following symptoms: (a) The '*hostel symptom*' thathas converted many communities as boardings and lodges. (b) The '*wrestlemania symptom*'that has given vent to conflicts, misunderstanding, indifference, and vengeance turning communities as fighting than fraternal, building borders than bridges and creating fissions than fusions. (c) The '*One-Man Show symptom*'that has ruptured communities, bred individualism, and prioritised personal success and vain glory over the mission mandate. If that mandate is ignored...you then cease to be a Gospel leader and have joined the secular band- an ugly caricature.[46] (d) The '*I am ok-you are not ok symptom*' that has created missionaries to whom without license one can't approach, who are more complex than mathematical theorems, and who claim superiority in culture, attitudes, and decisions . These have rendered 'Transforming Missionary Discipleship', 'Embracing Interculturality',and 'Journeying Together' with members of Arnoldus Family and Lay partners dysfunctional.

2.1.1.3. The 'Acedia' Syndrome:

The *Oxford Concise Dictionary of the Christian Church* defines acedia (or accidie) as "a state of restlessness and inability either to work or to pray."[47] Acedia is a sickness of the soul that is expressed in boredom, distaste for prayer, slackening or abandoning one's penitential practices, neglecting the heart, and indifference toward the sacraments.[48] This syndrome is exhibited thus: (a) The '*Schizophrenic symptom*' that has caused dichotomy in terms of what one says and what one is or acts, where congruence seems a myth, hoarding a passion, and exhibitionism, a power increasing mechanism. (b) The '*Gossip symptom*' "a sin against the foundational commandment of the Gospel to love others as God loves them"[49] that has turned many missionaries into cold-blooded murderers. (c) The '*Talking Tom Symptom*' where one's actions are neither an outcome of an integrated personality nor a product of discernment rather just a mere fulfilment of another's demand or command. This syndrome with all such symptoms transforms missionaries into mummies in a museum.

2.1.1.4. The 'Band-Aid' Syndrome

Band-Aid Syndrome is made visible through: (a) The *'Impatience Symptom'* that grips mission 'Me' to seek for instant gratification, runs away from challenging human and geographical situations, remains sluggish in terms of taking initiatives, and adheres to quick-fix solutions. (b) The *'Maintenance Mode Symptom'* that is contented in maintaining the status quo after the servant who buried the one denarius received from his master. These symptoms lead to dysfunctional creativity and novelty, visionary blindness, and passionless mission 'Me', nothing less than dead man walking.

The sum total of all these syndromes and symptoms isa 'funeral-faced hypocrite' whose pseudo-authenticity leads to 'mission buffering'. Housing all such syndromes drains all time and energy just in taking care of challenges *ad intra* that no time is left to attend to challenges *ad extra*. John Calvin had said, "When God wants to judge a nation, He gives them wicked rulers."[50] The Old Testament is a staunch witness to the fact that when the chosen people, by their disobedience, unfaithfulness, and moral autonomy to play god, had distanced themselves, God appointed wicked and cruel rulers to remind them of their pseudo-authenticity and spiritual worldliness. Hence, the actual challenge is not the rulers nor any factor but the pseudo-authentic mission called 'Me'.

2.2.   Unravelling the Authenticity of Mission in the Past

The history of the Church from the early period witnessed powerful spiritual and prophetic movements led by holy men and women.[51] Their authenticity was contained not only in fleeing from the world (*Fuga mundi*) and the worldly to lead a life of total dedication and consecration leaving their homes and dear ones but also in living in the world as a 'contrast-community'.[52] As persons freed by the power of the Gospel, responding to the radical call of the Gospel in their varied contexts, soaked and convinced by the values of the Gospel in the midst of a fractured and sick world, several consecrated men and women like Anthony of Egypt, Pachomius, Benedict, Francis of Assisi, Ignatius of Loyola, Vincent de Paul, Arnold Janssen and many more listened to 'His Voice' who from the "burning bush" of demeaning human conditions and corrupt practices called to challenge the existing systems and structures in Church and the society in order to "offer a more Gospel oriented vision of the world."[53]

2.2.1. Counter-Cultural Movements

The first three centuries were marked by itinerant preachers (wandering ascetics) and missionaries like the ones seen in the Gospel and the community ascetics who lived a life of communion inspired by Jesus' invitation- "If you wish to be perfect, go and sell your possessions and give the money to the poor, and you will have treasure in heaven; then come and follow me,"[54] and Paul's call "to pray at all times."[55]

The end of persecutions and the subsequent mass conversions to Christianity caused the institutionalization of the Church thereby a superficial Christianity. When martyrdom, the so thought authentic way of imitating Christ, was no more possible, fervent Christians like Origen claimed asceticism as the alternative form of martyrdom. Thus the two Egyptians Anthony and Pachomius made family and community asceticism into a new form of life in the Church which came to be accepted as a more perfect and radical form of following Christ,[56] that opposed the leniency, growing clericalism and sacerdotalism that had sneaked into the Church after the edict of Milan. Humility and submission of the celibate monks to the authority of the Church, especially the bishops who were often married and to the monastic rules was an expression of genuine humility. Thus monasticism, from the beginning, had an anti-institutional and anti-hierarchical slant.[57] On the long run monasticism instead of a radical movement emerged into a powerful institution in the Church that controlled the laity, enjoyed royal patronage and ascended as feudal lords.

2.2.2. *Poverty Movements*

A lay-awakening in the twelfth century against monasticism (the "life of perfection") arose against the staggeringly rich 'feudal monks'. Austerity was a myth and monastic life was much cosier than life outside the walls of the monastery. Stability and security were now means to hoard possessions. The authentic prophetic step as against the mortifying monasticism was to advocate wandering preaching so as to promote the virtue of poverty after Jesus and the apostles. Many wanted to live the radical life of the Gospel, "naked following the naked Christ" (*nudus nudum Christum sequi*), a saying of Jerome, but which became the slogan of many movements of the Middle Ages.[58]

By deciding to live by begging, adopting the rule of individual and corporate poverty, refusing to accept endowments or own property, the Mendicant Orders discarded seclusion and enclosure of monastic life instead plunged on active pastoral work. The message was authentically prophetic and crystal clear. "The brothers shall appropriate nothing to themselves, neither a place nor anything; but as pilgrims and strangers in this world, in poverty and humility serving God, they shall with confidence go seeking alms. Nor need they be ashamed, for the Lord made himself poor for us in this world."[59] The Waldensians,[60] the Humiliati[61], and specially the Dominicans, the Franciscans were the finest witnesses to *vita apostolica* and the proof of authentic consecration against the turmoil and unrest of the twelfth century.

2.2.3. The Empowered Beguines

As against the decree of Boniface VIII through the bull *Periculoso* (1298) that all religious women everywhere must be cloistered, the Beguines passionately embraced a new form of life that fused charity, mysticism and contemplation. The cloistered had a strict enclosure, could serve only inside the nunnery and go out only at times of fire or pest. The Beguines without sanctions of any religious order observed celibacy, renounced personal property, supported themselves with works like embroidery, weaving, sewing etc., and moved around freely, serving the needs of the sick and the poor. The motive for their penitential lifestyle was the desire to imitate Christ.[62] By doing so they challenged the domineering and misogynic organization of the Church. Due to the chronic conflict between institution and charism, the cancerously growing Beguines were seen as a threat to the hierarchical Church organisation and the Council of Vienne (1312) censured them.

3.   Revisiting the Mission called 'Me': Towards a Paradigm of Greater Authenticity

3.1.   Authentic Paradigm of Spirituality: 'Being' more than 'Doing'

The first area of renewal of the mission called 'Me' is spirituality, for without a solid spirituality, it is impossible to face the challenges of contemporary society.[63] Authentic spirituality is founded on *'what one is'* rather than *'what one does'*. The closer any spirituality is to the Bible, the more authentic it is.[64] Christ is therefore the embodiment of authentic spirituality and, quite logically, from our point of view spiritual life must be a participation in the mystery of Christ.[65]

Hence, authentic spirituality is a quintessence of interiority, austerity, simplicity of lifestyle, contemplation, hospitality, tolerance, adaptation and (in) inter-culturation that calls "to witness to a life of total dedication in its fullness with joy and integrity" to become 'being' persons, rather than only be 'doing' persons."[66] Unclear establishment of Trinitarian Spirituality as the basis for our missionary mandate can run the risk of plummeting missions to manifold activities of a social character, to projects for economic growth or progress, to political participation to endorse the liberation of oppressed peoples, or to a mere struggle against exclusion.

3.2.   Authentic Paradigm of Consecration

The evangelical counsels should drive missionaries to follow Christ faithfully and authentically. After all, "following Christ is not a passive herding of the onlookers, but a radical imitation (*imitatio Christi*) of the disciples."[67]

3.2.1. Authentic Paradigm of Poverty: A Call to Practical Solidarity

In the words of Pope Francis "poverty teaches solidarity, sharing and charity, and is also expressed in moderation and joy in the essential, to put us on guard against material idols that obscure the real meaning of life."[68] Our profession of poverty is a participation in the *kenosis* of Jesus (Phil 2:6-70). The Christological foundation of poverty "impels a follower of Christ into practical solidarity with those for whom poverty is not a matter of virtue but the condition of life and the situation exacted of them by society."[69]

3.2.2. Authentic Paradigm of (Chastity) Celibacy: A Call to Generate Spiritual Children

Chastity embraced for the sake of the Kingdom, is a sign of the world to come, a source of greater fruitfulness in an undivided heart.[70] It frees the heart of man [sic] in a unique fashion (1 Cor. 7:32-35) so that it may be more inflamed with love for God and for all men [sic].[71] Consecrated Celibacy is an 'opportunity' to grow in compassion (Mk 6:34) towards the orphans, isolated ones from families and marriage bonds, and to respond to the 'expectant' with love and belongingness in order to truly be a 'Father, Mother, Sister, Brother'. Thus, celibacy "can become a fruitful virtue which generates spiritual children in the Church."[72]

3.2.3. Authentic Paradigm of Obedience: A Call for Self-Emptying in Service

If for Jesus, obedience was the uncalculated and radical surrender of life to his *Abba,* then for missionaries, authentic obedience "is not an expression of feeble submission,"[73] instead the *kenosis* of solidarity with the crucified people of today and our humble move to shoulder their cross. It's a call, to take the same path of Jesus, who did not deem equality with God (Phil 2:6) and to give up our freedom to set others free without ruling out the possibility for dangers and misunderstandings.

3.3. Authentic Paradigm of Fraternity: A Call for Widened Fellowship and Networking

Pope Francis reemphasizes the spirituality of communion, emphasised by Saint John Paul II calling the consecrated to be "experts in communion."[74] As a special family in Christ,missionary communities and other religious and lay collaborators, "by their fraternal union, rooted and based in charity...are to be an example of universal reconciliation in Christ."[75]*Koinonia* and *kenosis* are the two pillars for authentic fraternity. *Koinonia* (communion) emerges from right relationships, belongingness, self-acceptance and other-centeredness where "criticism, gossip, envy, jealously, hostility...have no place in our houses."[76] Authentic communion is "constantly open to encounter, dialogue, attentive listening and mutual assistance...also called to true synergy."[77] *Kenosis* calls for "a self-emptying of our ego, giving up our claim to power, name, position, and joining in the washing of the feet of the poor and the oppressed."[78]Today, when governments market lies and throttle our democratic dissent, networking denotes the human enterprise of judiciously optimising resources by pooling together all the resources towards a single-minded prophetic purpose.

3.4. Prophetic Witness: The Paradigm of Authentic Mission

Mission as imitation of Christ as a particular form of Christian life "began as a prophetic protest against the domestication of Christianity and the practice of faith."[79] Prophetic mission is to be a witness to the radicalism of the Gospel, live the Christian faith amidst absurdities and re-discover, re-invent and renew ones faith conviction in the light of the changing and challenging times. A Church that hesitates to speak prophetically and sacrificially to the modern world is bound for a consequential loss of her sense of calling as a people with a mission in the world.[80] When we revolt against whatever is dehumanising and commit ourselves to the construction of a worthier future for human we are doing what the prophets did of old.[81]

3.4.1. Towards ingraining a Mystic-Prophet Authentic Personality

After Jesus the mystic, our prophetic mission, must have its genesis in the 'Abba Experience' arrived at through prayer (Mt 26:26; 27:46, 11:25-26,14:23; Lk 6:12-13; 5:16, 11:2-4) and silence (Lk 23:9; Jn 19:9). Jesus contemplated the face of God...in turn; the reflection of the Father's face was seen on Jesus' face.[82] George Soares Prabhu regards that Jesus' prophetic mission is deeply grounded in his experience of God and as a prophet he adopted the life of "an itinerant charismatic preacher identifies with the poor, despised, lepers, blind and the crippled,"[83] Every missionary must adopt a contemplation-action mode of operation. A mystical consciousness and a prophetic lifestyle are meant to serve each other because every true prophet is a mystic and every genuine mystic is a prophet.[84]

3.4.2. Towards being 'The Message' and 'The Voice'

The credible way of living out mission is to bear witness to an authentic life. The prophet presents a vision by embodying it and calls for conversion and transformation.[85] If life is not the 'message' then message has 'no life'. Modern man [sic] listens more willingly to witnesses than to teachers, and if he [sic] does listen to teachers, it is because they are witnesses.[86] Consecrated life will not flourish as a result of brilliant vocation programs ... (but) because they see us as men and women who are happy.[87] Missionaries must be charged with the conviction that, "it is not by proselytising that the Church grows, but by attraction."[88]

Today there is so much injustice in the world not because of the violence of some but because of the silence of many. Remember, prophets obtain from God the aptitude to scrutinize the period in which they live and to deduce events. Because they are free, they "tend to be on the side of the poor and the powerless, for they know that God himself is on their side."[89] They are able to discern and denounce the evil of sin and injustice.[90] In the words of Chittister:

What the world needs now, respects now, demands now, understands now, is not poverty, chastity and obedience. It is generous justice, reckless love, and limitless listening...a religious life that vows to be what the world needs most: reckless lover, a voice for the poor, a pursuer of truth. For only such things as this, for this kind of poverty, chastity, and obedience only, does the present battered, exploited, and poverty-stricken world wait and grieve and crave.[91]

3.4.3. Towards living the Mysticism of Encounter

Pope Francis calls the missionaries to live the mysticism of encounter i.e., for a "Prophetic Dialogue" that includes "dialogical acknowledgement of the presence of the seeds of God's Word in all cultures, and prophetic acknowledgement of those elements contrary to God's Reign (denunciation) and of blindness to God's movement (annunciation) in all cultures."[92] Missionary work consists not only of communicating a message but also of helping people to encounter Christ and to have an intimate experience of his love.[93]

3.4.4. Towards Lived Eucharist at the Peripheries with God, using Google, and GPS

Eucharist is not a ritualistic ceremony celebrated within the wall of a structure instead it is a clarion call to 'take', 'give thanks', 'break' and 'give' (Cf. Lk 22:19); an ongoing process lived daily not only at the centre of affluence but at the peripheries striven with poverty, pessimism, persecution, opposition, and rejection. Eucharist thus calls for adaptation, an insertion into the lives of the people, and for incarnation of Christian message in local cultures so as to embark on a mission of mercy and compassion, not by following the means and methodsof the past instead to be creative and innovative reading the signs of the times. A prophet strives to listen to God's Word, to discern God's presence in the signs of the times..., and to dialogue with the worldview and context of the people.[94] Pope Francis recalls the creativity with which various charisms have sparkled in the past and demands for "creative ways to catechize, to proclaim the Gospel and to teach others how to pray."[95] Mission 'Me' in this time of infotech revolution needs to be "as wise as serpents and innocent as doves" (Mt 10:16), and timely update oneself so as to be relevant.

Conclusion

The source of mission is summed up by St. John: "That...which we have heard, which we have seen with our eyes, which we have looked upon and touched with our hands, concerning the Word of Life.., we proclaim also to you, so that you may have fellowship with us; and our fellowship is with the Father and with his Son Jesus Christ. And we are writing this that our joy may be complete" (1 Jn 1:1, 3-4). The understanding of Mission today is 'Mission Me'. On the one hand, yes, "the harvest is plentiful" (Mat 9:37) but 'Mission Me' diagnosed with syndromes and symptoms, makes true the words of Jesus, "the labourers are few" (Mat 9:37). For today's challenging times and troubled situations there can be no method as useful as to embark on a paradigm of greater authenticity. This is not the end. Mission 'Me', like the rich man of the Gospel, needs to ask every day, "What must I do....." (Lk 18:18).

Endnotes

[1] Josef Alt, *Journey in Faith: The Missionary Life of Arnold Janssen* (Romae: Apud Collegium Verbi Divini, 2002), 57.

[2] St. Arnold Janssen is the founder of the three missionary congregations-Society of the Divine Word (SVD), the Missionary Sisters Servants of the Holy Spirit (SSpS), and the Missionary Sisters Servants of the Holy Spirit of Perpetual Adoration (SSpSAp). Against the background of the pervasive melancholy *Kulturkampf,* he wanted to establish a house for the foreign missions. When the Archbishop Paulus Melchers of Cologne seriously said: "We live in a time when everything seems to be shaking and sinking," St. Arnold gave the following answer.

[3] J.D. Bosch, *Transforming Mission: Paradigm Shifts in Theology of Mission* (Mary Knoll: Orbis, 1991), 34.

[4] John Paul II, Post-Synodal Apostolic Exhortation *Vita Consecrata,* 25 March 1996, n.1 (Vatican City: Vatican Press, 1996) 3.

[5] E. Mathews, "Christ and Kenosis: A Model for Mission," *Journal for Applied Missiology* 2 (1991), 1, in *http://bible.acu.edu/missions/page.asp?ID+415,htm*, 3 August 2015.

[6] J. A. Kirk, *What is Mission? Theological Explorations* (London: Darton, Longman and Todd, 1999), 69.

[7] Dale T. Irvin and Scott W. Sunquist, *History of the World Christian Movement*, (Bangalore: Theological Publications in India, 2004), 163.

[8] S. M. Michael, "Interculturality and the Anthropos Tradition," *Verbum SVD*, Vol. 54:1 (2013), 63.

[9] Kuncheria Pathil, "Church in Pilgrimage with Other Nations, Cultures and Religions," *Third Millennium: Indian Journal of Evangelization*, XIV (2011) 3 July-September, 60.

[10] *Ibid.*, 61.

[11] F. X. Clooney, "Roberto de Nobili's Response to India and Hinduism, In Practice and Theory, *Third Millennium: Indian Journal of Evangelization* I (1998) 4 October-December, 73.

[12] Augustine Sauliere, *His Star in the East*, (Anand: Gujarat Sahitya Prakash, 1995), 122-123.

[13] Franz Gmainer-Pranzl, "From "Inculturation" to "Interculturation": An Essay in Mission Theology," in Lazar T. Stanislaus and Martin Ueffing, ed., *Intercultural Mission*, Vol. 2 (Delhi: ISPCK & Germany: Steyler Missionswissenschaftliches Institut, 2015), 129.

[14] *Ibid.*, 130.

[15] "CBCI Message on Mission in India Today," (Delhi, February 25-March 2, 2994), in D.H. R. De Souza, ed., *Final Statements of the General Body Meeting of C.B.C.I (1966-2002)* (New Delhi: 2003), 142.

[16] Paul Hiebert, *The Gospel in Human Context: Anthropological Explorations for Contemporary Missions*, (Grand Rapids, Michigan: Baker Academic, 2009), 178.

[17] Justin Vettukallel, "From Inculturation to Interculturation: The Significance of Intercultural Theology for Mission in a Global Age," *Mission Today* Vol. XVI No.2 (April-June 2014), 137.

[18] Antonio Pernia, "Missio Inter Gentes," *Arnoldus Nota* (November 2009), 2.

[19] Heinz Kulueke and the Leadership Team, "Giving One's Body and Soul in the Peripheries," *Arnoldus Nota* (October 2014), 1.

[20] Heinz Kuluke and the Leadership Team, "Celebrating 50 Years of the Decree *AdGentes*," *Arnoldus Nota* (July 2015), 3.

[21] Documents of the XV General Chapter SVD 2000, *In Dialogue with the Word,* (Rome: SVD Publications Generalate, 2000), 30-31.

[22] *Ibid.*

[23] Antonio Pernia, "Cross-Cultural Mission Revisited," *Arnoldus Nota* (November 2010), 1.

[24] Second Vatican Ecumenical Council, Dogmatic Constitution on Divine Revelation *Dei Verbum,* 18 November 1965, n. 4, in *Vatican Council II: Conciliar and Post Conciliar Documents,* Vol I, ed. Austin Flannery, (Mumbai: St Pauls, 2010), 664.

[25] Philip Gibbs, "Encountering Difference: Interculturality and Contextual Theology," *Verbum SVD,* Vol. 54:1 (2013), 85.

[26] Kulueke and the Leadership Team, "Giving One's Body and Soul in the Peripheries," 2.

[27] Kuluke and the Leadership Team, "Celebrating 50 Years of the Decree *AdGentes,*"3.

[28] Kulueke and the Leadership Team, "Giving One's Body and Soul in the Peripheries," 2.

[29] Antonio Pernia, "The "Ad Gentes" General Chapter," *Arnoldus Nota,* (August-September 2012), 2.

[30] Francis, Apostolic Exhortation *EvangeliiGaudium*The Joy of the Gospel, 24 November 2013, n.40 (Kerala: Carmel International Publishing House, 2013), 38.

[31] Francis, *EvangeliiGaudium,* no. 49, 44.

[32] Francis, no. 273, 200.

[33] Chris Lowney, *Pope Francis: Why He Leads The Way He Leads: Lessons from the First Jesuit Pope,* (Mumbai: St Pauls, 2014), 66.

[34] Francis, *EvangeliiGaudium,* no. 259, 189.

[35] Francis, no. 25, 28.

[36] *The New Shorter Oxford English Dictionary*, vol I A-M, 1993 ed., s.v. "Authentic," by Lesley Brown.

[37] Francis, *Apostolic Letter to All Consecrated People* (21 November 2014), Cf. *L' Osservatore Romano*, Eng. ed., 5 December 2014, 17.

[38] "Gratitude, Passion, and Hope," *The New Leader* vol.128, No. 1 (January 1-15, 2015): 36.

[39] *Ibid.*

[40] *Ibid.*

[41] *Ibid.*

[42] Joan Chittister, "The Fall of the Temple: A Call to Formation," *InFormation*11:3 (2003), 9.

[43] Donald Senior, "Religious Life and Mission: Through the Biblical Eye," *InFormation*10:4 (2002), 5.

[44] Jacob Parapally, "Editorial," *Jeevadhara: Jesus and Consecrated Discipleship*, vol. XLV, No. 267, ISSN 0970-1125: 5-6.

[45] Henry Nouwen, *Making All Things New* (San Francisco: Harper & Row, 1981), 37.

[46] Tom Kunnunkal, "Diseases that Afflict the Church," *The New Leader*, vol.128, No.8 (April 16-30, 2015): 12-13.

[47] "Acedia", Wikipedia,*https://en.wikipedia.org/wiki/Acedia.html* as accessed on 24 August 2018.

[48] Robert Cardinal Sarah, *God or Nothing: A Conversation on Faith,* trans. Michael J. Miller (San Francisco: Ignatius Press, 2015), 237.

[49] Kunnunkal, 12-13.

[50] Felix Cabrera, *Is Donald Trump God's Judgement on America?,https:// www.christianpost.com/news/donald-trump-gods-judgment-america-159315. html*as accessed on 24 August 2018.

[51] ShaliniMulackal, "The Meaning and Significance of Consecrated Life as Women Disciples of Christ,"*Jeevadhara: Jesus and Consecrated Discipleship*, vol. XLV, No. 267, ISSN 0970-1125: 50.

[52] The idea of a 'contrast Community' was first used in reference to Israel by Norbert Lohfink, the German Old Testament scholar and later by Gerhard Lohfink, his brother, as a reference to the Church (*Jesus and Community: The Social Dimensions of Christian Faith* (trans. John P. Gavin; Philadelphia: Fortress Press, 1984) 122-31. Walter Bruggemann and George-Soares Prabhu picked up this concept.

[53] Isaac Padinjarekuttu, "Consecrated Life as Counter-Culture: Historical Impulses for Its Reinvention Today,"*Jeevadhara: Jesus and Consecrated Discipleship*, vol. XLV, No. 267, ISSN 0970-1125: 27.

[54] Mt 19:21.

[55] 1 Thess 5:17.

[56] Padinjarekuttu, 29.

[57] *Ibid.*

[58] Padinjarekuttu, 32.

[59] C.H. Lawrence, *Medieval Monasticism* (London, 1993), 247.

[60] Also called as "Poor Men of Lyons" was founded by the Lombards in Italy and Peter Waldo, a banker of Lyons and a wealthy cloth merchant

who having experienced a conversion, abandoned everything and embarked upon a career of itinerant preaching, supporting himself by begging. Later as they drifted into anticlericalism and an anti-hierarchical stance Pope Lucius in 1184 condemned them.

[61] A religious fraternity active in Italy that consisted of priests and literate lay people who dedicated themselves to the apostolic life. Pope Lucius in 1184 condemned this group.

[62] Charles J. Healey, *Christian Spirituality: An Introduction to the Heritage* (New York: St. Pauls, 1999), 163.

[63] Valerie, "Being Rather than Doing," *Consecrated Life in the Third Millennium: Challenges and Prospects* (Mumbai: St Pauls, 2004): 30.

[64] Jordan Aumann, *Christian Spirituality in the Catholic Tradition* (Great Britain: Sheed& Ward, 1985), 3.

[65] *Ibid*, 9.

[66] Valerie, 30.

[67] Joseph Xavier, "Call of Evangelical Counsels," *Vidyajyoti Journal of Theological Reflection*, vol. 79, No. 4 (2015): 252.

[68] Francis, "Address to the International Union of Superior Generals" (8 May 2013). 1, in *https://w2.vatican.va/content/francesco/en/speeches/2013/may/documents/papa- francesco_20130508_uisg.htm*, 12 August 2015.

[69] Xavier, 253.

[70] Can.599.

[71] Second Vatican Ecumenical Council, Decree on the Up-To-Date Renewal of Religious Life*PerfectaeCaritatis*, 28 October 1965, n. 12, in *Vatican Council II: The Conciliar and Post Conciliar Documents*, vol. 1, ed. Austin Flannery (Mumbai: St Pauls, 2010). 550.

[72] Francis, *Address to the International Union of Superior Generals* (8 May 2013). 1.

[73] Xavier, 255

[74] "Gratitude, Passion, and Hope," *The New Leader* vol.128, No. 1 (January 1-15, 2015): 38.

[75] Can.602.

[76] "Gratitude, Passion, and Hope," *The New Leader* vol.128, No. 1 (January 1-15, 2015): 38.

[77] *Ibid*.

[78] Helen Mendonca, "Contrast Community for the Third Millennium," *Consecrated Life in the Third Millennium: Challenges and Prospects* (Mumbai: St Pauls, 2004): 65.

[79] Xavier, 256

[80] Sherman Kuek, "The Call of Consecration: Renewing Discipleship in the Church in Modern Asia," *East Asian Pastoral Review*, vol 46, No.4 (2009): 329.

[81] Sebastian Kappen, *Jesus and Freedom* (New York: Orbis Books, Maryknoll, 1977), 54.

[82] Francis X. Clooney, *His Hiding Place is Darkness: A Hindu-Catholic Theopoetics of Divine Absence* (California: Standard University Press, 2014), 21-22.

[83] John, 12.

[84] Sebastian Painadath, *We Are Co-Pilgrims: Towards a Culture of Religious Harmony* (Delhi: ISPCK, 2006), 19.

[85] John, 21.

[86] Paul VI, Apostolic Exhortation *EvangeliiNuntiandi*, n.41; quoted in P. R. John, "Jesus and Consecrated Discipleship: The Mystical and Prophetic Dimension of Consecrated Life in the Indian Context,"*Jeevadhara: Jesus and Consecrated Discipleship*, vol. XLV, No. 267, ISSN 0970-1125: 17.

[87] "Gratitude, Passion, and Hope," *The New Leader* vol.128, No. 1 (January 1-15, 2015): 37.

[88] Francis, Apostolic Exhortation *EvangeliiGaudium*The Joy of the Gospel, 24 November 2013, n.15 (Trivandrum: Carmel International Publishing House, 2013), 19.

[89] "Gratitude, Passion, and Hope," *The New Leader* vol.128, No. 1 (January 1-15, 2015): 37.

[90] *Ibid.*

[91] Joan. Chittister, *The Fire in These Ashes: A Spirituality of Contemporary Religious Life* (Kansas City: Sheed& Ward, 1995), 102-103.

[92] Schroeder, 17.

[93] Sarah, *God or Nothing: A Conversation on Faith,* 234.

[94] Roger Schroeder, "Interculturality and Prophetic Dialogue," *Verbum,* vol. 54, No. 1 (2013): 15.

[95] "Gratitude, Passion, and Hope," *The New Leader* vol.128, No. 1 (January 1-15, 2015): 38.

Bibliography

"Acedia", Wikipedia,in *https://en.wikipedia.org/wiki/Acedia.html* , 24 August 2018.

"CBCI Message on Mission in India Today," (Delhi, February 25-March 2, 2994), in D.H. R. De Souza, ed., *Final Statements of the General Body Meeting of C.B.C.I (1966-2002),* New Delhi: 2003.

Alt, Josef, *Journey in Faith: The Missionary Life of Arnold Janssen,* Romae: Apud Collegium Verbi Divini, 2002.

Aumann, Jordan, *Christian Spirituality in the Catholic Tradition,* Great Britain: Sheed & Ward, 1985.

Bosch, J.D., *Transforming Mission: Paradigm Shifts in Theology of Mission,*Mary Knoll: Orbis, 1991.

Cabrera, Felix, *Is Donald Trump God's Judgement on America?, in https://www. christianpost.com/news/donald-trump-gods-judgment-america-159315. html,* 24 August 2018.

Chittister, Joan, "The Fall of the Temple: A Call to Formation," *InFormation* 11:3 (2003), 9-15.

_____, *The Fire in These Ashes: A Spirituality of Contemporary Religious Life,* Kansas City: Sheed & Ward, 1995.

Clooney, F. X., "Roberto de Nobili's Response to India and Hinduism, In Practice and Theory, *Third Millennium: Indian Journal of Evangelization,* I (1998) 4 October-December, 72-80.

Clooney, Francis X., *His Hiding Place is Darkness: A Hindu-Catholic Theopoetics of Divine Absence,* California: Standard University Press, 2014.

Documents of the XV General Chapter SVD 2000, *In Dialogue with the Word,* Rome: SVD Publications Generalate, 2000

Francis, "Address to the International Union of Superior Generals" (8 May 2013).1, in *https://w2.vatican.va/content/francesco/en/speeches/2013/ may/documents/papa- francesco_20130508_uisg.htm,* 12 August 2015.

_____, Apostolic Exhortation *Evangelii Gaudium* The Joy of the Gospel, 24 November 2013, Kerala: Carmel International Publishing House, 2013.

_____, *Apostolic Letter to All Consecrated People* (21 November 2014), Cf. *L' Osservatore Romano,* Eng. ed., 5 December 2014.

_____, Apostolic Letter to all Consecrated People on the Occasion of the Year of Consecrated Life, 21 November 2014, in "Gratitude, Passion, and Hope," *The New Leader,* vol.128, No. 1 (January 1-15, 2015): 35-39.

Gibbs, Philip, "Emerging Indigenous Theologies in Oceania," *Concilium,* (2010/5), 34-44.

Gmainer-Pranzl, Franz, "From "Inculturation" to "Interculturation": An Essay in Mission Theology," in Lazar T. Stanislaus and Martin Ueffing, ed., *Intercultural Mission,* Vol. 2, Delhi: ISPCK & Germany: Steyler Missionswissenschaftliches Institut, 2015, 125-154.

Healey, Charles J., *Christian Spirituality: An Introduction to the Heritage,* New York: St. Pauls, 1999.

Hiebert, Paul, *The Gospel in Human Context: Anthropological Explorations for Contemporary Missions,* Grand Rapids, Michigan: Baker Academic, 2009.

Irvin, Dale T., and Scott W. Sunquist, *History of the World Christian Movement,* Bangalore: Theological Publications in India, 2004.

John Paul II, Post-Synodal Apostolic Exhortation *Vita Consecrata,* 25 March 1996, Vatican City: Vatican Press, 1996.

Kappen, Sebastian, *Jesus and Freedom,* New York: Orbis Books, Maryknoll, 1977.

Kirk, J. A., *What is Mission? Theological Explorations,* London: Darton, Longman and Todd, 1999.

Kuek, Sherman, "The Call of Consecration: Renewing Discipleship in the Church in Modern Asia," *East Asian Pastoral Review,* vol 46, No.4 (2009): 313-333.

Kulueke, Heinz, and the Leadership Team, "Giving One's Body and Soul in the Peripheries," *Arnoldus Nota* (October 2014), 1-2.

Kuluke, Heinz, and the Leadership Team, "Celebrating 50 Years of the Decree *AdGentes,*" *Arnoldus Nota* (July 2015), 1-3.

Kunnunkal, Tom, "Diseases that Afflict the Church," *The New Leader* ,vol.128, No.8 (April 16-30, 2015): 10-13.

Lawrence, C.H., *Medieval Monasticism,* London, 1993.

Lowney, Chris, Pope *Francis: Why He Leads The Way He Leads: Lessons from the First Jesuit Pope,* Mumbai: St Pauls, 2014.

Mathews, E., "Christ and Kenosis: A Model for Mission," *Journal for Applied Missiology* 2 (1991), 1, in *http://bible.acu.edu/missions/page. asp?ID+415,htm,* 3 August 2015.

Mendonca, Helen, "Contrast Community for the Third Millennium," *Consecrated Life in the Third Millennium: Challenges and Prospects* (Mumbai: St Pauls, 2004): 64-66.

Michael, S.M., "Interculturality and the Anthropos Tradition," *Verbum SVD*, Vol. 54:1 (2013),60-74.

Mulackal, Shalini, "The Meaning and Significance of Consecrated Life as Women Disciples of Christ," *Jeevadhara: Jesus and Consecrated Discipleship*, vol. XLV, No. 267, ISSN 0970-1125: 45-56.

Nouwen, Henry, *Making All Things New*, San Francisco: Harper & Row, 1981.

Padinjarekuttu, Isaac, "Consecrated Life as Counter-Culture: Historical Impulses for Its Reinvention Today," *Jeevadhara: Jesus and Consecrated Discipleship*, vol. XLV, No. 267, ISSN 0970-1125: 26-44.

Painadath, Sebastian, *We Are Co-Pilgrims: Towards a Culture of Religious Harmony*, Delhi: ISPCK, 2006.

Parapally, Jacob, "Editorial," *Jeevadhara: Jesus and Consecrated Discipleship*, vol. XLV, No. 267, ISSN 0970-1125: 5-8.

Pathil, Kuncheria, "Church in Pilgrimage with Other Nations, Cultures and Religions," *Third Millennium: Indian Journal of Evangelization*, XIV (2011) 3 July-September, 51-74.

Paul VI, Apostolic Exhortation *Evangelii Nuntiandi*, n.41, quoted in P. R. John, "Jesus and Consecrated Discipleship: The Mystical and Prophetic Dimension of Consecrated Life in the Indian Context,"*Jeevadhara: Jesus and Consecrated Discipleship*, vol. XLV, No. 267, ISSN 0970-1125: 9-25.

Pernia, Antonio M., "Interculturality in the SVD," *Arnoldus Nota* (June-July 2012), 1-2.

Pernia, Antonio, "Cross-Cultural Mission Revisited," *Arnoldus Nota* (November 2010), 1-2.

_____, "Missio Inter Gentes," *Arnoldus Nota* (November 2009), 1-2.

_____, "The "Ad Gentes" General Chapter," *Arnoldus Nota,* (August-September 2012), 1-2.

Sarah, Robert Cardinal, *God or Nothing: A Conversation on Faith,* trans. Michael J. Miller, San Francisco: Ignatius Press, 2015.

Sauliere, Augustine, *His Star in the East,* Anand: Gujarat Sahitya Prakash, 1995.

Schroeder, Roger, "Interculturality and Prophetic Dialogue," in *Verbum SVD*, Vol. 54:1 (2013), 8-21.

Second Vatican Ecumenical Council, Decree on the Up-To-Date Renewal of Religious Life*Perfectae Caritatis*, 28 October 1965, n. 12, in *Vatican Council II: The Conciliar and Post Conciliar Documents*, vol. 1, edited by Austin Flannery (Mumbai: St Pauls, 2010). 545-555.

Second Vatican Ecumenical Council, Dogmatic Constitution on Divine Revelation *Dei Verbum*, 18 November 1965, in *Vatican Council II: Conciliar and Post Conciliar Documents*, Vol I, edited by Austin Flannery, Mumbai: St Pauls, 2010, 663-675.

Senior, Donald, "Religious Life and Mission: Through the Biblical Eye," *InFormation* 10:4 (2002), 3-12.

The New Shorter Oxford English Dictionary, vol I, A-M, 1993 edition, s.v. "Authentic," by Lesley Brown.

Valerie, "Being Rather than Doing," *Consecrated Life in the Third Millennium: Challenges and Prospects* (Mumbai: St Pauls, 2004): 27-30.

Vettukallel, Justin, "From Inculturation to Interculturation: The Significance of Intercultural Theology for Mission in a Global Age," *Mission Today* Vol. XVI No.2 (April-June 2014), 122-138.

Xavier, Joseph, "Call of Evangelical Counsels," *Vidyajyoti Journal of Theological Reflection*, vol. 79, No. 4 (2015): 245-258.

A Leaf out of Paul's Mission at Antioch

Arockiasamy Savarirayan SVD

One cannot but think of Saint Paul the moment one wants to reflect on Jesus Christ and his mission in the world both then and now. As an ardent admirer of Paul, I have always looked up to him for inspiration, model and example for missionary life. In my effort to comprehend the missionary journeys of Paul, I began to read Acts 13. This chapter narrates the first Pauline Missionary Journey which could be dated to 46-49 CE.[1] It is a chapter that narrates the presence of the Holy Spirit from the beginning to the end and all throughout. The Holy Spirit makes His presence in the community and reveals His choice known to the worshipping community (v. 2), "performing a liturgical service".[2] Barnabas and Paul recognize that they are being sent out by the same Spirit (v. 4); Paul speaks filled with the Holy Spirit (v. 9) and the disciples are filled with joy and with the Holy Spirit (v. 52). The stamp of the Holy Spirit is there all-around for all to see as the Church commissions her sons for the Antiochian mission. However, as I reached vv. 13 and the following, I thought I got to read a beautiful theological-historical and biblical summary of the Salvation History. By the time I arrived at vv. 25-26, I could realize that I am also reading a few summary statements of the Gospels. I could not proceed further as I was mesmerised by the content of Paul's first ever speech found in this chapter. The text that caught my attention, however, is Acts 13:13-52. It revolves around Paul's first missionary journey and his mission in Pisidian Antioch. At the centre of the pericope are found "a sample of Paul's synagogue preaching and a more detailed account of the opposition (he) experienced".[3]

This essay, in this context, is a humble effort to understand the evolving missionary efforts of Paul, his emerging leadership, the struggles within, the progress of the early Church and finally what has it got to tell us Divine Word Missionaries who are known as frontier religious missionaries. In my limited experience and knowledge, what happened to Paul as narrated in the pericope under investigation, happens to everyone who makes efforts to establish Christ's mission or rather the Kingdom of God either as a Congregation of Priests or Sisters or as an individual missionary. Thus, a rather detailed study of Acts 13:13-52 could inspire all the missionaries in the field and even those in formation. And thus, a leaf out of Pauline mission at Antioch could serve as a paradigm for a few areas of our missionary life.

1.   The Context of Acts 13:13-52

If we divide the Acts of the Apostles in two parts, Acts 2 is programmatic for the first half while chapter 13 does the same function to the second half. It is worth noting that Jesus revealed his mission statement in Luke 4:18-21 (Jesus' mission manifesto proclaimed in Nazareth) while Peter reveals the *Magna Carta* of his mission in Acts 2:14-40 in Jerusalem. Paul in his turn makes a powerful statement of his mission in the passage under enquiry. The events occur in Pisidian Antioch. Mission at Antioch was indeed an adventurous one. Paul was in for a few surprises since it was also his first ever mission attempt. There were events that hurt Paul to the core and exposed his human side of the story but there were also moments that would at the same highlight his courage and commitment to the mission entrusted to him. Thus, Paul becomes a prototype for all of us missionaries. As we move on to reflect on the speech delivered by Paul, we would immediately realize that unlike Peter's speech, Paul's is more evangelistic. It demonstrates how the Gospel of the Christians is different from the Jewish Scriptures.[4]

2.   Paul, the Undisputed Leader

We take for granted that Paul was the undisputed leader of the missionary team and that he began to organize the missionary journeys as he desired. It is far from the reality. Paul's leadership over the missionary team is something that evolved progressively in the course of time. An intent reading of Acts 13:1-2 might reveal that Barnabas was one of the well-recognized prophets and teachers in the church at Antioch. His name appears first in the list of the five persons of whom Saul is the last. Let us take note of the fact that Paul is still known as Saul.[5]In the context of prayer, the Holy Spirit revealed his intentions to set apart two people for the mission. The name of Barnabas appears first followed by the name of Saul: "Set apart for me Barnabas and Saul" (Acts 13:2). In his desire to hear the word of God, even the proconsul Sergius Paulus[6] invited Barnabas and Saul (cf. Acts 13:7). But a change of guard takes place once "Saul, also known as Paul, filled with the Holy Spirit" (Acts 13:9) admonished Elymas the magician. In v. 13, the name of Paul appears first ("Paul and his companions") suggesting the change of guard and Paul takes up the leadership role. Peterson opines that "Paul emerged as leader (of the group) after the demonstration of his prophetic authority in Cyprus".[7]

What makes Paul a leader, as suggested by the text, is his prophetic authority and the courage with which he tackled the magician. Someone may require many years of formation and training to don various leadership roles. Even if we contend that leaders are not born but are made, certain people may emerge as natural leaders for the way they conduct their lives and go about carrying out their responsibilities. The people around/under them recognize their inborn charisma and capabilities and begin to recognize their leadership abilities. Paul could have been one of those naturally born leaders who outshone the other members of the group, but the author of the Acts of the Apostles attributed Paul's ability as a leader to his prowess in prophesying and admonishing because of the powerful presence of the Holy Spirit. Both Barnabas and Paul received the same prophetic gift, but it was in Paul the Spirit of prophesying revealed Himself better.

People in the world today are looking for such kind of leaders who can not only lead the people forward but also possess moral and spiritual authority to guide them to God and to interior joy. The world looks forward to leaders who are doers and not mere chatterboxes. In the present political scenario, People of India have made it clear on more than one occasion that the world today needs not *bhashan* (speeches with rhetoric) but real *shashan* (good governance). As priests, religious and evangelisers, we need to be the missing link between the political leadership and religious leadership; between honest and dishonest leaders and promote leaders with genuine leadership traits.

One need not be in a mighty hurry to don leadership roles in order to perform. It is the other way around. When one goes about carrying out the assigned jobs in an exemplary manner, leadership roles will automatically come. One need not force through dishonest means and complicated, often highly misunderstood and misused *murmuratio* to achieve this target demonstrating to the world that there is no distinction between worldly political leaders and religious leaders.

3. John Mark and Paul's First Missionary Team

One of the FAQs in the classroom is 'What happened to John Mark that he left Paul and returned to Jerusalem during the first missionary journey?' This question is not merely an academic curiosity but one that touches some of the delicate issues that religious leadership faces today. It is a question that revolves around one's perseverance, commitment and also obedience of every individual consecrated person to the authority and the apostolate s/he is assigned to. It may also demand certain amount of respect and honour to the individual who goes through certain odds of life. How often have we heard of the so-called Assistants (at all levels) having difficulties with their immediate superiors? Many of them have also tendered their resignation in search of peace of mind or even for the common good of the congregation or diocese or the place of work. Certainly, every issue has to be seen from both the sides as every issue is like a coin.

There are also persons who are afraid to work in certain places or conditions or in the company of certain people. Some are terribly afraid to take some people as companions in ministry because of certain aversions. We are in no position to condemn John Mark and/or people who continue to behave like him even today. Keeping aside these intriguing aspects of priestly/Consecrated life, we take note that Acts 13:13 tells us that John Mark abandoned[8] the first missionary team and returned to Jerusalem. The reason for his departure is not found in this context but one has to wait for the end of this so called first missionary journey to find a satisfactory answer. R. E. Brown thinks that Barnabas could have been weighed down by the enormously adventurous side of the missionary journey.[9]

When we continue to attentively read Acts 15:36-39, we see Paul requesting Barnabas to accompany him in his return visit to all the cities where they proclaimed the word of God. When Barnabas expressed his desire to take his cousin John with him, "Paul decided not to take with them one who had deserted them in Pamphylia and had not accompanied them in the work" (v. 38). Did John Mark desert Paul? That is what Paul thought! Whatever may be the situation, the feeling of being deserted by a person whom we trust creates wounds. It may take years to heal such hurt memories, even if the deserter has enough and more reasons to do so. What happened then as a consequence? Luke reports that "The disagreement became so sharp that they parted company; Barnabas took Mark with him and sailed away to Cyprus" (v. 39). The fact that even Barnabas deserted Paul could have had devastating impact on the latter. Let us not forget that Barnabas was somehow Paul's mentor. It was he who introduced Paul to the super-apostles in Jerusalem. So, the first known missionary team of the 1st century CE did not stand the test of the times. There were only three members and they could not complete one missionary tour together. We may conclude this discussion by affirming that Paul considered John Mark as someone who deserted him although we don't know the reason behind Mark's action. Paul was in no mood to reconcile, neither with the situation nor with the person. Thus the first missionary team stood dismantled.

Since we don't have the account of John Mark, we are not in a position to analyse both the sides but we know for sure that Paul and John Mark reconciled with each other, even if we gather this news from Deutero-Pauline sources [Col 4:10 ("together with Paul, John Mark sends greetings to the Christians at Colossae"). It is a sign that John Mark was with him during his imprisonment) and 2 Tim 4:11(Paul requests Timothy to bring along John Mark and he believes that John Mark will be helpful to him)] and from Petrine correspondence which need not have come directly from Saint Peter (1 Pet 5:13: Peter addresses John Mark as his son). It is a sign that Paul buried all the differences and extended a hand of friendship and that John Mark reciprocated the good will of Paul. More importantly, John Mark never lost his missionary spirit. In spite of all the odds, Paul and Mark have sorted out their differences and lived together, thereby become worthy of our admiration and imitation, if not even emulation.

4.   Paul at Antiochian Synagogue

Paul in the synagogue of Antioch is reminiscent of Jesus at the synagogue of Nazareth (cf. Luke 4:16-20) at the beginning of his public ministry. We don't know the composition of the crowd at Nazareth but the author of Acts of the Apostles says that in Antioch were present both men of Israel and the God-fearing Gentiles.[10] He also takes note that the Gentiles were much more docile to the Spirit of God than the Jews themselves (cf. Acts 13:16). While Jesus stood to read Isa 61:1-2 and sat down to deliver his sermon, Paul preached standing. Drawing a comparison of this fact, Israel Abrahams says that Jesus interpreted Prophet Isaiah and it was purely an exposition of the Scriptures while Paul gave away only an exhortation.[11] Let us not forget that Jesus entered the synagogue at Nazareth at his will and the scroll of the prophet was given to him (cf. Luke 4:16-17) while Paul needed a special invitation from the synagogue official (cf. Acts 13:15-16).

The Master will always remain as Master and the student, as a student. Only Jesus could preach with authority (cf. Mark 1:22, 27). We can only share in his authority as we share in his humanity (cf. Heb 2:14-18) and are partners of/coheirs with Christ (cf. Heb 3:14). We may never become 'like' Jesus (akin to Jesus; having the same or nearly the same appearance, qualities or characteristics) but we should like Jesus in our lives, in the sense of loving him or choosing him or be pleased with him and it is then we would be like Jesus in the sense of resembling Jesus. As St. Jose Maria Escriva says, "We must, each of us, be *alter Christus, ipse Christus*: another Christ, Christ himself".[12]

4.1.   What Happened in the Synagogue?

Acts 13:14-16 gives the picture of what happened in the synagogue at Antioch, at least one that is in *diaspora* as narrated in the pericope mentioned above. Paul and Co., went and sat down. The main purpose of entering into a synagogue is to listen to the Sacred Scriptures and to reflect on their meaning. This process has to culminate in prayer. David G. Peterson says that "A typical Sabbath synagogue service would have included a recital of the *Shema'* (Dt 6:4-9; 11:13-21; Nu 15:37-41), the praying of the Benedictions with responses, readings from the Law (so ordered that the whole of it was read in a three-yearly cycle) and the Prophets following no continuous pattern), translation of the readings into Aramaic, an exposition related to the lessons if someone competent was present and the priestly blessings (Nu 6:24-26)".[13] As the text in question would vouch, Paul and Barnabas were recognized and addressed as fellow Jews/brothers and they are invited to give a word of exhortation. Persons of the stature of Paul and Barnabas could not go unnoticed. Their presence is felt strongly and positively by the synagogue officials who considered them as persons of repute, worth and competent to address the congregation.

We may highlight two important points over here. One is the procedure of a synagogue worship which is both founded and centred on the Word of God, mainly from the Torah, Psalms and Prophets and not so surprisingly they too made sure that some part of the

Sacred Scripture was available in the dialect of the people. Both Paul and Barnabas must have been well-read people who were ever-ready to plunge into the situation. Indeed, they grabbed the God-given opportunity with both the hands. It is an appropriate occasion for us to introspect about our own preparedness to grasp the occasions that come on our way and above all to make sure that the knowledge of the Bible (besides what is given from above; for we don't rely only on our knowledge but on the power of the Holy Spirit that is given from above. The Lord has promised us not to worry what to speak and what not to speak. All of these will be given at the right time. It is the Spirit that speaks as we read in Matt 10:19-20) is sufficient enough to meet the demands of sufficiently feeding the Christian flock in our care which hungers and thirsts for the Word of God.

We said above that perhaps the synagogue officials considered Paul and Barnabas as persons of great repute and competent. The time of our formation has to make us persons of certain moral authority, commitment and standard and that we are not like common men and women. There is something very distinctive about us. We are people chosen to bless others and pray for others. We are a people who have to a certain extent renounced the world and the worldly pleasures and desires. Indeed, we are different from others in so many ways.

5.   The Main Features of Paul's Speech

5.1.   Similarity with the Speech of Stephen

Scholars have found a similarity between the speeches of Stephen, the proto-martyr and Paul. Both Stephen and Paul possessed the Holy spirit but the contexts and the purpose of the speech is dissimilar. Paul's speech is a historical retrospect. Paul spoke of the choice of God and the Exodus event and the Davidic dynasty. From there, he moves on to Christ, possibly to exhibit the Davidic roots of Jesus. While speaking of David, Paul underscores the significance of David by citing 1 Sam 13:14 and Ps 89:20 that David was a man after God's own heart.

5.2. Paul and *Kerygma*

Although Paul's speech sounds like a confessional summary, it is certainly an Old Testament *kerygma*. The skill of Paul is made manifest when he employs the OT *kerygma* as a prelude to the NT *kerygma*.[14] The New Testament *kerygma* demonstrates that "the apostolic preaching took place as the sequel to God's dealings with His people in ancient days".[15] Obviously, at times Paul loves to look at the life of Jesus and the events surrounding him as a fulfilment of the Sacred Scriptures (cf. 1 Cor 15:3-4). And without any hesitation, Paul calls his preaching as "… Good News that … God promised to our ancestors" (Acts 13:32). Paul is very happy to bring the same to the people. One may ask: What is that promise of God? Paul may have many answers but the one that he instantaneously comes up with is what is written in the Second Psalm, "You are my Son; today I have begotten you" (Acts 13:33). This witness of God attests that Jesus is God's Son and that he was sent into the world by God Himself to do the will of God, the Father. It also discloses that Jesus is the point of focus, the point of connection, the point of departure and also the point of arrival.

5.3. The Resurrection is the Core

Paul proclaimed the resurrection of Jesus as a triumph of God over death and evil. It made Paul's preaching a joyful event. Without mentioning Jesus' Galilean appearances, Paul emphasizes the importance of being witnesses to Jesus' resurrection and Messiahship. Through the resurrection of Jesus God has fulfilled all His promises as one could read from Pss 2:7 and 16:10. Bruce opines that "The promises made to David and his posterity could not have been fulfilled apart from the resurrection of the crucified Messiah".[16] Although the fact of the resurrection of Jesus defies secular history, the common sense human thinking, unrelenting questions from the believers of other religions, it is understood that the resurrection of Jesus is the foundation of Christianity. Paul says very clearly, "And if Christ has not been raised, our preaching is useless and so is your faith" (1 Cor 15:14) and again, "And if Christ has not been raised, your faith is futile; you are still in your sins" (1 Cor 15:17). Therefore, our faith in the resurrection is the only way to give meaning to our lives as Christians and this is what guarantees the forgiveness of sins.

5.4. *Kerygma* Calls for Response

By highlighting the ministry of John the Baptist and his preaching on repentance, Paul challenged his audience to look into their lives. Paul says emphatically in Acts 13:26 that it is "to us[17] the message of this salvation has been sent" and calls for response. Naturally, the response to *kerygma* is faith in Jesus Christ. As we have just seen above and Bruce confirms, "The *kerygma* was regularly rounded off with a direct application to the hearers, calling for repentance and offering the forgiveness of sins to all who believed. So, Paul now proclaims through Christ the remission of sins, and goes on to add a word about justification as well".[18] Paul would always argue for and establish the power of the Gospel and faith in Christ as against what the Law of Moses is capable of.

5.5. The Response of the Jews and the Proselytes[19]

Paul's speech had two important features. They are expositions of Sacred Scripture and then moral exhortations. The core message was the exhortation that everyone continues to live "in the grace of God" (Acts 13:43). When the Jews and the proselytes showed intense interest in the teachings of Paul and Barnabas, the synagogue authorities were suspicious.[20]

6. The Envious Outcome of Paul's Speech

We have just seen above that the Gentiles responded well to the *kerygma* of Paul and Barnabas. Indeed, the whole Gentile population of the city was there in the synagogue on the next Sabbath day. The Jews were indignant and annoyed. The positive response of the Gentiles was something unacceptable to the Jews. They thought that Paul is a sheep-stealer. They feared that all those God-fearing Gentiles who regularly frequented the synagogue were becoming the followers of

Jesus Christ. They decided to refute Paul's teachings. As Bruce says, they "cast abusive aspersions on the two apostles, perhaps including the name of Jesus in their defamatory remarks" and naturally "Paul's complaint would have been that it was only the Jews' refusal to receive the gospel light that prevented them from being themselves light-bearers to the Gentiles".[21] That is what we get to see in Acts 13:47.

7.   Rejection, Expulsion and Exit from Antioch

As a necessary sequence, the Jewish community at Antioch played its negative role in not only preventing the believers of Jesus Christ to join Paul and Barnabas, they also made sure that they are chased away from their sight. Thus, the prophetic words of Jesus became a reality as the apostles "shook the dust off their feet in protest against them, and went to Iconium" (modern Konya in Turkey) (Acts 13:51; cf. Matt 10:14). All was not lost. In spite of the foul play of the Jewish community, we take note of positives. The civic and provincial authorities did not act upon the advice of the Jews and the women followers stood by their conviction to follow the path treaded by the apostles.[22] And more importantly, the text ends saying that "the disciples (the new followers in Antioch) were filled with joy and with the Holy Spirit" (Acts 13:52).

8.   The Takeaways

8.1 The believing community/parish or religious community/seminary has to make sure that the presence of the Holy Spirit is always there, and it is led by the same Spirit. That is what makes the community distinct from other gatherings of people. A Spirit-filled community will always be active and alive. More than anything, the presence of the Spirit makes a community sacramental. Sacraments are visible signs of God's presence and channels of God's grace. The believers are called to become channels of God's blessings to each other. A good and kind-hearted Christian will always wish the other wholeheartedly "God bless you!"

8.2 As Paul and Barnabas felt deep within that they are set apart, chosen, sent out by and filled with the Holy Spirit, all the men and women of God who have embraced and are eagerly waiting to be anointed (those in formation) must feel the same. It is a question of what has motivated us to consecrate ourselves. Have we purified the original, innocent, mundane aspects of our orientation and motivation to join the selected band of Jesus Christ and set our goals and priorities, right?

8.3 The question of leadership seems to haunt the church so much today. Young boys and girls who want to become priests, nuns, missionaries, saints and martyrs when they enter the seminary, soon after the ordination or the Final Religious Profession want to occupy the chairs of the principals, provincials and bishops. They tend to think that they know everything and there is no need to listen to the elders and thus obedience becomes very difficult. For some people, vocation to priesthood and consecrated life has become professions and sources of enriching themselves with money. Instead of working like professionals, these people have begun to play with their commitment to the Church and thus have wounded the Church beyond one's imagination.

8.4 The standoff between Paul, John Mark and later Barnabas demonstrate the human side of the men specially called to follow Jesus and evangelize the people of the 1st century CE. With due respect and honour to these great men, we realize that they reflect in many ways the men and women of today. There are many who are like Barnabas who spotted Paul, encouraged him to become an evangelizer and introduced him to the super-apostles. He also took the initiative to form the first missionary team. With all these great things he could not stomach the way Paul dealt with his cousin John Mark and so he decided to abandon Paul. That is what he is and we never know what happened to him although the Holy Mother Church declared him an apostle and celebrate his feast and consider him a model.

John Mark must have been inspired to become a follower of Christ when he witnessed the preaching and prayer services organized by Peter and company and other Christian missionaries in his own house in Jerusalem (cf. Acts 12:12). Indeed, the seed of vocation is sown at home and in the environment provided by the parents. When Barnabas asked him to join the first missionary team, he would have voluntarily joined Paul and his cousin. Whether it is the enormity of the adventure, as opined by R. E. Brown or for another unknown reason, John Mark left the company of the other missionaries. Without condemning him for what has happened, we may insist upon the gift and grace of perseverance as vocation is God's gift and also for the humility to reconcile with those who offend us. The Scripture attests that John Mark was helpful to Paul in his old age and imprisonment. It is something all the youngsters would have to take note.

Paul was a hardworking and committed person who could have been very strict with himself and could have applied the same yardstick with others as well. He could also have been very demanding and adamant as was visible in the text under enquiry. But then we too see him changing himself and his stance as the time changed. He has a large heart to reconcile with John Mark.

The human side of the story of these three men highlights two important virtues that are missing today. One is the ability to reconcile and the other one is healing the fruit of the reconciliation. God makes use of these weak instruments. There is something here for all of us to take heart. God will make use of us provided we are willing to collaborate with him.

Conclusion

At the end of a rather limited theological analysis of Acts 13:13-52, we realize that following the missionary exemplary life of Paul brings us a lot of encouragement and comfort. The one who follows the footsteps of Jesus Christ and commits his/her life to the mission of Jesus will never go disappointed. Those of us who are consecrated to the Lord are called to preach. The main purpose of this preaching is to make people respond positively, repent for one's sins, and place one's faith in Jesus. We should not be afraid of anyone as long as we do what we are supposed to do. St. Paul is one of the best missionary models proposed by the Church so that all the missionaries may look up to him without losing sight of Jesus Christ, the Master around whom our vocation to priestly and consecrated life and above all Christian life is built. May Saints Paul, Barnabas and Mark accompany us in all our efforts to preach the Word of God to the ends of the earth.

Endnotes

[1] Cf. R. E. Brown, *An Introduction to the New Testament*, Doubleday – New York 1997, 303.

[2] R. E. Brown, *An Introduction to the New Testament*, 303.

[3] David G. Peterson, *The Acts of the Apostles*, WM. B. Eerdmans, USA 2009, 383.

[4] David G. Peterson, *The Acts of the Apostles*, 383. Cf. F. F. Bruce, *The Book of the Acts, The New International Commentary on the New Testament*, WM. B. Eerdmans Publishing Company, Grand Rapids, Michigan 1987, 277 questions the authenticity of Paul's speech. Citing B. W. Bacon, he thinks that Paul's speech rehearses the speech of Peter at Pentecost, with a few variations. Ref. B. W. Bacon, *The Story of St. Paul*, London 1905, 103. This issue is open to different scholarly opinions.

[5] Acts 13:9 "But Saul, also known as Paul, filled with the Holy Spirit, looked intently at him". The text in a way reveals that the change of name signifies two things: Paul is filled with the Holy Spirit and he is able to tackle the magician.

[6] Some tend to think that Sergius Paulus could have inspired Paul and Barnabas to go to Antioch since he had a few of his relatives over there and that he wanted them to know the Living God.

[7] David G. Peterson, *The Acts of the Apostles*, 384.

[8] David G. Peterson, *The Acts of the Apostles*, 383, analyses that the participle *apochoresas* (Acts 13:13) can have the milder sense of left or the more negative sense of 'betrayed' or 'abandoned' (cf. 3 Macc 2:33). The latter sense is clearly brought out in 15:38 with the use of another participate (*ton apostanta*), describing John as one who deliberately deserted them.

[9] Cf. Cf. R. E. Brown, *An Introduction to the New Testament*, 304.

[10] Paul would meet a group of cultured Gentiles in Acts 17:22-31 and later a group of Christian leaders in Acts 20:18-35. In Antioch, he meets both these groups. Talking to a mixed group is always full of challenges. A message which is relevant for one group need not necessarily good for the other.

[11] Cf. F. F. Bruce, *The Book of the Acts, The New International Commentary on the New Testament*, WM. B. Eerdmans Publishing Company, Grand Rapids, Michigan 1987, 271.

[12] www.escrivaworks.org as on February 17, 2019 from a Website dedicated to the writings of Opus Dei's founder. Italics belong to the present writer.

[13] David G. Peterson, *The Acts of the Apostles*, 385-386, footnote 54.

[14] G. Ernest Wright, *God Who Acts*, SCM Press, London 1952, 76.

[15] F. F. Bruce, *The Book of the Acts*, 272.

[16] *Ibid.*, 276.

[17] It is noteworthy that Paul includes Barnabas and himself together with the Jews to whom the message has been sent. It is a statement inclusion and solidarity.

[18] F. F. Bruce, *The Book of the Acts*, 278.   A look at Paul's letters to the Galatians and Romans would tell us that it is not surprising that Paul anticipated these issues already in his Antiochean speech according to the Acts of the Apostles.

[19] A question arises with regard to the identity of the "devout converts to Judaism". Are they the "God-fearers" of vv. 16 & 26? Are they mere proselytes or devout proselytes? In the light of the discussion in Bruce, The *Book of Acts*, 280, I tend to understand them as the Gentiles who worshipped the God of Israel.

[20] Cf. F. F. Bruce, The *Book of Acts*, 280.

[21] *Ibid.*, 281.

[22] *Ibid.*, 284.

Church's Response to Social Concern:
Looking ahead in SVD Mission in India

S.M. Michael SVD

Introduction

In 1992, the Babri Masjid which was built in 1527 fell in the hands of certain Hindu fundamentalist groups. Communal riots between Hindus and Muslims occurred across India immediately following demolition of the mosque resulting in the death of an estimated 2,000 people. As a reaction there was a bomb blast at the Stock Exchange Building of Mumbai in March 1993, resulting in the deaths of an estimated 900 people.

Those days, there was an often-repeated slogan ""Pahale Kassayi bathme Ishayi" First the Muslims, then the Christians. This fear of attack on Christian community did not remain as a mere slogan, but it became true. On January 22, 1999, Graham Staines, who had lived and worked among some of the poorest Adivasi communities in Odisha – was burned alive along with his sons Philip and Timothy by a group of right-wing activists. Dara Singh, a member of Bajrang Dal, was in the forefront to unleash the attack against Graham, who had spent 35 long years as a Christian missionary nursing the leprosy patients in Baripada, Odisha. Then came the carnage of Christians in Gujarat in 2000 and the Kanthamal in 2008.

This situation in India urged me to undertake a research on the reasons for the attacks on Christians. I began to document the pronouncements made against Christians and incidents of attacks on Christians from five leading English newspapers in India.

After five years of documentation, I began to analyse the data for the reasons for the attack on Christians as stated by Hindu organizations and leaders. I also began to document the incidence of violence against Christians.

My findings are given below:

2.   Violence against Christians

Religious violence in India has been increasing steadily. It has increased and reached in a phenomenal level during the last few decades. According to government data, 111 persons were killed and at least 2,384 injured in 822 cases of sectarian violence in 2017 alone, the highest figure for the last three years. In 2016, 86 persons were killed and 2,321 injured in 703 incidents of religion-based violence. In its investigation by NDTV in 2018 on the increasing polarization of Indian public due to "Hate Speech", it found that the use of hateful and divisive language by high-ranking politicians has increased almost 500% in the past four years. The data was collated from public record, internet, network of reports, scanned articles of 1,300, and cross-referenced databases.

Numerous reports have revealed a clear pattern of rising religious intolerance against Christians in India. Alliance Defending Freedom (ADF) - India, an organization defending Christian rights in the country stated that between January and October 2018, there were 219 incidents of Hindu violence against Christians reported; mostly affecting women and children.

If we look back a little, a quick survey on violence against Christians in India over the years   indicates that the trend of such attacks has increased since about March 1998. According to the United Christian

Forum for Human Rights (UCFHR), in the last 32 years between 1964 and 1996, the number of registered cases of communal violence against Christians was 38. This rose to 15 in the year 1997 alone. In 1998, the number rose to 90 (see Examiner, May 20, 2000, p.8). Gujarat was the major theatre of violence. Under the BJP rule, Hindu fundamentalist organizations like Vishwa Hindu Parisad (VHP) and Bajrang Dal had a field day with burning Bibles, chasing missionaries, crying the slogan, "Hindu jago, Christi bhago" (Awake Hindus, pack up Christians). In the month of July 2000, the Christian missionaries working in the century's worst drought hit areas of Saurashtra in Gujarat have been assaulted and threatened with dire consequences if their "anti-Hindustan community" continues relief work for the drought-affected impoverished villagers. They forced the missionaries in the village to open their ware-house and then took away 144 gunny bags of wheat and oil meant for drought-affected villagers, saying that the Hindus in the village did ot require any help from these *foreigners*. In another occasion, the Vishwa Hindu Parishad secretary B.L. Sharma 'Prem', rationalised the rape of four nuns in Madhya Pradesh as the expression of the "anger of patriotic Hindu youth against anti-national forces". The Kandamal violence against Christians is still fresh in our memory. The unabated violence in August 2008 that continued for seven weeks killed some 100 people, rendered 56,000 homeless and destroyed 6,000 houses and 300 churches. In other parts of India also nuns have been raped, priests executed, Bibles burnt, churches demolished, educational institutions destroyed and religious people harassed. Calls of "Christians – Quit India" were often heard.

2.   An Analysis on the Prevailing Situation

a)   Why this Violence?

Several fact-finding reports by Non-Governmental Organizations seem to indicate that the main instigators appeared to be from bodies associated with the Hindu Right, namely, the Rashtriya Svayam Sevak Sangh (RSS), the Vishwa Hindu Parishad, the Bajrang Dal, and the Hindu Jagran Manch. Together with the BJP, these are often described as the Sangh Parivar, i.e. the Hindu Nationalists' Organizations (see the reports: "Then They Came for the Christians – A Report to the Nation," by AIFOFDR, 1999: Report of the United Christians' Forum for Human Rights, 1999; Violence in Gujarat – *Hindu Jago Christi Bhago* by Kamal Mitra for National Alliance of Women, 1999).

As said earlier, the research undertaken to understand the reason behind the violence against Christians, by documenting the statements and comments made against Christians in five main-line National news papers in English all over India; and the analysis of the data on the news items, pronouncements, comments, editorials and statements made on the reasons for the violence against Christians and Muslim minorities by the Hindutva Organization and its related Institutions revealed that the main issues raised by them against Christians are related to three main issues of India, namely "CULTURE", "NATION" and "CONVERSION".

In the perception of Hindutva, India is a Hindu nation; the Christian mission is an unwanted and foreign body and therefore to be eliminated from the holy soil (*Punya Bhoomi*). Harsh Narain says: "Hindu culture alone deserves the credit of recognition as the national culture (*abhimanin*) of this country, as the culture owing and possessing this great nation, along with other Indian-born cultures like Buddhist and Jain cultures as its sub-cultures; Muslim and Christian cultures being in the nature of tenant-cultures" (see Noorani, 1999:127).

The concept of a 'Hindu Rashtra', governed entirely by the principles of Sanskritic Hinduism, has been widely promulgated in recent years. The idea was put forward in February 1999, in the forty point "Hindu agenda" during the Eight Dharma Sansad (Religious Heads) of Vishwa Hindu Parishad held in Ahmedabad. The demand was that Bharat should be reinstated in its true *Sanatan* (heritage) and righteous form. K. N. Govindacharya, the then BJP and RSS ideologue, declared that India is "geo-culturally" a "Hindu Rashtra" (Times of India, January 30, 1999). To be Indian is to be a Hindu. According to Hindutva ideology, to be an Indian is defined by one's religion.

For several centuries, there have been constant efforts to homogenize the culture of India in terms of an upper caste, Sanskritic, Brahmanic Hinduism. Anything outside this cultural orbit is denied legitimate existence in Indian society. Proponents of Hindutva believe that" Hinduism is superior to any other faith, that Hindus are the original and only creators of Indian culture and are exclusively, the Indian nation". (see Fishlock, 2000:13). The process of Sanskritization of the Indian sub-continent has been going on ever since the Aryan migration/invasion.

The name Hindutva and its explicit political and ideological formulation is a product of the late 19th and early 20th centuries (see Michael, 1996). Anti-Muslim and anti-Christian sentiments are consistently used to project a political ideology of Hindu dominance. In actual fact; however, Hindutva is a "mix of Brahminical Hinduism with nationalism, reflecting the interests of upper castes" (Ram, 1999:34).

3.   Reality Check on the Cultural Identity of India

In order to respond to the Hindutva vision of India, we need to study the cultural reality of India. This analysis may also shed some light on the real motive behind the violence against Christians in India.

(i)   *The Question of National Identity and Cultural Foundation of Modern India*

While the available anthropological knowledge on India reveals that India is a multi cultural, multi-racial, multi-lingual and multi-religious country, the Sangh Parivar questions this and proclaims India to be a Hindu nation. Anybody who does not subscribe to this vision of the Sangh Parivar is considered an enemy of the nation.

This is a very serious and grave error and an injustice to the citizens of India. The inspiration behind the Hindutva ideology, 'to be Indian is to be Hindu' can be traced to Swami Dayananda Saraswathi (1824-1883), one of the first Hindu revivalists of modern India. When several Indian elite raised the question of the cultural foundation for the modern India, some reformers were of the opinion that recreation of modern India should be on the basis of incorporating science and rationality into Indian culture. For example, Rammohan Roy (1772-1833) recognized some of the evil practices in Hindu society such as Sati, child-marriage and idol worship, and insisted on the need for reform in Hinduism and its society. He founded the Brahmo Samaj to restructure Hindu culture in terms of modernity. This challenged the presuppositions on which the orthodox Hindu system of conduct was based.

Opposing the modernist views, Dayanda Saraswathi urged a regeneration of Hindus through adherence to a purified "Vedic faith". The Vedic Aryans are described by Dayananda as a primordial and elect people to whom the Veda has been revealed by God and whose language – Sanskrit – is said to be the "Mother of all languages". They would have migrated in the beginning of the world from Tibet – the first land to emerge from the Oceans – towards the Aryavarta. This territory, homeland of the Vedic civilization, covered the Punjab, Doab and Ganges basin. From this position, the Aryans would have dominated the whole world till the war of the Mahabharata, a watershed, opening a phase of decadence. The national renaissance implied precisely, for Dayananda, a coming back to the Vedic Golden Age.

The chief object of the Arya Samaj he founded in 1875 was to bring about social and religious revival through the renaissance of early Hindu doctrine; its favorite mottos being "Back to the Vedas" and Aryavarta for the Aryans" (Smith, 1938:57). This view simply equated Indian culture with Hinduism and Hindu culture; all non-Hindu aspects were regarded as contaminating influences. The Arya Samaj is probably the first movement in India defining nationalism in terms of ethnicity.

These views of Dayananda Saraswati are the basis from which the later Hindu movements and organizations such as the Hindu Mahasaba, R.S.S., Shiva Sena, V.H.P. , Bajrang Dal and BJP are formed (see Michael, 1998a: 20-34). The leaders of the Hindu nationalist movement based on a revival of Hindu culture openly acknowledged their identification of nationalism with Hinduism. Vivekananda, Aurobindo Ghose, Tilak, Savarkar, Hedgewar and Golwalkar are some of the prominent Hindu nationalists who identified India with Hindu. Golwalkar for example, one of the prominent ideologues of the RSS made it crystal clear that India is a Hindu nation. He suggested that Muslims and Christians be placed behind bars during the time of national crisis. His idea of the best solution to the minorities' problem is contained in one word – assimilation. According to him they should be "wholly subordinated to the Hindu nation, claiming nothing, deserving no privileges, far less any preferential treatment – not even citizen's rights" (Golwalkar, 1947:55-56).

In an interesting speech, a Hindu Mahasabha leader attempted to list the cultural changes which Indian Muslims would have to undergo in order become acceptable nationals of the Indian (Hindu) state of the future. First, they would have to accept the **Ramayana** and **Mahabharata** as their epics and reject the Arabic and Persian classics. They would have to regard Ramachandra, Shivaji, and the Hindu gods Rama and Krishna as their heroes, and condemn various Muslim historical figures as foreign invaders or traitors (Deshpande 1949:10).

The present Sangh Parivar members express similar views about Christians in India. For example, the Bajrang Dal has been threatening Christian-run educational institutions in Karnataka and other states with dire consequences if they did not "Hinduise" them by installing an image of Saraswati and begin the day with Saraswati Vandana (Ram, 1999:2). Rashtriya Swayamsevak Sangh leader Rajendra Singh at a RSS camp in Meerut on November 22, 1998, declared "Muslims and Christians will have to accept Hindu culture as their own if Hindus are to treat them as Indians" (The Asian Age, November 23, 1998).

The above position of the Sangh Parivar goes contrary to the historical data. A simple scrutiny on Indian civilization will reveal that since the middle of the second millennium B.C. several streams of migrant groups and communities from different parts of the world migrated to the Indian sub-continent. The advent of the Aryans, the Tibeto-Burman speaking Mongoloid groups, the Kushans, the Sakas, the Greeks, the Huns, the Arabs, the Persians, the Turks and the Mongols at different points of time testifies to the pervasiveness of the migration process during the successive periods of Indian civilization (D'Souza, 1999: 64-74). The migrant groups and communities brought their respective traditions and behavior patterns from their native lands. In course of time, they lost contact with their places of origin and underwent an extensive process of indigenization. The process of adaptation and interaction among the various groups brought about on the one hand, India's characteristic diversity and on the other, a composite cultural tradition. This fact is borne out by historical sources and contemporary surveys as well as researches in folklore.

Since the above facts of the social emergence of Hinduism in India go against the very interest of the Sanskritic Hindus, there are attempts today, to deny the Aryan migration (or invasion) into the Indian soil. The Hindutvavadis are beginning to assertively propagate the idea that the Aryans are the indigenous inhabitants of this land. They founded the rich urban Indus Valley civilization. This claim is very important for Hindutva-oriented historians because it helps them to demonstrate that the present-day Hindus are the lineal descendants of the Aryans and the rightful inheritors of the land from time immemorial.

Since 1920, archeological excavations at Harappa have documented that the rich urban civilization of the Indus Valley is much older than Aryan culture in the Indian subcontinent. This left the Hindu nationalists with no recourse but to seek to incorporate the Harappan civilization into the Vedic literary tradition. In this enterprise, the antiquity of the Vedas had to be pushed back several centuries and the Vedic river Sarasvati had to be assigned a greater priority than the Indus as a cradle of ancient civilization.

Yet the numerous well-established linkages between the Rigveda and the Avesta firmly rule out the Indian origin of the Aryans. Dr. Stephen Fuchs' study on the "Vedic Horse Sacrifice in its Culture-

Historical Relations" (1996) also shows that the Aryans have been migrating from inner Asia to India and Europe and thus giving birth to the Indo-European language groups which include most European languages and many languages of western Asia, including Sanskrit and Hindi. "Equally definitively, it is simply inconceivable that the Harappan civilization could have been Aryan. A number of arguments are advanced in support of this assertion, one among them being the absence in known Harappan sites of any well-testified remnants of the horse, a crucial animal in Vedic lore" (Muralidhran, 2000:75; also see Mahadevan 1977 & 2000; Thapar, 2000).

But recently the Hindutva ideologues have claimed that the Indus script has been deciphered and that the language of Harappa was 'late Vedic Sanskrit' (see Rajaram and Jha 2000; Rajaram and Frawley, 1997; Rajaram, 1999; Rajaram 2000). They have also been claiming that the Harappan civilization gives religious significance to the horse and thus should have been an integral part of Aryan civilization.

The above claim of RSS historians has been clearly refuted by international scholarship. In the year 2000, in a cover story article titled, "Horseplay in Harappa – The Indus Valley Decipherment Hoax", in the Frontline Magazine dated October 13, 2000. Michael Witzel, a Harvard University Indologist and Steve Farmer, a comparative Historian, debunked the claims of N.S. Rajaram and N. Jha in their co-authored book, "The Deciphered Indus Script". The book establishes a connection between the Rig-Veda and the Harappa civilization on the basis of inter alia a fabricated horse seal. International scholarship has in this question been supported by the reputed Indian historian Romila Thapar and Iravatham Mahadevan the leading Indian expert on the Indus Valley script and one of the world's foremost scholars in the field (see Frontline October 13, October 27, and November 24, 2000). The international scholars Michael Witzel & Steve Farmer have challenged to offer $ 1,000 to any Harappan researcher who is willing to defend Rajaram's claims. "Not one has taken us up on our offer. So far as the scholarly world goes, nothing is left of Rajaram's

Hindutva 'revisions' of history than an `*va-s*` *ava* – in plain English, a dead horse" (Witzel and Farmer, 2000:129).

These attempts of the Sangh Parivar to `rewrite history' has come under great criticism by other eminent scholars and by the public (see The Times of India News Service, January 3, 2001:6; United News of India, January 1, 2001:4; Chattopadhyay, 2001).

In recent times, new evidences have emerged on the migration of Aryans to India. In its title page of *India Today*, in August 2018 edition, the main article, "*4500-year-old DNA from Rakhigarhi reveals evidence that will unsettle Hindutva nationalists*" clearly gives sufficient evidence to the fact of the later migration of Sanskrit speaking Aryans to India. This revelation is part of the long-awaited and much-postponed results of an excavation conducted in 2015 by a team led by Dr Vasant Shinde, an Archaeologist and Vice- Chancellor of Pune's Deccan College (for the full article, refer India Today). Similar conclusions have been arrived at by 92 leading scientists through their new genetics study (see Indian Express "*The Long Walk: Did the Aryans migrate into India? New genetics study adds to debate*"). (see Sowmiya, Ashok and Adrija Roychowdhury, 2018; see also Tony Joseph, 2017).

The Hindu nationalists want to deny the above fact for the simple reason that it goes against their interest of preserving the pre-eminent position which they are enjoying in the Hindu caste social order at the expense of tribals, Dalits and other lower castes who are mainly Sudras. A quick look at the composition of Indian society will speak for itself. The Brahmins of India form only 6 per cent of Indian society; the other upper castes are 14 per cent. The Backward castes (Sudras) are 52 per cent; Dalits are 16 per cent and Tribals are 8 per cent of the Indian population (Time, April, 1992:11). Since there is no Census Data on this, many social scientists say that the population growth is in similar line even now.

The subaltern groups mainly the backward castes, Dalits and tribals view India completely differently from that of the Brahmins and other upper castes who dominate the Sangh Parivar. The leaders of the subaltern masses such as Jotiba Phule, Ramaswamy Naicker, Ambedkar and Swami Achchutanand incessantly and systematically exposed and condemned Brahminical Hinduism as a religion and culture of social slavery, and therefore an enemy of the people struggling to emerge as a modern nation (see Michael, 1999). The ideals, values, the customs and injunctions of Brahminical literature – the Vedas, Upanishads, Ithihasas, Puranas and Dharma Shastras – as interpreted and upheld within the competitive politics of Hindu nationalists appeared to these men as a preemptory call to reinforce and re-establish the Varna ideology of discrimination against the lower classes.

As a result of these conflicting visions on modern India, we today observe the emergence of two opposite socio-political and cultural forces in the Indian political arena. On the one hand, backward castes and classes are in search of a culture based on an egalitarian social and economic order with greater political participation; on the other hand, upper caste Hindus (Sangh Parivar) are equally strong in trying to retain control of their present position of privilege and dominance by reasserting ancient hierarchical Brahminic Hindu values. Thus, the contrasting interests of the upper and lower groups have polarized cultures in India, the former vigorously clinging to their traditional status and the latter fighting for justice, equality and human dignity.

It may now be easy to understand why Christian missionaries are attacked by the Hindu nationalist organizations such as RSS, VHP, Bajrang Dal, Shiva Sena, etc. The work of Christian missionaries among the downtrodden people of this country will go against the interests of the upper castes. That is why Pastor Rev. Graham Stewart Stains who was working among the lepers in a remote part of Orissa was burned to death, the nuns who are working in the remotest parts of India are raped; Christian educational and Social Institutions are ransacked and missionaries are humiliated.

(ii)   The Issue of Conversion and Human Freedom

Another important issue on which Christians are targeted is on conversion. Almost every day, there is one or the other news item in the Indian Newspapers on the above subject. A number of statements have been made by different Hindu organizations. For example the 8th Dharma Sansad of the Vishwa Hindu Parishad (VHP) demands strict anti-conversion laws and a white paper by the Central Government on the 'foreign conspiracy', behind conversions. The Prime Minister, Atal Behari Vajapyee, demanded a 'national debate on conversion' thereby implying that attacks on Christians are due to their conversion activities. Mr. Vajpayee said, "If Christian missionaries continued religious conversions, the government cannot stop reconversions". VHP's Ashok Singhal argued that Professor Amartya Sen's Nobel Prize is a Christian conspiracy to open more missionary-run educational institutions to convert the poor. It was alleged that missionaries use force, fraud and allurements to convert people to Christianity. Funds obtained for welfare activities are used for conversion. At the same time, conversion from Christianity to Hinduism is encouraged and supported by the Sangh Parivar as "Gharwapasi" or homecoming.

We need to analyze the issue of conversion impartially. Usually, when conversion is discussed in India, it is done in the context of conversion to Islam and Christianity alone. In reality, however, conversion has been going on all through the history of India (see Michael, 1998). There have been cultural and religious encounters and interactions over the ages. India has been a sub-continent with a vast population of diverse levels of culture. Anthropological studies on India show that through a process of absorption and assimilation and conquest, a process of Sanskritization has been taking place in ancient India. Adivasis or Tribals and other indigenous people have been drawn into the orbit of a sanskritic world-view.

Jayant Lele explains this process: "The Brahminic worldview had succeeded on several occasions in the past in capturing the diversity of cults, deities, sects and ideas (by making many compromises) under the rubric of **sanantana dharma**" (1995:xviii). Explaining this process of Brahminic incorporation, reinterpretation, appropriation and assimilation of tribal and other cultures, N.K. Bose says: "Once a tribe came under the influence of the Brahminical people and was converted into a caste enjoying monopoly in a particular occupation, a strong tendency was set up within it to remodel its culture more and more closely in conformity with a Brahminical way of life" (Bose, 1967:214). Like the tribals who were assimilated to Hinduism, the non-Aryan i.e. the **Sudras** and **Ati-Sudras** were also assimilated and Sanskritized. The powerful upper-castes of a particular area exercised such an influence on the lower castes and outcastes that they also wanted to be integrated into the caste hierarchy by adopting the values and practices of the upper castes. This process is described as "sanskritization" by the well known anthropologist M.N. Srinivas (1989:56). According to Romila Thapar, this "first step towards the crystallisation of what we today call Hinduism was born in the consciousness of being the amorphous, undefined, subordinate, other" (2000: 5). Even today this process of Hinduization of tribals is going on with full political support by the State and Central Governments (see Patel, 1999:186-212).

While the Hindu fundamentalist organizations through their assimilation policy claim the tribals and dalits to be Hindus, the tribals and the dalits on the other hand reject this superimposed identity. The upper caste Hindus while trying to get the services of the dalits and tribals paid little attention to alleviate their deprived conditions. They are addressed as "Backward Hindus" (see Ghurye, 1963). Rejecting this identity, the tribals and dalits have found their own ways to move up in the social ladder of Indian society. The conversion movements among the Dalits and tribals have shown the potential of social change in religion (see Natarajan, 1977; Snaitang, 1993).

Sociologically, conversion is a process of change from one religion to another. It is something that is used by the individual to move forward in society, to free themselves from inherited shackles, to better themselves and their children (see Moon, 1989). These shackles might be those of caste, of illiteracy, of economic slavery, of psychological apathy. Yet all these factors are always inter-linked and no one of them should be considered in isolation. The converts did not always perceive the spiritual and material components of conversion as separate identities but as a single phenomenon. For them, it constituted no contradiction to use conversion as a leverage for upward social mobility.

Forceful conversion should be condemned and unacceptable. Yet, is it wrong if a group of people change their religion when they realize that their poverty and social degradation are due to the legitimized religious values and the structures of a given society? The prospect of radical change can only seem subversive to those who are committed to the status quo. It is understandable that the beneficiaries of the status quo resent radical changes. But to the oppressed and downtrodden, change is the lever of hope. At a time when the 'right to informed choice' is upheld even in routine matters, how can the right to freedom of choice be denied to millions in matters of ultimate significance?

Blaming the Church for accepting poor people to Christianity does not hold ground in the context of Indian democracy. Such sayings are an insult to the dignity of the poor. There is the condescending paternalism in this idea that denies the poor the ability of making rational and intelligent decisions. Does our Constitution discriminate the poor from voting and choosing their representatives to the parliament? Indian elections have proved the power and the wisdom of the poor and the ordinary. They have their own wisdom to choose and pick up in spite of pressures and coercion. Hence, any underestimation of the capacity of the poor and the downtrodden by the upper caste Hindu fundamentalists is unwarranted.

Moreover, conversion movements are not only towards Christianity but also to other religions. In reality, Buddhism and Jainism were widespread in India, but today they are reduced to small minority religions because of the missionary activities of Brahminic Hinduism. Hence, a deeper study will show that the idea of conversion is part and parcel of the Indian tradition. The Arya Samaj and other Hindu organizations like the Vishva Hindu Parishad promote conversion and reconversion in their programmes not only in India but all over the world (see Jorden, 1977). The *Ghar Vapsi* (Home coming) movement of conversion of Christian tribals and dalits to Hinduism initiated by Dilip Singh Judev, the then B.J.P. Member of Parliament from Jashpur targeting Chotanagpur plateau in Madhya Pradesh (now in Chhatishgarh) and portions of Bihar, Orissa and West Bengal is well known (see The Asian Age, 1997:4). The Sikhs and Buddhists believe in a process of conversion towards human dignity and emancipation. In this context, the Hindu fundamentalists recognize as valid only one kind of conversion, namely reconversion to the Hindu fold. This attitude is out of tune with Indian tradition and contradicts the fundamental rights of the people of India.

Let us not forget the revolt of Dr. B.R. Ambedkar against Hinduism and his mass conversion to Buddhism in 1956. A deeper look into the history of India would reveal that Buddhism and Jainism were widespread in India, but today they are reduced to small minority religions because of the aggressive missionary activities of Brahminic Hinduism. The Arya Samaj and other Hindu organizations like the VHP promote conversion and reconversion (*Ghar Vapsi*) in their programs not only in India but in many parts of the world. There is so much misunderstanding, misinformation, rumors and political overtones with regard to Christian conversions. Hindu fundamentalists do not recognize the pluralistic nature of Indian society. Hence, they politicize even the very idea of conversion to Christianity. Behind this politicization there is a big agenda of Hinduization of India. This attitude is out of tune with the pluralistic tradition of India and contradicts the fundamental rights of the people of India.

3. The Constitutional Vision of India

At the dawn of India's freedom movement during colonial rule, there have been several contending visions of Indian identity. The complexity of Indian cultures and their efforts to construct a modern nation was a complex one. An analysis on the controversies of the culture of Indian people in modern Indian nationalism clearly proves the difficulties and multiple approaches to modern India. The Indian Constitution grew out of these challenges and contending visions for the future of India's cultural, religious and ethnic plurality. The secular Constitution of the Republic of India is the outcome of conflicting views on the secular form of the modern state and various religious claims on Indian identity.

The debates in the Legislative Assembly before independence of the country reflected the paradoxes of the Indian situation. The failure to reach a satisfactory conclusion on the question of Indian identity resulted in the separation of Pakistan from India. Mahatma Gandhi fell a victim to excessive and narrow nationalism. In spite of these setbacks, after almost three years of deliberation, the Constituent Assembly of India on 26 November 1949, our founding fathers crafted a historic document, the Constitution of India that promised us liberty, equality and fraternity. The founding fathers of the Indian Constitution defended the notion of a pluralistic society and a neutral state based on equal rights and citizenship. The Indian Constitution may justifiably be described as secular and multicultural. Recognition and protection was offered to religious, cultural and linguistic minorities. Equal respect, fairness and non-discrimination were to be the guiding principles of state policies towards minorities.

Differences were recognized but so are the values of equal citizenship and equal rights. After protracted discussions in the Constituent Assembly, the Constitution was passed upholding ethnic, linguistic, cultural and religious pluralism in India and promising recognition and protection for all and non-discriminatory state policies. It articulated a secular and inclusive nationalism of equal opportunities and equal liberty for all, regardless of their religious affiliations or social status. It meant that the state itself was not to become partisan to any particular group, nor does it privilege any particular religion. The Constitutional vision of India is respect and recognition of all the citizens of India with their cultural and religious identities.

4.   Conclusion

According to Amartya Sen, one of the eminent economists of India, despite being the fastest-growing economy, the country has taken a "quantum jump in the wrong direction" since 2014. He considers that due to moving backwards, the country now second worst in the region. In his considered opinion the government has deflected from issues of inequalities, the caste system and the schedules tribes. Sen shows disappointment with regard to the health care system in India.

This year in 2019, we are celebrating the 70th Republic of Indian Nation. Republic means the supreme power of the people living in the country to govern themselves and to build their future according to the vision and foundations of the Indian Constitution. As a a sovereign nation, with its own written Constitution, the solemn pledges of the Founding Fathers, it is a document especially treasured for the broadness of its vision and the egalitarian values. This Constitution is drawn and promulgated in the context of the debate on the pluralistic nature of Indian society. The Founding Fathers of the Indian nation were well aware of the multi-cultural, multi-religious, multi-lingual and multi-ethnic nature of Indian society. Hence, it is very important to affirm the pluralistic nature of Indian society; and no religious group could claim India to be theirs.

Analysis on the violence against Christians for the last few decades indicate that there is a conflict between the Constitutional vision of India and that of Hindutva with regard to the identity of India of its culture, nation and religious freedom. Hence, it is very important to affirm the pluralistic nature of Indian society and culture, and its traditions; and that no religious group can lay claim to India as their exclusive property.

In constitutional negotiations, Indian Christians gave up the request for separate electorates, and came under the general voters' roll; this is in view of their love for the country as Indian Christians who are actively involved in the political process of the development of the country. The critical part of the Constitution, adopted in 1949, was Article 25, under 'Fundamental Rights'. This said 'Subject to public order, morality and health and to the other provisions of the Part, all persons are equally entitled to freedom of conscience and the right freely to profess, practice and propagate religion.'

So, Christians in India should actively involve themselves in the reconstruction of modern India with the values of equality, fraternity and social justice. As citizens, Christians should actively participate in politics and people's movements which are promoting human dignity and promotion of life. Indian Christians must show more courage to stand for their faith defending its freedom and to safe guard its Constitutional rights enshrined in the Constitution.

At the same time, it is also very important to urge Christians to develop sensitivity on the issues of culture, nation and conversion in India. The Church must actively collaborate with government agencies and other secular organizations to bring more life to the downtrodden people of India. In this context, the Christians in India can learn a lot from the pronouncements of the Holy Father Pope John Paul II (now St. John Paul) who visited India in November 1999. Since the issue of religious conversions had formed a core part of the controversy about Papal visit, the Pope John Paul had done well to clarify the position of the Church on the issue. The Pope said freedom constituted the noblest prerogative of the human person and one of the principal demands of freedom was the free exercise of religion in society. "No state, no group has the right to control either directly or indirectly a person's religious convictions, nor can it justify claim the right to impose or impede the public profession and practice of religion, or the respectful appeal of a particular religion to people's free conscience" (as reported in Deccan Herald, 8 November, 1999:1).

Speaking about the relationship between Church and cultures, the Holy Father points out that the Church has been imbibing positive elements of other religions apart from renewing cultures from within. "This engagement with cultures has always been a part of the Church's history. But it has a special urgency today in the multi-ethnic, multi-religious and multi-cultural situation of Asia where Christianity is still too often seen as foreign," the Pope said during the concluding session of Asian Synod, an assembly of Asian bishops.

The Pope's call for dialogue is also very vital and relevant in the Indian context. This dialogue is to strive to discern whatever is good and holy in one another to promote peace and guarantee the world's future. The dialogue, the Pope advocated was not intended to "attempt to impose our own views upon others, since such a dialogue would become a form of spiritual and cultural domination". However, this religious and spiritual interaction can be done without abandoning one's own convictions. "Holding firmly to what we believe, we listen respectfully to others, seeking to discern all that is good and holy, all that favours peace and cooperation".

To conclude, we may say that the cultural context of evangelization in India is related to three main areas of Indian reality, i.e. culture, nation and conversion. As these issues are highly politicized today, Christians need to be sensitive to these issues without compromising the vision of Jesus, dialoguing, inculturating and discerning whatever is good and holy in other religions and cultures to promote peace and guarantee the world's future.

References

Bose, Nirmal Kumar, *Culture and Society in India*, Bombay: Asia Publishing House, 1967.

Chattopadhyay, Dhiman, "ASI projecting Vedic civilisation the RSS way", *The Times of India*, 2001, Feb.24, p.9.

Communalism Combat, 1998.

Deccan Herald, November 8, 1999, pp.1 & 9.

Deshpande, V.G., *Why Hindu Rashtra?* New Delhi: All India Mahasabha, 1949.

Friese, Kai, "An Inconvenient Truth: The Findings of Highly Anticipated Study of Ancient DNA from the Graveyard of the Historic Indian Town of Rakhigarhi Reveal Evidence that will Unsettle many Hindutva Nationalists", *India Today*, September 10, 2018, pp.24-35.

Ghurye, G.S., *The Scheduled Tribes*, Bombay: Popular Prakashan, 1963.

Golwalkar, M.S., *We or Our Nationhood Defined* (4th ed.). Nagpur: Bharat Prakashan, 1947.

India Today, "The Explosive Truth: DNA analysis of 4,500-year-old skulls like this one found in Haryana produces politically inconvenient revelations on the origins of Indian civilization", *India Today*, September 10, 2018, pp.24-35.

Jordens, J.T.F., "Reconversion to Hinduism, the Shuddhi of the Arya Samaj", *Religion in South Asia*. G.A. Oddie (ed.), New Delhi: Manohar, 1977, pp.145-161.

Kamal, Mitra (1999), "Violence in Gujarat – Hindu Jago Christi Bhago", *The Church and Conversion: A Study of Recent Conversions to and from Christianity in the Tamil Area of South India*, National Alliance of Women Wingate, Andrew, Delhi: I.S.P.C.K., 1977.

Lele, Jayant, *Hindutva: The Emergence of the Right. Madras*: Earthworm Books, 1995.

Mahadevan, Iravatham, *The Indus Valley Script: Texts, Concordances and Tables*. New Delhi: Memoirs of the Archaeological Survey of India, 1977.

_____ "One sees what one wants to", Frontline, 2000, November 24, p.125.

Michael, S.M. *Anthropology of Conversion in India,* Mumbai: Institute of Indian Culture, 1998.

_____ "Culture, Religion & Politics in India: Rise of Hindu Cultural Nationalism", *Dharma Rajya*, 1998a, March, Vol.2, No.1, pp.20-34.

_____ *Dalits in Modern India: Vision and Values*. New Delhi: Vistaar Publications, 1997.

_____ "Conversion, Empowerment and Social Transformation", *Understanding Indian Society: The Non-Brahmanic Perspective,* Ed. By S.M. Dahiwale, 2004, Delhi: Rawat, pp.153-181.

Moon, Vasant, *Dr. Babasaheb Ambedkar Writings and Speeches*, 1989, Vol.5, Bombay: Education Department, Government of Maharahstra.

Muralidharan, Sukumar, "Questions about the Aryan identity", *Frontline*, 2000, December 22, 2000, pp.73-75.

Natarajan, Nalini, *Missionary among the Khasis*. New Delhi: Sterling Publishers, 1977.

Noorani, A.G., "RSS and Christians", *Frontline*, January 1, 1999, pp.123-127.

Patel, Arjun, "Hinduisation of Adivasis: A Case Study from South Gujarat", *Dalits in Modern India. Vision and Values*. S.M. Michael (ed.), New Delhi: Vistaar Publications, 1999, pp.186-212.

Puniyani, Ram, "The Other Cheek", The Examiner, 1999, May 20, p. 8.

_____ *In the Name of Religion. Truth Behind Conversions and Acts of Violence*, Mumbai: EKTA, 1999.

Rajaram, N.S. and N. Jha, *From Sarasvati River to the Indus Script*. Bangalore: Mitra Madhyama.1999

_____ *The Deciphered Indus Script: Methodology, readings, interpretations*. New Delhi: Aditya Prakashan, 2000.

Rajaram, N.S. and David Frawley, *Vedic Aryans and the Origins of Civilization*. New Delhi: Voice of India, 1997.

Report of the United Christians' Forum for Human Rights (UCFHR) 1999

Snaitang, O.L., *Christianity and Social Change in North East India*. Shillong: Vendrame Institute, 1993.

Smith, William Roy, *Nationalism and Reform in India*. London: Yale University Press, 1938.

Sowmiya, Ashok and Adrija Roychowdhury "The Long Walk: Did the Aryans migrate into India? New genetics study adds to debate", *Indian Express*, 2018, April 16.

Srinivas, M.N., *The Cohesive Role of Sanskritization and Other Essays*. New Delhi: Oxford University Press, 1989.

The Asian Age, November 23, 1998.

The Examiner, (1999): "The Endangered Species – I", May 20, pp. 50-7.

_____ (2000): "Update: Attacks on Christians", September 16, pp. 6-7

The Frontline, 1999, January 1.

The Frontline, "Horseplay in Harappa. In the ` Piltdown horse' hoax, Hindutva propagandists make a little Sanskrit go a long way," *Frontline*, Oct.13, 2000, pp.8-14.

_____ "Horseplay in Harappa", *Frontline*, Oct.27, 2000, pp.5-9.

_____ "New Evidence on the 'Piltdown Horse' Hoax", *Frontline*, November 24, 2000, pp.32-38.

The Hindustan Times, August 6, 1998.

The Indian Express, August 12, 1998

The Indian Express: "RSS extends swadeshi to churches now", October 8, 2000, p.1.

Then They Came for the Christians – A Report to the Nation by AIFOFDR, 1999.

The Times of India News Service, "Amartya hits out at Sangh Parivar for trying to 'rewrite history', *Times of India*, January 3, 2001, p.6.

Times of India, January 30, 1999.

Time Magazine, "The Revolution Against Caste", *Time, 1992,* April 13, pp. 11-16.

Thapar, Romila, "Hindutva and history", *Frontline*, 2000, October 13, pp.15-16.

Tony Joseph, "How genetics is settling the Aryan migration debate" *The Hindu*, June 16, 2017.

Tony Joseph, "How genetics is settling the Aryan migration debate", A writer and former editor of Business World. *Twitter: @tjoseph0010.*

United News of India, "RSS attempts rewrite history", *The Indian Express*, January 1, 2001, p.4.

Kamal Mitra, *Violence in Gujarat – Hindu Jago Christi Bhago*, 1999, by for National Alliance of Women

Witzel, Michael and Steve Farmer, "Horseplay in Harappa: The Indus Valley Decipherment Hoax", *Frontline*, 2000, October 13, pp.34-39.

_____ "New Evidence on the 'Piltdown Horse' Hoax", *Frontline*, 2000, November 24, pp.126-129.

Contributors

Arockiasamy Savarirayan SVD, Rector, *Khrist Premalaya* Regional Philosophate, Bhopal.

Babu Karakombil SVD, Manager, *Sat Prachar* Press, Indore.

Clarence Srambical SVD, Editor, the Word Among Us, Indore.

Dixson Lawrence D'Souza SVD, Treasurer, *Ishopanthi* Ashram, Puri.

G. Lazar SVD, Director, *Sanskruti*, Habsiguda.

Ignatius Soreng SVD, Director, *Sanskruti Kendro*, Sundargarh.

Ivan D'Silva SVD, Parish Priest, Ambassa, Tripura.

Joy Thomas SVD, Professor, St. Joseph's College, Kohima.

K. Jose SVD, Director, *Sanskriti*-NEICR, Guwahati.

Lazar T. Stanislaus SVD, General Mission Secretary, Rome.

Libnus Kullu SVD, Dean, SVD Vidya Bhavan, Bhopal.

Nirmal Lawrence SVD, Doctoral Scholar, Institute of Indian Culture, Mumbai.

Richard Quadros SVD, Director, *Sarva Vikas Deep*, Maharashtra.

S.M. Michael SVD, Director, Institute of Indian Culture, Mumbai.

Thomas Chacko SVD, Former Director, *Panorama* – Centre for Spirituality and Counselling, Bhopal.

Thomas Malipurathu SVD, Rector, Divine Word Seminary, Pune.

www.ingramcontent.com/pod-product-compliance
Lightning Source LLC
Chambersburg PA
CBHW060431030726
47495CB00003B/836